THE PEBBLE IN THE POND

THE PEBBLE IN THE POND

A Tale of Stuarts Landing

SUZANNE GROVES

atmosphere press

To all the women I have known and to all the women I will meet–friends or foes though we may have been or might become–this book is for you.

"In a gentle way, you can shake the world."
– Mahatma Gandhi

"Just as ripples spread out when a single pebble is dropped into water, the actions of individuals can have far-reaching effects."
– Dalai Lama

After locking up their house and handing the keys to the bank representative, Miriam Llewelyn helped her husband George load the red cooler full of snacks and soft drinks into his truck in preparation for their seven-hour drive to Stuarts Landing, Virginia. Taking one last look at the home she had cherished for the last five years, Miriam fought back tears as she remembered all that had transpired over the past seven months to result in their leaving Lexington, Kentucky, for an unknown community in a different state.

As George eased out of the driveway, Miriam closed her eyes and replayed the scene in their kitchen, just a few weeks back. A few months before her granddaddy's death, a loss she continued to mourn, George suggested she needn't worry about the business of their hardware store and, instead, spend as much time as she could with him. After his death, George stopped mentioning the business altogether, which she believed was his attempt to give her space to process her ravenous grief. *I know I should care*, she would chastise herself. After all, her grandfather had given them the seed money to open their store. But the abyss created by her grandfather's passing devoured her interest in anything else, including their business.

One night, while Miriam was half-heartedly ironing George's work shirt, she noticed him hunched forward at the kitchen table, his head in his hands. Worried, she took a seat next to him, alarmed by his solemn demeanor.

"What's up, honey?"

"We're in trouble," he had said, waving his hand at the stack of paperwork spread before him.

"What do you mean?"

"We can't make payroll. And we can't make our loan payments. Got this letter here from the bank," he said, picking up an envelope. "Says we're overleveraged. I'm not exactly sure what that means, but we're in trouble, Mim. And we still have our mortgage payment to make too—it's already late. But we don't have it. We don't have the money." His lips twitched, and his eyes pooled with tears.

Her stomach had woven itself into a tight knot as she fought back despair. Losing their business felt like losing her grandfather all over again. They wouldn't have been able to get Llewelyn's Hardware up and running without his help, and now they had nothing to show for his support except hearts broken and dreams dashed.

"We're going to lose the house, Mim. I'm sorry. I know I've let you down," he said.

In the ten years they had been together—eight of them as a married couple—she had never seen George cry. Not when he buried his parents, not when he lost his left pinky in an accident with a timing belt, not even when they were told they couldn't have children. She sat helplessly, quietly, her mind racing to find a solution. And then, she recalled her granddaddy Rusty's deathbed plea: to move to Stuarts Landing. At that moment, Miriam took charge, but now she found herself wondering how George felt about it all.

"Honey?" she said, reaching over to turn down the radio. "Are you okay, you know, with all this?"

George looked at her with a smile. "Don't have a choice, do I? Once we lost most everything, why not embrace a new adventure?"

Miriam patted his knee and thought, not for the first time,

that while she continued to miss her granddaddy dearly, she would always be able to count on George—bankrupt or not.

"You know we did the best we could, right?" she said softly.

"Some things aren't meant to be permanent, Mim. Let's just see what the future holds in Stuarts Landing."

She didn't realize she had drifted off until George gently nudged her.

"We need to find a service station," he said. "I forgot what a gas guzzler this old girl is on the highway."

Miriam rubbed the sleep from her eyes before peering over at the gas gauge. "Looks like we have a little bit left," she said.

"A little bit." George kept his eyes on the highway, but Miriam could see his jaw muscles clench and unclench. *He's taking this harder than I thought.*

"We'll be okay, honey. We always are, aren't we?"

George didn't respond, so Miriam let him concentrate on the road. A few minutes later, he pulled into a Phillips 66 station and they both let out sighs of relief.

"I'm going to use the ladies' room," she said. "Need anything?"

"All set for now. After I finish with the gas, I may hit the head before we get back on the road."

After washing her hands, Miriam perused the small store and found, to her delight, a *Virginia Almanac*. She purchased a copy, along with a candy bar, and all but skipped back to the truck.

"Look at what I got!"

George smiled before heading toward the men's room inside the station. When he returned, Miriam pulled out the soft drinks and egg salad sandwiches she had packed, and George pulled back onto the highway.

"This is really interesting," Miriam said as she ate her lunch, the magazine splayed in her lap catching the errant breadcrumbs.

"What's that?"

"I'm reading here that Stuarts Landing was established in the early 1800s as a farming community. Mostly tobacco and soybean farms. Have you ever had a soybean?"

"Can't say as I have, at least that I know of."

Miriam laughed. "And there was a sawmill that used to be the largest employer. Guess that means there's a bunch of trees there, right?"

"I'd imagine."

"And get this—it says most of the homeowners there hold professional jobs in Richmond, which locals call 'the city.' That's funny. It's what they call a 'bedroom community.' I wonder what that means," Miriam said, taking the last bite of her egg salad sandwich.

"I think it means people work in the big city but maybe lead sleepier lives in a smallish town?"

"Well, that sounds... fancy," she said, returning her attention to the magazine. "Gee whiz, honey, some of the homes pictured are like museums!" George didn't respond, so she kept flipping the pages in silence. She felt anxious but assumed she was just excited about this new adventure.

An hour later, George pulled into the lot of the Cardinal Motel, just off the state highway leading into town. Stiff from their nearly eight-hour drive from Lexington, Miriam stepped gingerly from their truck and shook out her hands and legs, like a freshly washed dog shaking the water from its coat. "I'll be back in a sec," she said before closing the truck's door. The motel didn't look like much, with maybe ten rooms in total, and she assumed it was there for truckers and road-trippers who merely needed a clean bed for the night. She knew their situation was quite different, but she hoped she could make it a home for as long as it took them to get situated in this new place, this new life.

She found the front office empty, so she looked around

and took note of the stained carpet, the fraying curtains, the yellowed 1978 wall calendar, and the lingering smell of cigarette smoke. *This is no time to be picky*, she thought before seeing the silver desk bell, its domed cover pitted and scratched. She tapped it twice, and within a few seconds, a curtain parted, revealing a wizened Black man chewing on a toothpick. "Howdy," he said with a toothy grin. "What can I do you for?"

Miriam fiddled with the straps of her handbag, trying to hold back the anxious tears that sprang from nowhere. The man looked kind, reminding her of her granddaddy, reminding her of Lexington. *Maybe this was a bad idea,* she thought. *Was I foolish to bring us here without any real plan?*

"My husband and I," she began, then removed a tissue from her purse to dab her eyes. "We, um, we need a place to stay for a while." He squinted his eyes as he seemed to appraise her.

"Ya'll in some kind of trouble?" he asked, cocking his head thoughtfully.

"Yes. I mean, no. Well, both?"

"Nothing with the law?" His eyes narrowed further.

She realized how she must have sounded. "Oh, no! Nothing like that. We're moving here from Kentucky. Lexington, actually, and we need a place to stay while we look for a place to rent."

He folded his arms. "You have any kind of business here? Family?"

Miriam couldn't decide if she was being interviewed for a room or if he was merely curious, so she decided to give him the benefit of the doubt... like Granddaddy had always taught her.

"No on both counts," she said. "Well, that's not entirely true. My grandfather grew up here but then moved to Kentucky. He died seven months ago." It still hurt to talk about him, and her eyes welled with tears. "He told us we should come here someday, and well, here we are." She shrugged.

"I'm sorry to hear about your granddaddy," he said as he removed a key from the pegboard behind him. "How long you think you'll be here?"

Miriam quickly calculated how much money they had in cash—only two thousand dollars—and tried to run the numbers, assuming they both found jobs quickly. "Well, I'm not sure, but I don't think it will take long before we find jobs and a place to rent. Maybe a few weeks?"

"I see," he said, placing the key on the counter. "Might take a bit more time than that. Both jobs and rentals is pretty scarce in these parts. Do you have a credit card?"

She felt her face flush with shame. They had lost all their credit when forced to declare bankruptcy, but she was loath to share that information.

"Just cash," she said with all the confidence she could muster.

"That's fine, but I'll just need a deposit. How does two hundred dollars sound?"

Miriam gulped, then stifled a cough. "Sure, I guess that's okay." She removed two crisp one-hundred-dollar bills from her wallet and placed them into his wrinkled, outstretched hand.

"No parties, no loud music, no smoking anything, and no inside grill. We provide clean towels and sheets, but you gotta keep the kitchen clean. That's about it for my rules," he said. "Meant to say, my name is Milo. Welcome to Stuarts Landing. We're mostly good people here. Mostly." He gave her a friendly wink, then removed the toothpick from his mouth. "I've been living here most my life. I probably even knew your kin. What was granddaddy's name?"

Miriam felt her stomach turn. She remembered her grandfather's dying words, how he'd been forced to leave town followed by his claim of innocence. But she didn't know what he'd been accused of, and she wavered. *Should I disclose his name*

to this stranger? A person I'll need to depend on until we find our footing. But what if he holds an important clue as to why Granddaddy told us to move here? She might as well plow ahead.

"His name was Russell Benson." She watched with dread as his expression changed.

"Lordy. Haven't heard that name in a long time. And if I was you, I wouldn't share that with no one else," he said.

"Well, my grandfather was a wonderful man—he all but raised me by himself," Miriam said, feeling her hackles rise in her grandfather's defense.

"That may be well and good, but that's not what folks know around here."

Miriam didn't know whether to be confused or angry. "What did he do? What happened?"

"He worked at the sawmill, right?"

Miriam had a vague memory of him mentioning how much he loved working at a sawmill, but he'd never said where it was. *Why didn't I ask him more about his life?* she thought ruefully.

"I'm not really sure," Miriam said. She could feel her pulse racing.

"Well, there was some trouble, and he mighta been involved. That's all I'm sayin'. And just know that folks around here have a long and unforgiving memory. You don't want to get off to a bad start, ya hear?"

Miriam nodded, half hoping he'd say more and half hoping he wouldn't. She took the key from the counter, her hands shaking slightly. "Room eight?"

"Yes, missus...?"

"My apologies. My name is Miriam Llewelyn, and my husband out there," she said, turning to point to the truck parked out front, "that's George."

"Real pleased to meet you. If y'all want, you can park your trailer around back where it's hidden from the road."

Seems that's not all we'll have to hide, she thought, although she wasn't quite sure what needed to be kept secret.

She gave him a wan smile. "Much appreciated, Milo. Have a good night." She walked heavily toward George's truck, again questioning her own judgment about their relocation until she heard her grandfather's soft words again. *"Stuarts Landing. I was happy there, for a time. You will be too. That's where you will find answers, honey. Promise me? Promise me you'll go and when you do, be sure to look for the flowers... most colorful in town. You can't miss 'em."* All these months later and she still couldn't make sense of what he was asking of her, nor the unspoken question he thought would be answered in her new community.

Trying to order her thoughts, Miriam shifted her eyes to the fiery sunset, seeking in its glow a divine reassurance they could be happy here. Straightening her shoulders, she grinned as a soft breeze tousled her hair. *When did my grandfather ever lead me astray?*

As she put her hand on the door handle, she noticed a shiny green pebble—the color of her eyes—on the asphalt beside her feet and bent to pick it up and put it in her pocket, smiling. *Think of it as a reminder that God's gifts are everywhere,* she remembered her grandfather saying any time they found special treasures on their walks.

"How'd it go?" George said when she climbed into the truck.

"We've got ourselves a room, and it even has a little kitchen!" she said with false bravado yet clearer-headed than she had been in some time. "Milo, the manager, said we can leave the trailer in back for a while. Let's do that then go find us a place for dinner. I could go for some chicken-fried steak. How's that sound?"

"Whatever you wish, my love," George said, giving her hand a gentle squeeze. "Whatever you wish."

Louise Winston Caldwell's first introduction to Miriam Llewelyn was through Louise's friend, Bitsy Butler, with whom she co-wrote the weekly church bulletin. The women had been friends since their sophomore year in high school when Bitsy's family moved to Stuarts Landing. Bitsy was a beautiful, gregarious girl–if not a bit flighty at times–and Louise had taken her under her wing. With time, Louise's "project" had yielded results–Bitsy had become the perfect protégé, and Louise loved having her as her dutiful social sidekick.

One Friday afternoon, Bitsy came flying into the small office while Louise glared at the mimeograph threatening an eruption of purple ink. Feeling fuzzy from the fumes, Louise had just opened a window and was fanning herself with an invitation to the upcoming Stuarts Landing Women's Auxiliary Annual Fashion Show, of which she was a co-chair. *These invitations won't address themselves,* she thought. *And I can't count on Kay. What's the point of a co-chair, anyway?*

Bitsy's brunette curls had been windblown into a haystack, and the armpits of her Lilly Pulitzer shift were damp with perspiration. Smoothing her hair, she breathlessly took a seat across from Louise.

"Where's the fire?" Louise asked, casually taking a sip of her Coca-Cola.

Bitsy pulled a lacey pink handkerchief from her purse and dabbed her lips. "When was the last time someone new came to town?" Bitsy said. "Can you remember?"

"I can't say as I do," Louise said. She walked to the vending machine and bought a bottle of root beer for her friend. Placing it on the table, she returned to her chair behind the desk. "At least no one of our kind."

Bitsy rolled her eyes, then took a long pull from her root beer before speaking.

"Well, I wasn't exactly 'your' kind when I first moved here either," Bitsy countered.

Louise chuckled at the memory. "You were darling. You just needed some guidance as to how things are done around here. And you know as well as I that you wanted to be popular. I mean, who doesn't? And we got you there, didn't we, Miss Homecoming Princess?"

"For Pete's sake, Louise. You were the homecoming queen, so really, I was just standing in your shadow."

"But you were on the same stage, so doesn't that count?" Louise smiled as if a languid feline relaxing in the sunshine.

"Well, anyway, I was just at the Piggly-Wiggly, thumbing through the magazines while waiting to check out. Did you know that terrible woman, Gloria Steinem, is on the cover of *The Ladies' Home Journal* this month? What's become of this country?" She sighed, taking another sip of soda.

"And?" Louise said, examining her fingernails. She found it difficult to be patient with Bitsy, who, while her closest friend, could be quite excitable and often annoying.

"This woman was in line behind me. Her basket was full, I mean, brimming over with cookies and Sara Lee poundcakes–poor thing probably can't cook–and bologna and, can you imagine, store-brand white bread!"

"Downright criminal," Louise muttered.

"And she had yogurt. Imagine... yogurt!"

"Did she look like a hippy?" Louise asked, her lips curling with amusement.

"No, not at all. Though her hair was kind of unkempt, and

she was carrying a tote bag that looked like it was made from a flour sack. And get this—she had opened her box of Lemon Coolers and was eating one, right there in line! Powdered sugar all down the front of her polyester blouse!"

"Indeed," Louise said, conjuring the vision. "Polyester, of all things. Tell me about her shoes."

"Oh, crazy. Hiking boots! Like the ones men wear when they go dove hunting!"

"So, maybe she's just visiting?"

"I thought that, too, at first. You know me... I had to find out, so I struck up a conversation. She and her husband just moved here. They're staying at the motel for now, but they're looking for a place to rent," Bitsy said, crinkling her nose. "Rent! Can you believe it?"

"I don't know how that's going to work here," Louise said, arranging the invitations and corresponding envelopes into even stacks.

"Her name is Miriam. Miriam, um, Llewelyn," Bitsy said. "I invited her to church this Sunday. Told her she could join us and help set up breakfast."

Louise shook her head slowly. "Bits," she said, "we really don't have time to teach someone how we do things. We have our routine! And the Webster sisters, well, I'm not sure how they're going to respond. You know how they are."

"Oh, I bet they'll like her right away. She seems, I don't know, eager to please. She's actually really nice," Bitsy said.

"The very worst kind," Louise said matter-of-factly. "Everything's fine just the way it is now. I'm glad you invited her to church, Bits, but people must earn their place here. You know that."

That Sunday morning, Louise strode into the community hall with her basket of homemade muffins, a mixture of blueberry and apple cinnamon, all from Caldwell family recipes dating back generations. Greeting her fellow parishioners with air kisses and compliments, she moved to the covered banquet table to arrange her baked goods on a silver platter, then tucked the basket away for safekeeping.

"Louise," Bitsy said, walking up to her. Louise noticed Bitsy was followed by a round, red-faced woman, eyelids painted blue, and lips frosted with bright pink, looking at her expectantly. Her limpid green eyes reminded Louise of her father's favorite tabby cat, Maggy. *That animal was worthless,* she thought.

"I'd like to introduce you to Miriam Llewelyn," Bitsy said, stepping back so Miriam could move in. "Miriam, this is Louise Winston Caldwell, one of my oldest friends and the co-editor of the church bulletin, among so many other things around here."

Louise extended a manicured hand, her gold bangles jangling as Miriam gave her a hearty handshake. "Welcome to Stuarts Landing," she said. "And welcome to our church. If you'll excuse me, I have a few more things to attend to before service begins."

"I'm happy to help, if you'd like," Miriam offered, following Louise like a wayward stray.

"Don't be silly," Louise said, turning around to size up this new species. "You're our guest, after all."

As Bitsy escorted Miriam toward the chapel, Louise watched the newcomer amble along in her sensible shoes and obviously homemade dress.

This will be interesting, Louise thought before popping a Jordan almond into her mouth. *Very interesting, indeed.*

3

Miriam unlocked the door of their sparse room at the Cardinal Inn and headed directly for the kitchenette. She pried open the box of Sara Lee poundcake, peeled back the foil pan, and sliced off a two-inch piece. Sitting on the edge of her bed, she devoured the snack in four bites while considering her options.

George had elected not to attend church with her, despite her pleas. "I think God's done with me," he had said the night before over dinner. "Besides, I don't really feel I'd be accepted until I have a job."

Miriam couldn't argue with his feelings, but it pained her to see him so forlorn. He had lost so much—not just their business but most of their possessions, which they had sold to afford the move to Stuarts Landing. He kept his tools, some of his fishing gear, and, of course, his clothes. She kept her sewing machine, fabric, and the most essential cookware and dishes. What few loved collectibles and jewelry she owned were now in other homes... with two exceptions, one of which was her wedding ring. She looked at her left hand with its modest gold band and felt grateful they were still together. *We can get through this.* She wished she had someone to talk to, but so far, she was confused by the women she met at church. They seemed exotic and unapproachable, like hothouse flowers that might just be poisonous. *What's the deadliest? Oleander?* she thought. Something about "flowers" tickled her memory, but she discarded the thought. She was on a mission.

Opening the *Weekly Gazette*, she searched for something interesting or useful that would help them understand this new place.

Newspaper sprawled across the small table, she had just begun reading about the Women's Auxiliary Annual Fashion Show when George opened the door, carrying an ice chest. He seemed genuinely happy for the first time in months.

"Boy, the fish were biting this morning! Better than anything I ever saw back in Kentucky," he said, kissing Miriam on the cheek before placing the cooler on the counter. "Met a guy named Gus on the dock. He said the new car dealership needs a mechanic. I told him about myself—well, not the bankruptcy part—and he said the owner is his cousin. Told me to go by tomorrow, talk to him, see about working there. What do you think, Mim?"

He looked at her hopefully, nearly bouncing on his toes with enthusiasm. Smiling, she stood and gave him a hug, then looked inside the cooler.

"I think this is a whole lot of trout for just two people!" she said. "Thanks for cleaning them. You know how much I detest that part." She washed her hands, drying them on her apron.

"Of course," he said, going into the bathroom to rinse his face and hands. "But the dealership, Mim," he hollered. "What do you think?"

It had been years since George had come home with grease on his hands and coveralls. She closed her eyes, remembering the many nights she spent trying to remove the stains, usually to no avail. He was a much younger man then, and he hadn't done much in the way of physical labor since starting their hardware business, but they needed the money.

"Will it make you happy?" she asked when he emerged from the bathroom to grab a clean shirt.

"Anything would make me happy at this point. Anything

that pays, anyway."

"Then I think it sounds great. You know, I could look for work too," Miriam said, though she wasn't sure this town offered many options for women, especially those who had only taken a few community college pottery classes. "I do have retail experience, obviously!" She was warming up to the idea. "I worked when we had the business, didn't I? And I enjoyed it until, well, you know." Miriam couldn't abide whining, yet here she was.

"But I don't want you to have to work, Mim," George said, sinking down onto the sagging couch. "I'd rather see you get involved, make new friends, enjoy yourself for once."

"I'm not finding the people here too friendly just yet. I get the feeling, I don't know... it seems they're a different breed. So, the 'make new friends' part might be harder you think. I'd rather get a job, if that's okay with you," Miriam said.

"You don't need my permission, honey. But I do need your encouragement. It would be nice to let someone else be the boss for a change," he said with a chuckle. "As long as they can make payroll."

"Of course, George. I'm happy for you." She hoped she meant it.

***

The next morning, George dressed in his only suit, the short-sleeved shirt Miriam had pressed the night before, his best tie from JC Penney, and the black loafers he had spent an hour spit shining. He was standing in the bathroom, practicing his smile in the mirror, when Miriam wrapped her arms around him.

"You'll be the most handsome mechanic they've ever had," she whispered in his ear. "I'm proud of you. Let's say a quick prayer."

George turned, and while holding hands, they asked for divine direction before saying, "Amen."

"I'd like to take the truck today. Are you okay with the Pinto?" George said. While it had been affordable and reliable, she thought the car was hideous.

"Absolutely, take it! Good luck! I love you!" she said as he opened the door. With one last glance and a wink, George was on his way. He looked just as confident as he had when they met so many years earlier. She smiled at the memory before turning her attention to her own plans for the day.

One hour later, Miriam pulled into the parking lot of the Stuarts Landing Chamber of Commerce, which, according to the phone book, housed the Stuarts Landing Women's Auxiliary. She wore her very best dress, a basic sheath she had sewn from a Butterick pattern using a bold plaid fabric she had rescued from the clearance bin. She had done her best to style her unruly red hair into an updo, and though her suntan pantyhose sported a run up the back of one leg, she hoped no one would be looking that closely. Gathering her handbag, she walked purposefully into the Greek Revival building to begin her campaign. As she approached the receptionist, she heard a symphony of polite laughter down the hallway.

"Are you here for the lunch meeting?" the receptionist asked, peering over her glasses while seeming to appraise Miriam's attire. Miriam detected a smirk but elected to ignore it.

"Yes, I am," she said. She hadn't known a luncheon was going on, but she might as well dive in headfirst.

"Name?"

"Miriam Llewelyn."

The receptionist opened a folder and ran her pen down the list.

"I'm afraid your name isn't here. Did you RSVP?" she asked, tapping the pen on the desk.

"No, I'm new here and thought I'd like to visit. I saw the

ad in the gazette, the ad for the fashion show? I thought it would be fun to help out," Miriam said.

"I see. Do you have any acquaintances with the auxiliary? Any friends, perhaps?" Miriam took a step backward, thinking perhaps she should leave, when a voice called her name.

"Miriam, nice to see you!" Bitsy said, walking daintily toward her with kitten-heeled steps.

"She says she's here for the luncheon, but her name isn't on the list," the receptionist said.

"Well, Lila, please put her on the list as my guest. I'll settle up later, okay?" And with that, Bitsy linked her arm through Miriam's and escorted her down the hall, stopping at a set of double doors near the end.

"Are you sure?" Miriam whispered before Bitsy reached for the doorknob.

Bitsy patted her arm. "Absolutely. It will be fun! They don't bite... mostly," she said with a grin.

When they entered the room, Louise was at the podium, flanked by mocked-up posters advertising the annual fashion show. Resplendent in a lilac silk dress and opera-length pearls, she looked regal and very much in charge. Miriam's eyes met hers, and she saw Louise shift her glance to Bitsy, press her lips together, and subtly shake her head. In response, Bitsy shrugged slightly and smiled, putting her hand on Miriam's back and guiding her to a table.

"Fortunately," Bitsy said as they took their seats, "one of my guests was unable to attend today, else I'd have to find another spot for you. Now we can get better acquainted with each other! Would you like some sugar for your iced tea?"

"No thank you," Miriam said. "Do they have any artificial sweetener?"

Bitsy looked confused, then brightened. "Just ask the waiter when he comes."

Miriam tried to ignore the other six women completing

their table, each sneaking glances, then covering their mouths with their napkins. *Are they laughing at me?* Maybe she'd just drink her tea unsweetened.

The waiter served their lunch—a trifecta of chicken, ham, and fruit salads—artfully arranged on porcelain plates, along with a basket of warm muffins. Miriam placed one on her plate, then searched the table for some butter, but seeing the others pass, she pushed her muffin aside.

"This fruit salad is delicious!" Bitsy said. Miriam nodded, chewing her chicken salad. *This needs more mayonnaise,* she thought, taking a sip of unsweetened tea to wash it down.

"Have you found a place to rent yet?" Bitsy said, cocking her head with interest.

"Not yet. We want to get a better feel for the town," Miriam said, taking a bite of ham salad.

"Well, I'll help if I can. I believe our cleaning girl rents too. I'll see if she has any leads," Bitsy said. "What will your husband be doing in Stuarts Landing?"

Miriam's throat tightened—that was a question she had hoped to avoid.

"He actually has a meeting about an opportunity today," she said carefully.

"How wonderful! Where, might I ask?"

"He met a man yesterday who said his cousin owns the Ford dealership in town. He's—"

Before Miriam could finish, Bitsy began laughing. "Oh, that must have been Gus!" she said, shaking her head. "Such a character, that one. Yes, he's my husband's cousin on his father's side."

Miriam took a gulp of her tea before responding. "Your husband..."

"Yes, Bobby Butler. That's his dealership. Actually, it's *our* dealership, but I let him think he's in charge," she said with a wink.

"How remarkable," Miriam said, unsure how to continue.

"Is your husband interested in sales?" Bitsy said, taking another bite of fruit salad.

Miriam noticed that was all she was eating. *No wonder she's so thin.* "He actually has experience, much earlier in his life, as a mechanic," she said, trying to sound confident while assuming they were being judged.

"You know, we don't give tradesmen enough respect," Bitsy said, dabbing her lips before placing her fork on the plate. Within seconds, the waiter had silently removed it.

"That's true. I come from a long line of tradesmen. Where would our country be without them?" Miriam said proudly.

"I couldn't agree more. But is he good with people?" Bitsy cocked her head once again, reminding Miriam of an exotic parrot.

"We used to own a business, so yes, he's very good with people."

"Hmm. Let's see what we can do, shall we? I'll be right back." She excused herself from the table and left the room.

Miriam looked around the table to see if anyone else was interested in chatting, but they were embroiled in their own conversations. She turned her attention to the front of the room, where Louise was gliding back to the podium.

"Ladies," she said, tapping the microphone twice. The room quieted immediately. "Welcome to the bi-weekly meeting of the Stuarts Landing Women's Auxiliary. I do hope you've enjoyed your lunch. If we have any visitors today, I'd like you to stand so we can welcome you," she said, staring directly at Miriam with a dangerous smile.

Without Bitsy, Miriam felt vulnerable in this room full of well-heeled strangers. She took a deep breath, then scooted her chair out far enough that she could stand without bumping the table. But when she stood, her napkin fell from her lap to the floor, making her blush with embarrassment.

Seeing every eye was on her, she pushed it under the table with her foot and offered a wan smile.

"Hello and welcome. Might we learn your name?" Louise asked.

Of course, you know my name, Miriam thought with irritation. *I met you twenty-four hours ago!* "My name is Miriam Llewelyn. My husband George and I have just moved here from Lexington. Lexington, Kentucky," she said. The room erupted in giggles.

"I wasn't aware there was more than one Lexington, dear," Louise said, and the laughter grew louder. Feeling publicly shamed, Miriam sat back down, immediately wishing she had said, "There's a Lexington in Missouri." Somehow, though, she knew Louise wasn't one to be challenged.

"We're glad you're here, Miriam." And with that, Louise began working through the agenda, inviting subcommittee chairwomen to the podium to provide fashion show updates. Miriam found it tedious, but she tried to remember each woman's name.

Ten minutes later, Bitsy returned to the table, breathless. "Oh, Miriam!" she whispered, but not softly enough. Louise shot her a glare from the dais, so Bitsy cupped her hand around Miriam's ear.

"Bobby said he's going to offer George a job running our service department. Isn't that wonderful?"

Miriam let out a grateful sigh. "Thank you," she said, smiling.

"Isn't that what friends are for?" Bitsy blinked wistfully before taking Miriam's hand in her own. "And I do want us to be friends," she drawled. "No matter what Louise might think."

After meeting a few women on her way to the reception area, Miriam thanked Bitsy once again—for her hospitality and for her help—then walked to the Pinto. Though she saw several

women clearly laughing at her car, parked among late-model Fords and Oldsmobiles and Cadillacs, she shrugged it off. She had taken the first step in building a new life in Stuarts Landing. That's all that mattered, at least that day.

When she opened the door of their motel room, George was sitting at the table drinking a beer. She glanced at the clock–it was only one thirty. She put her handbag on the couch and took a seat next to him.

"How'd it go today?" she asked carefully, wondering if Bitsy had been wrong.

His face broke into a wide grin. "Mim, you're talking to the new service manager of Butler Automobiles!"

"Congratulations! This is the answer to our prayers, George! I'm so proud of you!" She rose and wrapped her arms around his neck.

"There's no looking back! Stuarts Landing, meet the Llewelyns!" George said, toasting the air before taking a pull on his beer.

"Now, we just need to find a place to live," Miriam said, her eyes brightening at the prospect.

"Let me get my first paycheck, Mim." George laughed, patting her bottom. She playfully swatted his hand. *It's so nice to see him happy, for a change.*

"I think we should celebrate properly," he said. "Red Lobster?"

"Honey, we have a freezer full of trout," Miriam said, still worried about their finances.

"But we don't have lobster. And you, my bride, deserve lobster."

Louise eased her baby blue Cadillac sedan into the driveway and took a moment to gaze at her exquisite home. Designed in the Beaux-Arts style, the Winston House—as it had been known since its completion in 1905—was considered a precious gem in Stuarts Landing. A beacon of aspiration for many, the stately home telegraphed wealth and refinement that was not so much acquired as it was inherited. She noticed, with a twinge of displeasure, that the topiaries framing the front balustrade were in dire need of pruning. *I don't have time for this,* she thought.

As she walked up the front steps, she heard the distant sound of exuberant barking from the backyard. Her beloved German shepherds, Olga and Zeta, always knew she was home before her car made it to the driveway. *At least someone's glad to see me,* she thought as she unlocked the front door and stepped inside. When she saw the enormous bouquet of coral roses, stargazer lilies, and white hydrangeas displayed on the mahogany side table in the foyer, she didn't have to read the card to know they were from her husband, Clifton, who was in Richmond arguing a case. Perhaps he was feeling guilty about spending so much time away—hence, the flowers.

Feeling on edge, especially after seeing Bitsy with that awkward Miriam person, Louise called out for her housekeeper. "Pearl?"

The older woman appeared from the kitchen, drying her hands on a tea towel. "Yes, ma'am?" she said, concern

etched on her face.

"Would you be a dear and make me some of your special lemonade?" Louise said, moving to her escritoire to sort the day's mail.

"My special lemonade, ma'am? But it's only two o'clock."

Louise ignored the look of censure on Pearl's face and glanced at her Cartier watch. "So it is. Can you make sure the ice is crushed?" She smiled at her housekeeper, who had been with her family since Louise was in middle school. When Louise's widowed father, Edward Winston, took his retirement south to Myrtle Beach eight years ago, he deeded over the family home to Louise and Clifton before passing away. She had promptly asked Pearl to stay on as their housekeeper. "No one knows this house like you do," she had told Pearl at the time.

"And no one knows *you* like I do, neither," Pearl had replied with a hearty chuckle. Louise had chosen not to argue with her.

While waiting for her cocktail, Louise heard the familiar staccato sounds of her two prized companions trotting through the tiled kitchen into the great room. She turned her attention from the mail to their beautiful amber eyes, looking at her beseechingly for some ear scratches.

"Aren't you the best girls?" she said, petting each of their velvety heads as they looked at her adoringly. She flicked the handfuls of dog hair onto the Aubusson rug. "Are you blowing your coats again, my precious babies? Are you?"

Olga, the older of the two dogs, tossed her head and ran to get her favorite toy, which she dropped in Louise's lap. Zeta took the opportunity to engage in a game of chase around the expensively decorated room, challenging Olga as they jumped on and off the silk divan. Louise just laughed, enjoying their boundless energy. "Girls, let's calm down, okay?" The dogs ignored her command—the only beings on the planet she would allow to do that–and continued their canine shenanigans while Louise watched, smiling.

When Pearl returned with a Waterford crystal highball glass, swaddled in a starched cocktail napkin, Louise daintily removed the mint sprig, *lovely though annoying*, took a healthy sip, and closed her eyes with pleasure.

"How I needed that, Pearl," Louise said. She could feel her shoulders begin to uncoil.

"I'm glad you like it," Pearl said. "You know, Emma will be home any minute, right? And look at all the hair those dogs have left all over the rug!"

"Mm-hmm," Louise said, rubbing her neck. She wasn't going to have yet another discussion with Pearl about her dogs and redirected the conversation. "With my luck, my daughter will hopefully have dinner at Debbie's."

"Emma's just going through a phase, Miz Caldwell. You didn't act much different at that age, always backtalking your daddy. But he never stopped loving you, not once, even after you lost your grandma's gold locket."

"That was not my fault," Louise retorted. She finished her drink, finally beginning to feel more relaxed. "It fell off somewhere at the football game. I've told you that."

"All I'm saying is that Emma's doing what comes natural to girls. Just keep on loving on her. That's what I did with my Jackie, and with you, and you both turned out all right," she said, beaming.

"Yes, I know Mrs. Butler is very happy with your Jackie," Louise said. "It's hard to find reliable help anymore." She held out the glass. "Might I have one more, please?" She gave Pearl a warm smile. Pearl took the glass and dipped an eyebrow, but said nothing as she left the room.

***

Two hours later, Louise was sitting at her desk in the solarium, working on the plans for the fashion show. She barely noticed the sound of a slamming door. Pearl's special lemonade had soothed the feathers ruffled by that woman. *What was her name? Oh yes, Miriam. Definitely not our kind.* But she jumped when Emma blew into the solarium like a horse bolting back to the barn. Removing her reading glasses, Louise glared at her daughter, a puzzle of angles and awkwardness and attitude.

"I just can't believe the nerve!" Emma said, flopping onto the chintz chaise.

"I've told you not to use the servants' entrance, Emma," Louise said. "That's for Pearl and the gardener when he must come in the house. That reminds me, I need to give Moses a call. Can you believe how he's let our topiaries go?"

Emma made a show of rolling her eyes.

"Attitude, missy. Watch it, please," Louise said, turning her attention back to her notes.

"Don't you care what I have to say?" Emma said, her voice growing shrill. Louise swiveled around in her chair to get a better look at her child.

"Of course," she said, letting out a sigh.

"Debbie said her dad is planning to make a commercial for his dealership, a TV commercial," Emma said, picking at a cuticle.

Louise tried to ignore her daughter's nervous habit. *So unladylike.*

"Well, that sounds exciting! Good for him," she said, inwardly cringing at the gaucheness of it all.

"And she said he's going to let her be in the commercial, along with a few of her friends," Emma said, her eyes beginning to well up.

"Okay..."

"She's already asked Caroline and Mandy. Can you believe it? They're not even cheerleaders! And I'm her best friend!"

"They are quite pretty," Louise mused, failing to see the flash of impatience in Emma's eyes.

"So, I asked if I could be in it, and do you know what Debbie said?" Emma had moved to the edge of the chaise, resting her elbows on her knees like a benched football player.

"I couldn't possibly," Louise said.

"She said, and I quote, 'My mom thinks it would look like favoritism to have her best friend's daughter in the ad and could turn away some of her friends in the auxiliary.' Why do *we* have to care about what *your* friends think? But her dad put her mom in charge of the shoot, and that was her decision. Like her mom even knows what she's doing!" Emma began to cry.

Instinctively, Louise moved to comfort her daughter, sitting next to her on the chaise and trying to take Emma's hands in her own. Emma pulled away.

Louise was taken aback but refused to let it show. Pretending nothing was wrong, she changed her tactic. "I'll tell you what. I think days like this call for a manicure. What do you say? I'm sure Laverne can fit us in—it's only four o'clock."

Emma stared at her sullenly, but Louise persisted.

"Is that a 'yes'?" she said, standing up and smoothing her dress.

"Whatever," Emma said. "And please don't say anything to Mrs. Butler."

"I don't intend to because I think she did you a favor, really. Young ladies with your background don't parade around in front of cameras to sell cars, of all things. Someday, you'll thank me." Louise could not decide if Bitsy made her decision in consideration of others or as a jab to Louise, but she knew it would blow over in time... at least, for Emma.

"But, Mom..." Emma began. Louise put a finger to Emma's lips.

"When have I ever let you down?"

Emma reared back her head. "You're letting me down *now*! Don't you care what I want?"

Louise considered her borderline hysterical daughter for a moment, seeing in her eyes a wild fury that reminded her of her own mother before, well, before.

"I care that you want the *right* things. Now, let's go."

Even though Stuarts Landing had grown to nearly 40,000 residents, largely because of its proximity to big city life in Richmond offset by its residual small-town vibe, it was still difficult to be anonymous. At least for the daughter of Louise Winston Caldwell, whose family had been at the top of the community's hierarchy for three generations straight. Born into a carefully curated cache of etiquette and expectation, Emma's destiny had been charted before she took her first step. Or so she believed.

It was a Saturday morning, so her parents were gone—her mother to an emergency meeting about the fashion show and her father to his weekly golf outing in the city. Normally, she would have spent the night at Debbie's or invited Debbie to spend the night at her house, but Emma had distanced herself over the whole commercial brouhaha. *Why can't my mother just let me be me?* she thought, taking a seat in the kitchen while Pearl, the one person she trusted, did the breakfast dishes.

"Pearl, has my mother always been, you know, like she is now?" She reached down to scratch Olga's ears. Zeta was preoccupied watching a squirrel on the other side of the bay window.

Pearl softly chuckled and set a glass of freshly squeezed orange juice on Emma's linen placemat. "You hungry, honey?" she asked.

"Not really," Emma said, taking a drink of the pulpy liquid. "But my mom, why is she so controlling?"

Pearl shook her head ruefully, but said nothing as she returned to the counter, her back turned so Emma couldn't see her expression, and began drying one of the porcelain teacups. Impatient, Emma rose from the table and hopped onto the butcher's block where she could look Pearl in the eye.

"I don't understand her, Pearl," she said.

Pearl seemed to consider Emma's question before speaking. "Your mama is a very proud woman, honey. She's proud of her heritage, she's proud of her home, she's proud of her family—especially you—and she's proud of the good work she's gone and done for Stuarts Landing," she said, folding the dish towel and hanging it over the dish rack. "It ain't easy being a Winston, that much I can tell you."

Emma twirled a lock of her tawny hair around her index finger, noticing with dismay several split ends. She was surprised her mother hadn't noticed. *Not yet anyway.*

"It's not like we have anything to prove, Pearl. Why does she care what people think?"

"I wish it was that easy," Pearl said, pulling a chair next to the sixty-year-old butcher's block and taking a seat. "People 'round here are funny about tradition. Seems they're of two minds. You got the folks who will do anything they can to keep things the way they always was, and you got the folks who think it's time to shake things up." She scratched the back of her head through the tight kerchief she always wore.

Emma wasn't sure if Pearl had gone gray because she had never seen her hair. *How old is she, even?* But she pushed any thought of Pearl aging from her mind. She couldn't imagine being without her and quickly refocused. "Which one are you?"

"That's a mighty dangerous question, honey," Pearl said, lifting her chin. "But I know this for true—when you're someone like your mama, with the name and the status and all this lifestyle, people both admire you and want to see you fail.

They want to be like you. And they want to pull you off what they reckon is your 'high horse' 'cuz it makes them feel even better about their own lives."

"Why can't people just live the way they want and let others do the same?" Emma asked, picking at her recently manicured nails.

Pearl cleared her throat and nodded at Emma's hands. "Don't go ruining them nails," she chided but tempered it with a smile.

Emma shrugged and stopped picking. "I wish we could just move away," Emma said with a sigh. "It'd be easier to live somewhere new."

"Now that there is foolish thinking, Miss Emma," Pearl said, leaning forward. "Your mama's gonna be your mama no matter where you live. Thing is, your mama's smart. She knows she has a lot of power here, but she also knows to be careful about who to trust."

"I don't want to be like that, Pearl. So rigid all the time! Worried about how I look and what I say and being judged before people even get to know me. You know, she's already talking about what sorority I should pledge, and I've still got two more years until I even graduate high school! It's ridiculous," she said, dropping her head.

"Just be yourself, sweet girl, and you'll do just fine." Pearl reached over to pat Emma's arm. She looked as though she might say more. Emma waited, raising her eyebrows at Pearl in invitation as the dogs nuzzled her knees. She stroked their heads silently.

When Pearl remained silent, Emma said, "But I still don't understand her. I mean, can't you tell me something? Anything?"

Pearl let out a long sigh. "Miss Emma, your grandmother—your mama's mama—she didn't come from the same world as the Winstons," she began carefully. "I didn't start working for

the family until your mama was a bit younger than you is now. Fact is, they didn't have a housekeeper at all, not until…" Pearl's mouth closed with a snap when Louise dramatically entered the kitchen.

"What a lovely day! Is there any coffee left, Pearl? And good morning, sleepyhead. Or should I say, good afternoon? Getting your beauty sleep, I see," she said before leaning down and kissing each dog on her head. "Oh, and please get down from the butcher's block. That's not for sitting. You know better."

Emma jumped down, took her orange juice, and scurried from the kitchen to the library for refuge… but not before hearing her mother's low voice.

"Pearl, just leave it alone. You hear me?"

6

Miriam could scarcely believe her good fortune, but her mother always said there was no such thing as coincidence. "Just God's way of remaining anonymous." That morning, Miriam made her trip to Piggly-Wiggly, coupons in hand, and managed to save almost ten dollars while buying enough to fill the small refrigerator and pantry of their kitchenette. She even bought fresh flowers, which she placed in her mother's chipped ceramic teapot and displayed on the small table. Though it was Saturday, George would be at work until five, giving her several hours to prepare a celebratory dinner. She decided on a small roasted chicken, mashed potatoes, and fresh green beans. She had splurged and picked up a three-dollar bottle of Chablis, a rare luxury but more fitting for the occasion than iced tea or Shasta cola.

She made herself an olive loaf sandwich, poured a glass of buttermilk, and sat down at the table to read the *Weekly Gazette*. She noticed, with pride, an advertisement for Butler Automobiles and smiled. In his first week, George had already come up with ideas to make the service area more welcoming. *I'm rubbing off on him after all*, Miriam thought. The key, she had told him, was to make the service area feel more like a lounge, with fresh coffee and snacks arranged in pretty baskets. George took the idea to Mr. Butler, who clapped him on the back. "I'm surprised Bitsy didn't think of that. She's got her hands in everything," he had said, rolling his eyes.

George had recounted the exchange that evening, just three days into his job.

"Nothing we went through was in vain, Mim," he had said. "Thanks for staying positive, even when I couldn't."

"Together, we can make it through anything, George. Just you wait and see!" she had responded.

Nibbling her sandwich, she turned the page and saw a picture of Louise at the luncheon earlier that week, encircled by the subcommittee chairwomen and smiling from the podium. It was a practiced pose, or so it seemed to Miriam. *Her mouth is smiling, but her eyes sure aren't. I wonder if she's happy.*

The caption read, "Stuarts Landing ladies on a mission with style. The Women's Auxiliary Annual Fashion Show expected to raise enough money to begin restoration of the old sawmill, with ultimate plans of converting it to a museum."

Miriam's hands inexplicably began to shake. She didn't remember hearing that information at the luncheon, probably because she had been so nervous under Louise's piercing stares. *Surely, there are more important causes here,* Miriam thought, her pulse quickening with panic, though she didn't know why. *Why the sawmill, and why now?* Remembering her brief exchange with Milo when she first checked into the motel, her thoughts turned anxiously to her grandfather and his possible connection to the mill. She placed her hand over her heart to calm her breathing, then vowed quietly to stay focused on the unexpected blessing of the day. "Let go and let God," she said aloud, then opened a fresh box of Lemon Coolers for a taste of comfort.

***

When George unlocked the door, Miriam had just finished mixing the potatoes.

"Mmm, smells like you've been busy!" George said,

removing his clip-on tie and unbuttoning his work shirt before taking a seat at the table.

"I've got a chicken roasting, and the green beans are in the Crock-Pot," Miriam said, bringing him a beer. "You don't have to work tomorrow, so why not?"

"Well thanks," he said and took a long pull. "Pretty flowers," he said. "Just like you!"

"Aw, George, you're sweet," Miriam said, taking a seat next to him.

"Wine, Mim?" he said, raising his eyes at the glass she had set on the table.

"Why not?" she laughed. "I don't have to work tomorrow either. Laundry's all done. Besides, it's time we start enjoying life again!" She took a small sip, then leaned back in her chair. She wanted to draw things out as long as possible.

"So, tell me about your day," she said.

"It was a good day, all things considered. Had a few folks who weren't so happy with the wait time, but the complimentary pretzels and cold sodas did wonders. Oh, and Mr. Butler added a television, so they could at least watch the *Wide World of Sports*," he said.

"Did you get your first paycheck?" Miriam said, idly rearranging the flowers. She was worried. Their bank account was running low, and they still needed to find a place to rent.

"I did!" George said, reaching into his shirt pocket. He handed her the folded check, which she put in her purse.

"I'll deposit it Monday," she said, trying not to scowl. His check was much less than she thought it would be, especially since George was a manager. But she decided not to mention it—she knew George was proud to be working again.

"How was your day, honey?" he asked, taking off his loafers and rubbing his feet. "Still getting used to standing all day," he said with a smile. "It's been a while."

"You can soak them in Epsom salts after dinner," Miriam

said. She took another taste of Chablis. "Today was interesting. I went to Piggly-Wiggly. Those coupons really helped–I saved almost ten bucks," she said.

"Well, you have to factor in the flowers and the wine, hon," he said. "So, you really didn't save, did you?"

Miriam felt a stab of irritation. She couldn't tell if he was being serious. She hoped not, since he had never questioned her spending, not even with the hardware store.

"Oh, and I got you your favorite strawberry ice cream. You can have it with some pound cake for dessert."

"You take such good care of me, Mim," he said, smiling.

"That's my job. And speaking of jobs, listen to this. When I first got to the store, I grabbed a basket and was walking by the community bulletin board," she said. "And I saw a flyer posted."

George had closed his eyes, so Miriam cleared her throat loudly.

"I'm listening, dear," he said, but his eyes were still closed.

Frustrated by his apparent lack of attention, she raised her voice slightly. "The flyer was for a job at the store. It said, 'Full-time cashier wanted. See the manager for details.' I was curious, so I asked to speak with the manager. His name is Roy. Nice guy–he looked like he must have played football once upon a time. He was huge!" she said with a laugh.

That did the trick. George's eyes flew open, and he sat up straighter in his chair. "Who was huge?"

"Pay attention, George. I was talking about Roy. I introduced myself, told him we were new here. I mentioned you were working for Mr. Butler, and he said the man was a straight shooter. Then I told him about our hardware store and that I had customer service experience. George, he offered me the job, right on the spot!" She took a sip of wine and looked at her husband expectantly. "What do you think?"

George seemed to be engaged, but his reaction wasn't

what she expected. "I think you are truly remarkable, Mim. But I don't want you to feel like you need to work," he said, slumping back in his chair. "Don't you think I can take care of both of us?"

"What if I like working?" she asked, her voice shaking with frustration. "I don't want to live in this motel forever, and if I'm making money, we can find a place sooner. Isn't that what you want too?"

George ran his hand through his thinning brown hair, then reached out and took Miriam's hand.

"I just think you're better than that is all," he said.

"We're not above anything, George. It's a starting point. It could lead to something else, who knows? For now, I just want to feel useful."

"You're always useful to me," he said.

"Is it wrong to want more?" she said, trying not to sound petulant. George remained silent, picking at the label from the beer bottle.

Saddened by his lack of support, Miriam rose from the table to begin plating their dinner. The chicken, she realized with dismay, was slightly overcooked, and her green beans had turned mushy, but the instant mashed potatoes were perfect. She decided to improvise. She mixed the beans with the chicken and served it over the potatoes, using juices from the pan to make a gravy of sorts.

"Delicious," George pronounced after taking his first bite. "Different but tasty. About the job, Mim. If that's what you want, I support you."

She looked up from her plate to see if he looked sincere. "Thanks, honey. I'm ready to meet some ordinary people here since I clearly don't fit in with the high-society ladies."

"Give it time, Mim. And if they don't want to be your friend, it's their loss."

Pleased he was trying to make amends, Miriam took a bite of the impromptu hash and smiled. *Sometimes, you gotta make it up as you go along,* she thought. She tried to put the women's auxiliary out of her mind, but something about their plans for the sawmill unnerved her.

Of all her philanthropic work, Louise least enjoyed her service as a trustee for the Fulton Academy, a private school her maternal great-grandfather, Harold Fulton, had founded shortly after his daughter, Nora, and her husband, Charles, moved from Manhattan to Stuarts Landing in 1911. As her grandmother Nora had explained, Harold Fulton wanted to ensure his grandchildren received an elite education so they would be well-prepared to attend Ivy League schools. Louise knew Nora had enthusiastically coordinated fundraising events that helped the academy become one of the finest prep schools in the region. Despite Nora's prodding, her daughter-in-law, Deirdre, never shared the same passion for the academy or anything else in the community, so Nora tended the familial obligation until Louise was old enough to step into the assignment. Though routinely bored by the countless meetings and exhaustive fundraising drives, Louise continued to serve so she could ensure Emma got the most from her time there.

Walking down the marbled hallway on her way to the Fulton Academy headmaster's office, Louise stopped to look at the framed black-and-white photo of her 1957 graduating class. Her eyes surveyed the other photos and newspaper clippings in the display case, and she smiled at an old article announcing her election as class president. *I was the first girl to ever be in charge,* Louise reminisced. As had been the case since they met their sophomore year, Bitsy was stationed directly to

Louise's right, smiling as she handed Louise a bouquet. Bitsy had gladly accepted Louise's invitation to be her campaign manager. *Everyone loved Bitsy*, Louise thought, taking out her compact to quickly powder her nose. *Even though she always tried to bring her strays into the pack. Still does, obviously.*

She entered the anteroom of Dr. Blevins's office and checked in with Olivia, the headmaster's secretary.

"I'm afraid he's running a few minutes behind, Mrs. Caldwell. Please make yourself comfortable. May I get you a cup of coffee? A glass of water? Iced tea?"

Louise sat down on the Chesterfield couch. "Iced tea would be lovely. Thank you, Olivia."

She had just picked up a copy of the *Fulton Forecast*–the academy's monthly progress report to its alumni and donors–when she heard familiar footsteps approaching the door. Her husband walked in, nodded at Olivia, and took a seat next to Louise. She looked at him in surprise. "Clif, why are you here?" she asked, furrowing her brow.

"Blevins called and asked that I join you," he said. "I'm not quite sure why, actually. I assume it has something to do with the capital campaign. Isn't it always about money?" he said. "Did you make this appointment, or did he?"

"He left a message with Pearl that he wanted to see me today. I imagine he wants me to serve as president of the board of trustees, and honestly, I don't have room on my plate for one more thing," she said, primly smoothing her shiny blonde bob. "This fashion show may be the death of me."

"I appreciate how hard you work, Lu," he said, patting her knee. "Is there dissent among the committees? Let me guess. There's a dispute over denim?" he asked, chuckling at his own joke.

"Keep your voice down, please. And it's not funny, Clif. Trying to get these women to agree is like presiding over a feral cat race. Everyone's claws are out, and I'm not exaggerating. But to answer your question, the conflict is over the theme, which, as you know, sets the tone for what the ladies will model," she said. "It's critical we strike the right balance."

"Don't you include the theme on the invitation? I thought those had already been printed," he said. Louise assumed he was patronizing her, just as she did him when he talked about the specifics of a case, but she was grateful to have his ear.

"No, we never include the theme so it will be a surprise on the day of the event," she said. "I truly don't understand what has gotten into some of these women. I proposed the theme of 'Resplendently Red,' with every outfit a varying shade of the color."

"How very creative, Lu," Clifton said, adjusting his tie.

"The Webster sisters objected," Louise said. "Loudly."

"Well, they've always had strong opinions. That's what makes them interesting."

Louise ignored his comment, though she knew he had to be diplomatic since they were one of his biggest clients and Stuarts Landing royalty to boot. "You can't imagine their rationale for nixing my idea. Downright ridiculous if you ask me."

"What, the color hurts their eyes?" His eyes sparkled with laughter.

"*No.* Communists. They said it would make us look like Commies!"

Clifton threw back his head and guffawed. "Well, we are in the middle of the Cold War, sweetheart," he said, wiping his eyes with his handkerchief.

"Nobody thinks about those things here. At least not in the women's auxiliary." She sniffed imperiously.

"Apparently, the Webster sisters do."

"They proposed an alternative, which at least half the membership supports. We will take a vote at our meeting this Friday. I must get a handle on this before they

ruin everything!"

"What's their idea?"

"It's so awful, I'm not sure I can say it out loud," Louise said, shuddering at the very thought.

"I'm waiting."

Louise inhaled dramatically, then leaned forward to look Clifton in the eye.

"Disco," she whispered.

Before Clifton could react, the headmaster opened the oak door to his office. "Good afternoon, Mr. and Mrs. Caldwell. I'm sorry to keep you waiting. Please, come in."

Dr. Blevins held the door as Louise led the way. After the door was closed, they took their seats in the cordovan leather wingbacks facing his desk. He sat down, then clasped his hands over a manila folder.

"I'm sorry to have asked for a meeting on such short notice, so I appreciate your availability. I know how very busy you both must be," he said, adjusting his glasses.

"It's the least we can do," Louise said. "The academy means the world to our family. You know that."

"Indeed, I do, which is why this conversation is difficult for me," Dr. Blevins began.

Clifton cleared his throat. "If this is about the capital campaign, I do believe we've already made a sizeable contribution," he said, looking at Louise for affirmation.

She nodded. "Yes, I brought the check to our last trustee meeting."

"As always, we appreciate your family's generosity," Dr. Blevins said. "But that's not why I asked you here. We need to talk about Emma."

Louise glanced at Clifton, but he merely shrugged.

"Is this about her grades? She's seemed a bit distracted lately," Louise said.

"Her grades could be better, to be honest, but she's still

an above-average student," Dr. Blevins said. "No, this is more of a conduct issue, I'm afraid. She is causing some disruption among her classmates."

"Well, I know she and Debbie Butler had a bit of a falling out over the TV commercial for the dealership," Louise said, taking a sip of iced tea. "But you know how girls can be!" She raised her eyebrows.

"That may have something to do with it, perhaps. The truth is," Dr. Blevins said, opening the folder and taking out a handwritten flyer, "Emma has called for a boycott of the spring cotillion." He passed the flyer to Louise.

She snatched the paper and held it in front of her so she and Clifton could read it simultaneously. The message was brief. "Tradition Oppresses! End Classism & Kill Cotillion!" Louise gasped.

"This couldn't possibly have been Emma," Louise said, pushing the flyer back to the headmaster. "Our daughter would never do such a thing!" She expected support from Clifton, but he only sighed loudly before looking at his watch.

Dr. Blevins sat back on his veritable throne. "Olivia saw her taping the flyers around campus," he said, stroking his chin. "We've removed as many as we've found, but we don't know how many she may have stuffed into lockers."

"Everyone wears the same uniform. How can she be sure it was Emma?" Louise said.

"She had the flyers in her tote bag embroidered with her name," Dr. Blevins said. She heard Clifton trying to suppress a chuckle, and she became annoyed. *Why am I the only parent who takes things seriously?*

"We'll have a talk with her when we get home," Louise said.

"I think it's important to tell you that Debbie Butler is the student liaison to the cotillion committee," Dr. Blevins said. "And the committee isn't taking this well."

Clifton finally spoke. "Who's the chair?" he asked in his courtroom voice.

"Bitsy Butler."

"I'll take care of it." Louise closed her eyes and absent-mindedly stroked her pearls. *Here we go,* she thought.

the automatic door to let her in. "Morning!" he said, locking the door behind her. "You're early! That's good! We don't open until eight thirty, so we have plenty of time to get you situated. Follow me," he said, walking through the produce section. He continued through the metal double doors marked "Employees Only" and led her to a break room.

"You can put your bag in one of these lockers," he said, then placed a plastic bag on the bench next to her tote. "And here's your apron!" *It was brand new!*

Miriam squealed with joy. "I'm so happy to be part of the Piggly-Wiggly family!" she said.

"Miriam," he said, holding up his hand with mock seriousness. "Around here, it's called The Pig." His mouth widened into a toothy grin.

"Got it, Roy," she said with a mock salute. "Oink!" She tied the red apron around her waist, looping the ends into a bow in front.

"It's going to be a busy one," Roy said as employees began entering the room. "Double-coupon day! Hey gang, gather round—let's give a Big Pig welcome to Miriam, our new cashier!"

One by one, the aproned employees extended their hands while Miriam tried to memorize each name tag. For the first time since they arrived in Stuarts Landing, she felt like she belonged.

"Let's get you checked out on the register," Roy said, moving through the double doors.

"Is it a Victor?" Miriam said as they approached the checkout line.

"The one and only! You know how to use it?"

"Sure do," Miriam said with a smile. "I'm ready to go!"

"Doors open in five," Roy said. Women were already lined up. "We're running a deal on ground beef," he said with authority. "And remember, double coupons. Hit the—"

"Times two button," Miriam said, finishing his sentence.

He patted her on the shoulder. "Glad you're here. Should you need me, just press the intercom and say, 'Manager requested at checkout,' and I'll be here in a jiffy."

***

At twelve thirty, Roy tapped her on the shoulder as she was ringing up an elderly gentleman's purchases.

"Afternoon, Reverend," Roy said, nodding his head.

"And to you, Roy," he said. "I like your new employee here. She's a real firecracker. Got me thinking about yogurt. Maybe next time!" He took his two bags and ambled toward the door.

"Have a nice day!" Miriam called out behind him. He held up his hand and waved.

"You get a thirty-minute break. I'm sure you're ready," Roy said. "I'll cover your line. Go eat some lunch."

"I have to admit, I should have had breakfast." Miriam giggled. "Every time I saw a box of Little Debbies, my stomach started growling!"

"Hazard of the trade," Roy said, patting his round stomach.

Miriam went into the break room and took her timecard from its slot, clocking out before opening her locker to get her lunch. After hours of checking groceries, her peanut butter and sweet relish sandwich didn't seem as appealing, but it was all she had. She peeled back the top slice of white bread, opened her bag of potato chips, pressed them into place, then put it all back together before taking a healthy bite.

"I thought I was the only person who did that," a young woman said, taking a seat across from her. "I'm Gloria," she said. "I work in produce."

"Nice to meet you! I'm Miriam," she said after swallowing. "It's my first day as a cashier."

"How you like it so far?" Gloria said, opening the lid of

her microwaved Cup O' Noodles and fanning away its steam.

"Very much," Miriam said. "People seem really nice!"

Gloria rolled her eyes. "The folks who work here mostly are," she said, blowing on her soup. "Some of the customers, well, you'll see," she said, daring to put a spoonful of noodles into her mouth. Miriam was impressed Gloria didn't flinch, though she opened her mouth and exhaled loudly.

"Tab?" Miriam said, pushing the pink can toward her. "I haven't opened it yet."

"That's real sweet, thank you. But I'm okay," she said. They sat quietly while finishing their respective lunches. Miriam looked up at the wall clock–her break was nearly over.

"Nice meeting you, Gloria. I look forward to getting to know you better," Miriam said, clocking back in.

"Ditto," Gloria said. "Just remember, our customers can be first-rate bitches. Don't let them get under your skin."

While Miriam was surprised by her candor, she wasn't surprised by the warning. She had already met Louise Winston Caldwell. *How much worse could it be?*

Roy was right–it was a hectic day at The Pig with a full run on ground beef, steak, and laundry detergent, all of which were on sale. Enjoying a brief break in the action, Miriam realized she hadn't taken anything out for dinner. *Maybe we can order a pizza,* she thought drowsily. She was ready to get off her feet.

Two teenaged girls, sporting matching outfits and feathered hairstyles, put their hand basket on the conveyor.

"Hi there," Miriam said as she rang up the first item–a bottle of Sun In. "Is this stuff any good?" she asked, looking up with a smile. The girls were ignoring her, flipping through *People* magazine instead.

"Like, I can't even believe what a weirdo she's become," the tawny-headed girl said, shaking her head. "Who does she think she is, trying to do away with cotillion? I've worked my butt off trying to organize everything. Talk about an embarrassment to her family! My mom is furious."

"I guess if you're part of the Caldwell family, you can pretty much get away with murder," the brunette said. "Man, Kevin Costner is hot!" She lifted the magazine close to her lips as if to kiss the picture.

"Not as hot as Patrick Swayze."

Miriam rang up their suntan lotion, lip gloss, hair spray, diet sodas, and tampons while eavesdropping.

"My mother said she'll see to it that Emma gets suspended," the first girl said.

"Don't you think that's a bit much, Deb?" her friend asked.

"My mom looks like a sweetheart, but don't be fooled, Caroline. She likes to shake things up, but you'll never see her coming," she said, putting the magazine on the conveyor. "She's stealth."

"What do you think she'll do?" Caroline asked.

"She asked Daddy if the dealership would underwrite cotillion," she said with a sly smile. "Make it an even bigger event, maybe even offer up a car for the raffle."

"And what does that have to do with Emma?"

Debbie smirked. "It's all part of the deal, Caroline. I think Mom calls it 'quid pro quo.'"

"What does that mean?"

"Basically, 'I'll scratch your back if you scratch mine.' Dr. Blevins would sell his soul to bring the academy more money," Debbie said.

"I worship at your mom's feet," Caroline said, laughing.

Miriam had no idea who they were discussing, but she instinctively felt sorry for the poor girl on the other end of this teen drama.

"Will that be all, girls?" Miriam said. They nodded, not even looking at her.

"That will be nineteen dollars and thirty-eight cents,"

she said.

Debbie reached into her wallet, pulled out a pre-signed check, filled it out, and handed it to Miriam, who simply raised her eyebrows.

"I have permission," Debbie said defiantly. Miriam looked at the name across the top: *Robert Butler.* Her husband's boss and... *Bitsy's husband? This is their daughter?* She placed the check into the register, then handed Debbie the receipt.

"Have a nice day, girls," Miriam said as they picked up their grocery bags and left the store, ignoring her.

They sure start 'em young here, Miriam thought, shaking her head. *Must be in the water.*

When Emma got home from cheerleading practice, she was surprised to see her parents perched on the silk damask couch in the great room. Her father never arrived before at least six each night, and it was only five o'clock now. She noticed they each had a cocktail.

"Emma, we'd like to have a word with you," her mother called as Emma tried to sneak past them to the staircase.

"Gah, Mom. Can I just take my stuff upstairs first?" she said. Her arms were laden with her purse, book bag, and pom poms and she was desperate for an icy cold drink.

"Please, just set your things down and join us," her mother said. "Pearl?" A moment later, their housekeeper appeared. "Will you be a dear and bring me another lemonade, please?" *Who did she think she was fooling?* Emma thought with derision.

"Yes, Mrs. Caldwell. Sir, may I bring you anything?" Her father just held up his hand and shook his head.

"I'm all set for now, but thank you," he said.

"Could you bring me a can of soda, Pearl?" Emma said. Her mother shot her a look.

"Emma, we've talked about this," she said after Pearl had gone to the kitchen. "Your legs aren't broken, best as I can tell. You could have gotten the soda yourself."

She opened her mouth to object, but her father interrupted her by motioning to the Queen Anne armchair. "Sit down, Emma."

She flounced across the Aubusson rug and dropped her bags loudly to the floor before flopping onto the antique chair, catty-corner to her father but within glaring distance of her mother. Everyone remained quiet while Pearl served the drinks in what felt like slow motion. Once she exited the room, Emma tried to analyze her parents' expressions. *They're scary-serious,* she thought. *Are they getting a divorce? Is someone sick?*

Her mother took a sip of her drink, then set it down primly on the coffee table. She looked at Emma's father, raising her eyebrows and cocking her head. Her father stayed silent, merely returning a subtle nod. Her mother sighed, then tucked a lock of blonde hair behind her ear.

"Dr. Blevins asked to meet with us today," her mother said. Emma could hear her own heartbeat pounding in her chest.

"Well, that sounds like fun," Emma said, taking a sip of her drink. She was aiming for a grin from her dad, who failed to deliver.

"It wasn't, I assure you," her mother said. "We were very surprised to learn of your little campaign at school. What on earth, Em? Haven't you got the sense that God gave a goose?!"

Emma looked to her father for some type of defense. He sat back against the silk pillows and crossed his legs casually, *as if settling in for a good movie,* Emma thought. Her mother remained on the edge of the couch, staring directly into Emma's eyes.

"Is that a question?" Emma said.

"I will not have you smarting off like that, missy. I certainly hope you're not as impertinent with your teachers as you are with me."

"C'mon, Em," her father said. "You're smarter than this." *Smarter than challenging the mighty Louise Winston Caldwell, or smarter than standing up for what I believe?*

"What compelled you to wage war against cotillion, of all things? Why, it's a time-honored tradition at the academy, dating back to the 1930s," her mother said. "It's a rite of passage, after all."

"Passage into what, Mom? Your life? Marrying well? Volunteering? Going to the country club? Coordinating fashion shows? Having servants?"

Her mother glared at her, her lineless face wearing a look of sheer contempt, then glanced at Emma's father. His expression remained blank. *Does he even care?* Emma wondered.

"It seems to me our lifestyle suits you just fine," her mother said, setting her lemonade down loudly. Emma saw the muscles twitching along her jawline. "But to answer your question, cotillion is where your manners become more refined, with the help of the instructors."

"Oh, you mean ladies like Bitsy Butler? We're taking lessons from her?" She heard her father suppress a chuckle.

"Why are you so wound up about this? I don't understand you," her mother said. "You're not just from any old family around here, you know. 'To whom much is given…'"

"I know. 'Much is expected,'" Emma said. "But the world is changing, Mom. Why are you so hell-bent on maintaining tradition?"

"Language," her father said. Emma folded her arms across her chest.

"Tradition is what gives society structure," her mother said in her annoying, preachy tone. "It's what reminds people of their history while perpetuating the very best of our standards for future generations."

"Did you hear that at your DAR luncheon?" Emma said with a sneer. "Don't you know how ridiculous this sounds? I mean, whose standards are you talking about? Rich people? We're not the majority, you know."

Louise crossed her arms in front of her chest. "It has nothing to do with money, young lady. It has to do with class and breeding."

"We're not horses, Mom," Emma said. Her father began to laugh.

"That's not funny, Clifton. A little help here might be nice."

Her father sat up, putting his palms on his knees. "Look, Emma, while I'm glad to see you have a questioning mind, I don't see the point of fighting a battle you can't win. By taking on what is considered a sacred cow, you're placing a target on your own back. Is that really what you want?"

She considered his question before nodding. "There are two kinds of people in this world, Dad," she said, "those who will do whatever they can to preserve tradition and keep everything the same and people who will do what they can to shake things up so the world can change."

Her parents eyed her with interest. "And what type are you, pray tell?" said her mother.

"That's a dangerous question," Emma said, remembering her talk with Pearl.

"What's wrong with the way things are here?"

"Would Pearl's daughter have been admitted to the academy?" Emma said. Her mother inhaled sharply.

"Don't be silly, Emma," she said, picking up her lemonade and taking a drink. Her father cleared his throat.

"You just answered your own question. Classism is oppression, plain and simple," she said. "May I be excused, please?" she said, rising from the armchair.

"Not yet," her father said. "We're not quite finished."

Emma sat down. *What now?*

"Dr. Blevins has asked that you write a formal apology to the school and the cotillion committee," her father said. "And read it at the assembly this Friday."

Emma considered her options under her mother's hawkish stare. "No way," Emma said. "That would make me look even worse, like I've been managed or something. Gagged.

I'm not doing it," she said, picking at her thumbnail.

"Then, according to Dr. Blevins, you will be suspended for three days, starting tomorrow. You will be home tomorrow, Friday, and Monday, but you will still be expected to stay current on your homework. Your mother can pick up your assignments tomorrow," he said. "Hopefully, we can get this expunged from your permanent record."

Emma rolled her eyes and let out a dramatic sigh.

"I'm sorry you've made this decision, Emma," her mother said. "But it's important in life to pick your battles very carefully. And this one, I do believe, was foolhardy. You're clearly learning nothing from me, despite my best efforts. I assumed that might be your choice, though I had hoped differently, so I've arranged for you to spend tomorrow afternoon with the Webster sisters. Maybe they can teach you a bit about tradition."

"But Mom!" Emma looked at her frantically. "They're ancient, and those cats! You know I'm allergic!"

"Just trying to shake things up a bit," her mother said, rising from the couch and striding out of the room.

Emma stood up and looked down at her father, still seated on the couch. "Why can't you be on my side?" she asked.

"I am on your side, honey. And so is your mother, in her own way," he said, then reached for his newspaper.

"That's the problem," Emma said, catching a glimpse of Pearl just outside the doorframe. "What if I don't want the same things she wanted? What if my values are different?"

"Let's see what you pick up from the Websters," he said, "then we can resume this conversation afterwards."

10

The next morning, Louise showered, applied her department store makeup and Chanel No. 5 perfume, then opened the door to her walk-in closet—one of the few renovation projects she and Clifton had undertaken once Winston House became theirs. She didn't want to do anything that would compromise the historical integrity of the family estate, but she drew a line when it came to properly storing her clothes and accessories. With a full day of meetings, as well as Emma's drop-off at the Webster sisters, she wanted to look elegant (as always) while feeling comfortable. She stood in her closet and evaluated which of her options would allow her a break from panty-hose. Opting for a pair of tan slacks, a pink cashmere twin set, penny loafers, and a Hermès scarf she tied stylishly around her neck, she was ready to face the day. Or so she thought.

Clifton was sitting at the breakfast table reading the *Richmond Times-Dispatch* and drinking his coffee when she entered and sat down. Pearl quickly and wordlessly served Louise her daily breakfast of half a grapefruit, dry toast, and black coffee. Louise felt an indescribable gloom hanging over the house.

"Where's Emma?" she asked no one in particular.

"I haven't seen her this morning, ma'am," Pearl said. Clifton shrugged.

"It's eight thirty," Louise said. "Just because she's not going to school doesn't mean she can treat this as a holiday. For Pete's sake." She screeched back her chair, threw her napkin on the table, and marched upstairs to her daughter's room.

Opening Emma's door, she realized she hadn't ventured into her room in months, having thought it appropriate to give Emma her privacy. While the French Provincial-themed room, awash in floral bedding and complemented by apricot-colored walls and turquoise silk drapes, had once been immaculate, it now looked every bit the province of a petulant teenager. Louise grabbed the wicker wastebasket and began loudly crumpling the empty soda cans littering Emma's desk and vanity. The lump in the queen bed stirred, and Louise remembered, for a moment, how it felt the first time her daughter had moved while in utero. She sat down on the bed and nudged her daughter awake, then noticed a poster tacked—*tacked*—onto the closet door.

"Emma, wake up!" she said. Her daughter's head appeared from under the comforter. Rubbing the sleep from her eyes, she looked at Louise and scowled.

"What are you doing in here?"

Louise stood up and folded her arms. "I came to wake you up. You're not going to lounge around all day, especially since you only have a few hours before going to the Websters. But what on earth made you put that on your closet?" She pointed her well-manicured index finger at the objectionable piece.

"God, Mom, that's Jimi Hendrix! Only the greatest guitar player in the world, unless you count Carlos Santana. I've been trying to sound out some of his riffs on my Fender," she said, sitting up.

"It's druggie music and has been for the last ten years," Louise said, putting her hands on her hips.

"Whatever. I love him," Emma said. She got out of bed and walked to her *en suite* bathroom, shutting the door loudly behind her.

"You can love him all you want, but you will not—and I repeat, *will not*—use thumbtacks on my walls or my doors!"

Louise commanded through the door.

"It's my room!"

"Are you paying rent?"

"You're being ridiculous, Mom!" Emma said before flushing the toilet.

Louise strode to the closet door and removed each thumbtack, then placed the poster on Emma's bed. She would save round two for later since she was already running late.

***

When she arrived at Dr. Blevins's office, Louise was surprised to see Bitsy seated on the Chesterfield, chatting casually with Olivia. They quieted as Louise approached the secretary.

"Good morning, Mrs. Caldwell," Olivia said with a wan smile. "How's, you know, everything?"

"Everything is just fine! I'm here to pick up Emma's assignments," she said, smiling cordially. "I was assured they would be waiting for me."

Olivia handed Louise a manila envelope. "Everything should be here except for the biology assignments since they're doing a practicum. Dissecting an earthworm, I believe," she said, wrinkling her nose. Louise heard Bitsy laugh.

"Remember when we had to do that?" Bitsy said to Louise. "You were so calm holding the scalpel. I was a nervous wreck."

"I guess that's why I got an A," Louise said.

"And that's why I didn't!" Bitsy giggled.

"I'll see you tomorrow, Bits," Louise said. "We have to get this week's church bulletin ready to go. Olivia, thank you again. Have a lovely day."

Louise was walking down the hall when she heard footsteps behind her.

"Is Emma all right?" Bitsy said once she caught up with Louise. "Is she ill with something?"

Louise stared at her oldest friend, wondering for the first time if she really knew Bitsy at all. *Why was she feigning ignorance?*

"She's just fine, but thanks for asking. She'll be back at school next Tuesday."

"I'm glad to hear that, but I can't imagine what set her off with that whole cotillion business. You must be so angry with her! As mothers, we must stick together and do what we can to keep our girls on the right track," she said in a conspiratorial tone. "I mean, she upset the entire committee and for what? To make a point? If so, I guess I missed it."

"Look, Bits, I'm sure you think this was her retaliation for your excluding her from your little commercial for the dealership. Trust me when I tell you, she didn't care in the least," Louise lied. "As I've learned, though, people can surely surprise you."

Bitsy stopped walking and folded her arms. "Louise, look. Bobby gave me the responsibility to coordinate our advertising because he knows I can do it. For goodness' sake, I know *I* can do it! And for once, well, I just wanted the opportunity to do things my way, without your influence. I figured if Emma was in the ad, you'd end up calling the shots. Truly, I didn't mean to hurt her. Or you. I hope you can see things from my perspective."

Louise considered Bitsy's words as she watched the woman fiddle with the strap of her handbag. But only for a moment, before looking at her watch. "The day is getting away from me. I must run—I'm supposed to be at the auxiliary meeting in thirty minutes," she said, doing her best to remain unflustered by Bitsy's disloyalty. Clearly, Bitsy was nervous about speaking her mind. *And why shouldn't she be? Doesn't she remember who brought her this far?*

"Did I miss an announcement? Am I supposed to attend?" Bitsy asked, pulling her pocket calendar from her bag.

"No, this is for the fashion show, and as I recall, you elected

not to serve on an auxiliary committee this year due to chairing the cotillion committee," Louise said with an innocent smile. "Everyone has their limits."

"That's rich, my dear. You seem to juggle everything, just like you always have."

"Again, everyone has their limits, Bits. You'll see. Bye for now." Louise wiggled her fingers in a wave, then proceeded toward the exit. *I need to read up on Judas,* she thought as she slipped behind the wheel of her Cadi.

***

Her committee chairwomen were gathered around the conference table, nibbling on donuts and talking animatedly when Louise glided into the room. "Good morning, ladies!" she said, placing her designer purse next to the bouquet on the credenza. "Are you all ready to make some decisions?" she said, clapping her hands enthusiastically. The women nodded and smiled. *What else could they do?*

After pouring herself a cup of coffee, she took her seat at the head of the table.

"Are you ready to take notes, Kay?" she asked her co-chair.

"Of course," Kay said, holding up her yellow legal pad. "As a reminder, our show is exactly one month from tomorrow on April twenty-first. We have a lot of work to do."

"Thank you," Louise said abruptly, cutting Kay off. "Let's get started by addressing the elephant in the room. Our theme." She looked down the table with a smile at the Webster sisters, who co-chaired the silent auction committee as they had done for years. "The proposed theme is 'Resplendently Red,' a color long associated with power and strength. But it has come to my attention this theme could be misconstrued into something political." She looked around the table for comments.

"I dare say, any reference to red could be seen as political, honestly," Rose Webster said, looking at her sister for agreement.

"Indeed, though this community is solidly Republican," Iris Webster said.

"True enough. Which is why we're decidedly anti-Communism! Haven't you heard the phrase, 'Better dead than red,' for goodness' sakes? We don't need that kind of negativity splashed upon the auxiliary," Rose said before taking a bite of her pastry.

"But it would be so visually inspiring," Louise countered. "And the photos, can you imagine? I think it was Audrey Hepburn who said something like, 'There's a color of red for everyone.' It could be so chic, though I must admit, it's not a color I've typically worn."

"Rose is right, dear. It's Communist," Iris said. She looked around the table and smiled when coiffed heads slowly nodded. She looked back at Louise, seemingly waiting for her ruling.

"The alternative theme that has been presented is 'Disco Landing,'" Louise said, trying to keep her expression blank. "Though to my knowledge, we don't have a disco nightclub in the vicinity."

"They've started teaching a class at the Y," Iris said, nudging her sister. They giggled in unison.

"Isn't disco kind of on its way out?" Kay asked innocently.

"Not at all!" Rose said. "Just imagine, an entire fashion show of satin and sequins. Like a Studio 64 right here in Stuarts Landing!"

"And the music!" Iris said. "Think about it–'I Will Survive!' And the Bee Gees!"

Louise looked at the sisters and wondered if the septuagenarians had become senile. She was unfamiliar with the songs and uncomfortable with the possibility of such a garish production.

"Are you taking classes, ladies?" Louise asked. The Websters nodded with delight.

"Alphonso is a very gifted teacher," Iris said. Rose giggled.

"Very," Rose echoed.

Louise looked across the table at Kay, who merely raised her eyebrows.

"We have two choices to consider, ladies," Louise said. "I don't think it's a good idea to open the floor to any further ideas. If we can reach consensus on the theme here, we don't need to take it to the full membership for a vote tomorrow. To summarize, we can vote for 'Resplendently Red' or 'Disco Landing.' Is there any further discussion?"

She paused as the ladies looked around the room, waiting for additional commentary.

"Hearing none, let us vote. All in favor of 'Resplendently Red,' please raise your hands."

Kay's hand went up, as did Louise's. A newer committee chairwoman, Cindy, raised hers as well.

"All right. Those in favor of 'Disco Landing,' please raise your hands."

The Webster sisters shot their arms into the air, as did the remaining nine women. Louise wasn't surprised as no one ever challenged the Websters, but her ego was bruised just the same.

"Kay, what say you?" Louise asked formally.

"The theme for the 1979 Women's Auxiliary Annual Fashion Show, with proceeds benefiting the conversion of the sawmill into a museum, will be 'Disco Landing.'"

The room exploded with applause. The Webster sisters did some sort of synchronized motion, pointing their right index fingers high in the air, then crossing down across their chest, then back in the air. *Were they impersonating John Travolta? Or having some type of geriatric episode?* Louise was struck by the irony of using a flash-in-the-pan trend to fundraise for historic preservation, but the decision had been made.

"We will need to move forward with the styles to be modeled. Are our style chairwomen here?" Louise said, looking at Kay.

"They're on vacation," she said.

Louise rolled her eyes. "But we must move quickly!"

"I'd be happy to help," called a familiar voice behind her. Louise rotated in her chair to see Bitsy entering the room. The Websters clapped their hands.

"How very gracious of you," Louise said, tamping down the anger building in her chest.

"I simply love disco!" Bitsy said, grinning widely. "It will be fun!"

"Oh yes, yes it will," Louise said. *Bitsy is becoming unmanageable. What happened to the friend who used to worship me?*

Though it was only her second day at The Pig, Miriam had already begun feeling like her old self—someone comfortable with greeting everyone she knew as if they were familiar friends, just as she had done at their hardware stores. The day was slightly slower than her first, mostly elderly shoppers she assumed were retired and who traversed the aisles as couples. She smiled, daydreaming about her golden years with George. Maybe they, too, would run errands together, selecting their produce and contemplating what new meal they might prepare. *That is, if I could get him interested in learning to cook. A girl can dream!*

"We've got a special on homemade pies in the bakery," Roy told her that morning. "I've tasted them all. Cherry is my favorite, but the apple's pretty good too. Be sure and tell the customers before they're finished checking out!"

"I do love a good pie," Miriam said. "Maybe I'll bring one home for George."

"Don't forget about your employee discount," Roy said. "Comes in real handy. Remember, if you need me, just call me on the intercom. I'll be in the back office putting together next week's schedule."

"Yes sir, boss!"

The early afternoon was slow. With no one in line, Miriam moved to the magazine rack by the grocery conveyor to ensure everything was arranged neatly. She had just picked up the latest issue of *Good Housekeeping* featuring a story on

"The Cabbage Soup Miracle Diet" when two elderly women approached her checkout line. Miriam quickly took her place behind the register and watched as they gingerly placed their items on the conveyor. She had never seen anyone like them, not even in the movies. Their pixie hairstyles shone like liquid silver, and their lips and nails were painted fire-engine red to match the psychedelic colors of their respective tunics. Miriam knew the designer must be Pucci, and vintage at that, because she had once tried to create her own version of the look. It was an unfortunate mess. The women's skeletal forearms were stacked with silver bangle bracelets, and other than in pictures of Native Americans, Miriam had never seen anyone wearing turquoise beads, which were the size of gumdrops. She breathed in heavily, trying to place their fragrance. *Ah, yes, patchouli.* They were the most exotic women she had ever encountered... birds of paradise personified.

"Good afternoon, ladies! I hope you found everything you were looking for," Miriam said as she began ringing up their items. "And in case you missed it, we're running a special on our homemade Piggy Pies today. Half off!"

The women turned to one another, then put on the eyeglasses hanging from their necks to peer at Miriam.

"Thank you, dear, but we prefer cakes. Don't we, Iris?" said the older-looking of the two.

"In limited amounts, of course," Iris replied. "But we thank you for the reminder." She continued unpacking their basket, taking great care with the produce.

"Be careful with the tomatoes!" the older woman said to Iris. "We saw you at the auxiliary luncheon. So, you're new here?" she asked, turning her attention to Miriam.

"Yes, my husband and I just moved," Miriam said, beginning to bag the groceries she already had rung up. "My name is Miriam. Miriam Llewelyn." She extended her hand.

"Pleased to meet you. I'm Rose Webster, and this is my

younger sister, Iris." Rose took Miriam's hand and shook it warmly. *What an apt name... her skin is as soft as a rose petal,* Miriam thought.

"Hi, Miriam. Welcome to our community! What brought you here, if I may ask?" Iris said.

"My husband George and I owned a business in Lexington. We were doing well, and then we weren't," Miriam said with a shrug. "We decided a change of scenery would be good for both of us, so here we are!"

"Well, now, that's a right shame," Rose said. "What kind of business was it?"

"Hardware," Miriam said, double bagging the carton of eggs. "But that's behind us now."

"How on earth did you choose Stuarts Landing, of all places?" Iris asked, pushing the empty cart forward. Rose began loading the bags.

"Oh, please, Miss, or is it Missus, Webster? I can do that," Miriam said.

"It's Miss, and nonsense. It's good for my upper arms!" Rose said with a throaty laugh.

"We, um, we just heard really good things about the area and so, yeah. We made the move." Miriam's instincts told her to keep quiet about her granddaddy.

"Any children?" Iris asked.

Miriam shook her head. "Not in the dear Lord's plan for us," she said, ringing up the last item.

"And is your husband working?" Rose asked.

"We're not trying to pry, dear," Iris said. "We just haven't met anyone new here in ages!"

Miriam nodded. "That's okay. My husband just started working last week at Butler Automotive. He's the service manager," she said. The sisters turned to each other, and their shared look appeared to be telegraphing something, but they remained silent.

"He's really happy there. And I love working here."

"That's wonderful to hear," Iris said. "This is a very tight community, as you can imagine. Too tight if you ask me."

"Uptight is more like it," Rose said, pulling her envelope of coupons from her macrame bag and handing them to Miriam.

"We should invite you over for lunch," Iris said. "What days are you off?"

Miriam began subtracting the coupons from their total. "I'm not sure just yet. My boss is working on schedules as we speak."

"Well, if you would, please write down your address so we can send you a proper invitation," Iris said. "We would love to get to know you!"

"That is so kind of you. Your total today, with coupons, is forty-two dollars and eleven cents."

Rose wrote out the check and handed it to Miriam. "Groceries are getting so expensive!" she exclaimed while Miriam placed their last bag in the cart. "We usually have our man Jasper do the shopping, but for some reason, we felt called to do it ourselves today."

"Well, I'm sure glad you did. Would you like help out?" Miriam said with a smile.

"Thank you, but no," Iris said. "Did you write your address on the receipt?" She had replaced her eyeglasses with a pair of red cat-eye sunglasses.

"We don't have a permanent address just yet," Miriam said. "We're staying at the Cardinal Inn until we can find a place to rent. Ultimately, we want to buy, but we're just not there yet."

Iris removed her sunglasses and looked at Rose, who had taken charge of the cart. Once again, Miriam watched as the sisters seemed to communicate wordlessly. She knew twins had their own secret language, or so people said, but was the same true for all sisters? *These women are unique, indeed.*

The sisters nodded to one another, then grinned.

"As it happens," Iris said, "we have a guesthouse on our property that has been empty for too long..."

Rose interrupted her. "It was the servants' quarters, actually, back when the tobacco farm was still in the family."

"Ancient history," Iris said with a sharp look. "It's got two bedrooms, a nice kitchen, a living area, a bathroom, of course, and room for a garden around back."

"It sounds lovely," Miriam said, closing her eyes to imagine canning her homegrown vegetables.

"It would require a great deal of work," Rose said. "But I do believe you might like it. Would you like to come by after work and take a look?"

Miriam couldn't contain her enthusiasm. "Yes, I'd love to!" she said, grinning and clapping like a cheerleader.

"Don't forget, we have Emma coming to the house at two," Iris said, looking at her watch.

"That's right... but we'll be finished with her in a few hours," Rose said.

Iris removed a card from an engraved silver case and handed it to Miriam. *The Webster House, 1 Webster Way*. Miriam furrowed her brow. "I'm not sure I've been on that road," she said.

"Oh, you wouldn't have. It's a private drive," Iris said. "Take Main Street north until it ends. Turn right, then go about two miles. You'll see our driveway on the left."

"We have a historical marker too," Rose said, smiling.

"That's so interesting! For what?" Miriam asked.

The sisters looked at each other and laughed.

"For being the first family to own land and build a home here," Iris said.

Miriam let out a low whistle. "So, you're like Stuarts Landing royalty?" Miriam asked.

"Some might say so," Iris said, twirling her sunglasses

mindlessly. She gave Miriam a wink.

"We'll see you this evening then?" Rose asked.

"I get finished at five," Miriam said.

"Then we'll see you at five fifteen," Iris said. Miriam was enchanted.

Things are looking up. I just hope it stays that way.

12

Emma was sitting in the den, snacking on corn chips and watching *All My Children*, when her mother seemed to appear from nowhere. She wore an expression Emma didn't recognize, and it was giving her the creeps, honestly, so she unfurled her legs and rose to turn off the television.

"Here are your assignments," she said, placing the manila envelope on the ottoman. "I told you to be ready by one forty-five."

"I am ready," Emma said with a sigh. "Do I really have to do this?"

"I've had more than my fill of opposition today, young lady. Yes, you really have to do this. Let's get going," her mother said, turning around and marching from the room.

Nestled in her mother's Cadi, Emma looked cautiously at her mother.

"Everything okay?" she said.

"I'm surprised you're wearing cutoff shorts, Emma," her mother replied, maneuvering out of the driveway and onto Maple Lane. "A dress would have been more appropriate, don't you think?"

"It's not like I'm going to high tea with the queen," Emma said, rolling her eyes.

"Close enough," her mother said, shaking her blonde head. "These women are something else."

"What happened now?" Occasionally, she found her mother entertaining. Especially when she was in a snit.

"People just need to know their place," she said. "Certain things simply aren't done."

Emma knew all about the right time to wear white shoes, madras, and linen, and she understood butter should always be applied to the bread dish instead of the roll directly. The other "rules," though, what was even the point?

"You don't just storm into a committee meeting you're not part of and volunteer without being asked!" her mother said, her porcelain face flushing with anger. "And 'Disco Landing,' of all things. It's preposterous!"

"What are you talking about, Mom?" Emma said, playing with the fringe of her shorts.

"And to think we've been best friends since high school," her mother continued. "The sisters, well, they can do what they like."

"I'm sincerely confused," Emma said.

"So am I, Emma. So am I."

At precisely two o'clock, Louise pulled into the mile-long drive leading to Webster House. Emma had only been there once, some ten years ago when the sisters hosted a holiday party for the children of auxiliary members. She remembered it as a magical occasion, with the great room transformed into a scene from "The Nutcracker." Everyone received either a handmade nutcracker soldier or a Clara doll, depending on their gender. Emma had asked for the nutcracker; her mother corrected her and said those were just for the boys.

The estate hadn't changed since then, and it probably didn't look much different than when it was first built, Emma imagined. While their own home was quite palatial, Webster House reminded Emma of a museum. Constructed of red brick, the two-storied main house sat as the centerpiece amidst beautifully landscaped gardens and carefully tended parterres, which looked like swirls of paisley to Emma's untrained eye. The gabled roof, three dormer windows, and two brick

chimneys gave the estate a look of permanence, impervious to change.

Her mother pulled into the circular drive and parked. Emma grabbed her tote bag. "Let's just get this over with," she said, getting out of the car.

They walked up the steps and used the lion's head doorknocker to let the crones know they had arrived. Emma fidgeted with the hem of her denim shorts while her mother stood patiently. The door opened with an explosion of color quite unexpectedly, Emma thought, given the stately nature of the home's exterior. She knew the sisters weren't twins, but they certainly seemed to have coordinated their ridiculous outfits.

"Welcome, welcome!" Iris said, opening the door. "Be careful of the cats—the little devils are always trying to escape. Please, come in," she said, taking a step back. Rose was right behind her sister, holding what appeared to be a scrapbook.

"Thank you so much for having us over," Emma's mother said, stepping into the foyer. "I'll just be here for a moment, then I'll pick Emma up around five, if that's okay."

"That's exactly what we had discussed, dear," Rose said. "Won't you sit with us for a moment?"

Emma looked at her mother, who seemed less agitated than before. "I'd be happy to, but then I really must run," she said, glancing at her Cartier.

They followed the sisters through the varnished pocket doors to the front parlor, the décor of which was not at all what Emma expected. The turquoise walls, complemented by the brilliant white wainscoting, were replete with several abstract paintings, equally jarring and hypnotic. The hardwood floors were covered with ample Persian rugs in shades of cerulean, red, gold, and black, and the bookshelves were full to the brim with an assortment of what looked like first-edition manuscripts and a collection of Native American pottery. The furniture was upholstered in white, save the red velvet chaise lounging atop a zebra hide in the far corner. Emma took a seat on the couch but not before marveling at the painting behind it.

"Is that…" Emma said, looking at Iris in awe.

"Yes, it's a Picasso, dear," she said. "Lovely man, really. Isn't that right, sister?"

"Absolutely. We had such a time with him in Cannes, didn't we? That was a summer we won't forget," Rose said.

"How did I not know you had met him?" Emma's mother asked, sitting down next to Emma.

"I suppose it's never come up in conversation, come to think of it," Iris said. "But then there's quite a bit we've never really discussed." She looked Emma's mother directly in the eyes. Her mother coughed nervously, or so it sounded to Emma.

"Shall I ring for our refreshments?" Rose said. Her sister nodded.

"I really should be on my way," Emma's mother said, standing. "Ladies, thank you, again. I know Emma will enjoy her time with you."

Iris stood and extended her bejeweled hand to touch Louise's arm. "Are you quite all right after the meeting today, dear? I know how much you like everything to be orderly," she said, chuckling.

"I'm just fine! Things will work out as they're supposed to," Louise said, walking toward the foyer.

"They always do!" Iris said with a knowing smile.

"I'll be back at five. Emma, please mind your manners," she said before leaving. Emma rolled her eyes.

Once her mother was gone, Emma sat back on the couch and continued looking around the Bohemian room, unlike anything she'd ever seen. A blue-point Siamese jumped into her lap unexpectedly, and Emma yelped.

"Oh, Diva won't hurt you," Rose said, sitting down in one of the two club chairs across from the sofa.

"I think her claws got me," Emma said, gently pushing the cat aside and checking her unprotected thighs for scratches.

"Great beauty can often inflict great pain," Iris said. "Ah, thank you, Jasper," she said as an intriguing young man set a wooden platter on the rough-edged coffee table. He struck Emma as another work of art.

"Iced tea, dear?" Rose said, using the silver tongs to place a lemon wedge in the cobalt-blue glass. Emma nodded.

"Is Jasper..."

"He's our housekeeper," Iris said brightly. "Isn't he darling? And he's a writer!"

"A very talented one at that," Rose said, nodding. "Much better than I ever was and, goodness knows, I tried. Hummus, dear?"

Emma leaned forward to examine the crystal bowl full of tan goop with some kind of flat bread arranged in a basket beside it.

"What is it?" she said, trying not to grimace.

"Oh, it's called 'hummus,' and it's divine. Basically, it's pureed chickpeas," Iris said, "with a few more ingredients I can't remember. Jasper makes it himself." She placed a dollop of hummus and a few bread triangles on her plate. "He makes the pita bread too," she said, dipping her bread into the hummus and popping it into her mouth.

Not wishing to appear rude, Emma served herself a spoonful of hummus and two pita quarters, then took a cautious bite.

"Mmm! I've never tasted anything like it!" she said, her mouth still full. "It's, it's so nutty tasting!" Rose pumped her fist into the air while Iris laughed.

"So, your mother explained your current situation," Iris began. "We'd like to hear what you have to say." She leaned

back in her chair and crossed her legs.

"Yes, dear," Rose said, scratching the chin of a black Persian sprawled across her tunic. "Clue here is interested, and so are we. Do tell."

Emma took a sip of her iced tea, which tasted like ginger, then began.

***

"As I understand it," Rose said thirty minutes later, "you decided to take what you believed to be a righteous stand against a time-honored tradition. That must have taken great courage." Iris nodded enthusiastically.

"Tradition is a funny thing," Rose continued. "Folks tend to cling to tradition if it benefits them in some way, or they tend to question it if it benefits them in some way. Your friend, Debbie, for example. Didn't you say she was the student liaison to the cotillion committee?"

Emma nodded, serving herself another scoop of hummus. Jasper appeared wordlessly, refreshing the carafe of iced tea. *Is he wearing gauze pajamas?* Emma wondered, watching as he practically floated from the room.

"The success of the event, then, is in her interests," Rose said. "Is this about her?"

Emma began picking at her thumbnail. "Not really, though she wasn't the friend I thought she was. She basically told me her mom said it would look like favoritism if I got put in the commercial because our moms are best friends. But that just doesn't seem to make any sense." She lowered her head in despair.

The sisters looked at each other and began laughing. Emma looked up, shocked they were being so insensitive.

"I don't see why that's funny," she said.

"Oh, sweet girl, we're not laughing at you," Iris said.

"Debbie's mother has been competing with your mother since they were your age. No matter how hard she tried, Bitsy always ended up playing second fiddle to Louise. I wonder if Debbie feels that way about you?"

"That's what I think too," Rose said. "Not including you in the commercial may just be Debbie's way of thinking she finally has something you don't, and that gives her a little bump in self-esteem. Didn't we see something about that on *Phil Donahue*?" she asked, looking at her sister.

"I think it was *Good Morning America*," Iris said. "I love Joan Lunden, but David Hartman should do something about those teeth," she said, shaking her head. "Like the mouth of a horse, really."

Emma listened to the sisters bantering, wondering why on earth her mother thought spending time with them would be helpful. *Although the hummus and ginger tea are quite nice.* Diva jumped back onto the couch, proceeding to lift her hind leg and give her privates a bath.

Iris noticed and said, "That just means she's comfortable with you."

Gee, I'm honored, Emma thought, mentally rolling her eyes.

"So, Emma, back to your situation. Are you really that opposed to cotillion or simply the idea that Debbie is in charge?" Rose asked.

"It's just so stuffy and outdated. I don't know, it feels like the idea is to put us all in these perfect little molds that are a hundred years old," Emma said. "Tradition is oppressive, don't you think? I mean, isn't this elitism based on money and class?"

Iris cleared her throat. "Money and class are not one and the same, dear." She cast a knowing look at Rose.

"Emma, you are fortunate to have been born into a family with both. I'm not sure the same can be said for some of your peers, whom I shall not name. But that's not the point. I believe one earns the right to buck tradition, only after fully understanding the consequences of doing so," Rose said.

"Well, your grandmother, for example—"

Rose quickly interrupted her. "Iris!" Rose said. "That's not your story to tell!"

Emma sensed a shift in the air, so she decided to change the subject. "I just wish my mom would let me follow my dreams, but she says they're impractical," she said as Diva curled up next to her. Emma's eyes began to water, and then she sneezed.

"Oh, dear. Are you allergic?" Rose said. Emma nodded then sneezed again. Rose stood up, walked to the mantel, and hit the Tibetan gong. Jasper appeared as if from thin air.

"Would you be a dear and take the girls to their cat-a-tat, please?" Jasper bowed, picked up Diva in one arm and, with some effort, pulled Clue from her perch on Rose's chair before floating from the room. Emma watched, intrigued by this silent—but very handsome—man.

"What are your dreams, dear?" Iris asked.

"You know how there are all these rock bands, and they're all men?" Emma said.

"Well, of course. We absolutely adore Led Zeppelin," Iris said.

"Don't forget the Stones," Rose said. "We've seen them a few times!"

"So, you get my point," Emma said, even more impressed by these women. "The only female rock group I know of is Heart. And they're sisters. I want to start a girl band someday, so I've been teaching myself to play the guitar. Daddy got me a Fender last year, but Mom doesn't approve."

"Why, playing music is wonderful for the brain!" Rose said.

"And it's great for the soul too," Iris said.

"It's the only thing that really makes me feel, I don't know, like myself," Emma said, shaking her head. "But it's not

practical. At least according to her."

"While it's unfortunate your mother doesn't seem to support your interests, you don't have to let her discourage you. You're allowed to pursue your passions. It's 1979, after all! Some of us didn't have that luxury," Iris said, leaning her head back against her chair and closing her eyes.

"What's in the past should stay in the past, dear," Rose said, leaning over to pat her hand. Emma was doing her best to read between the lines, but she felt there was a bigger story at play she may never hear.

Before Emma could speak, they heard a knock.

"That must be your mother," Iris said to Emma. "Would you please let her in?"

Emma uncoiled herself from the couch to answer the door.

"Hi there!" her mother said, entering the foyer. She seemed in much better spirits.

"We so enjoyed our visit," Rose said with Iris at her side. "Emma is welcome to visit any time, and if she does, I'd love it if she'd bring her guitar."

Emma noticed her mother wince at the mention of her prized instrument but chose to ignore it. "Yes, ma'am. Thank you for your hospitality," she said before following her mother to the car. She looked over her shoulder and saw the two women waving from the landing, their tunics billowing like wildflowers in a soft breeze.

Her mother started the engine while Emma buckled her seatbelt.

"What in the world is he doing?" her mother said, inclining her head toward the parterre, where a figure clad in white was practicing tai chi.

"Oh, that's just Jasper being Jasper," Emma said with a giggle. "Doing his tai chi. It's a martial art."

Her mother ran her manicured fingers through her freshly coiffed hair before donning her sunglasses.

"Does it work by boring the opponent to death?" she said under her breath.

"Mom! You're so close-minded!"

"And I'm okay with that," Louise said, putting the Cadi into drive.

They were halfway down the narrow lane when they saw a clunky blue car approaching from the opposite direction. It was the ugliest vehicle Emma had ever seen. *Who would be caught dead driving such a disaster?*

As they got closer, Louise slowed down to see which of the two would move onto the grass so the other could pass. Realizing the other driver wasn't going to yield, Louise maneuvered her car to the right. The blue car inched by but not before they could see who was driving.

Louise gasped. "It's that woman!" She peered into her rearview mirror as the visitor made her way to the house.

"Who?"

"I believe her name is Mary or some such. She's new in town. Definitely not Stuarts Landing material," Louise said with a sniff. She moved back onto the drive and sped up.

"That was elitist," Emma said, reaching to turn on the radio.

"Not today, Emma. Not today."

Emma changed the station in time to catch Blondie belting out "Heart of Glass." She grinned as her mother groaned.

13

Bitsy was flipping through the *Richmond Yellow Pages* when she heard Louise's clipped footsteps prancing down the hall toward the church office. If a criminal lineup used sound rather than sight, Bitsy would be able to pick out her friend's walk with complete certainty. *Like a dressage horse in Andrew Geller heels,* she thought with a smirk. Louise sat down at the desk and opened her can of Tab, taking a long sip before putting a sheet of paper in the typewriter.

"Do you have the pastor's weekly message?" she said.

"And good morning to you," Bitsy said. "Here it is," she said, giving Louise the handwritten document. "About yesterday. I didn't mean to upset you. I was just—"

"We've known each other a long time," Louise said, her fingers flying over the keys. "I expected more from you, to be honest."

Bitsy rolled her chair over to sit directly across the desk from her co-editor. "I thought about what you said, you know, my not volunteering for this year's fashion show because of cotillion, and I felt guilty," she said in her best peacemaking voice. "I was going to wait until after the meeting, but I heard the panic in your voice about the style co-chairs..."

Louise stopped typing and leaned across the table, her eyes squinting like a viper. "I never panic, Bitsy. Never."

Bitsy knew she was only making things worse, but she kept talking.

"You may have been right about the red theme," she said,

taking a different angle. Louise's expression softened, though she crossed her arms across her chest.

"Really? How so?"

"I was looking for boutiques in Richmond that might carry disco outfits," Bitsy said. "There certainly aren't any in Stuarts Landing."

"Of course not. I can't believe you would have thought otherwise," Louise said.

"I did find a few places where we can get disco balls for the ceiling, though," she continued, hoping for Louise's praise.

"How tacky," Louise said, returning her attention to her typewriter. "Besides, you're not on the decorations committee. Actually, you're not *formally* on any committee. But you are welcome to help until Natalie and Gigi return from their vacations." She resumed typing as Bitsy tried to read the situation.

"Well, I didn't find any disco boutiques in Richmond, but I can make a few calls," she said, pulling the phone closer to the Yellow Pages.

"No long-distance calls from the church phone, Bitsy. I would think you'd know better. About a lot of things," Louise said, pursing her lips.

"Such as? I'd love to hear it," Bitsy said, taking an emery board from her purse and leisurely filing her thumbnail to soothe her nerves. She had never been the subject of Louise's anger, at least as far as she knew. *I can't let her intimidate me,* she thought, *like she always has.*

"For one thing, you know how I feel about loyalty," Louise said, folding her hands in her lap. "That you would deign to disparage Emma yesterday was beyond the pale, even for you."

"I just thought you'd want to get ahead of it before people start gossiping about you," Bitsy said, putting the nail file back in her purse. "I know how sensitive you are about such things."

Louise's eyes narrowed, and she smiled slowly, though it

felt more like she was baring her teeth in a sign of aggression. Bitsy's palms began to sweat.

"Is that so, Bits? Please, tell me more." She leaned forward, put her elbows on the desk, and cupped her chin in her hands. Her eyes were flashing like warning flares.

Bitsy shifted uncomfortably in her chair as she contemplated how best to extricate herself from the situation.

"You've worked hard to maintain your dignified reputation, Louise, and you've earned everyone's respect," she said.

Louise smiled and nodded. "Go on."

"And I know we shouldn't be judged by what our children do. Nor should our children be judged by what we do. You, of all people, know that firsthand," Bitsy said. Louise's smile faded as Bitsy stepped into dangerous territory. "And it's wrong."

"Please don't," Louise said, holding up her hand.

"While I can't say I understand why Em would make such a stink about cotillion, I understand why she thinks she needs to separate her identity from yours, in a way," Bitsy said. "You do have a very strong personality, and you cast a long shadow. I've stood in it for years."

Louise sat back and crossed her long legs, her eyes unblinking. "For what it's worth, Bits, I don't believe I could have been any different. You know what my family's name means around here. It comes with certain expectations."

"I sort of think you felt the need to compensate for your mom's, well, for your mom," Bitsy said.

"When did you turn into a shrink?" Louise asked, crossing her arms and cocking her head.

"I've started reading *Ms.* magazine, and the articles are quite enlightening," Bitsy said.

Louise began laughing, and soon, the tears were streaming down her cheeks. "Bitsy," she said, "you're just full of surprises, aren't you?" She dabbed her eyes with a tissue, shaking her head. "What's wrong with *Ladies' Home Journal?*"

"I'm just trying to keep up with the times is all," she said with a shrug.

"Which brings us back to the present matter. Disco. Of all the absurd ideas," Louise said.

"Look, Lu, I'm sorry about yesterday," she said with all the sincerity she could muster. "Please forgive me," she said, reaching her hand across the desk. Louise stared at her for a moment, then took Bitsy's hand into her own.

"Of course, Bits, but only because you can't seem to help yourself. Now, about the fashion show."

"If we can't find store-bought outfits, we may have to make them ourselves," Bitsy offered, flipping through the Yellow Pages while electing to ignore Louise's snide comment.

"I can't fathom people paying good money to see a bunch of homemade clothes. They can see that every week at church," she said with a smirk.

"Wow," Bitsy said, holding up her hands and curling her fingers like claws. "Seriously, we could turn it into a competition, maybe? Run an ad in the *Weekly Gazette* to see who'd like to serve as our designers? It could be fun!"

That was nowhere close to Louise's vision, and Bitsy knew it, yet their options were limited.

"The show is in less than four weeks, Bits. I'm not sure we can pull it off."

"We just need a few people who can sew and give them each a budget for patterns, fabric, and notions. I would think Cloth World has everything they would need. Maybe the store would even agree to be a sponsor?" Bitsy said, growing more enthusiastic about her idea.

Louise looked at her, mental wheels obviously spinning as she drummed her index finger on her chin. "I can't speak for you, but I've never been to Cloth World." Louise wrinkled her nose. "All I know is we need ten outfits. Ten. Those of

us modeling will need to be fitted at least a week before the show, which leaves less than three weeks to find the so-called designers, approve their patterns, and see the finished products. Do you really think that's possible?"

Bitsy took a deep breath. She wasn't sure her idea would work, but she was willing to take the chance. After all, Louise was the co-chair, so she would either get the credit or the blame. "We can do this. It will be unlike any show the auxiliary has ever produced."

"All right. You win. Can you put together the ad copy? If we submit it today, that should be enough time to be in Monday's edition."

"I'm on it!" Bitsy said, pulling a legal tablet from the desk.

Louise continued typing up the pastor's message while Bitsy worked on the advertisement. "Do you think we should put up flyers too?"

Louise nodded. "If we have them by this afternoon's meeting, we can ask the ladies to post them around town."

"And we want people to know this is open to everyone, not just members," Bitsy said. "Does Pearl sew?"

Louise glared at her. "Do you really think that's appropriate?"

"Do you?" Bitsy asked. *Honestly, I have no idea,* she thought. *But why not?*

"Speaking of help," Louise said, bolting upright. "When I went to pick up Emma from Webster House yesterday, I saw the strangest thing. That young man with a ponytail, Jasper, was wearing a white floaty ensemble and doing some kind of exercise in the front garden. Can you imagine?"

"But was he cute?" Bitsy said with a giggle. "The Websters—you have to give them credit!"

"Well, as the oldest family in Stuarts Landing, they can be as eccentric as they wish, I suppose," Louise said. "My grandma Nora adored them. My mother, well..."

Bitsy interrupted her, then wished she hadn't. "Why was Emma there?"

"We thought she should learn a bit more about tradition."

"From the Websters? You're joking!" Bitsy said.

"They know more than you might think. Remember, I've known them my entire life, Bits. They'll be a good influence on Em."

"If you say so," Bitsy said.

"And there's one other thing that was odd about yesterday," Louise said. "When we were driving down the lane from their home, this blue clunker–it almost looked like an egg on wheels–was coming from the opposite direction. Didn't even have the courtesy to maneuver to the side so I could pass. I had to pull over. It was like that game of chicken the fellas used to play on the Strip. Ridiculous! You'll never guess who it was."

Thanks to her husband, Bitsy knew a fair amount about cars, and that particular description didn't sound familiar. "No idea," she said, rubbing her neck.

"It was that new woman you brought to church. Mary, I think it is?" Louise sniffed.

"Oh, you mean Miriam!" Bitsy said with a smile. "She's a doll. So authentic! I wonder what she was doing there?"

"Well, we know the sisters already have a housekeeper," Louise said.

Bitsy was growing more intrigued by this newcomer. *I have an idea, and I just know Louise will hate it.*

"I'm going to invite her to lunch," Bitsy said. "She may be just what we need around here." When Louise clenched her teeth, Bitsy was certain her idea was a good one.

14

When George arrived home to the motel room on Thursday night, Miriam was in the kitchenette, dancing awkwardly to a Donna Summer tune on the radio. He closed the door, startling Miriam, who spun around and brandished a wooden spoon. "Oh, it's you!" she said with relief, turning down the music and placing the utensil back on the ceramic spoon rest. "I'm making spaghetti for dinner, and we have pie! Half price today, and they look sooo good."

"Hi, sweetheart," he said, removing his Butler Automotive vest and draping it over the chair. "Were you expecting someone else?" he asked with a grin.

"Just lost in thought," Miriam said, her eyes twinkling. "Beer?" For the second time in a week, Miriam was having a glass of wine.

"That would be nice," George said, taking a seat at the table and loosening his tie. "Long day. Crazy busy, what with it being near the end of warranties on the 1974 models. Otherwise, all I can say is, boy, it must be nice to be rich."

Miriam joined him at the table, bringing over their drinks. "That's an understatement," she said, "but what makes you say that?"

"Bobby is donating a brand-new Ford Fairmount to the Fulton Academy for their annual raffle. Some big to-do, I imagine. His daughter goes to school there," he said, taking a swig of his beer. "Mm. Hits the spot!" He belched for emphasis.

"How much does a car like that sell for?" Miriam asked,

recalling the conversation she had overheard the day before.

"The MSRP is about fifty-four hundred bucks," he said.

"I suppose they can afford it," Miriam said. She opted not to tell her husband about Mrs. Butler's purported *quid pro quo* with the headmaster to get some poor girl suspended. It wasn't really her concern, though she wouldn't have expected such a thing from the woman she first met at The Pig. *She seems so nice. Maybe I misunderstood what those girls were saying.*

"How was your day?" George said. "Other than scoring some half-priced pie."

"Well, don't forget about my discount," Miriam said.

"Every penny counts." He took another swig of beer.

While she wanted to wait until dessert, Miriam couldn't contain her news.

"George, we have been blessed, once again!" she said, her eyes sparkling with delight.

"As long as I'm with you, I'll always be blessed, honey," he said, patting her hand.

"Why, thank you, George. And ditto. But you can't possibly guess what happened today! I met these two older women in my checkout line, as colorful as peacocks, wearing the most flamboyant outfits I've ever seen. And their jewelry—all silver and turquoise. Nary a diamond or pearl on either of them!"

"Okay..."

"And they were really interested in me, asking me all kinds of questions about where we're from, what brought us here, and so on," she said.

"That must have been nice," George said. "You've always been so good with people."

"It gets better, George. They wanted to invite me to lunch, but they needed my address to send a formal note, I guess. I explained where we're living and that we're looking for a place to rent," she said, her excitement growing. "And get this!"

George leaned forward, folding his hands on the table.

"They have a guesthouse. Well, technically, it was once servants' quarters. But they said it's been empty, and they'd be happy to rent it to us!"

"That's certainly one option to consider, Mim," he said.

"I'm not finished," she said with a grin. "They invited me to come see it, so I went after work. That's why we're having store-bought sauce instead of homemade—I ran out of time."

"Everything you make is wonderful, Mim. But the house... did you like it?"

"George, I've never seen such an estate. It even has a historical marker! It's on Webster Way, and I swear, I think the main house sits about a mile from the entrance. It was so grand, honey, with gardens like something from Versailles."

"That sounds quite nice, but what's in it for them? From what you're describing, I wouldn't think they'd need the money," George said, furrowing his brow.

"Maybe they're just being good Christians, dear. They do seem a bit eccentric, but I found them refreshing after the other people I've met here. I must admit, it felt good to be welcomed," she said, pleating the skirt of her apron.

"How is the guesthouse?" he asked. "And how close is it to their house?"

"I wouldn't call their home a 'house.' It's more like a mansion, actually... it's enormous. The guesthouse, though, is probably about a quarter mile away. It's got plenty of space, beautiful hardwood floors, and enough room for a garden in back. The front porch is splendid—I can imagine sitting there on some Adirondack chairs, drinking our morning coffee. It just felt peaceful, you know? And the furniture is old, but it's still nice, so we won't have to buy much."

He was quiet for a moment, and she knew it best not to oversell the idea. The few times she had, well, things hadn't worked out as she had expected.

"What's the catch?" he said, ever the cautious one.

"The house does need work," Louise said. "It could use a fresh coat of interior paint, that much I could tell. Maybe a few other cosmetic improvements. But the sisters—Iris and Rose—said they would deduct the cost of supplies and our work itself from the rent." She sat back, smiling triumphantly.

"Honey, with our work schedules, we don't have a lot of free time," George said.

"Please, try and see this as an opportunity, George. With our background in hardware, we know what we're doing, right? And we can think of the improvements as a hobby we can share. Wouldn't that be special?" She nodded, subliminally encouraging him to agree.

"And it's a full-sized house, you say? What are they asking for rent? I'm not sure we have enough cash for a deposit and the first and last month, if that's what they want," he said.

Miriam let out a squeal. "They're asking only two fifty a month," she said, clapping her hands. "No deposit, no rental agreement, no first and last month's rent! Isn't that the most wonderful thing?"

"Almost too good to be true, Mim," he murmured. "Why are they doing this?"

"I don't know; maybe they're lonely. But I do believe they just liked me," she said, taking a sip of wine.

"Who doesn't?" George said, smiling at his bride.

"Not too many around here, it seems," she said under her breath.

"How did you leave it with them? Iris and Rose, you said?"

Miriam nodded. "We can move in in a week," she said, grinning ear to ear.

"Well, if you think this best, let's do it! Another Llewelyn adventure," he said with a chuckle. "I should never underestimate you, sweetheart. Another beer, please?"

"With pleasure, dear husband."

15

"I don't feel like going to church today, Mom. Can't I just go back to sleep?" Emma whined from beneath the covers. Louise put her hands on her hips, considering her daughter's request. She thought about her conversation with Bitsy and wondered if she was on to something, if Emma really was trying to distance herself from her mother. *That's what I did, but for different reasons. Obviously.*

"Sweetheart, I think it would be good for you. C'mon, get up, please," she said, picking up a pile of dirty clothes and placing it in the wicker hamper.

"I don't want to see Debbie," Emma said, pulling the top sheet over her head.

"I understand, though you're going to see her in two days when you go back to school. And trust me, there are plenty of people I don't enjoy seeing, but that's not the point. We're there to give thanks for our blessings," Louise said, sitting on the edge of her daughter's bed and pulling back the sheet.

"You really believe that?" Emma scoffed. "It's just another social event, with everybody judging everyone else. I don't see the point. We can be grateful in the comfort of our own home." She burrowed her head under her pillow melodramatically, as only a teenaged girl can do. Louise suppressed a chuckle.

"Well, you can be different, then," Louise said. "Get dressed—we leave in fifteen minutes."

***

"Looks pretty crowded today," Clifton said, maneuvering his Mercedes through the parking lot. "I'll drop you ladies by the door, then I'll meet you in the sanctuary after the men's prayer group, okay?" Louise leaned over and kissed his freshly shaved cheek.

"Always the gentleman," she said, patting his leg. "See you inside." Louise opened the passenger door. "Emma, out!"

Louise wasn't on that week's hospitality rotation, so she would have plenty of time to mingle before the service began. Emma followed her sullenly into the hall, keeping her head lowered like an animal on its way to slaughter. Louise looked over her shoulder at her petulant child. "Can you please just try to be pleasant?" she said. "It's only an hour and a half. Please."

Scanning the room, Louise saw the Webster sisters by the buffet, chatting with Bitsy and... Miriam?

What in heaven's name? Louise said to herself.

"Can I wait in the sanctuary?" Emma asked.

"Wouldn't you like a muffin and some juice?" Emma shook her head. "All right then. Sit in our regular pew, please." She watched her daughter quickly escape the crowded room before approaching the sisters—and company.

"Well, good morning, dear! Don't you look lovely in corn-flower blue? It suits your eyes," Iris said.

"And your beautiful complexion," Rose added.

"Why, thank you," Louise said. "As usual, you both are the most colorful women in the room." The Webster sisters smiled and gave each other a high five. Louise raised her eyebrows; Bitsy just laughed.

"Hi, Bits," Louise said. "Is that a new dress? It's stunning." Bitsy pretended to preen, fluffing her hair like a 1940s movie starlet. "How are we doing with the flyers?"

Bitsy smiled. "As it turns out, we have quite a helper! You remember Miriam. Miriam Llewelyn," she said, looking nervous.

Louise took a deep breath. *Be gracious.* "Yes, nice to see you again," Louise lied, looking briefly at Miriam. "Are you getting settled in?" Appraising the plain woman, she couldn't find anything to compliment, though that was an unspoken rule in her social circle. She caught herself doing exactly what Emma had criticized earlier–judging this poor woman for her unfortunate floral dress that bunched awkwardly around her ample hips. *She would be better suited in a solid color, Louise thought. And maybe a more flattering hairstyle. Stop it!*

"Everything is going perfectly," Miriam said. "We've been so blessed already! George–he's at home, packing–he's working at the dealership for Bitsy's husband. And we've found a place to live!"

Louise smiled politely.

"That's right," Iris said. "They move in next week!"

Louise's eyes widened, and she looked at Bitsy, who was beaming. "I beg your pardon?" Louise said, trying to keep her voice level.

"We met at The Pig," Miriam said happily. "I'm working there as a cashier for now. The sisters were so friendly. One thing led to another, and they invited me to see their guesthouse."

"The servants' quarters, you mean," Louise said.

"We don't refer to it as such, not anymore," Rose said, looking at her sister. Iris nodded solemnly.

That will be a topic for another occasion, Louise thought.

"It's just darling," Miriam said.

"And as it turns out, Miriam here is quite the seamstress," Bitsy said, placing her hand gently on Miriam's shoulder.

"I do love to sew," Miriam said. "I make most of my own clothes."

Well, that explains a lot. "And did you make," Louise struggled to contain a sneer, "did you make this?" she said, gesturing at Miriam's dress.

"I did. You know, polyester is hard to manipulate because it's so slippery, but I got a new running foot for my Singer, and it keeps the stitches from breaking." She looked at the women and nodded. "It's been a godsend."

Louise had never worn polyester, so she could only smile. "How wonderful for you."

"Lu, Miriam and I were talking about the fashion show," Bitsy said, "and how we're looking for designers to create some of the outfits? Anyway, she volunteered to take on three ensembles. Isn't that grand?"

"Well, shouldn't we see who all applies?" Louise said, staring at her oldest friend with a look intended to telegraph, "Are you quite mad?"

"I think it's delightful you want to help," Iris said. "You can set up your machine in our dining room if you'd like. Right, sister?"

"Oh, yes." Rose fluttered her arms. "It will be so much fun. We can put some disco music on the hi-fi for inspiration!"

"That might ruin Jasper's Zen," Iris said, chuckling. "We'll do it anyway!"

"Are you working full-time? At 'The Pig?'" Louise said, making air quotes. Because Pearl did their grocery shopping, Louise wasn't familiar with the establishment, nor did she care to be.

"I am," Miriam said. "And I just love it. I even get a discount."

"I would think that between working and moving, your time might be limited," Louise said, looking to Bitsy for agreement.

"She's already posted our flyers at The Pig," Bitsy said.

"And all the other stores in the shopping center," Miriam added.

"We certainly appreciate it," Louise said with as much sincerity as she could muster.

"Louise, I do believe Miriam should be on the show committee," Iris said. Louise winced internally—she had just been backed into a very uncomfortable corner.

"That would be so helpful!" Bitsy said as if Miriam wasn't there.

Louise looked at Miriam thoughtfully. "While I think it's an interesting idea, we're just under four weeks from the event," Louise said.

"All the more reason," Bitsy said. "As they say, 'Many hands make light work,' right?"

"Not to be unkind, but she's not a member of the women's auxiliary," Louise said. "We do have our bylaws." She looked at the Websters for assistance. They, along with her grandmother Nora, had written the rules, so they should know.

"I hereby nominate Miriam Llewelyn for emergency membership into the Stuarts Landing women's auxiliary," Iris said with a smile. "Do I have a second?"

"Second!" Rose sang, dramatically drawing out the syllables.

"That's, um, that's not really the way this works," Louise said. "You know that."

Miriam stood quietly, fidgeting with her ruffled sleeve. She clearly felt out of place. She couldn't help feeling a pang of compassion for this poor woman who, for some reason, had captivated the sisters. Yet, Miriam's apparent lack of concern for what other people thought gnawed at her, churning up unpleasant feelings she didn't understand.

"As president emerita, I do believe I am entitled to make this appointment, dear," Iris said, peering over the top of her cobalt-blue eyeglasses.

"We have an official membership application," Louise said.

"Phooey," Iris said.

"I'd be happy to fill it out," Miriam said.

"I can meet you at the chamber tomorrow," Bitsy said. "Remember, where our luncheon was?"

"I'll be at work until five," Miriam said.

"Then I'll bring the application to you!" Bitsy said, clearly ignoring the holes Louise's eyes were boring into her forehead.

"Thank you all so very much," Miriam said, turning her attention to Louise. "I look forward to helping make the show a success!"

"And you will," Iris said with a proud smile. "Welcome aboard." She looked at Louise and gave her an encouraging nod.

"Bitsy can fill you in on the details," Louise said, realizing she had been outmaneuvered.

Three mellifluous chimes indicated the service would begin in five minutes.

"Ladies, lovely visiting with you. Enjoy the service," Louise said before moving toward the sanctuary.

"I'll walk with you," Bitsy said. Louise picked up her pace.

"Really, Bitsy? What's gotten into you?" she hissed.

"Honestly, Lu, I'm surprised at your attitude, especially since your daughter wanted to—what were the words? 'Shake things up' by trying to ruin the cotillion. I guess I'm just trying to do the same, for the good of the auxiliary, of course," she said with a smirk.

"You just made this personal," Louise said through clenched teeth.

"Ah, I see Bobby and Deb. Talk to you tomorrow!" Bitsy said, patting Louise's back.

Louise could feel the invisible bullseye as if she had just been branded.

16

Miriam draped her three fashion show outfits, each carefully encased in the plastic bags she bought from the dry cleaners, over her left arm, locked her car door, and headed toward the women's auxiliary office. The last three weeks had been a blur of working at The Pig, getting settled in their rental house, and dedicating every spare moment to her sewing in the Websters' dining room. She had tried to devote her evenings to George, but with such a tight deadline looming, George was often left to eat what she had made in the slow cooker while she worked feverishly to ensure her three ensembles were perfect. She hoped her "models" would be pleased with her creations. She also knew these women could be difficult. Taking a deep breath, she entered the office, hung the outfits on the clothes rack, and helped herself to a glass of iced tea.

"Miriam, my dear, I'm so happy to see you," Bitsy said, giving her a quick hug. "I can't wait to see what you've created. You've been a busy little bee!"

"I can truly say it was more of a challenge than I expected," Miriam said, taking a seat at the conference table. "Trying to get that sequined fabric to cooperate was darn near the death of me. I even broke a couple needles on my machine, but at least I managed not to sew through one of my fingers, so that's a plus."

Seeming to dismiss Miriam's story, or finding it unworthy of comment, Bitsy sat next to her and leaned in, conspiratorially. "The measurements I gave you for the sequined dress?

They're Louise's. Isn't that a riot? I don't think she's ever worn a sequin, much less flaming red, in her life! She's going to lose her mind."

Miriam had sensed some tension between Bitsy and Louise, and as she understood it, Bitsy was responsible for someone getting suspended from the academy, but she didn't think her capable of deliberately embarrassing her supposed best friend. Not that her dress, unto itself, was anything to be ashamed of. It was quite glamorous, in fact, at least to Miriam's eyes.

And the Webster sisters loved it. "Nothing says disco quite like a ruby-red sequined halter dress," Iris had said with squeals of delight.

"And with that slit down the side!" Rose added.

"Don't forget the bare back—simply intoxicating. Wait until Alphonso sees it," Iris said. "Maybe this will help increase enrollment in his dance classes!" Miriam was torn between basking in the sisters' lavish praise and wondering if they were just being nice because she was their tenant, but their approval seemed genuine.

However, Miriam wasn't sure how to read Bitsy's decision to put Louise in such a racy design; it suddenly felt like a mean joke about to be played at Louise's expense. "I don't mean to poke my nose into your business, Bitsy, but I thought you and Louise were best friends," Miriam said.

"Oh, you know, every relationship has its challenges." Bitsy removed her diamond rings before slathering her hands with lotion. "She's been so accustomed to getting her way, for as long as I've known her, that it's kind of refreshing to see her squirm," she said.

"Squirm?"

"Well, Louise's daughter, Emma, committed quite the faux pas, trying to get her classmates to boycott cotillion," Bitsy said, sliding her rings back into place. "I mean, I'm this year's chair, for gosh sake. And Debbie is the student liaison.

The headmaster put Emma on suspension. Maybe that will teach her not to buck tradition," she said with a chuckle.

Miriam stared at her, speechless. So, the girl who Bitsy's daughter and friend had been talking about at The Pig was Emma, Louise's daughter? She remembered what the girl had said about her dad donating a car for the raffle in exchange for a favor. *How could someone hurt a child, especially their best friend's daughter? Could anyone here be trusted?*

"Please excuse me," Miriam said, scooting back her chair. "I need to get ready for the fittings." She left the office to get her sewing basket from her car, and as she was walking back to the building, she heard Louise calling her name.

"There you are," Louise said, walking briskly to reach Miriam's side. "How's our little seamstress?"

As always, Louise was beautifully appointed in a navy linen suit, a triple strand of pearls, and spectator pumps. Miriam looked down at her denim A-line skirt and pink eyelet blouse, both homemade, and felt like a country bumpkin, but she had tried her best.

"I'm doing well, Louise. Busy, for sure. How about you?"

"Ready for this show to be over," Louise said. "And before I can even take a breath, we must tackle the auxiliary's annual cookbook next. We're already behind because it needs to be completed, printed, and bound before Labor Day. They always make such lovely holiday gifts."

As they reached the doors to the chamber, Miriam stopped abruptly. "I just had an idea," she said. Louise looked at her intently. "I wonder if The Pig would be willing to sponsor the printing of this year's cookbook. You know, as long as we included some of their name brands in the recipes? Maybe we could even include coupons in the back? I imagine it would really help sales. Everyone likes a bargain."

Louise began twirling the pearls around her index finger, her peach-tinted lips pursed together.

"You really are quite a surprise," Louise said. Miriam wasn't sure if that was a compliment, so she offered Louise a hopeful smile.

"First, you jump in to help with the fashion show. Now, you have this big idea for the cookbook," she said, waving her hand dramatically in the air. "We have our traditions here, as I'm sure you know, and now, Stuarts Landing feels like a snow globe getting all shaken up."

Miriam didn't know how to respond. "Never mind," she mumbled. "It was just a thought." *What makes you think you can be on the same level as Louise Winston Caldwell, anyway?*

Louise put her cold hand on Miriam's arm and gave her a pat, followed by a sudden smile, as if she had just had the most marvelous idea. "I don't really know much about you, but you seem like someone who could use a sponsor. A mentor, of sorts, who can help you—how shall I say? Fit in here." Her smile broadened as she seemed to consider the project standing before her.

Miriam wanted to feel flattered that someone like Louise would give one whit about helping someone like her, yet she could not miss the implied message: as she was now, Miriam was inadequate. She could feel the back of her eyelids beginning to burn with embarrassment. She bit her lip to keep from telling Louise what she could do with her idea, but she held herself to higher standards. Her granddaddy's standards. *It never pays to be unkind,* he always said.

"I suppose I should thank you, yet I'm not sure why I need to be groomed," Miriam said, striving to keep her voice as steady as possible. "Granddaddy always said it's better to be a work horse than a show horse. I know who I am, Louise, and I'm not cut out for winning ribbons when there are more important things to care about."

Her blue eyes flashing like a comet, Louise seemed momentarily taken aback by Miriam's retort, then just as quickly, her

countenance softened.

"And what might those things be?" she asked with what seemed like sincerity.

Miriam inwardly recoiled both at feeling interrogated and at feeling she needed to explain herself, yet she knew enough about life to know that, in Stuarts Landing, Louise was the queen bee. *What did Granddaddy tell me? Worker bees will turn on their queen if they perceive her as a threat to the hive's survival. Something worth remembering...*

Interrupting her own thoughts, Miriam shifted her sewing basket to her other arm and collected herself.

"You know, I care about what everyone cares about. Being a good person, being loved, making a difference, having friends..."

"And that's where I can help you, dear," Louise said, nodding her head toward the chamber doors. "A relationship with me will do wonders to help you move into the right circles."

Miriam raised her eyebrows. Clearly, Louise thought having friends meant having the *right* friends. But before she could think of how to respond, Louise continued. "So, here's what I propose. How would you like to co-chair the cookbook committee with me?"

"What all does that entail?" Miriam said, trying to suppress her suspicions. Something didn't feel right about this proposal, but she couldn't find words to explain why. Not yet, anyway.

"Working with the ladies to cull out the best-possible recipes. We really try to put an emphasis on family, you know, and this year's theme is 'Love in Every Bite.' I'll be submitting my mother's shepherd's pie recipe," Louise said, patting her nonexistent stomach. "It's quite delicious but dangerous for the waistline."

"Sounds like my kind of meal," Miriam said, warming to the idea. Maybe Louise's intentions were genuine after all.

"Louise, I need to tell you something before we go in for the fittings." Louise folded her arms and cocked her head.

Miriam lowered her voice. "Bitsy assigned me the patterns she wanted me to use and left me to select the fabrics and notions." She was nervous about how to proceed.

"And?"

"Well, I only had the basic patterns and the measurements for my three models. I didn't know who would be wearing what and... well, based on what Bitsy said inside, I'm worried she may have selected what I just learned is your outfit to, um, embarrass you."

"That wouldn't surprise me. She's been nipping at my heels for some time now. Promise me I'm not wearing a white satin tuxedo," she said with a snicker.

"No, Kay's wearing that one," Miriam said. "It came out real nice. Your outfit is quite something. The sisters think it will be a showstopper even."

Louise took a deep breath. "That's certainly saying a lot," she said, exhaling.

"It's a halter dress," Miriam blurted. "A red-sequined dress with a very low back."

"How low?"

"You can still wear a strapless bra, I think. But you're not worried about the sequins or the color?" Miriam asked, puzzled.

"Even if I were, I would never say," Louise said with a mischievous glint in her eyes. "I look forward to trying it on."

Thirty minutes later, all the models had donned their outfits. The designers were making their adjustments with arsenals of pins, chalk lines, and fabric tape to show what needed to be taken in or let out. Bitsy paused at each one, acting (in Miriam's eyes) like Bill Blass assessing his newest collection as she made notes on her clipboard. Miriam bit her lip to keep from laughing. Bitsy had already approved Kay's white satin

tuxedo and Gigi's teal Quiana wrap dress. Fortunately, only minor alterations were needed.

"Louise, dear, aren't you just the vision in red!" Bitsy said, her eyes darting like a hawk to Miriam, then back to Louise.

"Hello, Bitsy," Louise said with a mock curtsy. "Isn't this simply divine?" she said, twirling. "I've never worn anything quite like it!"

"It's quite bold," Bitsy said. "Like Diana Ross!" Miriam heard a few of the models tittering behind her.

Louise studied Bitsy with raised eyebrows, then turned her attention to Miriam. "Miriam, you're a genius. I do believe this is my new favorite color. And I ended up getting to have my resplendently red theme after all, thanks to you."

Bitsy's cheeks flushed, and she turned on her heel.

"Anything else you'd like to offer?" Louise called out sweetly. Bitsy continued walking toward the door.

"Could you please unzip me? Now, about the cookbook committee," Louise said as she gathered her suit from the clothes rack to change out of her dress. "Would you like to come to my home this weekend for a planning session? I can have Pearl make us lunch."

Of all the ways Miriam thought this day would play out, receiving two invitations from Louise was more than she could have fathomed.

"That would be nice, Louise," she said. "Thank you for giving me a chance." She felt tears welling in her eyes, but she was confused about why. Louise merely nodded.

"I'll see you Saturday at noon," she said before moving behind the dressing curtain. "Oh, and the dress really is something else."

Though she didn't have to go to work, Miriam rose early Saturday morning to make George's breakfast before getting ready for lunch with Louise. After giving him a quick kiss goodbye, she drew a hot bubble bath and soaked, breathing in the soothing fragrance as she thought about the past week. Louise had seemed cold—even condescending at first—but maybe it just took her some time to trust people. Miriam was now in the early stages of a relationship with her, so she still had time to get to know the real Louise (if there was one). Bitsy, though... Bitsy was another story. She was the first to welcome Miriam into the community—even inviting her to church—yet that business with Louise's daughter continued to eat at her. "Eventually, people will always show you their true colors," her mother had always said. *Best to just let things play out,* she thought as she rinsed her hair.

Taking a cue from the women in the auxiliary—well, everyone except the Websters—Miriam replaced her regular bright-colored eyeshadow with a light peach tint she had just bought at The Pig, then applied only one coat of mascara instead of her usual three. A dab of blush, and she looked as fresh as a flower. After drying her hair, she did her best to fashion the unruly curls into a chignon, then spritzed herself lightly with her prized Emeraude perfume before getting dressed.

A few days earlier, after she had finished the alterations on her three outfits, Miriam had gone to Cloth World and

splurged on a Vogue dress pattern, notions, and three yards of emerald linen. She spent the next two evenings piecing the sheath dress together, and though it looked a bit plain to her tastes, it fit her curvaceous figure beautifully. The only thing missing to complete her new look was accessories, so she decided the occasion warranted wearing her mother's brooch, the only piece of jewelry she owned besides her wedding ring. It had been a gift from Miriam's grandfather, so in Miriam's mind, it was an heirloom. She didn't know what type of flower it depicted, but she thought the white and green enamel would complement her latest creation. Taking one last look in the mirror, she quickly applied her coral lipstick before making her way to Louise's house.

Once she turned onto Maple Lane, she slowed down to gape at the extraordinary mansions, each framed by perfectly manicured gardens and shaded by curtains of red maple and green ash trees. She felt transported to a different world, one of quiet wealth steeped in its stratified air, dignified and strong, classic and permanent, impermeable. Pulling into the driveway, Miriam's confidence faltered. *I don't belong here. But I'm here, just the same. Here we go.*

Walking up the front steps, she noticed an elderly gentleman wearing overalls and a wide-brimmed hat, humming as he trimmed the topiaries lining the balustrade. As she passed, he tipped his hat. "Afternoon, ma'am," he said.

"Good afternoon!" Miriam said, wishing she could join him in the garden instead of having lunch with Louise. Already nervous about the afternoon, she wondered if he could tell she was an outsider, maybe even an imposter.

"I'm here to have lunch with Louise," she said, then chided herself for feeling the need to explain her presence.

"Well, that's just dandy," he said, continuing to snip the branches. "Reckon Miss Pearl gonna make you a real fine lunch," he said. "She a good cook, that's for sure. Them Caldwells is right lucky to have her."

"My name is Miriam. Miriam Llewelyn," she said.

"I'm Moses," he said. "Nice to know you." He turned his attention back to his work, which Miriam took as a signal he wasn't much interested in chatting.

"Have a nice day," she said, then approached the intimidatingly grand front door and rang the bell. Within a few seconds, the door opened, and an older woman answered, stepping back so Miriam could enter. She was wearing a starched black dress and an equally stiff white apron, reminding Miriam of the servants on *Upstairs, Downstairs.*

"Hi," Miriam said, smiling and extending her hand. "I'm Miriam Llewelyn."

"Yes, the missus is expecting you. Please follow me to the solarium," the woman said politely, ignoring Miriam's outstretched hand. She withdrew it. *Had she done something wrong?*

"Are you, by chance, Pearl?" Miriam said as she followed the woman through the great room, trying not to gawk at the paintings, the oriental vases, the grand piano, the fancy-looking rugs, the sheer splendor of it all.

"Matter of fact, I am. How you know?" she said with a throaty chuckle.

"Moses just told me you're one of the finest cooks around," Miriam said, knowing she was exaggerating, but she felt herself wanting to be liked by this woman.

"That old fool," she said. "He'd say just about anything if he thinks I'll go on a date with him. He outta his ever-lovin' mind."

"I do look forward to lunch," Miriam said, not sure it appropriate to inquire further about Moses's apparent crush.

"Should be real fine. I whipped up a salad niçoise with shrimp, some lobster bisque, fresh crescent rolls, and raspberry sorbet," Pearl said.

"That sounds like lunch for a queen!"

Pearl merely grinned, then tilted her head toward the solarium, where Louise was sitting on what appeared to be a rattan throne. Pearl wiggled her eyebrows playfully at Miriam before announcing her arrival.

"Miriam! Please join me. It's so nice to see you," Louise said, rising from her chair and gesturing to its twin. Miriam sat down carefully, hoping the chair wouldn't creak under her weight.

"Now, that is an exquisite dress," Louise said, sitting back down and crossing her long legs. "Where did you find it? Wait, let me guess. Thalhimer's?"

Miriam shook her head. "Heavens, no. That's way out of my league," she said. "Actually, I made this." She smoothed the dress over her knees. It had become wrinkled during her fifteen-minute drive from the Websters, but she was pleased with it, nonetheless.

"You are clearly quite talented," Louise said. "Have you ever considered opening your own sewing business? Once people see your outfits at the fashion show, I'm certain you will be in high demand."

Pearl appeared with a silver tray, which she set on the coffee table.

"Chablis?" Louise said to Miriam. *At lunch?* Miriam thought. *Well, as long as I'm out of my comfort zone...*

"Yes, thank you," she said. Pearl filled a crystal goblet and handed it to her, then did the same for Louise.

Louise held up her glass. "Here's to a new partnership!" Miriam followed suit, and they clinked glasses. "Cheers," they said in unison.

"I've actually owned a business before," Miriam said after taking a sip of the tangy chilled wine. "Well, me and George."

Louise looked at her with a surprised expression. "Really? How ever did I not know that?"

"We haven't really had too many personal conversations,"

Miriam said, then, not wanting to sound critical, she added, "what with all the hustle and bustle at the auxiliary, of course."

"What type of business was it, if I may ask?"

"Hardware store," Miriam said. "It was going real well for a few years, then, well, life just sorta happened, and we had to shut down." She took another sip of wine, not wishing to expound on the events that led to their failure. "I'm not sure I'm cut out to be an entrepreneur."

"Well, think about it, perhaps," Louise said. "Canapé?" She gestured regally at the porcelain plate of assorted crackers covered with exotic-looking spreads. Miriam selected what looked like salmon and placed it on one of the starched cocktail napkins, glancing at Louise to ensure she wasn't breaching etiquette in some way.

"Oh my heavens, this is fantastic," she said after swallowing her first bite.

"Pearl is quite gifted," Louise said. "We're indeed fortunate to have her as part of the family–she's been with us since I was a teenager."

"So, she has all the secrets then?" Miriam said, feeling playful.

Louise sat up straighter and smoothed her hair, then cocked her head. "What an interesting thing to say," she said coolly, her blue eyes turning gunmetal gray.

"Oh, I was just being silly," Miriam said. "Please forgive me."

Louise's expression relaxed.

"I'm not sure what we shall do once Pearl decides to retire. Her daughter, Jackie, works for the Butlers, and I wouldn't dream of trying to recruit her. That would most certainly start World War Three," she said with a wry grin.

Miriam finished her wine, then daintily ate another canapé. From nowhere, Pearl appeared to refill her glass before Miriam could decline.

"Thank you, Pearl," Miriam said, dabbing the crumbs from her lips. "So, you and Bitsy, you go back a long way?"

Louise uncrossed her legs, then began fiddling with her gold charm bracelet. She leaned over to show Miriam.

"This is the seal from the academy," she said, pointing to the embossed gold coin. "We've been friends since our sophomore year there, right after her family moved here from Charlotte. Her daddy came to join my daddy's law practice, but he left a few years later to open his own firm, just a few buildings down the road." She sat back and took another sip of wine from her half-empty glass.

"That must have been awkward," Miriam said.

"Well, it certainly irritated my father but only for a moment. I remember him saying, 'Ingratitude is always a kind of weakness. I have never known men of ability to be ungrateful.' I believe that was Goethe," Louise said. "Bitsy's dad's firm didn't last more than a year. People around here are many things, but disloyal isn't one of them."

Miriam shifted in her seat, wondering if what she was about to say would fall under that description. She cleared her throat.

"I've never been one to meddle in other folks' business," she said, taking a large sip of wine for courage. "But you know that feeling, of knowing something bad and not knowing what to do about it?" She hoped she wasn't slurring, as the wine had gone to her head.

"Oddly enough, I do," Louise said. Miriam waited for her to continue, but she didn't.

"My second day working at The Pig, these two teenaged girls were in my checkout line, talking about another girl who had done something to stop cotillion," she said.

Louise clasped her hands in her lap and looked at Miriam through darkening eyes. "Please, go on," she said.

"One of the girls said her mom had convinced her daddy

to donate a car to the school raffle. She implied it was a kind of bribe to get the poor girl suspended," she said. "I put two and two together and realized it was Bitsy. So, I already felt sick, knowing she could do such a thing. And then..."

"And then you found out the girl who was suspended is my daughter, Emma," Louise said, massaging her knuckles.

I hope she's not going to punch me. "Right. I'm sorry, I just didn't feel like it was fitting not to tell you," Miriam said.

Louise fluttered her perfectly manicured hand in the air. "What's done is done," she said with a feline smile. "Bless her heart."

"You're not angry?" Miriam said.

"Better than that," Louise said. "I'm resolute."

As they were rising from their chairs to take a seat at the table, Louise stopped and stared at Miriam's brooch.

"What an interesting piece," she said, moving closer to get a better look.

"Oh, this was my mother's," Miriam said, touching the enameled pin.

"Was she from around here, then?"

"I don't know," Miriam said. "She was adopted, and as I understand it, the brooch had belonged to her birth mother. My grandfather gave it to her. That's all I can say. Why do you ask?"

"Well, that's the state flower of Virginia—dogwood," Louise said. "That very design was the first logo ever created for our women's auxiliary by someone who was local at the time."

"I was wondering what kind of flower it was," Miriam said, confused by how uncomfortable she had suddenly become.

"Wouldn't it be fascinating to know how it came into your grandfather's possession?"

Miriam nervously took a seat at the beautifully decorated table. "May I have another glass of Chablis?" she asked

as Pearl began serving the lobster bisque. She was ready to go home.

While they were not participating in the fashion show as models, Iris and Rose arrived at the chamber feeling quite proud indeed of their ensembles. They knew Miriam must have been exhausted after creating three different outfits in an astonishingly short time, but Iris had asked her sweetly if she'd whip up two additional looks for them. And, as they expected, she was more than happy to oblige.

"We'll pay you, of course," Iris had said as Miriam took her measurements.

"Please, it's the least I can do, especially since you let me turn your dining room into a workshop," Miriam had responded.

"The House of Llewelyn!" Rose had proclaimed from her seat at the head of their dining room table.

As they were checking in, Iris and Rose were aware people were staring, as they always did, but they held their silver-haired heads high as they scooped up their swag bags.

"Ladies, you look like you should be models! But I'm afraid I don't see you on the program," Louise said, checking their names off her list and handing them their swag bags. "At the minimum, you'll be perfectly attired for your next dance class."

"Thank you, dear. I've never worn a jumpsuit before, but this might just be my new favorite thing!" Iris said.

"Orange is a lovely color on you," Louise said. "Or is it more of a tangerine?"

"Definitely tangerine," Rose said. "What would you call mine?"

Louise looked at her thoughtfully. "I would have to say heliotrope."

"I agree," Iris said with a nod.

"And this fabric, it's so flowy. I do believe I could dance the night away!" Rose said with a laugh.

"That's right, sister. We're gonna boogie woogie oogie 'til we just can't boogie no more!" Iris laughed, giving her sister an impromptu hip bump.

Thanking Louise and wishing her luck for the show, the sisters ambled into the ballroom to find their reserved seats, which, of course, were in the front row. A handsome young man approached as they settled into their chairs, asking if they would care for Champagne.

"Most certainly!" Rose said, nudging Iris, who was perusing the program.

"Yes, please," she said, adjusting her fuchsia reading glasses. "Would you look at this? Bitsy's definitely making a play of some kind."

Rose leaned over to see what Iris was referencing. Butler Automotive had purchased an ad, congratulating the auxiliary and, in particular, Bitsy Butler for "curating the designs to be featured in this evening's show." She sat back and let out a whistle. "That's not going to sit well with someone we know and love," Rose said.

"She could at least have included Louise and Kay as the official co-chairs," Iris said.

"Maybe she's finally liberating herself from Louise's influence," Rose said, closing her program and removing her glasses.

"She should have done so already, but I can't see Louise idly letting this go," Iris said, nodding.

"Hopefully, everything will work out without too much

drama," Rose said, though she knew better.

After the waiter served their champagne, the sisters watched the room begin to fill. As usual, it was a diverse crowd, predominantly female except for the spouses of those women taking the stage.

"Oh look, there's George!" Rose said, waving at him from across the room. He replied with a double thumbs-up, and she smiled.

"He's such a good man," Iris said, taking a sip of her champagne. "He obviously adores Miriam."

"And with good reason," Rose said. "I'm so glad they live with us!"

"They don't, technically," Iris said. "But they are beginning to feel like family, yes."

"He's done some beautiful work on the house already," Rose said. "Quite the craftsman and so very devoted. Kind of reminds me of someone." She shot a stealthy look at her sister.

"You know better," Iris said. "That's ancient history."

The house lights dimmed as the stage came aglow in a pageantry of color. Rose clapped her hands.

"This is going to be so exciting!" she said. Iris simply nodded, her mind obviously elsewhere.

Louise and Kay glided up the steps to the podium, just left of the main stage, to the Bee Gees singing "Stayin' Alive."

"How marvelously apropos," Iris whispered. Rose giggled.

"I can't wait to see Louise's outfit," Rose said. "She's listed as going last. That means hers must be the most spectacular!"

"Good for Miriam," Iris said. "She deserves to be noticed."

After the co-chairs welcomed everyone to the event and reminded them to place their silent auction bids before six o'clock, Louise turned the audience's attention to the projection screen. A black and white photo appeared of the old sawmill before its demise.

"As a reminder, all proceeds from this evening's event will go toward renovating the sawmill and turning it into a museum," Louise said.

Iris turned in her chair and gave Rose a pained look. "In all the excitement about the theme and the designs, I think we missed this. Sister, I'm worried about what this will dredge up. Whatever shall we do?"

"Let's not jump to any conclusions," Rose said. "Things will work out as they should."

"Oh, dear," Iris said, fanning herself with the program.

Louise and Kay exited the stage, and the music resumed as the deejay warmed up the audience before announcing the first design.

***

An hour later, the sisters sat up expectantly when Louise's name was announced.

"Modeling the last outfit of the evening, created by Miriam Llewelyn, is Louise Winston Caldwell wearing 'Inferno,'" the deejay said.

The music changed as Louise appeared on stage, afire in her crimson sequined halter dress. She stood for a moment, not moving.

"What's wrong with her?" Rose whispered. Iris shrugged.

As Donna Summer belted out "Last Dance," Louise looked at someone offstage, her hands splayed at her side as if to say, "Are you kidding?" She took her first halting step, then gained her composure and moved down the catwalk, posing at the edge as the photographer took pictures. She smiled, then blew a kiss at the sisters as she floated back to greet Miriam with a brief hug. They both bowed before exiting.

"And that concludes this evening's fashion show," Kay said from the podium. "Remember, if you don't find something you like at the auction, you're still welcome to contribute to the Old Sawmill Renovation Fund by dropping a check in the basket at the registration table. Thank you all for coming!"

Iris stood up first, then held out her hand for Rose. "Let's go find Louise," she said.

They walked gingerly through the crowd, stopping to chat with various auxiliary members before making their way backstage.

They first saw Miriam holding a bouquet of flowers, her eyes wet with tears.

"Hello, my dear," Iris said. "And well done! We are so proud of you! George, I'm assuming you're the one to compliment for those beautiful flowers."

He nodded and shrugged. "She deserves them," he said. "I do believe her outfits were the best, but what do I know?"

The sisters nodded in unison. "Of course they were!" Rose said. Miriam was dabbing her eyes.

"Whatever is wrong, Miriam?" Iris said.

Miriam blew her nose loudly, then handed the flowers to George before subtly pointing at Louise and Bitsy, standing several yards away. From their body language, it appeared a confrontation was underway.

"What's going on?" Rose said.

"I really don't understand their friendship," Miriam said. "First, Bitsy tried to embarrass Louise by selecting the outfit she wanted me to create..."

"Which was magnificent, by the way," Iris said.

"Thank you. I know Louise was a bit reluctant, but once she saw how beautiful she looked, I was excited to see her take the audience by surprise."

"And I do believe you both accomplished that!" Rose said.

"Then, that ad," Miriam said. "Louise tried to pretend it didn't bother her, but it must have."

"That was a rather tacky move, unusual for Bitsy.

She's typically so kind," Rose said as her sister nodded.

"As I said, I think she's thrown down the gauntlet with Louise," Iris said, giving her sister a worried look.

"But the music, that was just too much," Miriam said, blowing her nose once again.

"I love that song," Rose said.

"It was deliberate, Rose. That wasn't the song that was supposed to be played. She didn't rehearse it even. Bitsy switched the music at the last minute," Miriam said.

"What was the song supposed to be?" Iris said.

"'Fly, Robin, Fly.'"

"I'm not sure I see the issue, but perhaps I'm being dim," Iris said.

"That other song, it's about last chances and anticipated endings," Miriam said wistfully. "I think Bitsy was trying to send a message." She reached out to hold George's hand.

The sisters looked at each other once again.

"I do believe it's going to get interesting around here, sister," Rose said.

"Oh, goody," Iris answered with a chuckle. "Let the fire-works begin."

19

Louise arrived at the chamber for the bi-weekly auxiliary meeting wearing her new suit of armor, otherwise known as crimson red—dress, nails, and lips. Her shoes, though, had to be taupe. She knew where to draw the line on taste, after all, but she credited Miriam (and Bitsy, indirectly) for giving her the courage to move away from the pastel colors that had been her wardrobe staple. After taking Sunday to recover from the show, Louise had spent Monday shopping in Richmond, followed by several hours at the spa. She felt like a new person and was greeted as such.

"Well, look at you, lady in red!" Miriam sang out as they met in the lobby. "Wow!"

Louise smoothed back her hair and smiled.

"I always thought red was too aggressive," Louise said. "I must say, if Bitsy thought she was going to embarrass me, she has another think coming. I do believe this is my new favorite color."

"It absolutely suits you, Louise, especially with your porcelain skin and blonde hair. You're the spitting image of Grace Kelly. Lucky girl," Miriam said, fidgeting with the elastic waistband of her skirt.

"You're very kind, Miriam. Enough about that, though. We need to have a quick chat before we select the cookbook committee." She took a seat on the couch and patted the cushion, signaling Miriam to join her.

"I'm afraid you got a rather unfortunate peek behind the curtain of how certain people in the auxiliary conduct themselves. Some women will do just about anything to get what they *think* is the upper hand. They're short-sighted, though. They're playing checkers, but I play chess," Louise said with a chuckle. "Someday, they'll learn. Strategy before tactics, always."

"I know I'm new around here, but I was flabbergasted," Miriam said. "Honestly, I was so shocked, I went home and cried. How can so-called friends behave that way? It hurt my heart. I couldn't even enjoy my evening pound cake. I went straight to bed. Were you upset?"

Louise recrossed her legs, considering Miriam's question. "That's not the word I would use," she said, licking her lips. "I might say, 'enlightened.'"

"How so?"

"Bitsy tried to employ a tactic—a few, actually—to humiliate me. As I reflected upon it during my massage, I realized she was trying to use my own preferences—my 'trademarks,' if you will—against me. An interesting attempt, to be sure, but a gift in disguise," she said, examining her stack of gold bangle bracelets.

"I'm not sure I understand," Miriam said. Women had begun entering the chamber for the meeting. Miriam lowered her voice. "How was it a gift?"

"Two-fold," Louise said, leaning closer. "First, I had the opportunity to consider some of the rules I've always lived by. Tradition. Not wearing certain colors and garments. Always adhering closely to the standards of etiquette I've known since birth. The social mores I inherited and that I believe to still be relevant. Second, Bitsy thought if she could make me look foolish, I would lose my temper. She was wrong, though," Louise said. "And now I know where we stand."

Miriam looked at her with a confused expression. "I never thought friendships were supposed to be so complicated. That's not at all the way I grew up."

Louise smiled and patted her hand. "You may not have been aware of it, dear, but this is the way of women since time immemorial. I imagine it was there, but you were just too nice to notice."

Miriam looked at her Timex. "The meeting starts in ten minutes," she said. "What did you want to discuss?"

Louise leaned back and smiled. "You and I must be in absolute lockstep on this year's cookbook," she said. "Any disagreements we may have, we keep between us, first and foremost."

"Okay," Miriam said.

"We will keep the committee to four people, including us," she continued. "Someone will oversee collecting the recipes, someone will oversee transcribing them, someone will be responsible for marketing, and someone will coordinate the luncheon to launch the book. Which of these sounds appealing to you?"

"I'd like to collect the recipes," Miriam said, "so I can cross-reference ingredients people can buy at The Pig."

"You do have a flare for public relations, Miriam," Louise said. "That's simply brilliant. I'd like to handle the luncheon where we will feature selected recipes on the menu. That just leaves transcription and marketing. One thing I must emphasize is that Butler Automotive will have nothing, and I repeat, nothing to do with the cookbook," she said in an impassioned tone.

"Butler Automotive or the Butlers in general?" Miriam said, eyeing her sideways.

Louise stood up and smiled. "Shall we go in?"

When the two entered the ballroom, auxiliary members were scattered about, chatting in small clusters. The room

became silent for a moment, followed by soft murmurs and a few audible gasps. Smiling broadly, Louise maneuvered with the grace of a prima ballerina through the various groups on her way to the refreshment table. Miriam followed closely behind. The sisters were there, loading their plates with finger sandwiches and shortbread cookies.

"Whom do we have here?" Iris said, looking Louise up and down, then letting out a low whistle. Louise smiled and bowed her head.

"Where are the firemen?" Rose added. "We've got us a four-alarm right here!"

"I've been inspired," Louise said. "And I'll leave it at that."

The women began taking their seats as Kay called the meeting to order. After asking the members to move to approve the minutes from the last meeting, Kay gave Louise the floor. She heard women whispering as she strode to the podium, and it gave her an unexpected jolt of adrenalin.

"Good afternoon, friends," she said, focusing her gaze directly on Bitsy seated in the second row. "Before we discuss this year's cookbook, I would like to congratulate the auxiliary on a very successful fashion show. I couldn't have been happier with how it turned out." Her lips widened into a bright smile as she continued staring at Bitsy, who had dropped her head. "Though we haven't tallied up all the proceeds, I hazard a guess this was the most profitable show we've had. Please, give yourselves a round of applause!"

The women responded dutifully, though Louise winced as Rose let out a whoop.

"And now, onto our next project—our annual cookbook. I'd like to introduce my co-chair for this year's cookbook. Miriam Llewelyn, please join me," she said, clapping. She heard more whispering, though several women joined in the warm welcome. Miriam rose from her seat and walked to the podium, standing awkwardly to the left and slightly behind Louise.

"Don't be nervous," Louise whispered, covering the mic. "Just follow my lead." Miriam nodded, looking like she was about to be sick.

"The theme of this year's cookbook is 'Love in Every Bite,'" Louise said, happy to see most of the women nodding their heads in approval. "The recipes must be family recipes, ideally those handed down through the generations. And we'd like each recipe to include a family memory or tradition associated with that dish. Can't you just taste the love?"

Rose raised her hand. "Yes, Miss Webster?" Louise said. Rose stood up, jingling her silver bracelets as she put on her purple glasses. "We don't cook," she said, "but Jasper has some wonderful recipes. Might they be accepted?"

Louise looked over her shoulder at Miriam and urged her to come forward. "Co-chair, what are your thoughts?"

Miriam shuffled nervously to the mic. "Good afternoon," she said. "I'm honored to be Louise's co-chair, and as you can tell, I love food!" She smiled and patted her hips. The women responded with good-natured chuckles.

"In response to the question, I think it would be appropriate to include those as long as the recipe, or recipes, have a sentimental connection," she said, looking to Louise for agreement.

"I agree wholeheartedly," Louise said. "We do have a few other stipulations that must be duly noted. First, no shortcuts in the recipes. That means no Velveeta, no canned soups, no Bisquick, no pre-made pie crusts... you get the idea."

Several women groaned loudly as others giggled. Bitsy raised her hand.

"Mrs. Butler, you have a question?" Louise said, her eyes shooting lasers toward Bitsy's permed head.

"I do, in fact," Bitsy said, standing and fluffing her hair. "What if the only family recipes someone has include those

items?" She looked around the room for support.

"It's quite simple then," Louise said matter-of-factly. "They won't be included. Any other questions?" She smiled as Bitsy sat down, looking deflated.

"Miriam and I have decided to keep this year's committee as small as possible since everyone seems to be busy this time of year, what with summer vacations and the like. I will be handling the luncheon to launch the cookbook," she said, placing her hand across her heart. "Miriam?"

Miriam stepped forward. "I will be responsible for gathering all your wonderful family recipes," she said. She looked at Louise, who signaled her to continue. "That leaves two other spots. First, we need someone to take on the critical task of transcribing the recipes," she said. "And perhaps most importantly, we need someone to handle marketing." She yielded the podium to Louise.

"Wonderful," Louise said, giving Miriam a warm smile. *I'm glad she's doing what I told her to. This couldn't be better if we had rehearsed it.*

Once again, Bitsy raised her hand. Louise raised her eyebrows and tilted her head. "Yes, Mrs. Butler?"

"I volunteer to be in charge of marketing," she said, looking around the room. Louise folded her hands on the podium and smiled.

"How lovely of you," Louise said. "You certainly know how to make an impression, after all." She paused as she watched Bitsy become flushed amidst the quiet snickering.

"However, I believe Gigi is the perfect candidate, especially since she worked briefly as a journalist. Gigi, wave your hands so I can see you!" Louise said. Gigi was seated in the back, but she stood and gave a mock salute.

"Delighted," she called out. Bitsy folded her arms, scowling.

"Well, I shouldn't have to say it," Bitsy said. "But the dealership would certainly be willing to underwrite all the production costs if I'm in charge of marketing."

Louise looked over her shoulder and gave Miriam a wink. "We have something much better up our sleeves, Mrs. Butler. But we thank you, we sincerely do," Louise said with a smirk. Bitsy dropped into her chair and glared at Louise.

Iris raised her hand.

"Yes, Miss Webster?"

"Rose and I would simply love the opportunity to help transcribe these precious recipes, wouldn't we, sister?" Rose nodded enthusiastically.

"What would the auxiliary do without you two?" Louise said. "You are truly our greatest treasures. But may I ask, do you have a typewriter?" She hoped she hadn't embarrassed them.

Rose stood up. "Jasper does," she said. "He's writing a book! I'm sure he'll let us borrow it, right, Iris?" Iris nodded.

Louise looked back at Miriam, who gave an almost imperceptible shrug.

"Perfect," Louise said, clasping her hands. "I do believe everyone has their assignments. Miriam, today is May tenth. When would you like everyone to submit their recipes?" Louise knew they hadn't discussed this, but she trusted her co-chair to think quickly on her feet.

"Give me a sec," Miriam said, chewing her bottom lip. She used her fingers to count out the months. "May to June, June to July, July to August, August to September. Hmm. We want to launch right after Labor Day, and we need several weeks to print and bind, right?" Louise nodded patiently. "I'm thinking, well, here's a deadline that everyone can remember. Please give me your recipes no later than July fourth," she said confidently. Louise patted her arm.

"Outstanding, thank you. Any further questions before we conclude?" She waited, keeping her eyes affixed on Bitsy. "Hearing none, thank you, everyone!"

Kay took the podium and worked her way through the remaining announcements before banging the gavel to end the meeting.

"Well done," Louise said to Miriam as they moved toward the refreshments. "I'm famished!"

"All this talk of food will do that," Miriam said, gazing at the cookies.

Louise had just scooped some fruit salad onto her plate when Bitsy appeared at her side. "That was a low blow, Louise, even for you," she practically spat.

Louise turned and smiled. "How's our resident stage manager?" Louise narrowed her eyes. "Or should I say, musical interventionist?" she added with a smirk.

Bitsy's eyes widened in what was clearly insincere contrition. "About that, Louise. I told you Saturday, and I'll say it again, the deejay made a mistake, not me. But I think you pulled it off, don't you?" Bitsy looked over at Miriam, who was focused on devouring a petit four. "You really did steal the show. But then, you usually do, isn't that right?" She crossed her arms in front of her synthetic breasts.

"I suppose that's one way to put it," Louise said. "I'm curious. Is it tuna casserole night at the Butlers? You know, with your cream of mushroom soup and Velveeta?" Bitsy walked away in a huff but not before giving Louise the finger.

"I'm not sure what to say," Miriam said, rejoining Louise. "That whole scene was quite... something."

"Watch and learn, Miriam. Watch and learn."

20

That evening, Miriam was watering the hydrangeas she had planted in the front garden when she saw the Webster sisters pedaling toward her on a bright red tandem bicycle. Rose squeezed the horn as they slowly approached while Iris waved enthusiastically from the second seat, even daring to take both arms off the handlebars and outstretch her arms. "Look, no hands!" she hollered as Rose reached around and swatted her knee.

"Do you really want me to fall off this thing and break a hip?" Rose yelled back. Miriam turned off the hose, smiling as the ladies came to an awkward stop.

"You brake when I brake, Iris! Like I told you!"

"How was I to know you were braking?" Iris said.

"Well, because we've reached our destination, maybe?" Rose got off the contraption, smoothing her tunic over her white clamdiggers. "Sisters! Jeez!" She waited to give her younger sister a hand. Iris ignored her, stepping off the bike and walking toward Miriam.

"We just thought we'd pay you a call," Rose said, "to check on you."

"What a nice surprise," Miriam said. "I've missed spending my evenings with you now that the show is behind us. Please, have a seat." She gestured toward the Adirondack chairs on her front porch. "Might I interest you in a glass of lemonade? Iced tea?"

"Would it be too much to ask if I may have a gin and tonic?" Iris said, taking a seat. "It is after five." She turned away from Rose, who was giving her a stern look.

"I'm afraid we don't have gin or tonic," Miriam said, drying her hands on her apron. "George doesn't drink the spirits—just wine and beer in our house. And, of course, soft drinks!"

"Prosecco, then?" Iris asked. Miriam hadn't a clue what that was. She shook her head. "Iris, you're being rude," Rose said. "I'd simply love a lemonade, dear."

"I do have some Chardonnay in the refrigerator," Miriam said to Iris, who nodded enthusiastically.

"Perfect, that will work just fine. Thank you. I do hope I wasn't being impertinent," Iris said, raising her chin as she looked at her sister from the corner of her eye.

"Not at all!" Miriam said, opening the creaking screen door to the guesthouse. "Be right back." She quickly draped a placemat on her wooden serving tray, poured a glass of wine and two mason jars full of lemonade, then cut a few slices of her beloved pound cake and placed them on her Coronet plate. She knew it wasn't the most elegant presentation, but she wasn't prepared for an impromptu visit either.

Using her rear end, Miriam opened the screen door and set the tray on the old wooden trunk she had repurposed for a coffee table. The door slammed behind her, and she jumped, nearly knocking over the wine glass. "I'll get used to that old door one day!" She laughed, sitting down in the rocking chair she had recently found by the side of the road. With a touch of white paint, it was right as rain, at least in her eyes.

"How charming," Rose said, taking her drink from the tray. "I don't know as I've ever seen mason jars used in such a clever manner!" She took a sip of iced lemonade. "I think this may be the best I've ever had. Whatever do you use, Miriam?"

Miriam took a taste of her lemonade before answering. "Well, lemon peel, of course, to make the syrup, but I do add just a pinch of shaved fresh ginger root to give it a bit more bite. Mama's old secret," she said, remembering her mother's love for experimenting in the kitchen. She never committed her creations to paper, so if Miriam didn't watch her prepare something, she couldn't replicate it. *How I wish she had written down her recipes*, Miriam mused. Fortunately, lemonade was a staple in their house until... she didn't like the memory of her mama's untimely passing.

"This wine is very refreshing, dear," Iris said, nibbling on a sliver of pound cake. "A very nice pairing, indeed." Miriam didn't know what Iris meant, but she smiled, nonetheless.

"To what do I owe the pleasure?" Miriam asked.

"Well, we just got our new bike, and we wanted to take her for a spin but not so far as to run into trouble. Not yet, anyway," Iris said with a wink.

"I've never seen such a thing," Miriam said. "But I do believe it suits you both!"

"Rose wouldn't agree to Harleys," Iris said, rolling her eyes. "This was the one compromise we could reach."

Miriam shook her head, laughing as the tears began rolling down her cheek. The sisters just chuckled, making Miriam laugh all the more. "You ladies... I want to be you when I grow up!" she said, wiping her eyes with the back of her sleeve.

"Oh, honey, be so very careful what you wish for," Iris said. "As they say, 'it just may come true.'"

"We really came by to see how you're doing, especially after today's little performance," Rose said, idly swirling the ice in her mason jar.

Miriam considered Rose's question. "I suppose I'm still learning the rules of the road around here, but I've truly never seen friends treat each other so—what's the word? So..."

"Cattily?" Iris offered with a grin.

"Yes, like that," Miriam said. "But then, I haven't had a lot of close friends in my life. We moved around a fair amount."

"Is that so? I can't imagine. We've been here, on this very property, since the day we were both born. Though we have traveled quite extensively," Rose said.

"I think I most enjoyed Sedona, at least when I think about our domestic trips," Iris said. "After all, that's where we found Jasper, isn't it, sister?"

"Absolutely," Rose said, dabbing her forehead with a handkerchief she pulled from her waistband. "He was guiding our group through the sacred rock formation where our chakras got cleansed."

Miriam didn't know if she should laugh because she didn't know a chakra from a hole in the wall. "Did it hurt?" she said.

Iris nearly choked on her wine, trying to swallow before answering.

"It was more spiritual," Rose said, drawing out her syllables as she made a floating motion with her hand.

"So, we offered Jasper a job with us!" Iris said. "Now, our chakras are always in good shape."

"Indeed," Rose added.

"Back to the auxiliary," Iris said. "You've seen enough to know a lot of unspoken rules of engagement exist, many of which can be quite mysterious to an outsider."

Rose interrupted her. "You mean 'newcomer,' dear."

"Quit correcting me," Iris snapped back.

"As she was saying, there are women in Stuarts Landing who have quite lengthy histories together, and with that comes the periodic drama," Rose said.

"Louise, for example. Her family—the Winstons—was one of the first to move here after our family, of course," Iris said. "We first met her grandmother, Nora, at church when we were quite young. She and our mother became friends."

"Nora was a lovely woman, Miriam, and such a beauty," Rose said. "But she had a backbone made of steel. No one challenged her. Not ever."

"That's right. She founded the auxiliary, along with Mama, which we were invited to join once we turned twenty-one," Iris said. "And we've been members ever since. But I digress. Nora played an active role in Louise's upbringing, and her standards were absolute. She fiercely upheld tradition and expected the same from everyone else."

"What about Louise's mother?" Miriam said, though she felt guilty for prying into her new friend's private life.

The sisters looked at each other, then set down their drinks.

"Deirdre, Louise's mother, wasn't from around here," Rose said. "Louise's daddy followed in his father's footsteps, attending Harvard Law before joining the family practice in Richmond. Deirdre, on the other hand..."

Iris cleared her throat. "Deirdre's family immigrated from Ireland," she said. "Very much working class."

"Louise's daddy met her at a pub in Cambridge where she was working at the time. Deirdre always said it was love at first sight," Rose said. "By the time he graduated, they were already engaged. They married at our church..."

Iris interrupted. "Very formal High Mass. All the smells and bells!"

"But she was never really accepted here," Rose continued. "She didn't like living in the Winston family home..."

"The one Louise and Clifton inherited," Iris said. Miriam knew that.

"And she resented Nora's interference, as she called it, always being told what to wear and how to act and what committees to serve on. As I understood it from Nora, Deirdre was quite unpredictable and often 'difficult.'" Rose made air quotes with her hands.

"Eventually, she began to crack, like a car windshield," Iris said. "That crack continued to spread, and one day, she gave up."

Miriam looked at both women, blinking her eyes as she tried to understand where the story was going.

"What do you mean, 'gave up'?" Miriam said.

"She became a recluse," Rose said. "Never left the house and I mean, never *ever*. Nora had hired Pearl to help Deirdre, as much as anything, but as Nora shared with us, Deirdre stopped bathing and wouldn't change out of her housedress."

"Such a pity," Iris said.

"And such a waste," Rose added. They both tsk-tsked, then took sips of their beverages.

"And then what happened?" Miriam moved to the edge of her rocking chair.

"At Nora's insistence, Louise's daddy took Deirdre to a doctor in Richmond who prescribed some pills to help her with her moods," Rose said. "That was the beginning of the end."

"Eventually, she had to take more medication to get through each day, and finally, they sent her to a sanitarium upstate," Iris said.

"She never came back," Rose added.

"I don't understand. Didn't she get better?" Miriam asked.

"I'm afraid not, dear. Within a year, she died," Iris said. "Louise's daddy always blamed himself, but really, Deirdre was a fish out of water here, and he should have known it before throwing her into a world she didn't understand."

"How old was Louise when Deirdre died?" Miriam asked, her mouth agape.

"She was thirteen," Rose said. "Nora took over the job of raising her."

That's how old I was when Mama died. I know how she must have felt. Maybe this is why she's so rigid? "Did Louise know what happened to her mother?"

"I do believe she did," Iris said, "but the story was her mother died of cancer." She held her index finger to her lips.

"Shh," she pantomimed.

"How awful for her," Miriam said, shaking her head.

"She's a true-blue Winston, Miriam, just like her grandmother, meaning she's resilient. She wasn't going to let her mother's situation, or anything else, define her..."

"Or hurt her," Rose said. "That is, until Bitsy's family moved here."

Now, Miriam was even more confused.

"May I refresh your drinks, ladies?" she said as she stood. Iris held up her wine glass. "Rose?" Miriam asked. She shook her head.

"I'll take a glass of wine, actually," she said. "All this history..."

"Indeed," Iris said.

Miriam returned with the bottle.

"I'm sure this will sound absurd, but it needs to be said. Bitsy's family was 'new money,' which, for many people around here, is an invitation to shun," Rose said, shrugging. "The Winstons included. Nora didn't want Louise to have anything to do with Bitsy, who was enrolled at the academy, but the girls became fast friends."

"She's a smart cookie, that Bitsy, and she obviously figured out Louise's family had serious social standing here... the kind that can't be bought. Theirs was a symbiotic relationship, though. Seeing in Bitsy an opportunity to expand her sphere of influence, Louise enveloped Bitsy into her circle, and soon, they were darned near inseparable," Iris said.

"Until Louise caught Bitsy making the moves on Clifton when they were all at the University of Virginia," Rose said in a quiet voice. "Louise and Clifton were already pinned."

"Pinned?" Miriam said.

"He gave Louise his fraternity pin, which represents an intention to propose," Iris said. Miriam nodded, though this was all so foreign to her.

"And then what happened?" she said, thinking Stuarts Landing should have its own television show.

"Louise asked Bitsy to be her maid of honor," Rose said. "Beautiful wedding, wasn't it, sister?"

"People talked about it for years," Iris said, swirling her wine glass thoughtfully.

"Wasn't Louise angry? Why did she have Bitsy anywhere near her wedding? I can't believe Bitsy would do such a thing!" Miriam said.

"Oh, darling, that's what we're trying to tell you," Rose said.

"Louise learned several valuable lessons from Nora, one of which was, 'Keep your friends close...'"

"'And your enemies even closer,'" Rose finished.

"So, Louise and Bitsy aren't really friends?" Miriam said.

"It depends on what day you ask, dear," Iris said. "But if you ask *me*, they never really were."

"Then what were they?" Miriam said.

"Two women trying to fill voids in their lives," Rose said, smiling sadly.

"I do believe they still are," Iris added.

"That's why they're so politely vicious to one another," Rose said. "In some weird way, they need each other, and they both hate it."

Miriam felt emotionally exhausted from it all. "I guess I'm glad my grandfather moved away when he did," Miriam said, taking a generous sip of wine. "Whew, what a story. I can't imagine Mama living here. She wasn't one for drama."

Iris leaned forward and furrowed her brow. "I beg your pardon?" she asked, looking over her glasses at Miriam.

"My granddaddy once lived here," Miriam said cautiously. She immediately wished she had stayed quiet.

"I'm surprised you never mentioned that, dear," Rose said.

"Well, he had to leave town in a hurry," Miriam said.

"That's all I really know, so it's not really something I was comfortable sharing with just anyone, but I feel I can trust you both to keep it to yourselves. I don't know all the particulars, but it seems he was wrongly accused of something. He said he had nothing to do with it, and I believed him, yet he knew there would only be trouble if he didn't skedaddle." She shrugged. "So, he moved to Kentucky. That's where he adopted Mama."

"And what became of your parents?" Iris said softly.

"I didn't really know my dad—he abandoned us not long after I was born. Then, Mama died when I was thirteen. Pneumonia," she said, twisting her wedding ring to keep from crying. "So, it was just me and Granddaddy until I met George at church."

"And... and what of your grandfather?" Rose said.

Miriam felt her upper lip quiver as it did any time she remembered their last conversation. "He died last year. Heart failure," she said softly.

She looked up from her hands to see Rose rubbing Iris's arm.

"Miriam," Rose said, "may I ask your grandfather's name?" Miriam noticed Iris closing her eyes.

"Russell Benson," Miriam said. "Folks always called him Rusty..."

"On account of his red hair," Iris whispered.

"Did you know him?" Miriam said, sitting up hopefully.

Rose looked at her watch. "Oh my," she said, "we've stayed much longer than we intended. We can continue another time. Iris?" She stood and extended her hand to her sister. "Do you want to be in front?"

Iris stood and gave Miriam a warm hug. "Thank you so much for the refreshments, dear," she said, solemnly following Rose to the bicycle resting in the grass.

"Yes, thank you," Rose echoed as she walked. Taking their seats, the sisters began pedaling back to their mansion as George's truck pulled into the drive. He gave them a quick honk, to which they replied with half-hearted waves.

"Hi, sweetheart," he said, joining Miriam on the porch. "What was that all about?"

Miriam shook her head, still staring at the retreating figures. "I have absolutely no idea."

21

"Would you prefer taking supper on the veranda or in the dining room?" Rose asked Iris, handing her a dampened towel for her forehead. When they got back from Miriam's, her sister had immediately taken to the red velvet chaise lounge in the front parlor.

"I'm not hungry," Iris said, covering her eyes with the towel. "I'd still like a gin and tonic, though. Would you tell Jasper?"

Rose nudged Iris's hip to move her over, then sat next to her. "Do you want to talk about it?"

"We can talk about it over a gin and tonic," she said.

"I'm afraid you must be in shock, dear. May I at least convince you to have a snack?" Rose asked.

Iris knew her sister would keep haranguing, and frankly, she wasn't up for an argument. "Fine, Rose. Maybe some Boursin with melba toast? And a gin and tonic," she said, moving the towel from her eyes to her neck.

Rose walked to their mantel and used the wooden mallet to strike the Tibetan gong. Within seconds, Jasper appeared in a black linen caftan, barefoot as always.

"Please be an angel and prepare us a tasting plate," Rose said. "Iris would like melba toast and the Boursin. Might you add some mixed nuts and an olive assortment?"

Jasper put his hands together and bowed. "Oh, and we'd both like a gin and tonic too," Iris said, confident Rose would conveniently forget.

Rose sat down on her wingback chair, which they had recently reupholstered with a bold dragonfly print fabric they ordered from London. Admittedly, they both agreed the pattern clashed with the zebra rug, but they didn't care—both sisters enjoyed the parlor immensely, quirky though it was. She strummed her fingers on the gilded table beside her, obviously waiting for Iris to say or do something. Anything. But instead, Iris remained silent, staring at the ceiling.

Jasper wafted back to the parlor, silently placing the sterling silver tray on the coffee table before handing each woman her cocktail.

"Perfect, as always," Iris said, lifting the crystal glass with appreciation. Because her hand was trembling, she sloshed some of the drink onto her lap but hoped no one would notice. Of course, she knew Rose did. "Thank you, Jasper."

After he left, closing the French doors behind him, Rose sat back and crossed her legs, her eyes affixed on Iris.

"I can feel you staring," Iris said. "Stop it."

"I took care of you then, and I'm here to take care of you now, dear," Rose said, popping a green olive into her mouth.

"Well, I didn't need it then, and I don't need it now, so there," Iris said, inching herself into a more upright position.

"What are the odds?" Rose said. "This all feels so surreal, you know?"

"I feel like I'm in an F. Scott Fitzgerald novel," Iris said. "Good thing we have plenty of gin." She tipped her cocktail to her lips again.

"Now I understand why we were so drawn to Miriam from our very first encounter," Rose said. "There was just something so familiar about her."

"She is very down to earth, which I find quite refreshing. Unassuming. Just like Rusty was," Iris said. "And so very talented, a true Renaissance man."

"You know it never would have worked between the two

of you," Rose said carefully.

Iris sat up, her demeanor quickly changing from a quiet river to a raging ocean. "Only because Daddy never would have allowed it to," she said. "I will never forgive him for accusing Rusty of a crime he absolutely didn't commit. Never."

"I think Mama had more of a say than you remember, sister," Rose said. "She did not believe him worthy of you."

"Only because he had no money." Her rage toward her parents was as fresh as it was in 1927, which startled her.

"No money, no breeding, no family name, no education—shall I continue?" Rose said. "I'm not saying what they did was right because I saw how much it hurt you, but you know how things were then."

"And they really haven't changed all that much around here," Iris said. "Look at the whole cotillion kerfuffle. So much ado about nothing, and so typical for Stuarts Landing. As for Rusty, he may have been lacking on paper, but he more than made up for it with his keen mind and generous heart. He deserved better than how he was treated."

Rose spread some of the Boursin on a piece of melba toast and handed it to her sister with a cocktail napkin. "Please, take a bite, Iris."

Iris swung her legs over and propelled herself into a full sitting position, begrudgingly taking the canapé and biting into it loudly. "Happy?" she said through a full mouth.

"What on earth are the odds," Rose said once again, shaking her head slowly. "But now that we know things worked out as well as they could have, well..." She seemed at a loss for what else to say.

"I'm happy she had Rusty's love, and I am even happier Rusty had hers, but also, I can't help feeling jealous. We didn't have a chance to say goodbye. What if he thought I didn't love him? We just disappeared—poof! Into thin air. He never even knew where our parents sent me." Her hands shook violently

as she dabbed her eyes with her napkin.

"You mean, where they sent us," Rose said. "There was no way I was going to let you go to Frankfort, Kentucky, by yourself. The convent was much nicer than I had expected, though. Honestly, I never thought we would speak of this again. But now that the subject has presented itself, I need to confess something." She set her cocktail on the side table and leaned forward to take Iris's hand.

"I'm not sure I can take much more," Iris said. "My head is already reeling."

"I contacted Rusty when we got to Frankfort," Rose said.

"How did you find him?"

"Oh, Iris, this is difficult," Rose said. "So many years of secrets. I know you hated Daddy for running Rusty out of town, but what you don't know is that Daddy wrote him a letter of introduction and gave him five hundred dollars so he could start anew. Once he found out you were in the family way, that is. He also warned Rusty to never contact you again. Just before we left, I heard Mama and Daddy talking. He said Rusty had found employment at a mill outside of Lexington. When we got to Frankfort, I asked one of the sisters about mills near Lexington, and she gave me the address of the only one in the area."

Iris's heart lurched at the thought of the only two men she had loved enmeshed in some kind of devil's bargain.

"Daddy paid Rusty to leave me? I can't believe Rusty would have taken the money," Iris said, getting off the chaise and grabbing her drink. She began pacing like a caged lioness. "I think that's even worse than accusing Rusty of something he would never, ever do."

"It wasn't quite like that, honey," Rose said, watching her sister move in circles. "Deep down, Daddy knew you loved each other. In some strange way, I think it soothed his conscience to help Rusty land on his feet."

"So, you found where Rusty worked? Then what?" Iris asked.

"I wrote him a letter telling him where we were, at the convent. I explained how long we would be there before setting out for Europe," Rose said, wringing her hands in her lap.

Iris returned to the chaise and sat down heavily, looking at her sister with an expression of confusion.

"Why, Rose? Why would you have done that?" A single tear rolled down her flushed cheek.

"Because I thought he deserved to know," Rose said.

"I don't believe that was your place! As I recall, you weren't particularly fond of him–at least the idea of my seeing him."

"I wasn't, well, not at first," Rose said. "But I saw the way he made you smile whenever you were near each other. Remember the fall carnival at church?"

"I do." Iris smiled at the memory. "He brought me a caramel apple and invited me to join the hayride. I sat next to him."

"And tried to hide the fact you were holding hands under the quilt," Rose said with a chuckle. "I saw!"

"Did he ever respond? To the letter?" Iris said, reaching for the silver bowl of mixed nuts.

Rose shook her head. "No, he never did. I assumed he either had moved somewhere else or didn't want to have any further contact. Times were tough then, remember? Beginning of the Depression and so many people had lost their jobs, I just thought maybe that had happened to him. Besides, we had other things to focus on," she said, giving Iris a gentle look.

"I didn't want to hold her," Iris said, her eyes filling with tears. "She was just perfect, though, and I had to know what she felt like in my arms. I knew, in that moment, I would never feel such love again."

"Perhaps that will change," Rose said. "Now that, well..."

"There's something I never told you. When you left the

room to give me a private moment with the baby before the nuns took her away," Iris said, wiping her eyes, "I pulled out the brooch Rusty gave me for my birthday. You know, the enameled dogwood flower?"

"The one you used as the template for the auxiliary's first logo? I didn't know that was from him," Rose said, leaning forward.

"The very one. That was the only gift he ever gave me," Iris said. "It must have cost him a full paycheck from the mill." She shook her head, smiling at the memory. "That was the night we…"

"No need to explain," Rose said, holding up her hand.

"In the servants' quarters," Iris continued.

"You mean the guesthouse."

Iris nodded. "We only met there a few times, when Mama and Daddy went to Richmond."

"I never really knew the particulars," Rose said. "I guess we've both had our secrets."

"Yes, well, the other secret is that before the nuns took the baby, I pinned the brooch to her blanket, and I asked that it go with her when she got adopted. I wonder what became of it?" Iris said, finishing her cocktail.

"So, you know we're both thinking it. Rusty adopted Miriam's mother. Do you think that was her? His daughter and yours? Could it be? Is Miriam your granddaughter? She must be!"

"I don't know. I can't even fathom that possibility. But even without that, Miriam grew up with Rusty, a man who captured my heart."

"What a strange twist of fate," Rose said. "This changes everything, you know."

Iris rose and walked to the mantel, hitting the gong to summon Jasper.

"Miriam seems happy," Iris said, returning to the chaise.

"Why must we change anything?"

"Because she deserves to know the connection and the possibility of where she comes from, sister," Rose said. Jasper entered the room, quietly placing two fresh cocktails on the table. "Thank you, dear," she said as he glided from the room.

"I don't believe anyone ever suspected what happened," Iris said.

"People just thought we were taking the Grand Tour. We were gone for a full year, as you remember. I do believe our trip to Cannes was the highlight, don't you?"

"That's why you bought the Picasso," Iris said. "To try and cheer me up." She stood and moved toward the painting, running her index finger down the side of the frame.

"Actually, I thought simply meeting him would cheer you up," Rose said with a smile. "The painting was just a very nice souvenir."

"What are we going to do? And do you think we'll ever know for sure?" Iris asked.

"I don't know, but we're going to have to tell her about your connection to Rusty," Rose said. "When the time is right."

"And when might that be?"

"We'll know," Rose said, joining her sister in front of the painting. She put her arm around Iris's slender waist. "We'll just know. You'll see."

Louise was organizing stacks of announcements when Bitsy sauntered into the church office, thirty minutes late (as usual). They looked at each other warily, but only for a moment before Bitsy slung her bag over the chair and took her seat at the conference table.

"Anything new?"

Louise recognized the game—*Lord knows we've been playing it for more than twenty-five years,* she thought. "Nothing that I know of," she said, handing Bitsy the outline for that week's bulletin. "You?"

Bitsy opened her soda and took a long swig. "I'm thinking of replacing Jackie," she said casually.

"Why on earth would you do that?" Louise said. "You've said she's a hard worker, just like her mama, Pearl, who's been with my family for twenty-five years. I couldn't possibly do without her. Nor would I want to."

Louise took a drink of her black coffee, then put a sheet of mimeograph paper in the typewriter. She knew Bitsy was trying to re-engage her, and as usual, Louise rose to the occasion. *Better to keep some semblance of peace, particularly with my auxiliary aspirations.* "Pastoral Ponderings," she typed at the top of the page, turning her mind to transcribing the weekly message from Father Phillips.

"She is a hard worker, no question," Bitsy said, interrupting Louise's concentration. "But she wants to go to community college, and I told her we'd be happy to pay for it, as long as we could find a replacement for her. She's considering it, so I'm just thinking about possible options."

"Mm-hmm," Louise said, squinting to decipher the priest's unusually sloppy handwriting.

"Looks like you might need readers soon," Bitsy said. Louise ignored her. "I was thinking about offering Jasper the job."

Louise stopped typing and took a measured breath. This latest fancy was so typical of Bitsy who, other than having silicone breast implants and regularly permed hair, hadn't really changed over the years. *I suppose I haven't either. But at least I've got good manners and impeccable taste. Unlike some people.*

"Why am I not surprised, Bitsy? You've always wanted what you can't have," she said, holding up her left hand to flaunt the heirloom diamond ring Clifton had given her when he proposed.

"That was unnecessary," Bitsy said, blinking like a dog momentarily blinded by a flashbulb. "I never really wanted Clifton, anyway. A little too bland for my tastes but obviously perfect for yours."

Louise knew Bitsy was trying to goad her, so she focused on appearing unruffled. "Yes, he is just perfect. But as for your thoughts about replacing Jackie with Jasper, I believe there are a few things you should consider, though you didn't ask my advice."

"I rarely do anymore," Bitsy said, mindlessly stroking her curls.

"Another foolish decision on your part," Louise said. "Even so, I don't believe you have a snowball's chance in you-know-where to steal him away from the Websters, and even if you did, you'd be making enemies for life."

"How much longer do you really think they'll be around? Aren't they nearly eighty?" Bitsy said, taking a sip of soda.

"They're seventy-three and seventy-two," Louise said.

"And from the looks of it, in quite excellent health."

"I heard Jasper makes them health food," Bitsy said. "Stuff like tofu and alfalfa sprouts. And someone said he was teaching them tai chi. Don't you think that would be more beneficial for me than for them?"

Louise shook her head. "You're something else, Bitsy. Just leave it alone."

"I have no idea how much they pay him, but I can double it," Bitsy said, lifting her chin proudly.

"Your background is showing, dear," Louise said. "I suppose that's just your nature, thinking you can throw money at something to get your way. Like donating a new Buick for the academy raffle."

Bitsy stared at her, aghast. "What's the point of having money if you can't use it to make things happen, not just for yourself but for others?"

"Oh, give me a break, Bits. You just made my point," Louise said with a smirk. "One other thing about Jasper you probably didn't consider–he's young, probably no more than twenty-eight. And while I make it a point not to notice other men, he's quite handsome. Just imagine what people might say if you hire him." She smiled. "I wouldn't think that would be good for your reputation, nor for your husband's."

Bitsy sat back in her chair and folded her arms defensively. "That doesn't seem to be an issue for the Websters, now does it?"

Louise elected not to give Bitsy the benefit of a response and instead resumed typing.

"Speaking of what people are saying," Bitsy said. "You've been quite the topic of conversation lately, in case you didn't know."

Though curious, Louise didn't want to dignify the comment with a reaction. She rose and walked to the coffee pot, refilling her monogrammed mug.

"I guess you don't care," Bitsy said. "Though you have always been so very concerned about your image."

Louise returned to her seat. "I don't really care, but I know you're just dying to tell me," Louise lied, adjusting the paper in the machine.

"The girls are all wondering why you've taken such an interest in Miriam, almost like she's your pet," Bitsy said, her eyes sparkling with mirth. "Let's face it, Louise, I introduced the two of you, and initially, you treated her like a leper. What's changed? Did you find out she's some eccentric heiress who's just slumming it for laughs? Or does she have something on you..."

"Don't be ridiculous, Bitsy, if you can possibly help it. She showed her true colors when she stepped up for the fashion show, as so many people did," Louise said, narrowing her eyes.

"Well, you have me to thank for that, as you may remember."

"She has fresh ideas and, more importantly, a kind heart. Why wouldn't I want her as a friend?"

"That's not the Louise of old," Bitsy said, cocking her head.

"Call it wisdom. I've learned it's important to surround yourself with people who can lift you up," she said. "And Miriam is a woman with many talents. Besides, I believe I can help her. Just like I helped you, all those years back."

"I knew it. You're just using her, aren't you?"

"Only you would say something like that," Louise said. "I believe Miriam will bring a lot of value to the auxiliary. If you thought about anything other than yourself, you'd see that. Maybe you should look a little deeper."

"That's rich, coming from you, Louise. You're one of the most judgmental people I've ever known," Bitsy said. "What's that you always say? 'They're not our kind.' Hmm. Has your 'kind' suddenly changed?"

Louise sat straighter in her chair, removing her cardigan and tying it around her shoulders.

"Are we finished here? I really need to finish typing this column so I can meet Miriam at the club for lunch."

Bitsy opened her mouth to speak, but nothing came out. Louise smiled and went back to typing.

Miriam was waiting in the lobby when Louise arrived at the country club, walking purposefully as if she owned the place. *It's possible*, Miriam thought as Louise gave her a breezy air kiss. "Hi there!" Miriam said. "Thank you so much for inviting me, Louise. It's nice to really relax on my day off."

"It's absolutely my pleasure," Louise said. "Would you like to have lunch by the pool or in the clubhouse?"

"I think it may be a bit too warm outside," Miriam said, self-conscious about perspiring too much. "I should have worn short sleeves, I guess."

"The weather these days," Louise said with a grin, "seems to be as unpredictable as some of the people around here! Come with me," she said. "Hopefully, my regular table will be available."

Miriam had never set foot in a country club and was already worried she wouldn't know how to behave. As they walked down the corridor, she breathed in the heavenly scent of lavender mixed with vanilla. "It smells so good in here!" Miriam said. "They should bottle and sell it."

"They do," Louise said. "In the shop. Would you like to see?" Miriam nodded happily, so Louise guided her to the mahogany staircase. "It's downstairs, between the dressing rooms," she said. "I'm afraid we don't have an elevator, though," she said, giving Miriam a concerned look.

"That's just fine," Miriam said. "Now I'll be able to justify dessert!"

The shop could have been plucked from Paris, Miriam thought as they walked into the beautiful confection of soft pinks complemented by black and white striped tablecloths. Along the walls, glass shelves brimmed with assorted potions and lotions, candles, picture frames, fragrances, and pot-pourri... a feast for the senses.

"Good afternoon, Mrs. Caldwell," said the teenager behind the counter.

"Hello, Jenny," Louise said. "Please meet my guest, Mrs. Llewelyn."

"Nice to know you," Miriam said, extending her hand. Jenny looked surprised but graciously offered her own.

"Are you looking for anything special?" Jenny said.

"Mrs. Llewelyn was quite taken with the scent in the lobby," Louise said.

"It does smell nice. Would you like the candle or the room spray?"

Miriam shrugged. "Which do you recommend?"

"Why not both?" Louise said. Miriam couldn't tell if she was teasing, but she followed Jenny to the display of Lavanille products.

"They're from France," Jenny explained as Miriam picked up the candle sample. "Mmm," Miriam said. Jenny handed her a small can of room freshener.

"Go ahead, give it a spritz," she said. Miriam sprayed the air, then sneezed loudly.

"You're probably better off with the candle," Louise said, chuckling. Miriam nodded, so Jenny removed a boxed candle from the lower shelf. "Would you like to keep looking?"

"We're on our way to lunch," Louise said. "Miriam?"

"I'm ready," she said, following Jenny to the register.

"That will be seventeen dollars and twenty-three cents," Jenny said. Miriam inhaled quickly and raised her eyebrows, realizing she had put herself in a terribly awkward position.

She only made four bucks an hour at The Pig. Was a candle worth half a day's pay?

"I should have clarified, dear. Please put it on our account," Louise said. "Consider it my early thank you for being my cookbook co-chair."

Miriam didn't know how to respond—was this another part of the Stuarts Landing code? "Well, thank you," Miriam said as Jenny wrapped the box in pink tissue, then tucked it in a bag.

"Here you go," Jenny said. "Enjoy!"

"I've never had such an expensive candle!" Miriam said as they walked back up the stairs to the clubhouse, where the hostess seated them at a table overlooking the golf course.

"I'm sure you'll enjoy it," Louise said, perusing the menu. "Please, select anything you'd like. I've never been disappointed here."

After giving the waiter their orders—a spinach salad for Louise and a cheeseburger with onion rings for Miriam—Louise took a leatherbound journal and sterling silver pen from her tote bag. "Ready to talk cookbook?" she asked.

"I was thinking, while we were downstairs, could we sell the cookbook here? In the gift shop?" Miriam said. She watched Louise tap her chin with the pen.

"You have such a mind for business," Louise said. "I admire that about you. Wonderful idea. Now, have you thought about what recipe you're going to provide? Something special from your family?"

Miriam shook her head. "Mama didn't write down any recipes," she said sadly. "She just whipped things up from her imagination, and most of the time, it worked." How she wished she had cared to learn more from her mother while she still could have. *No use thinking about that now.*

"That's a shame," Louise said. "My mother liked to cook, though most of her meals were simple. Her family was Irish,

so she liked to boil almost everything. Unless it could be baked, that is, like her shepherd's pie, which was divine. But our housekeeper prepared most of our meals," she said.

"Pearl?" Miriam asked.

Louise shook her head. "Pearl didn't come to work for us until I was thirteen. We had Augustine first, then Pearl. Right about the time Mama died."

While the Webster sisters had already told Miriam about Louise's mother, she thought it best to feign ignorance.

"I'm so sorry, Louise. That must have been difficult at such a young age."

Louise nodded, making absent-minded doodles in her notebook. "She got sick, and that was that," she said. "How about your mother? Were you all close?"

"We were," Miriam said. "On account of her having been adopted, she always said she wanted to be the mother she never knew and the mother she never had, so she gave it her all. She was my very best friend." Her voice broke as she choked back her tears.

"I suppose I'm a bit confused," Louise said, furrowing her brow. "She didn't have a mother? Wasn't she adopted by a family?"

Miriam dabbed her eyes with her napkin. "Yes, my grandfather and grandmother adopted her right after they married, but then my grandmother died when Mama was quite young— around ten, if memory serves. Grandpa pretty much raised her," she said. "We were thick as thieves, the three of us."

"So, he never remarried?" Louise asked, taking a sip of lemon water.

"Oh, heavens no," Miriam said, eyeing the basket of rolls the waiter placed on the table. "He always said he had been blessed by two deep loves, his first and then my grandmother. He said that was good enough for two lifetimes." As she was reaching for the basket, the waiter returned with their plates.

"Enjoy," he said with a bow.

"Thank you, Charlie," Louise said. "I don't mean to pry, but why didn't he marry his first love?"

"He said it wasn't in the cards for him," Miriam said. "And he said his marriage, while brief, was a happy one. Honestly, I didn't think any more of it."

"Interesting," Louise said, idly looking out the window. "Oh, goodness. Will you take a look at that?"

Miriam had just taken a bite of her cheeseburger, but she turned her head in time to see Jasper driving a golf cart with the Websters swinging their legs wildly from the bucket seat in back. They appeared to be laughing, and they were hardly dressed for golf.

"Are they wearing caftans?" Miriam asked, staring at the paisley robes billowing in the breeze.

"Only the Websters," Louise said, shaking her head. "Whatever would we do without them?"

"I didn't know they played golf," Miriam said before taking another bite of her burger.

"They don't," Louise said, picking at her salad.

"Then what are they doing?"

"Joyriding. It is Friday, after all," Louise said.

Miriam supposed that made some kind of sense, as much as anything did in Stuarts Landing. She shrugged. "They really know how to live," Miriam said. "I envy them."

"When you're from tobacco royalty and your family were among the community founders, you can do whatever you like," Louise said. "They never have to prove anything to anyone, so they don't even try."

"That must be nice," Miriam said. "Not to care what other people think."

"I wouldn't know. That's not a luxury I've had the pleasure of enjoying."

Miriam took another bite of her burger, washing it down

with a sip of soda. "But your family, the Winstons, weren't they founders too?"

Louise looked at her thoughtfully while chewing her spinach salad. She wiped the corners of her mouth primly before answering.

"Yes, but the difference is, like Clifton, my grandfather and father were attorneys, which meant they went to work every day. We had to be conscious of our reputations, always, so we wouldn't do anything to compromise their ability to attract new clients. The Websters owned numerous tobacco farms as well as the old sawmill, but they didn't labor themselves," Louise said, setting down her fork.

Miriam considered the women's extremes–the Websters completely carefree, the Winstons/Caldwells compulsively careful. *Perhaps happiness lies somewhere in the middle.*

"A few days ago, the sisters dropped by while I was in the garden," Miriam said before biting into an onion ring. "They rode over from their house on, of all things, a tandem bicycle!"

"Of course they did," Louise said, squeezing more lemon into her water.

"It was quite odd, actually," Miriam said. "They were asking about my family, and when I mentioned my grandfather had once lived here, it seemed like they couldn't wait to leave. I kept thinking I said something wrong."

Louise put the lemon wedge on the side of her salad plate. "Really? I didn't know that. I wonder if my parents knew him?"

Miriam shook her head. "I doubt it," she said. "He was a laborer at the mill. Left town to pursue better opportunities in Kentucky." She suddenly felt uncomfortable and wished she had kept her mouth shut.

"I've only been to Kentucky for the Derby," Louise said, thankfully moving the subject away from Miriam's grandfather. "Everyone should go at least once. Have you been?"

Miriam shook her head. "We never had that kind of money," she said. "But on television, it looks quite fancy!"

"Oh, it is, to be sure. We went with Bitsy and Bobby, let me think, about ten years ago," Louise said, placing her fork and knife on her plate. "That reminds me. You'll never imagine what Bitsy said this morning when we were working on the church bulletin."

Miriam put down the last of her cheeseburger and wiped her hands on her napkin. She was surprised Louise would gossip, especially to her.

Louise leaned closer, lowering her voice though the clubhouse was nearly empty. "She told me she wanted to steal Jasper away from the Websters. Of all the nerve!"

Miriam raised her eyebrows and mouthed, "Wow," conveying her horror at such a move even she knew was classless. "That's mighty bold," she said, shaking her head.

"Not exactly the B-word that came to mind," Louise said, chuckling. "She'll never do it, though."

"Why not?"

"All I had to do was suggest how people might perceive her, a married woman, at home with a handsome young man each day," she said, winking. "The power of suggestion is so amazing, don't you think?"

Miriam finished the last of her burger, silently vowing to remember Louise's veiled warning.

24

"I'm glad we got out of the house yesterday, aren't you, dear?" Rose asked Iris, who was sitting in front of her easel in the sunroom, working on a watercolor painting of their backyard flower garden. Iris used the same landscape every season, as she enjoyed capturing the changing light and blossoms–fading or flourishing, depending on the month. Their desk in the study–the one that had belonged to their grandfather–was full of Iris's work because she didn't believe it necessary to share with anyone but her sister. Her painting was hers alone.

Iris looked over at Rose, who was sitting on the brocade divan fashioning a macrame plant hanger with turquoise beads, and realized she had not responded. "I suppose it was good to get out." She rinsed her paintbrush and dried it on her canvas smock.

"Have you given any thought to what recipes we should supply for the cookbook?" Rose asked casually as she manipulated the rough jute.

"Not really. We have plenty of time, I believe. And we certainly have other more pressing concerns." She closed her paint set and placed the brush in a terracotta pot they had purchased in Tuscany.

"I was wondering when you would mention it," Rose said. "It's been several days now, and we haven't seen Miriam since. Do you think you might tell her?"

"I thought you said we would know when the time is

right," Iris said, giving her sister a pointed look. She rose from her table to pour a glass of cucumber water from the crystal pitcher on the credenza.

"That seemed like the right thing to say at the time, but I can't recommend with any certainty how we go about it," Rose said. "I don't have much experience in this area, after all."

"I'm not doing this by myself, sister, so we need to determine how we are going to handle it," Iris said.

"Do you think Rusty ever told her much about his life here?"

"I didn't get that impression, no," Iris said, unbuttoning her smock and laying it on the papasan chair in the corner. "This lady palm looks unhealthy." She ran her hands through the fronds of the tall tree. "I'll ask Jasper to work his magic."

Rose put down her macrame and leaned forward, resting her arms on her knobby knees. "You just gave me an idea," she said as her face broke into a smile.

"Oh, dear," Iris said, pouring some of her flavored water into the flowerpot.

"What if we went to a psychic? Or maybe to someone who could do a tarot card reading, something like that?"

"To accomplish what, exactly?" Iris said, now trimming the dead ends from the majestic plant.

"Are you sure you're not doing more harm than good to that poor plant?"

"That's what I'm afraid of with Miriam, actually," Iris said. "She gave no indication of being unhappy with how she grew up. What if we inadvertently open Pandora's box by telling her that Rusty and I were, were..."

"A tarot card reading might give us the answer about what we should do. I really like this idea, Rissy. I do!" Rose said, clapping her hands.

Iris lowered her glasses and shot her sister a perturbed

look–Rose only used Iris's childhood nickname when she was throwing down her big-sister dominance card. "I don't know," Iris said. "I've been praying about it, and I'm not exactly seeing a burning bush. If God doesn't have an answer for me, what makes you think some con artist with a head scarf will?"

Rose threw back her head and laughed, snorting for punctuation. "That sounds like a look you might favor, dear sister!"

"Maybe Jasper knows how to read the cards," Iris said, rubbing her chin.

"That won't help much since he doesn't speak," Rose said. "I rather admire that about him, honestly. I could never take a vow of silence. I think we should take a drive to Richmond. With all the colleges there, I'm sure we could find someone. Jasper can take us. The old Bentley is due for an adventure, after all."

Iris walked back to her painting table and sat down heavily. "I just don't know," she said, massaging her right hand now throbbing from her arthritis.

"Looks like you might need another acupuncture session," Rose said in a worried voice before changing her tone. "But maybe you could look at it this way. If you tell Miriam about you and Rusty, that will give you the opportunity to learn what she might know. Wouldn't you like that? After all these years?"

Iris took off her glasses and rubbed her eyes. "I'm afraid," she said.

"Of what, honey?"

"That it will hurt too much," Iris whispered. "If her mother was our child, then I have to face the fact that my daughter is dead."

"Won't it hurt more to have your possible granddaughter living on our property and never having the chance to enjoy family we didn't know we had?"

"You're my family," Iris said softly.

"As you are mine. But don't you think Miriam would want to know the full story of where she came from?"

"What if she judges me for what I did?" Iris said, leaning down to pick up Diva and put her in her lap. She stroked the cat's velvety gray ears and felt comforted by the percussive sounds of her purring.

"And what if she doesn't? She may be a romantic, just like you, dear. So, when do you want to get your reading?"

"Let's go on Monday, if you absolutely insist," Iris said.

Rose nodded. "That's a good girl."

Iris swatted her sister on the behind. "Don't think you've won," Iris said.

"I wouldn't dream of it, sister." Rose's eyes were beaming. "That would be ever so foolish, wouldn't it?"

"Go find the Yellow Pages," Iris said. "We can start looking today."

25

Louise was watching *60 Minutes* with Clifton when Emma flounced into the den and plunked herself down on the couch, wearing the same petulant expression that had become her signature look lately.

"Why is the trunk in my room?" she said to her mother. "I told you I'm not going!"

"Em, we're right in the middle of this segment about the Soviet Union," Louise said. "Can this wait until dinner, please?"

"Daddy! Please, tell her I don't want to!" Clifton set his Scotch on the side table and looked to Louise for guidance.

"Do I know what you're talking about?" he asked their daughter, holding his palms up plaintively.

"Camp Meadowbrook!" she yelled.

"Please do not raise your voice, missy," Louise said. "And you're going, just as you have since you were eleven. You always enjoy it, and it's a tradition in this family."

"Back to the tradition crap, Mom? Really?"

"Watch your language, honey," Clifton said.

"We've already paid the deposit, Emma, which, as you can imagine, is quite an investment for six weeks," Louise said, re-arranging the art books on the coffee table. "There," she said, satisfied. "I don't know why Pearl insists on stacking them at an angle. They look better this way, don't you agree?" she asked no one in particular.

"Summer camp is a privilege not all can afford to enjoy,"

Clifton said. "Think of all the new people you will meet! If I could take your place, I would. Spending my summer swimming and canoeing and telling stories by the campfire sounds pretty swell right about now."

"Besides," Louise said, "how else would you spend your summer?"

"Well, I thought it would be nice to spend time with you," Emma answered softly.

Louise started laughing, then covered her mouth as she looked at her daughter. "Okay, Pinocchio, now I've heard just about everything."

"Louise," Clifton warned.

"Why don't you ever listen to me?" Emma wailed. "You just want to send me away, so I'll be out of your hair, isn't that right?"

Louise cocked her head, looking at her beautiful daughter, who had morphed into some kind of alien overnight. "Honestly, young lady, I don't understand you," she said, taking a drink of lemonade. "And no, I don't want you out of my hair," she said as sincerely as she could. "I want you to be enriched through experiences, new friends, all the things I so enjoyed during my lovely summers there. Why can't you be grateful?" Louise almost added "for once" but thought better of it. She didn't want to further agitate this ticking time bomb sitting across from her.

Emma jumped to her feet, walked in front of the television console, and put her hands on her hips, glaring at Louise with a look of defiance.

"What if I don't want to be enriched? What if I just want to stay home and relax?"

Pearl entered the room quietly. "Supper's ready," she said, looking at Louise for acknowledgment.

"I have a question for you, Pearl," Louise said. "If you could have sent Jackie to summer camp, would you have done

so?" The corners of Pearl's mouth turned downward briefly as she wiped her hands on her apron.

"Mom! Are you out of your mind?" Emma said. "What a cruel question to ask! Gah!"

"It's okay, Miss Emma. That wasn't an option for us. Jackie started working every summer when she reached her thirteenth birthday," she said. "She right enjoyed having a little spending money, as most girls do." She gave Emma a toothy grin. "But you don't need to worry about that none." She looked at Louise, who simply nodded. "Go have yourself some fun."

"Thank you, Pearl. We'll come to the dining room in a moment." Louise watched their housekeeper head back to the kitchen.

"That was so insulting, Mom. Do you ever think about how you sound?"

"You will respect your mother, Emma," Clifton said in his courtroom voice. "She's only doing what's best for you, as she always does."

"Thank you, dear," Louise said. "Emma, I imagine there's another reason you don't want to go to camp, and it starts with a D, isn't that right?"

Emma dropped to the floor melodramatically. "Why does everything in your world always have to involve some kind of drama?"

Louise rolled her eyes at the irony. "C'mon. We don't want dinner to get cold."

"I'm not hungry," Emma mumbled.

"You will eat something," Louise said as they walked into the dining room. Pearl had placed the serving dishes on their walnut buffet–a platter of sliced pork tenderloin, a serving dish of au gratin potatoes, a bowl of haricots verts, and a basket of yeast rolls. Their Waldorf salads awaited them on the table.

"This looks delicious, Pearl," Louise said, serving herself small portions of all but the bread. Clifton had taken his seat, waiting for Pearl to prepare his plate. Emma dished herself a spoonful of potatoes and a single slice of meat. Pearl loaded Clifton's plate, and once she placed it before him, she quietly left the room.

"What if I stayed home and got a job," Emma said.

"Absolutely not," Louise said, taking a bite of her salad.

"I could babysit."

"Liability issues, Em. Not a good idea," Clifton said, buttering his roll.

"Then I could bag groceries at The Pig!"

"That's absurd," Louise said. "You're better than that. There are plenty of girls going to camp, Emma. If you like, I can arrange it so you and Debbie are in different groups. You'd rarely have to see her except for meals. Would that help?"

Emma pushed the potatoes around her plate with her fork. "I'm just worried she'll find a way to embarrass me, Mom. She always has to be at the center of everything. What if she spreads rumors about me? Or makes the other girls not like me?"

Louise put down her utensils. "Sweetheart, if I've learned anything in my thirty-nine years, it's this: people, and especially women, don't bother with those who don't threaten them in some way. Debbie is clearly jealous of you. I will refrain from commenting how much she's like her mother in that respect," she said, taking a sip of sauvignon blanc. "This is a wonderful opportunity to rise above it and make new friends. The only other advice I can give you comes from a French proverb—'Vous n'êtes insultée que si vous agissez insultée.' You know, 'You're only insulted if you act insulted.' Got it?"

Emma sat back in her chair and let out a heavy sigh. "Fine. I'll go. But please note for the record," she said, looking at her father, "I'm not happy about it."

"Wonderful," Louise said. "I do believe you'll change your tune once you get there. We can go shopping next weekend. How does that sound?"

"Like you're trying to bribe me," Emma muttered.

"Whatever it takes!" Louise said, smiling proudly. "I always get my way, Em. You should know that."

26

Miriam didn't think she'd feel so dejected at the thought of not having a family recipe for the auxiliary cookbook. Yet, as co-chair, she believed she needed to contribute something, else the other members would continue seeing her as an outsider. She was becoming friendly with several of them and didn't want to jeopardize that—honestly, she was not sure if it would or wouldn't. She chewed her meatloaf slowly, staring out the kitchen window as she wondered what to do.

"You're mighty deep in thought, Mim," George said, helping himself to another homemade biscuit and slathering it with raspberry jam.

"Oh, just thinking about the cookbook is all," she said. "I wish I had paid more attention when Mama was in the kitchen, but the only family recipe I can remember is her lemonade, and that won't cut it. Do you by any chance have any of Doris's recipes?"

"You know Mom wasn't much of a cook," George said with a chuckle. "Though she could make some fantastic Jell-O salads."

Miriam wrinkled her nose. "Definitely no, not for this crowd. Louise made it clear we weren't to provide any recipe that included a shortcut. Even though I love a good Jell-O salad. Maybe I'll make one this week now that it's getting hotter outside."

"Maybe the citrus layered one?" George said happily. "Lemon, lime, and orange—all done up in a pretty mold?"

"I'll have to dig my copper mold out from the storage shed," Miriam said. "But if that's what you'd like, I'll add Jell-O to my shopping list."

George sliced another hunk of the meatloaf and slid it onto his plate. "I think this is one of your best batches yet," he said, topping the slice with a mound of mashed potatoes. "Why couldn't you write up the recipe for this and just pretend it was your mom's?"

"Two things, honey. First, that would be lying..."

"It's not like they could verify it," George said.

"That's not the point. I would know, and it would ruin the integrity of the book. Laugh all you want, but I'm taking this project seriously. Second, I used stuffing, mix in this batch, so it wouldn't be accepted." She took a bite of green beans flavored with bacon and onion.

"Because it's a shortcut?" George asked. Miriam nodded. "Why not make homemade stuffing then use that instead?"

"Always the problem solver, aren't you?" Miriam said, smiling fondly at her husband. "It's still not a family recipe."

"You can say it's my recipe then," George countered. "But I think this is the best meatloaf I've ever had, honestly. Cookbook or not, it's a keeper."

"Speaking of solving problems," Miriam said, wiping her mouth. "The kitchen sink isn't draining properly. Can you look at it after dinner?"

"I guess you've already tried to plunge it?" George asked.

"Several times. Even used some Drano on it," Miriam said. "Honey, be sure and save room for dessert!"

"That's right—strawberry shortcake. I may have to let my dinner settle for a bit," he said, patting his protruding stomach. "Do you remember where you put your grandfather's tools?"

"I forgot you sold most of yours," Miriam said, giving him a sad look.

"I kept the essentials, but I think this job may take more than a hammer and a screwdriver," he said. "I'm sure I kept a wrench, too, but I have no idea where it is."

"Since I packed the boxes, let me go out to the shed and see what I can find," Miriam said, pushing back her chair. "After I clear the table."

"I can do that, Mim. After all you do for me," he said, leaning over to kiss her cheek, "least I can do is be your helper *and* handyman!"

"I love you, my sweet husband," Miriam said, getting up from her chair. "I'll be back."

"Watch out for spiders," George called as she opened the screen door.

"Gee, thanks," Miriam said, wiggling her fingers in the air.

She walked around the side of the house, stopping to smell the *Rosa virginiana* that was exploding with new blooms. The rosebush was more than six feet tall and had probably witnessed a lot in its long life. "I'll water you later," Miriam said as she headed toward the shed. At one time, the structure probably contained grain, maybe even hay, but now it only held the boxes Miriam had yet to unpack. She unlatched the handle and opened the double doors as wide as she could.

"If you're a spider, stay away from me," Miriam said loudly, then laughed at herself for behaving foolishly. She took a deep breath. "Going in!"

The boxes lined the walls and were carefully marked in her simple handwriting. Three of them contained her mementos from childhood through high school. She began opening one of them, then chastised herself. "Focus, Miriam. Focus." Several boxes held paperwork related to the hardware store and their bankruptcy—she opted to ignore those. Two boxes were dedicated to kitchen accessories—she opened the first and immediately found her fluted copper mold.

"One down, one to go," she muttered, wiping the dust off

her hands. She perused the remaining boxes until she found the one marked "Granddaddy." Though it was quite heavy, Miriam was able to maneuver it from the shed to the grass, then she sat down to unpack its contents. First, she lifted his navy peacoat from the box, bringing it to her nose and imagining she could still smell Old Spice on the neckline. Even though it was eighty degrees, she put it on and felt as though she was enveloped in one of his loving embraces. Next, she removed his well-worn Bible, thumbing through it to see passages he had marked, as well as favorites he had transcribed in the back. She was especially taken with the verse he had written from Exodus 14:14: "The Lord will fight for you, and you have only to be silent." Miriam hugged it to her chest as a tear slipped down her cheek. "You're coming inside with me," she said, placing it carefully in her lap. Finally, she took out a stack of files, setting them beside her, then placed the Bible carefully next to her before she stood to pull out the toolbox from the very bottom.

This must be at least seventy years old, she thought as she tried to open the rusted latch. Using her apron to protect her fingers, she carefully pried it open to find an assortment of woodworking tools, a hodgepodge of hammers, a couple of paintbrushes, and numerous wrenches. "Whew!" she exclaimed, wiping her brow. She was about to close the latch when she noticed a yellowed envelope, turned upside down and taped along the back of the toolbox. After taking out all the tools and setting them on the files, she carefully peeled away the fragile paper and removed it. Turning the envelope over, she saw his name and address beautifully written with perfect penmanship. And she felt something else inside—was it a coin?

She opened the envelope, and before reading the letter, she found a woman's ring—sapphire, Miriam guessed, mounted in a white gold Edwardian setting and obviously quite old. *This wasn't Grandma's,* she thought, remembering the pearl ring her grandmother always wore. She put the sapphire ring on her right pinky finger, then gently opened the letter.

"Dear Russell," it began, *"I'm sorry things have not turned out as you may have wished, but I trust my father's generosity has helped you realize a fresh start. Though I know you believed you could give my sister a good life, surely you know marriage was never a reasonable possibility given the vast disparity between your stations in life. I have yet to experience enough to know if this is right or wrong; it's simply the way things work. Yet, while I would most certainly be locked away in some remote dungeon if Father knew I contacted you, I felt it my duty to let you know I will be accompanying my sister for a short stay at the convent in Frankfort prior to our Grand Tour in Europe. Surely, you can deduce why a single young woman would need refuge with the nuns hundreds of miles from our home, but I can assure you, the child will be placed in the best possible home. Because my sister has told me about the love you shared, I wanted you to know. I have not told her I have written to you, nor can you ever contact her. I'm sure you understand. I wish you all the best, Rose."*

Miriam struggled to breathe, then she felt the blood drain from her head as she reread the letter. Things clicked into place. No wonder the two had acted strangely when she mentioned her grandfather's name. Despite wearing Granddaddy's coat, she began trembling as if taken with flu-like chills. *Was this supposed to be Iris's engagement ring?*

After a fitful night, Iris awoke feeling torn about the tarot card reading. She couldn't help but wonder if disrupting Miriam's reality was the right course of action, yet she also wanted to learn as much as she could about the daughter she had been forced to give up. Full of nervous energy, she turned her attention to the one thing she could control at that moment.

"What does one wear to a tarot card reading, dear?" Iris asked, standing in the middle of her cavernous closet, formerly one of their numerous guest bedrooms. "You know I don't like wearing all black, but does it suit the situation?"

Rose was reclined on the shell-pink divan, leisurely perusing the latest issue of *Connoisseur* magazine. "Have you heard of Patrick Nagel?" she said. "He's new to the art scene and he creates pop art, kind of like Warhol. I think we should acquire one before he becomes really famous."

"We already have two Warhols, Rose," Iris said, holding up a hand-painted silk kimono and a sleeveless, neon green jumpsuit. "What do you think?"

"I think you're distracting yourself from the purpose of our outing. We're going to look for an answer to our dilemma about what to say to Miriam. Or if we say anything. I know it's hard, sister. But we need to do this. And we don't have a Nagel," Rose said, holding up the magazine. "Look at his lines! And the color!"

"Whatever you'd like," Iris said, changing out of her white Gi and into the silk georgette jumpsuit. "Jasper sure put us through the workout this morning, didn't he? I think all this tai chi is helping my stamina!" She took a sip of her wheatgrass shake. "But I'm not sure I'll ever get used to this bilious juice." She made a gagging sound before sliding into the kimono. She added two strands of chunky beads—one coral, one turquoise—and a stack of silver bangles. "How do I look?" she said, twirling in front of Rose.

"Like you could wake the dead," Rose said. "Colorful?"

"Thanks," Iris said with a huff. She sat down next to Rose to put on her leather huaraches.

"You know when you walk in those, you sound like you're wearing a diaper," Rose said. "You're not, are you?"

"That was just rude," Iris said, taking off the sandals and replacing them with a pair of fuchsia sneakers.

"Better." Rose nodded. "How do *I* look?"

"A bit like Phyllis Diller, honestly, but with a better hairstyle," Iris said.

"Fair enough. Are you ready?"

"No, but let's do it anyway," Iris said, grabbing her Guatemalan bag from the shelf. "Let's go."

At Rose's request, Jasper had washed, vacuumed, and waxed their gold 1965 Bentley Corniche, which they kept cloistered in their five-car garage in favor of their go-to auto, an emerald Lincoln Town Car. "She looks positively radiant," Iris said to Jasper with a nod as she climbed into the backseat.

"I don't think she's aged a bit," Rose said, sliding in beside her sister. "I wasn't talking about you, dear," she said with a grin. As they pulled out of the drive, Rose asked what music Iris preferred for the drive to Richmond.

"Hmm," Iris said, putting on her Wayfarer sunglasses. "I'm feeling some sixties tunes." Before Rose could protest, Jasper had adjusted the radio. The Mamas and the Papas accompanied them from the estate onto the main thoroughfare.

"Do you know what you're going to ask?" Rose said,

putting her hand on Iris's knee.

"Isn't she supposed to know that?" Iris said.

"She's not a psychic, dear. She's a tarot card reader. You must have a question in mind."

"So many, dear sister, so very many," Iris said, rubbing one of her wrists.

"Narrow it to one," Rose said, leaning back and opening her magazine. "Now, back to Nagel. What do you think?"

***

Jasper pulled up to the door of Crystal's Crystals, then walked around the side to help the sisters from the sedan. "You'll join us, won't you?" Iris said, giving him an imploring look. He put his hands together and bowed, then held up one index finger. "Okay, we'll see in you inside," she said, as he returned to the car to park it in back. Taking a deep breath, she linked her arm through Rose's. "Let's get this over with."

As they opened the door, Tibetan chimes jingled, announcing their arrival. The air was hazy with incense—patchouli, Iris surmised, with a hint of jasmine. "What a lovely scent! We need to get some of that," Iris said, looking at the shelves lined with books, incense, incense holders, and crystals of all shapes and colors. "I feel calmer already."

"Good afternoon, ladies," said a middle-aged woman from behind the counter. Wearing a tie-dyed muumuu and sporting gray dreadlocks, she looked as though she had just returned from Jamaica. "I'm Sally. Are you here for something special?" They heard the chimes tinkle again as Jasper opened the door. Sally made an exaggerated fanning motion, then lowered her eyes. "My, my," she whispered. "He's a talk drink of water!"

"Oh, him? That's Jasper. He's with us," Rose said. She smiled as she watched him glide toward the book section.

"Lucky you," she said with a wink.

"We're here for a tarot card reading," Rose said. "For my sister, I mean."

Sally came around the counter and peered directly into Iris's eyes. "Are you a virgin?" she asked, placing her hand on Iris's shoulders.

Iris flinched. "What kind of a question is that?" she asked, pulling her bag over her stomach.

Sally laughed. "I should have asked it differently. Have you had a reading before?"

"She hasn't," Rose said.

"Please follow me," Sally said. "Bertie, would you watch the counter?" A lanky young man, reeking of marijuana, walked lazily from the back room to take his assigned post. Rose sniffed audibly.

"I apologize for that," Sally said. "That's why we have the incense." She laughed.

"I'm not bothered in the least," Rose said. "We might have to give it a try!"

"We already did, Rose. When we were in Amsterdam. Don't you remember?"

"No," Rose said, opening her bag to take out a Werther's candy and pop it in her mouth.

"There you go," Iris said. "You and ganja don't mix."

"Please be seated here," Sally said, pulling out the cane-backed chair at the card table covered with black velvet. "You are welcome to sit to the side," she told Rose before taking her own seat.

"May I start with your first name?"

"Iris," she said.

"Welcome, Iris. You're in a safe place, a sacred place. I invite you to close your eyes and reflect upon what you would like to learn from the cards today. Try to still your thoughts and focus on one question and one question only so the cards don't become confused."

Iris did as she was told, closing her eyes to see a slide-show of memories—the first time Rusty kissed her, the way he brushed the hair from her eyes, their first intimate moment in the servants' quarters, the last time she saw him before he left town without a goodbye. She shook her head to clear the images as a tear snaked down her cheek. *Miriam*, she thought. *I'm here about Miriam. Is it right to tell her who we are? Who she is?* Iris opened her eyes, wiping them with her sleeve. "I'm ready," she said, folding her hands in her lap. She looked to her sister for reassurance; Rose gave her a gentle nod.

"Very well," Sally said, shuffling the cards, then shuffling them again. "Please, hold the deck in your hand as you think about your question." Iris picked up the deck and cupped it in both hands—it was warm, and she could swear it was pulsing. She placed the deck back on the table.

"We're going to do a Celtic card spread," Sally said. "After I fan the cards, face down, on the table, I'd like you to select ten cards that speak to you."

Iris looked at her sister, rolling her eyes. Rose mouthed, "You can do this."

Iris did as she was instructed, then watched as Sally arranged the ten cards face up in the middle of the table in a cross formation. Sally tapped her fingernail on her front teeth, furrowing her brow as she evaluated the spread. Iris felt anxious and a bit queasy as she watched Sally's eyes dart from card to card.

"Interesting," Sally said. "I've not seen too many readings like this. You have five Major Arcana cards and five Minor Arcana cards in your spread. That's a rare balance. The Major Arcana cards represent life lessons, influences, and themes in your life," she said as Iris nodded, trying to follow Sally's words. "The Minor Arcana cards are all about subtlety and insights. You follow?"

Iris really didn't, but she nodded again, leaning forward.

"I've arranged the cards as you drew them. For your present self, you drew the Ten of Pentacles, which is all about permanence, satisfaction, and a signal that your legacy will endure," Sally said as Iris exhaled loudly. "The next card indicates the challenge you're facing—you pulled the Wheel of Fortune, representing a change in one or more relationships. Still with me?" She gave Iris a worried look.

"Just dandy," Iris said.

"I see in the past this card here, the Empress, who symbolizes motherhood in its simplest meaning, but it can also suggest maternal influences." Sally paused, looking over her glasses at Iris, who had dropped her head. "All good?" Iris nodded.

"Okay, continuing... this card, the Ten of Cups, signals what will happen in the immediate future, and it's all about family, togetherness, and joy," Sally said, smiling. "It's considered one of the happiest of the tarot cards and indicates you should feel good about the direction your life is taking."

Iris looked at her sister and smiled, nodding. Rose quietly clapped.

"Your fifth card, here, illustrates where your conscious mind is focusing right now. You drew the Four of Wands, which is a harbinger of happy families, reunions, and even surprises," she said, stopping to take a sip of water. "Is any of this resonating with you?"

Iris nodded, looking at her sister, who gave her a thumbs-up sign. Iris turned her attention back to the table.

"At an unconscious level, as expressed by this card, you have the Two of Wands, which symbolizes planning and making decisions. When we think of the unconscious in this instance, it's really about feelings, beliefs, and even values you may not completely understand. At least not yet," Sally said. "Your next card has to do with how you see yourself and how your self-image can influence how your situation plays out.

You drew the Strength card, which is more about compassion and determination. Still following me?"

"Yes, I think so," Iris said, pulling her kimono tightly across her chest.

"Okay, good. The next card addresses external influences—the world around you, your social environment, et cetera, and how others perceive you."

"Uh-oh," Rose said, laughing.

"Enough from the peanut gallery," Iris retorted.

"So, the card you have in this position is the Six of Pentacles, suggesting generosity and sharing." She paused to give Iris an encouraging smile. "It appears you are seen as quite the giver! Your hopes and fears are represented by the next card—that is, what you may secretly dread or deeply desire. You drew Death, the card indicating the end of one life phase and the beginning of another. Finally, what card represents the outcome to the question you posed? You drew Judgment, the sign for self-reflection and growth."

Sally sat back in her chair and cracked her knuckles.

"What does it all mean?" Rose asked, scooting her chair closer to the table and resting her chin in her cupped hands.

"Well, I see a very complex journey, one that involved your mother, perhaps, or even a lost child. You can be assured that in the present, the legacy you've created will endure, yet your greatest challenge is a change in one or more of your relationships. Perhaps, a new relationship will emerge. Consciously, you're focused on your wishes and dreams coming true—possibly a dream you never dared to imagine. Subconsciously, you know this will require some careful planning and making thoughtful decisions. Others see you as generous, willingly sharing yourself and your material fortune—I love that," she said, smiling at Iris. "And you see yourself as strong and capable, determined to rise to the challenge. As for your secret hopes and dreams, it appears one phase of your life will recede as a new one emerges. Finally, your outcome, at least as it relates to the question on your mind, is beautiful—self-reflection and growth."

Sally pulled an elastic from her wrist and fashioned her dreadlocks into a ponytail. "So, what do you think?" she said.

"I don't know what to say," Iris said, pushing away from the table. She looked at her sister. "What do you think?"

"I think we got our answer," Rose said, standing up and handing Sally a twenty-dollar bill.

"We did?" Iris said, her voice incredulous.

Rose nodded. "Care to look at the crystals, dear?" she said, taking Iris's arm.

"For your situation, I would highly recommend Amazonite. Would you like to see?" Sally said, walking to the glass case. The sisters followed her, then examined the variegated blue and green stone she placed on the counter. "This is called the Courage and Truth Stone. It represents feminine bravery, strength, and fearlessness. Isn't it lovely?"

"I'll take two," Iris said, pulling out her wallet. After Sally handed Iris her wrapped crystals, each nestled in a brocade pouch, she reached out and placed her hand over Iris's heart. "You have wonderful energy, Iris. Thank you for letting me work with you today."

"Thank you," Iris said. "I'm sure we'll return."

Rose motioned for Jasper, who was exploring the selection of Indian yoga pants. He nodded and came to the door to escort the women from the shop.

Once nestled against the sedan's buttery leather seats, Rose looked at Iris. "Did you get the answer you were looking for?"

"I already knew what I was going to do," Iris said, buckling her seatbelt.

"And that would be?" Rose asked.

"I need to talk to Miriam. It's that simple," she said,

shaking her head. "I hope she takes it well."

"Of course she will. Where next?" Rose asked. "Are you hungry?"

"Thirsty," Iris said. "Let's go have a martini."

"It's only one o'clock, dear," Rose said.

"Life is short. Jasper, please take us to the Jefferson Hotel."

He nodded and steered the Bentley toward downtown.

28

"You seem a bit distracted," Louise said, looking across the table at Miriam, who was idly pleating her paper napkin into an accordion fold. They were sitting at an outdoor café for drinks and a few nibbles.

"Tough day at work?" Louise couldn't imagine being on her feet all day, much less having to constantly deal with the public, yet at some level, she respected Miriam for doing what she must to make ends meet.

"I just have a lot on my mind is all," Miriam said softly, rubbing her temples.

"You know I don't like to pry," Louise said, though she was curious about Miriam's mood—it was as though she had lost some of her effervescence, like a soda gone flat. "Everything okay at home?" She took a sip of pinot grigio. "Oh, before I forget, thanks for meeting me on short notice."

"I always enjoy seeing you, Louise," Miriam said, bringing her glass of iced tea to her lips. "And things are fine at home, but I appreciate you asking."

Louise wanted to prod further, but something about Miriam's expression changed her mind.

"I brought you something," Louise said, reaching into her bag. "For the cookbook!" She handed Miriam a well-worn, folded sheet of paper. "Mama's recipe that, if memory serves, had been her mother's, transcribed from its native Irish." She handed it to Miriam. "That's Mama's handwriting."

Miriam opened it and smiled as she read. "Her penmanship is lovely," she said, licking her lips as she saw the ingredients. "Have you ever made this?"

"Oh, goodness, I don't personally cook," Louise said with a laugh, placing her hand on her chest. "That just wouldn't be good for anyone, especially me."

"What about Pearl, then?" Miriam asked. "Oh, and do you want me to take this?"

"Yes, please take it and add it to the file for the Websters to transcribe," Louise said. She noticed Miriam wince at the reference. "Though I'm pretty sure their housekeeper will be doing all the work. As for Pearl, I'm sure she would make it if I asked. I guess I just never got around to it."

Miriam seemed to consider what Louise said as she carefully folded the recipe and slid it into her tote bag.

"Did you write a blurb about why the recipe is important to you?" Miriam said, dipping a piece of bread into the olive oil mixed with balsamic vinegar, then popping it into her mouth. "Oh, crud!" She dabbed a spot on her blouse where the oil had dripped.

Louise sat back and crossed her legs as she considered Miriam's question, which was fraught with more complexity than Miriam could have imagined. "I'm not sure what I want to say, Miriam. It was so important to my family that her status of origin–as an immigrant, I mean–become buried once she became a Winston... I don't know, it almost feels like a betrayal." She lowered her eyes. "Grandmother Nora never did approve, you know."

"So, your family kept her background a secret?" Miriam said, her eyes moistening with tears.

"As I understand it, that was one of many conditions she had to agree to if she was going to marry Daddy."

"And she agreed?"

"She loved him," Louise said. "I believe she would have

done just about anything for him, until she couldn't any longer." She reached back into her bag, removed an enormous pair of black sunglasses, and put them on.

"Family secrets are hard," Miriam said, shaking her head. "Maybe it's best not to know, if that makes sense? Otherwise, they eat away at you."

Louise cocked her head. "Now you've piqued my curiosity," she said, happy to change the subject.

"I just meant, maybe it wouldn't be such a bad thing to share your mama's story," Miriam said. "It's 1978, after all. Almost a brand-new decade! Having an Irish mother is rather exotic, at least to me. I think it makes you even more interesting than you already are."

Louise nibbled on a piece of bread. "I think I'll just say the recipe was my mother's favorite, prepared by her family's cook when she felt poorly," Louise said with a resolute nod. "That should work, shouldn't it?"

Miriam put down her glass. "But that's not the truth, Louise," she said in a measured tone.

"Well, I'm making it my truth. All things considered, I loved her shepherd's pie, but really, it was always considered a peasant's meal. I need to treat it as a bit of a lark," she said. "Irony, even."

"Will it sound like you're making fun?" Miriam asked, her face awash with concern. "You know, of the 'commoners,'" she said, making air quotes.

Louise laughed. "Oh, Miriam, what a gentle heart you have. But honestly, I'm just bending the story a little. Mama's mama was her cook, and it was her recipe from the old country, so really..."

"If that's what you want to do, who am I to argue?" Miriam said, helping herself to another hunk of bread. "I wasn't raised in your world. What do I know?"

Louise smoothed her hair behind her ears. "I have learned,

all too well, that people will take advantage of any juicy tidbit they can find to assault your character. Best to be careful with what you share, and to whom, especially in Stuarts Landing," she said, patting the corners of her mouth with the checkered napkin.

"I guess we disagree, Louise. I don't think we should ever be ashamed of our backgrounds, such that we can make sense of them. That's who we are, isn't it?"

"Not always," Louise said, giving Miriam a knowing look. "Would you want people poking around in your past?" She didn't intend the question to be provocative, but she saw Miriam visibly squirm, the color draining from her face.

"Never mind. Would you like to order dinner?" Louise said, handing her the menu.

"Oh, it's later than I thought!" Miriam said, looking at her watch. "I must get home and make George's dinner. It's fried chicken night."

"That's fine, dear," Louise said, placing her American Express on the table for the waitress. "I really appreciate you joining me. I needed a moment to transition from my day at the auxiliary to the tempest that is my daughter, who's probably pouting at home. As usual. Thank God, she leaves for camp next week. I can only handle so much drama." She exhaled dramatically.

"Consider yourself blessed to be a mother," Miriam said, gathering her things. "That was never in the cards for me."

"Oh, heavens, forgive me," Louise said. "I... I don't know what I was thinking." She reached out to take Miriam's hand.

"My mama always told me to remain grateful, even when life isn't what you thought it would be," Miriam said. "Words to live by, I think." She gave Louise a look she couldn't decipher. "See you on Wednesday at the auxiliary meeting?"

"Yes, I'll see you there," Louise said, folding her napkin on the table and signaling the waitress. As she watched Miriam

shuffle to her car, Louise drummed her fingers in her lap, intrigued by what Miriam must be hiding. *I need to find out what it is. For her benefit, of course.*

29

By the time Miriam got home, George was already there, drinking a cold beer on the front porch. She noticed a charcoal grill positioned in the gravel to the side of the steps, and she could smell something cooking. "Hey," she said, taking a seat next to him. Pointing at the grill, she raised her eyebrows. "What's this?" As he continued rocking, his face broke into a wide smile.

"I thought I'd surprise you," he said. "I'm making dinner tonight."

"Why, thank you! Be right back—I need to get some iced tea." Miriam went inside, dropped her bags on the plaid recliner, kicked off her work shoes, and went to the kitchen. Sitting on the counter was a beautiful bouquet of red roses interspersed with pink dahlias and yellow snapdragons. Clasping her hands in delight, she leaned in to inhale the glorious fragrance. After pouring her tea, she returned to the porch, the screen door banging behind her.

"Today's not our anniversary," Miriam said as she sat down in the rocking chair. "So, beautiful flowers, a new grill, you making dinner... I'm confused. Grateful, don't get me wrong, honey, but should I be worried about something?"

George opened the cover of the grill to turn the chicken thighs before basting them with barbecue sauce. "Not at all. Just wanted to take care of my best girl!" he said, waving his tongs gallantly in the air. She smiled and raised her glass.

"Thank you, honey," she said as he returned to the porch.

"It's been a very long day." With a deep sigh, she mentally prepared herself to tell him about the letter she discovered the night before. Normally, she shared everything with her husband, yet she knew she needed time to process what she had learned. She wasn't sure how she felt, and twenty-four hours later, her thoughts remained convoluted. How would the sisters feel about her new knowledge of Rusty and Iris's relationship? And especially that she knew it produced a baby? Would they want to push Miriam away? Hide her like they did the baby Iris gave up? Would she and George have to find a new place to live? They were finally settled in, mostly, and had begun making the place feel more like their own. Her garden was thriving, and she looked forward to planting a vegetable garden in the next few weeks. The thought of starting over, once again, was more than she could fathom, especially with her responsibilities at the auxiliary and, of course, The Pig. She finished her glass of tea in three hearty gulps.

"Refill?" George said, reaching for her glass. Miriam looked up at him and smiled. "I'm not sure who you are, but I must say, I could get used to this!"

He returned with her tea and another beer for himself, taking the rocking chair next to hers.

"Well, I have news," he said, grinning mischievously. Miriam raised her eyebrows, deciding the news must be positive.

"Okay," she said, putting down her tea and holding onto the sides of her chair.

"I got a promotion today, Mim! Meet the new Service *Director* of Butler Automotive! And it comes with a nice bump in pay, maybe even enough to where you can quit your job. Would you like that?" he said, holding up his beer. Miriam lifted her glass and clinked his bottle.

"Oh, George, I'm just so proud of you," she said. "And in such a short time! You really are something, you know that?"

She leaned her head back against the rocker and closed her eyes. She couldn't possibly ruin his moment with her very emotional dilemma. She choked back her tears, though a single drop betrayed her, cascading down her freckled face.

"Sweetheart, what's wrong? You don't have to quit The Pig if you don't want to," George said, putting down his beer and taking both her hands in his own. "I just thought you might enjoy having more time for the auxiliary, you know, and your garden. But it's completely your decision." He gave her an imploring look.

"It's not that," Miriam said, wiping her eyes. "I'm just, um, I'm just so happy for you. That's all," she added, immediately feeling wretched about lying to him, even though it was only by omission.

"I need to pull the chicken from the grill," he said, rising from his seat. "I picked up some coleslaw and potato salad—they're in the fridge. Are you ready to move inside?"

Miriam stood up. "I'll get the table set," she said, glad to have a moment to collect herself.

"Oh, one more thing," George said as he placed the chicken thighs—slightly burned, from what she could see—on the cutting board. "We've been invited to join Mr. and Mrs. Butler at the club for dinner this Saturday night. To celebrate. How's about that?"

Miriam took a deep breath. "That's wonderful, dear. Maybe I'll whip up a new dress."

"Or you could go buy one!" George said. "I think we can afford it."

Miriam went inside to get their plates ready for dinner. She had some thinking to do.

***

After washing what few dishes they had used for dinner, Miriam joined George in the small den to watch television. "Care to sit with me on the couch?" George asked, wiggling his eyebrows.

"I'm a little warm, dear. I think I'll just sit in the recliner for a bit if you don't mind." George got up and walked to the television, turning it off.

"Don't you want to watch the baseball game?" Miriam asked, flipping through her latest issue of *Good Housekeeping*. She had splurged on a subscription and was delighted every time it arrived in their mailbox.

"Not nearly as much as I want to know what's going on with you, Mim. You don't seem yourself," he said.

"You're the second person today to comment," Miriam said, looking at her brittle nails. "Louise said I seemed distracted."

"When did you see her?" he asked.

"Oh, we just met for a snack. She called me at work and invited me to meet her after I clocked out."

"And how was that?"

Miriam looked up at her husband, whose face was so full of sincere compassion she felt her heart ready to burst. "It was fine, really. We discussed the cookbook, you know, and family. Well, mostly about her mother, really. And she mentioned her daughter, who she really seems to resent. I must admit, it made me sad to think how she seems to take for granted what so many of us wish we had," Miriam said as her head began to throb.

"A lot of folks are like that, Mim. They don't know how to be grateful until it's too late."

"Funny thing about Louise, well, one of many funny things about Louise is that I often feel she's speaking in code. Like she's giving me some kind of veiled warning that goes right over my head," Miriam said, picking at one of her cuticles.

"What did she say?"

"Something about people using information you've shared against you, to make you look bad," Miriam said, pinching the bridge of her nose. "She said to be careful who I trust. Honestly, why can't people just be genuine around here?" She rose to get some aspirin from her purse.

"Women are definitely complicated," George said with a wry chuckle. "I don't know how you do it. Having to keep so many versions of yourself straight must get a little complicated. I'm glad you're not that way."

Miriam swallowed the aspirin, then sat down next to him on the couch.

"I don't want different versions of myself, George. I'm just me, but I don't know if that's enough around here," she said. "Just when I think I'm starting to belong, things seem to shift, and I go back to feeling unwelcome."

George lifted her chin and looked into her eyes. "What aren't you telling me?"

So, she took a deep breath and told George everything—about the letter, about her conflicted feelings, about her fears the Websters would resent what she knew and push her away to keep their secrets buried. After all, they'd sped off on their tandem bike as soon as she mentioned her grandfather's name. It hadn't escaped her notice that she hadn't seen them since. They must be terribly embarrassed or worried Iris's secret would be exposed. Maybe both.

"She's seventy-two years old, George. I know they act like they don't care what people think, but that's because, as far as I know, they've never been the topic of gossip. No one would dare! Yet, if people knew Iris had gotten pregnant out of wedlock..."

George pulled her into a hug. "Mim," he said as he rubbed her back. "That was more than fifty years ago. I don't think anyone would care anymore."

"You don't know these women, George," Miriam said, pulling away from him and smoothing her hair. "They can be vicious. Honestly, I don't fit in here."

"You belong here as much as anyone. You're kind and caring. If people haven't figured that out yet, they will. Just don't give up."

Miriam exhaled slowly, then turned to her husband. "What should I do about the letter?" she whispered.

"Only you know the answer, sweetheart. But if you want my take, I think you should talk to Iris."

"I'll think about it," she said, wrapping her arms around a throw pillow.

"Better yet, maybe pray on it?" George suggested. Miriam took his hand and kissed it.

"I didn't want to ruin your big evening, honey. I'm sorry," she said as she rocked back and forth.

"We've been through a whole lot of life together, Mim. Why should today be any different? Or tomorrow? Or next week? Or next year?" he said, giving her a reassuring smile.

"I have a feeling things are going to change, George."

"Then we'll change too," he said. "Without losing the basics of who we are."

Miriam returned his smile. "I hope you're right, dear husband. I do hope you're right."

30

After the tarot card reading and two martinis each, Iris and Rose decided they would invite Miriam to lunch so they could explain what had happened back in 1928, when Miriam's mother was born. Iris wasn't sure how Miriam would react—what if she became angry or, worse yet, rejected them as her family? Despite her anxiety, Iris was keen to hear more about her daughter. Had she loved and been well loved? Had she been happy? Mostly, Iris hoped for some assurance, after all these years, that she—no, her family—had done the right thing.

"Do you know what I think would be nice?" Iris said to Rose, who was preoccupied with her loom, making yet another placemat. They already had at least ten in the pantry, but Iris knew the process was meditative for her sister, so she withheld her opinions about Rose's unfortunate color choices.

"What's that, dear?" Rose said, chewing her bottom lip as she tried to thread the yarn.

"Let's invite Miriam to a picnic lunch. The weather's been so nice lately, hasn't it? We can have Jasper prepare some of his delicacies, and of course, we'll need a nice sparkling wine—maybe Prosecco? We could have him drive us around one of our old tobacco farms to give her a sense of our history, perhaps. And we could take the convertible! How does that sound?"

Rose removed her hands from the loom and clasped them to her chest. "I think that sounds like a splendid idea, sister!

When were you thinking of doing this?"

Iris stood and walked to their grandfather's desk, then opened the bottom drawer to remove two dusty photo albums. "Well, today's Tuesday, and we don't know her work schedule, of course, but I was thinking maybe Saturday?" She took the albums and sat down at the antique double desk across from Rose and her table loom.

"I think that's a fine plan, and it gives us plenty of time to be thoughtful about how we approach the situation," Rose said, working a strand of metallic worsted yarn into her design. "Do you want to write her an invitation? We can have Jasper put in on her porch this afternoon."

Iris returned to the desk and pulled out her fountain pen and the stationery embossed with the Webster family crest. "Shall we say noon on Saturday?" Rose nodded. "Perhaps I should recommend wearing a hat? She is quite fair, after all," Iris said. "Just like Rusty."

***

That Saturday morning, while Jasper was in the garage detailing their 1967 turquoise Cadillac convertible, Iris sat in the solarium, poring through the photo albums she would show Miriam later. She smiled as she flipped through page after page of her and Rose, inseparable, whether on their horses, or dressed for cotillion, or playing tennis, or modeling their debutante gowns, or waving from the deck of a cruise ship. Her eyes became misty as she ran her fingers over the photographs of her mother and father, she draped in jewels, he outfitted in bespoke suits and elegant hats. She turned to the few pages they had of her grandparents, captured in sepia tones and stoic, lifeless, yet well-dressed, nonetheless. She squinted to see if she could find any of Miriam in any of the pictures, yet the only thing she seemed to have inherited was

Rusty's fiery red hair.

"Have you decided what to wear?" Rose said, interrupting Iris's reverie. Iris looked up to see her sister clad in madras clamdiggers, a chambray peasant blouse, an Hermes scarf, and lime green espadrilles.

"I hadn't given it much thought," she said, eyeing Rose's ensemble. "You look quite fetching, dear!"

"Wait until you see the hat I selected!" Rose said. Iris rolled her eyes.

Two hours later, Iris was ready to leave. She had opted for a demure look, which she thought appropriate given the story she was about to tell, so she dressed in a white eyelet sundress, a hand-knitted peach poncho, and a pair of ballerina slippers. Though she rarely wore pearls anymore—too dainty for her current taste—she removed a triple strand of Mikimoto pearls from her jewelry box and clasped them around her neck. As she smoothed the necklace into place, she remembered her sixteenth birthday when her father had given them to her. Her mother had objected, saying they were far too grand for such a young girl, but he had held firm in his decision, saying they would be perfect for her formal social debut (an event which never happened). *Life was so simple then.* She considered her appearance in the mirror, applied her frosted pink lipstick, and with one final look and a very deep breath, she was ready. At least as ready as she could ever be. She grabbed her wide-brimmed straw hat from the bed, then proceeded downstairs to meet Rose and Jasper waiting in the porta-cochère.

Jasper pulled the convertible in front of the guesthouse as Iris fanned herself nervously with the silk *abanico* her mother had purchased in Spain. She looked over at Rose, whose face was shielded by her black sunglasses and beribboned hat. "Isn't that the one you wore to the Derby?" Iris said, keeping her eyes on the Llewelyns' screen door.

"One and the same, dear," Rose said, reaching over to give

Iris's hand a squeeze.

"Should Jasper knock on the door?" Iris wondered if Miriam had decided not to join them.

"I don't think so," Rose said. "We can wait."

"Did she respond to the invitation?" Iris said, stroking her pearls.

Jasper shook his head.

"Maybe she's not coming then," Iris said, lowering her head.

She heard the screen door bang shut and looked up to see Miriam emerging from the porch, dressed in a pair of linen culottes and a gauze blouse and carrying a canvas hat. Iris smiled as her stomach did a flip. *My granddaughter,* she thought to herself, looking at Miriam anew.

Jasper got out of the car to hold the passenger door open for Miriam, who slid into the back seat next to Rose.

"Beautiful car," Miriam said as she placed her macrame tote on the floorboard.

"Good afternoon, dear, and thank you so much for joining us," Rose said. Iris leaned forward so she could see Miriam directly.

"Yes, we've been looking forward to this," Iris said as Jasper pulled out of the drive.

"Lovely day for a picnic," Iris said. Miriam simply nodded. "Jasper prepared a most delicious lunch for us, but that's no surprise," she said, laughing nervously. "We have a spinach and mushroom quiche, still warm from the oven, fresh fruit salad with kiwi, spinach salad, and, of course, two bottles of chilled Prosecco!"

"I've never had that," Miriam said, her eyes fixed on the road ahead.

"It's lovely," Rose said. "We first tried it in Florence, and we've kept some in the wine cellar ever since."

Miriam remained quiet. Iris looked at her sister, who gave

the most imperceptible of shrugs.

"How are things going at work and with the cookbook?" Iris said.

"I've cut back my hours a bit, but I still really like working there," Miriam said, putting on her hat and tying it beneath her chin. "As for the cookbook, I only have a few recipes so far, but we still have time."

"We're still trying to decide what to submit," Rose said. "I believe Louise agreed we could use one of Jasper's recipes?" Miriam nodded.

"It will be so difficult to decide," Iris added. "He's never made a bad meal."

Jasper turned off the main thoroughfare onto a country road, and soon, the landscape changed. Spanning for miles in each direction were row upon row of tobacco plants, their lush green leaves reaching hopefully toward the sun.

"Isn't it heavenly?" Iris said, breathing in deeply. "This land used to belong to our grandfather. He had six different tobacco farms, this one being the largest. What was it, Rose, a thousand acres?"

"A little more than that, if I remember correctly," Rose said.

"What happened to it?" Miriam said, looking at Iris for the first time.

"Well, I suppose the simple answer is that as Daddy got older, he didn't have the energy to oversee all six operations, even though each farm had several foremen. So, he sold to several of the big tobacco conglomerates," Iris said. "He never stopped loving the land, though. Said it would always be part of his blood. Ours too." She looked at Miriam and smiled, then noticed she was fidgeting. She gave Rose a concerned look, but her sister just patted her knee.

"Up ahead, Jasper, see the sign for the park? Please turn there," Rose said. Jasper nodded, turning on the blinker to make a right turn. He drove down the winding gravel road until they came to a clearing by a sparkling pond. "This is good. We can sit at one of the picnic tables."

Once the convertible was parked, Jasper jumped from the car to open the passenger door so the women could exit, then popped the trunk to remove two picnic baskets and a large beach tote.

"That table looks nice," Rose said, pointing to the one closest to the water.

"I agree, sister," Iris said, fumbling with her hat as the breeze picked up. "Let's sit down," she said. Rose and Iris folded themselves onto the bench facing the water, leaving Miriam to take the seat facing them. Jasper pulled three of Rose's woven placemats from the tote, placing them on the table, then set out the cutlery, dishes, and crystal flutes.

"These placemats are pretty," Miriam said, running her fingers along the woven fabric. Rose looked at Iris and beamed.

"Rose made them," Iris said. "She's very proud of her work, as you can see."

"As she should be," Miriam said. "It seems she always masters whatever she sets her sights on."

"She always knows how to figure things out. Always has," Iris said, ruffling her sister's shortly cropped silver hair.

"I would say," Miriam said, watching Jasper uncork the Prosecco. He filled all three glasses, then returned to a table behind them to plate their lunches.

"I'd like to propose a toast," Iris said, raising her glass. Miriam set down her drink and reached into her bag.

"To the truth?" Miriam said, her green eyes flashing as she placed the envelope with Rose's letter to Rusty and her enamel brooch on the picnic table. Rose leaned in to examine the items and let out a gasp. Iris began coughing once she recognized the dogwood pin.

"The only explanation I can find is that my mother was

your daughter, Iris," Miriam said gently, looking Iris directly in the eye.

"Forget the toast," Iris said, taking a hefty sip of her sparkling wine. "We didn't know, not until you told us about Rusty, and then we still couldn't be sure," she said. "But now, there's no question. I promise, I had no idea, Miriam. But I'm just so glad we found you. Or, that you found us. That we're finally together, anyway. That was the whole reason for proposing this little outing today, though we always love seeing you, of course. We wanted to talk to you on neutral ground, if you will, about our suspicions, which now have been wonderfully confirmed."

Miriam took a sip of her drink. "Did you look? Ever? I mean, for my mom... her name was Althea. Did you ever try to find her?"

Rose opened her mouth to speak, but Iris interrupted. "That would have been foolhardy," she said, taking off her hat. "My father never would have allowed it, and to be honest, I had to believe God had placed your mother in a better situation than we could have provided."

Miriam uncoiled herself from the table, rising to her feet. "Are you kidding? You all are richer than God! She would have had a wonderful life, one where she never had to worry about money, or belonging, or wondering why she wasn't good enough," Miriam said, pacing back and forth. "Mostly, she would have had her mother."

Iris tried to get up from the bench, but Rose held out her arm to stop her.

"Miriam," Rose said gently. "I need you to understand, times were different then. Iris never could have married Rusty, not without being cut off from the family."

"Did you love him?" Miriam said, rounding the table to confront Iris.

"More than life itself," Iris said, dropping her head as her eyes filled with tears. "But I had just turned seventeen. He was twenty and worked in the mill. My mother was busy trying to pair Rose and me with the most eligible bachelors in a three-county region. They saw Rusty as..."

"Low class," Miriam said, sitting back down and rubbing her eyes.

"I'm afraid so," Iris said, looking up at Miriam. "I saw him as the most interesting man I had ever met. Different from those in what I suppose was our parents' social circle. He had dreams, big ones, and he wasn't afraid to work with his hands. He wasn't concerned about what people thought. He just wanted to be happy, and he wanted us to be happy, together."

Jasper quietly placed the loaded plates on the table, then bowed and returned to his spot just behind them.

"Would you like some lunch, dear?" Rose said, putting her napkin in her lap.

"For once, I'm actually not hungry," Miriam said, taking a sip of Prosecco. "This tickles my nose," she added, sneezing. "Did you get to hold her? My mom, I mean." She began blowing her nose.

"For a moment. She was the most beautiful thing I had ever seen and warm as a summer's day," Iris said, dabbing her eyes. Rose put her arm around her sister's waist, pulling her into a hug.

"We really didn't have a choice, Miriam," Rose said. "But, as you obviously read in the letter, I wanted Rusty to know. It was the right thing to do, or so I thought."

Iris watched as Miriam seemed to fold in on herself, her shoulders slumped forward, her head in her hands. Iris watched and waited.

"You know, it's funny. When I first read the letter, I was worried about how you would react, knowing I'm the daughter of the daughter you had to give up. Without knowing how you felt about all that, I figured if you didn't want her, you

wouldn't want me either," Miriam said softly, dabbing her eyes.

"Oh, sweetheart, it wasn't like that at all! I wished, every single day, there could be a path that included Rusty, me, and the baby I was carrying... together, as a family. Rose and I spent many nights at the convent trying to figure out what we could do. In the end, I had to resign myself to what the sisters said: there were families who would be blessed by having your mother. I prayed that's what resulted," Iris said, folding her hands in her lap.

"We had some really tough times," Miriam said. "Mom married my daddy when she was eighteen. I don't think Granddaddy liked him too much. He was a drinker and a gambler who ran fast and loose with Mama's heart. She had me at nineteen, and by the time I was three, maybe four, he was gone."

Iris inhaled sharply. "What happened?" she said, giving Miriam a desperate look.

"All I know is he left, and Granddaddy was there to make sure we had enough to eat and a roof over our heads," Miriam said.

"I had wanted to ask if your mother was happy, but I guess I know the answer," Iris said, reaching across the table. Miriam cocked her head to one side, then reached out to take Iris's hand.

"I believe she was, despite what Daddy did," Miriam said. "When she died, I didn't think I'd be able to survive it, but Granddaddy was there to get me through the worst of it. Then I met George, and he was my safe place to fall. Still is."

"And your grandfather? Rusty?" Rose said.

"Died about seven months before we moved here. I was there when he took his last breath."

Rose looked at Iris, whose shoulders were shaking as she quietly sobbed, and back at Miriam, who was wiping her runny nose. She motioned for Jasper, who silently replenished their wine glasses, then noticed Miriam rummaging through her bag.

"Iris?" Miriam said softly while reaching for Iris's left hand. "I found this with Rose's letter. I believe this was meant for you." She slid the sapphire ring on her grandmother's left ring finger. Iris stared at the dainty piece, her expression changing from sadness to pure joy.

"Well, what do you know?" she murmured, holding her hand at different angles to inspect the modest piece. "If he kept it all this time, I guess that meant he never stopped loving me, just like I never stopped loving him. Knowing that heals a lot of wounds, Miriam. Thank you."

After a few silent moments, Rose lifted her glass. "Let's try this again," she said, tapping the flute with her knife. "I propose a toast. To family, to blood, to difficult choices, to survival, and to new beginnings. Please, Miriam, I know this is a lot to process, but allow us to be a safe place for you also."

Iris watched Miriam as her face burst into a smile. "I loved you guys from the moment I met you at The Pig," Miriam said, shaking her head. "I just thought you were two eccentric old women."

"That's for sure," Iris said with a chuckle.

"Oh, my gosh... how did I not piece it together?" Miriam said, her eyebrows raised and her mouth falling open.

"Piece what together?" Rose said.

"When he wasn't making any sense but told me we had to come to Stuarts Landing, Granddaddy told me to look for the flowers. He said I couldn't miss them! I thought he meant all the gorgeous gardens around here—yours, especially. *No!* He meant *you!* Iris and Rose. How could I be so stupid?"

Iris looked at Rose and they started laughing. "Sounds like something he would say," Iris said. "He saw things other people missed. One of the many reasons I loved him."

"Sometimes, I can be so dim," Miriam said. "But you are two women with remarkable strength. I can only hope to be like you both."

"Oh, sweetheart, you already are," Rose said. "Of course, this revelation changes things, as you must know," she added, looking at Iris.

"Yes, Miriam, we now have an heir, which means we will have to reconsider our final wishes," Iris said thoughtfully. "One day, you will be a very wealthy woman." She thought Miriam would be happy, but instead, she watched Miriam's face contort in anger.

"I never cared about money!" she all but spat, setting down her glass. "I only ever wanted to know my family." Tears exploded from her emerald eyes.

"I didn't mean to upset you," Iris said. "But it's the truth. That said, given the nature of this town and the way people judge others—usually for all the wrong things—I think it best if we keep our relationship to ourselves. At least for now, until we can revise our estate documents. Sister, you probably should make an appointment with Clifton." Rose nodded.

"I understand, but please know, this isn't what I wanted," Miriam said, pushing her plate away.

Iris's breath caught in her throat. "I know we may not be the family you had hoped for," she said.

"That's not what I mean," Miriam said. "I just wanted a family. I wanted to know where my people came from. I wasn't looking for anything more."

"Well, now you know," Rose said, lifting her glass once again. "Nothing need change, at least not anytime soon. But we're always here, for whatever questions you have, whatever you need... all you need do is ask. Dare I say, we love you, Miriam, and we're so glad to have found you."

"Ditto," Iris said, taking another sip of Prosecco. "Hardly eloquent, I know. But my heart is just so full, dear. Let us enjoy what time we have, together."

Miriam speared a piece of kiwi fruit with her salad fork and swirled it in the poppyseed dressing. "Do we still have to pay rent?" she said, grinning mischievously.

Iris threw back her head and laughed, her sides shaking with happiness.

"Only if you so wish, my beautiful granddaughter."

31

Miriam was so elated by her afternoon with the Websters—her family!—that she wished she and George could reschedule their dinner date with the Butlers, yet she knew it was an important opportunity for him. She dressed quickly in a black linen sheath she had finished making the day before and her only pair of high heels, which she bought right after finishing the dress. Smiling, she pinned the dogwood brooch near her shoulder, then secured her curls with two gold barrettes she picked up at The Pig.

"What a day you've had, Mim," George said as she emerged from the bedroom. He had taken the revelations from her afternoon well, surprised but thrilled by the family connections. "I guess we're celebrating a few things tonight! You look gorgeous." Miriam couldn't help but blush. She never tired of George's praise, though she rarely felt worthy of it. Today, though, today she felt different... as though she had finally found a piece of herself she didn't know was missing.

"About that, honey. We can't say anything to anyone about my relationship with the Websters," Miriam said, transferring her wallet, compact, and lipstick from her tote bag to a small black clutch she bought along with her shoes.

"I understand," George said, stepping behind her to kiss the back of her neck. Miriam giggled, then turned around and hugged him tightly.

"You haven't spent much time around Bitsy, have you?" Miriam said. George shook his head. "Well, let me just say, she can be quite a lot sometimes, but I do believe she has the best intentions, despite how she behaves around Louise. They have this strange relationship–like they're friends but they're not. Does that make sense?"

George scratched his ear. "Honestly, no. I can't say that it does," he said, chuckling. "What do you think?"

"I think it's best to remain Switzerland," she said. "Ready?"

***

The country club was abuzz with activity when the Llewelyns entered the lobby. Full of beautiful, expensively dressed people mingling about, it looked like a scene from a 1930s film, though in Technicolor. Miriam scanned the room, looking for their dinner companions.

"Oh, there's Bobby," George said, pointing to a man smoking a cigar and chatting amiably with another gentleman. She didn't see Bitsy, though.

"What do I call him?" Miriam said, placing her hand on George's arm. "I know Bitsy, but I've not met Bobby. Maybe I just don't use his name at all?"

"I'd say, let's leave it to him," George said. "Did I tell you how beautiful you are?"

It's as if he read my mind, Miriam thought. She was feeling out of place, intimidated by so much elegance–like a workhorse amidst a bucolic pasture of thoroughbreds. She took his hand and gave it a squeeze.

"Ah, here you are!" a familiar voice called from behind. Miriam turned to see Bitsy sauntering toward them, a vision in her red Thai silk cocktail dress. Strapless and form-fitting, it left little of Bitsy's figure to the imagination.

"Well, hello!" Miriam said, leaning in to give Bitsy an air kiss. Though she thought it silly, Miriam believed she had finally mastered this obligatory form of greeting.

"Don't you look stunning!"

"Thank you, Miriam—as do you! And you must be George," she said, extending her right hand and smiling sweetly. *Was she batting her eyelashes?* Miriam thought with a jolt. *Don't be ridiculous. That's just the way she is.*

"I've heard so much about you," George said, shaking her hand.

"Likewise," Bitsy said, turning her attention to Miriam. "Did you have to work today?"

"No, I don't work on Saturdays anymore," Miriam said. "I've cut back my hours."

Bitsy nodded, then looked across the room to catch her husband's attention. He gave her a wave, then held up a finger. "Bobby will be here in a moment," she said. "He appears to be in deep discussion, though I have no idea who that man is. Why don't we proceed to the dining room—Bobby will join us when he's finished."

They followed Bitsy through the maze to the maître d's stand. "Good evening, Mrs. Butler," he said. "We have your regular table ready if you'd like to be seated. Your husband?"

"He's in the lobby," she said. "Business, you know." She rolled her eyes and smiled playfully.

"Follow me," he said, leading them to a corner table. The dining room was not yet filled, but from their vantage point, they would be able to see everyone who entered. Miriam hadn't considered that everyone would be able to see them as well.

"Good evening," said the waiter, elegant in a summer tuxedo. "May I bring you some cocktails?"

"Hello, Bruce," Bitsy said, crossing her long legs. "I'll have an extra dry and dirty Stoli martini, please. You know how I like it." Bitsy gave him a wink, which made Miriam uncomfortable. Bruce didn't seem to mind.

"And for you?" he asked, turning to Miriam.

"Oh, um, how about a piña colada?" she said, looking at

Bitsy for approval. She subtly shook her head. "Wait, let me think. George, what are you having?"

"I'd like an old-fashioned," he said.

"Any preference on the whiskey?" Bruce asked. George shook his head.

"Ma'am?"

"I think I'll have a glass of Prosecco," she said, folding her hands in her lap. Bitsy raised her eyebrows and smiled, as if surprised by Miriam's choice.

"Right away," Bruce said, returning three minutes later with their drinks. After clinking glasses, they all took a sip, though Bitsy's was a bit heartier, Miriam noticed.

"I hear congratulations are in order," Bitsy said, beaming at George as she brought an olive to her lips, sucking on it provocatively before popping it into her mouth. Miriam noticed George shifting in his seat.

"My husband has always been a go-getter," Miriam said, placing her hand possessively over his while beaming at Bitsy.

Just as George was about to speak, several women appeared at their table, none of whom Miriam knew personally.

"Bitsy, you're simply genius," said a woman in pink chiffon. "Last night was nothing short of magical. You've forever raised the standard for cotillion!"

"Indeed," gushed a woman in sage taffeta. "Donating the car for the raffle was a masterstroke! Do you know who won?"

Bitsy shook her head. "I don't, really. But I'm glad you enjoyed the event. We so appreciate our parents!"

"I have to say, I was a bit taken aback by Louise's daughter," said a third woman in gray silk. She lowered her voice. "I can't believe she showed up in a burlap bag and tennis shoes, no less! How could Louise have let her leave the house like that?"

Miriam brought her napkin to her mouth to suppress her laughter.

"She should have just stayed home, particularly after her ill-fated attempt at waging a war on tradition," said Pink Chiffon. Sage Taffeta nodded, while Gray Silk made a "tsk tsk" sound, shaking her head.

"One can only imagine what goes on there," Bitsy said, taking another large sip of her martini. "You know how Louise is," she added in a conspiratorial tone, then signaled Bruce for another drink. Miriam felt like she was watching a *National Geographic* episode about predators in the wild.

"You look familiar," Gray Silk said, giving Miriam the once-over. "Have we met?"

Before Miriam could remind her they were both members of the women's auxiliary, Bitsy interrupted.

"Oh, where are my manners," Bitsy said. "You remember Miriam Llewelyn, from the auxiliary, and her husband, Greg."

"It's George," Miriam said, trying to keep the annoyance from her voice.

"I knew that," Bitsy said, finishing her martini. "Please forgive me." George nodded at the women circling the table, then took a sip of his old-fashioned.

"Well, we need to get to our table," said Pink Chiffon. "Lovely meeting you both, and, Bitsy, congratulations. You should be so very proud of what you did for the academy!"

Bitsy smiled as the women moved toward their tables. "A bunch of cheapskates, all of them," she said, nodding as Bruce set down her drink. "Not one of them bought tickets for the raffle. Can you believe it?"

"Maybe they don't need a new car," George said, then looked at Miriam, who smiled.

"That's not the point! You're always supposed to buy raffle tickets. Everyone knows that," she said, bringing the second martini to her lips, though from what Miriam could tell, she may have gotten an early start at home. Miriam wondered what had her so rattled. "It's, you know, a rule!"

"How much were the tickets?" George asked, though Miriam wished they could change subjects. The conversation must have been agitating Bitsy, whose tongue seemed to get thicker with each sip of her drink.

"They were a hundred bucks a piece," she said, fluffing the back of her hair with both hands. "Chump change, really, for a chance at a brand-new Buick Regal. Ah, here comes Bobby. Isn't he just so handsome? It's hard to believe he's ten years older than me. I swear, the man doesn't age, though I do what I can to keep him young. If you know what I mean," she drawled. Miriam cringed. *What has gotten into her?*

"Please forgive me," Bobby said, nodding at George and Miriam before leaning down and kissing Bitsy's bare shoulder.

"You must be George's better half," he said, extending his hand and giving Miriam a movie-star smile. "I'm Bobby."

"Nice to make your acquaintance," Miriam said, shaking his hand. "I'm Miriam."

"George, great to see you away from the dealership!" he said, taking his seat. Bruce appeared quietly, placing a Scotch–neat–in front of Bobby, who nodded but said nothing.

"We appreciate the invitation," George said.

"Are we all going with the chef's dinner?" Bobby asked, putting his arm around Bitsy's shoulders.

"Whatever you suggest," Miriam said. "We're your guests, after all."

***

The foursome had just finished their third course when Miriam saw the Caldwells entering the dining room. Louise, elegantly clad in a crimson silk shantung cocktail dress, walked behind her daughter, who moved sullenly with her shoulders slumped. A man, who must have been Clifton, followed at a close clip, dashing in his white dinner jacket.

Bitsy took a sip of her third martini, her eyes laser-focused on Louise, who had apparently just noticed them sitting at the corner table. Louise raised her eyebrows as she looked at Miriam with an expression Miriam couldn't read, though she suddenly felt guilty. She had no idea what to do.

"Miriam, I've been meaning to talk to you about something," Bitsy said, shifting her attention back to the table. "As you know, auxiliary elections are coming up," she said, her words now slurred.

"I guess I wasn't aware—I've been so focused on the cookbook," Miriam said, taking a final bite of her Beef Wellington. "Honestly, I'd like the recipe for this!" She wiped the corners of her mouth. She noticed Bitsy had barely touched her meal. Bobby and George were talking quietly about baseball scores, leaving Miriam on her own with Bitsy.

"I've been thinking," Bitsy continued. "Auxiliary needs new ideas, you know, some fresh blood in leadership positions. That's why I plan to nominate you for auxiliary president!" She bobbed excitedly in her seat, reminding Miriam of a cockatiel on its swing. Bitsy reached for her martini but accidentally sent it flying onto the carpet. "Oopsie!" She giggled, motioning for Bruce.

"Babe, I don't think you need another drink," Bobby said gently.

"For Christ's sake, Bobby. I'm not a child, so don't treat me like one!" The dining room fell to a hush. Bobby reached across the table to take her hand. "Don't!" she growled, sitting back and folding her arms. Miriam looked at George nervously. His face was expressionless, but she knew public scenes made him uncomfortable—particularly if they involved alcohol. He had endured enough of that as a child.

"About the auxiliary," Miriam said. "I don't feel qualified to serve as president. Besides, Louise really wants it. I couldn't do that to her." She looked at her glass of Prosecco, but her stomach had begun to roil. She opted for a drink of her ice water instead.

"You think she's your friend? Please, you're smarter than that. What's she ever done for you? Hmm? Asking you to be the cookbook co-chair? Big flipping deal. She knows you'll do all the work. I was the one who brought you into the fold, after all," Bitsy said, then wiped her mouth, smearing red lipstick across her cheek. "If anyone deserves your loyalty, it's me." Her eyes flashed like those of a coyote protecting its kill.

Miriam took a deep breath. "This feels uncomfortable, Bitsy. I like you very much, and I like Louise too. But I don't like feeling like a pawn in some game I honestly don't understand. Why don't you consider running?" she said. "Especially after your success with cotillion."

Bitsy adjusted the bodice of her strapless dress. "I'd rather be the power behind the throne," she whispered. "It's more fun that way."

"I'll think about it," Miriam said, hoping that would end the discussion.

"Nothing to think about. Trust me, Miriam. We can be a force. May the force be with us!" she added, raising her ringed hand to give Miriam the Vulcan greeting. Miriam wanted to correct her—wrong franchise—but chose to simply smile.

"I need to excuse myself," Miriam said. "Where's the powder room?"

"Down the hall, on the left," Bitsy said, hiccupping. "I'll go with you." She pushed back her chair to stand, though she was clearly unsteady on her feet.

"Let me help you," Miriam said, taking her hand. They walked through the dining room as Miriam felt judgmental eyes appraising her. It didn't occur to her their attention was on Bitsy, who could barely walk. *Why did she get so intoxicated?* Miriam wondered, then they passed the Caldwells' table and suddenly it made sense—Louise still had the power to make

Bitsy feel inferior. Nevertheless, Miriam nodded and smiled at Louise as they passed their table. Louise tilted her head and gave Miriam a puzzled look, cupping her hands—palms up—as if to ask, "What in the world?"

Miriam would deal with Louise later. For now, her only priority was to get Bitsy safely to the women's lounge. She opened one of the stalls so Bitsy could enter, then took another stall and latched the door. A moment later, she heard Bitsy violently emptying her stomach.

"Can I help?" Miriam called after flushing the commode.

"Bobby!" she said before heaving once more.

"I'll be right back," Miriam said, exiting the lounge and walking purposefully to the dining room. Her feet were aching from her new high heels, but she moved as quickly as possible.

"Miriam," Louise called out as Miriam passed their table. "A word?" She stood and motioned for Miriam to follow her to the lobby.

"I need to get Bobby," Miriam said as they left the dining room. "Bitsy's not well."

Louise turned around and stopped, then began laughing. "You're absolutely right, Miriam. Bitsy's not well. Not well at all," she said. "What are you doing here with *her*?"

"We were invited," Miriam said sheepishly. "I mean, Bobby is George's boss. And he just promoted George, so this was to be a celebration. Or so I thought."

"Congratulations to George," Louise said. "But you. I worry about you. You must be careful whom you let close." This wasn't the first time Louise had brought up the issue of trust with her, though in different words. Miriam wondered what made her so paranoid.

"I know you all have history," Miriam said. "Please don't put me in an awkward position, Louise. Please."

"Oh, my dear friend, you already are. You just don't know it yet," Louise said. "I'm only trying to look out for you, after all. Enjoy the rest of your evening. Oh, and one more piece of friendly advice." She stared at Miriam's dress, then whispered, "We don't wear linen after six." Turning on her heel, Louise walked back into the dining room, leaving Miriam to consider what sounded like another warning—the second such warning in less than a week.

32

Like many small towns, Stuarts Landing took the Fourth of July quite seriously. Rotary club members festooned Main Street with hundreds of yards of red, white, and blue bunting and ensured each business and home proudly displayed Old Glory by delivering flags to every address. The Chamber of Commerce organized the annual parade, always emceed by the mayor, and for a minimal price, organizations could enter their floats for a chance at the prize money—and bragging rights—to be awarded to the judges' favorite. Competition was typically fierce, and each year, the floats became more creative. After the parade, most people spent the remainder of the afternoon at the traditional picnic sponsored by The Pig, where they feasted on hot dogs, hamburgers, every type of salad imaginable, watermelon, ice cream, and gallons upon gallons of lemonade and sweet iced tea.

Independence Day fell on a Wednesday that year, but it did not inhibit the townspeople from enthusiastically celebrating. Louise was sorry Emma was still at camp, yet she knew her daughter would prefer swimming with her friends to riding on the auxiliary float with her mother. Though Louise was not on that year's committee, she was pleased they had chosen "Legendary First Ladies" as their theme, and at Kay's request, Louise was dressed as Jackie Kennedy—a woman Louise always admired and often tried to emulate. With Pearl's help, Louise had modified a white satin evening gown from her closet to approximate the sleeveless column dress the

First Lady wore at the Inaugural Ball. Completing the look with the gloves Grandmother Nora always wore to the opera and the rhinestone chandelier earrings her own mother wore only once, Louise felt positively royal.

She was standing in the shade as the floats lined up, nursing a cola, when Miriam greeted her. "Well, if it isn't Jackie O!" she said, giving a mock curtsy. Louise smiled broadly.

"And look at you, Eleanor Roosevelt," Louise said. "Brilliantly done!"

"What gave me away?" Miriam asked with a grin.

"The absolute sensibility of it all. No frills, no nonsense, just a proper black dress and, of course, the fox stole. Wherever did you find that?"

"Oh, the Webster sisters let me borrow it," Miriam said, "and I think this dress belonged to their mother."

"I just assumed you had sewn it yourself," Louise said. "Beautiful workmanship."

Soon they were joined by Martha Washington, Abigail Adams, Dolley Madison, and Mary Todd Lincoln. Bitsy had not been asked to represent the auxiliary that year—she was still paying the social price for her unladylike behavior at the country club, but she would be in the parade anyway, riding on the Butler Automotive float. Louise could see her in the distance, flitting about in a dress that could have been stolen from Scarlett O'Hara's closet and, of course, carrying a parasol.

"How very ridiculous," Louise said, fanning herself as she watched Bitsy flirt with the dealership's crew. "She really is shameless."

"Who?" Miriam asked as she loosened the fox stole and dabbed her damp neck with a handkerchief.

"Bitsy, over there," she said, ducking her head and surreptitiously pointing.

"Oh, she's just being friendly," Miriam said, though she appeared to keep her eyes on George, who was engaged in

conversation with Bobby. "That dress must be uncomfortable. Imagine wearing petticoats on a day like today. Poor thing. I wonder if she'll change for the picnic."

"I doubt it," Louise said with a sniff. "She's always loved being the center of attention, after all. Did you know she used to be in beauty pageants as a teenager?" She wrinkled her nose. "But that's ancient history. Tell me, did we get all the recipes we need for the cookbook? Today's the deadline, right?"

"Yes, I'm very happy with the response. We have about forty recipes, though most of them are either appetizers or desserts. I've made a few of them already, and I can truthfully say your mama's shepherd's pie is my favorite so far," Miriam said, licking her lips.

"I'm so glad you liked it!" Louise said. "Did you follow the recipe directly or did you improvise? I know lamb can be expensive."

"The only things I changed were substituting ground beef for the lamb, which, you're right, is pretty pricey, and making the mashed potatoes really cheesy," Miriam said. "I can never have enough cheese! The Websters devoured it." She smiled proudly.

Louise continued fanning herself as she wondered why the sisters were so taken with Miriam. *She is quite likable, obviously, but then, so am I,* she thought, surprised by a sudden stab of jealousy.

"You seem to be spending a lot of time with them," Louise said. "That's kind of you since they don't get out as much as they once did."

"I rather enjoy them, honestly. Iris is teaching me how to paint, though I'll never have her talent—she could sell her work, it's so good," Miriam gushed.

"As if they need the money," Louise said, then lowered her voice. "I have it on good authority they're worth tens of millions of dollars. It's a wonder they never married, honestly.

But at least they managed to avoid falling prey to gold diggers—smart choice on their part, though it's sad they have no heirs. We can only hope they leave their fortune to the Stuarts Landing Historical Society."

Miriam stared at Louise with a blank expression as she dabbed the perspiration beading above her lips.

"Maybe they never found 'the one,' at least the one that was eligible," Miriam said softly. "You and I are obviously blessed in that department. But enough about that. I've selected five dishes to serve at our auxiliary luncheon week after next. I wanted your opinion, as I thought it would be nice to have each person whose recipe I've selected prepare their dish themselves."

Louise sensed Miriam was uncomfortable discussing the Websters, but she couldn't imagine why. She considered probing further, then decided to leave it alone. For now.

"And what have you decided?"

"I thought we would serve Matty's crab terrine, Becky's Oysters Rockefeller, Janet's croissants, your shepherd's pie, and Jasper's chocolate almond torte," Miriam said. "How does that sound?"

Louise patted her stomach. "Fattening!" she said, chuckling. "No, that sounds lovely, but there's just one problem, Miriam. I don't cook. I've told you that."

Miriam smiled. "I thought you might say that, so I was hoping you'd let me prepare it. As long as you don't mind my leaving the cheese in the potatoes, that is. And substituting ground beef for lamb. Trust me. It's so yummy."

Louise pursed her lips as she considered Miriam's offer. On one hand, she was honored to have her mother's recipe showcased. On the other hand...

"Don't you think it's dishonest if I don't prepare it myself?" Louise said.

Miriam tilted her head to one side and smirked.

"Are you serious, Louise? After you convinced me to credit your mother's 'cook' for the recipe? Come on," she said, shaking her head. "No one will care who prepared the dishes as long as they taste good."

"Fine then. I appreciate your candor," she lied.

As the women began boarding the auxiliary float, Louise realized that conversation marked the first time Miriam had challenged her. *Something has changed,* she mused as she followed Miriam up the ramp. *She's supposed to be following my lead, not challenging it.*

33

Miriam had just taken the fourth casserole from the gourmet oven when Iris and Rose entered the kitchen, colorful as always in their floral caftans and matching turbans, each adorned with a gold brooch. The auxiliary luncheon began in an hour, leaving Miriam time to let the shepherd's pies cool enough to be safely packed in picnic baskets.

"Thank you so much for letting me use your kitchen," she said, taking off the quilted oven mitts. "It would have taken me twice as long in mine."

"No need to thank us, sweetheart. What's ours is yours, isn't that right, sister?" Iris said.

"Absolutely, positively," Rose said, leaning over the island to take a whiff of the casseroles. "These smell divine, Miriam. I do believe you've outdone yourself."

Miriam smiled and gave her great-aunt a hug. "Thank you, Rose," she said. They had all agreed it would be best for Miriam to refer to them by their first names, at least for the time being. "The credit goes to Louise's mother, though. This is her recipe, after all." She untied her apron and hung it in the pantry.

"Interesting," Iris said, adjusting her glasses. "Though it's delicious–at least the way you prepare it–shepherd's pie has always been considered a poor man's meal. Isn't that what the waiter told us in Dublin, dear, at that quirky little pub?"

"Oh, yes, I remember," Rose said. "The one where we tried Guinness for the first time?" She made a face. "It was like

drinking motor oil! Never again." She wagged her index finger at her sister before turning to Miriam. "She made me a bet I couldn't finish it. Guess who won?"

Miriam laughed. "I wouldn't care to speculate," she said, covering the casseroles with aluminum foil.

"Well, I'll give you a hint," Iris said with a devilish grin. "It wasn't Rose."

"What did you win?" Miriam asked, sitting down on the stool.

"An Irish sweater of my choice. I picked the most expensive one I could find," she said in a stage whisper. Rose made a raspberry sound at Iris, who responded by sticking out her tongue.

"You know what they say: 'You're only young once, but you can be immature forever.' My dear sister here has turned her immaturity into an art form," Rose said, giving Iris an innocent smile.

"Seems you're the one who insisted on buying the pinball machine," Iris said with a smirk.

"You have a pinball machine?!" Miriam said. "Where is it?"

The sisters giggled. "It's downstairs, in the wine cellar," Iris said. "I didn't want to have to hear it. It's ridiculous!"

"Would you like to ride with us to the luncheon?" Rose asked, pulling out picnic baskets from beneath the island.

"I would love to," Miriam said. "Do you think I should change clothes first?" she asked, looking down at her plain chambray shirtdress. The sisters looked at her and shook their heads.

"I think you look pretty. And besides, you have nothing to prove. Isn't that right, Rose?" Her sister nodded. "Anyway, all eyes will be on the pies!" Iris said, slapping her knee and laughing at her own cleverness. Miriam chuckled, but Rose simply groaned.

"Don't encourage her," Rose said, wagging her finger

once again. "Here, let me help you get the casseroles into the baskets."

Twenty minutes later, Jasper pulled into the chamber's parking lot, then helped the three women from the Town Car before popping the trunk to remove two portable carts on which he placed the picnic baskets. "I imagine we'll be ready to leave by one thirty," Rose said. "I believe we can take it from here. Thank you, Jasper!" He bowed and returned to the sedan, waiting for them to get inside before driving away.

"Here, let me," Iris said, taking one of the carts and beginning to push it forward. Rose took the lead so she could help open doors. Miriam followed behind with the second cart.

Bitsy was the first person they encountered on their way to the ballroom. "Good afternoon, ladies! Mademoiselles Webster, you look as remarkable as ever," she said, seemingly oblivious to their tolerant but polite smiles. "And Miriam, how wonderful to see you again! I've missed you, but you must know, of course, we've been on holiday, Bobby and I. Debbie is away at camp, so we had the chance to spend a week alone together. Nantucket is just so perfect this time of year!" She prattled on as the women pushed the carts down the hallway.

"I hope you had fun," Miriam said. "You got a really nice tan! Hey, would you mind taking over for Iris, please?"

"Oh, where are my manners?" she said, her heeled sandals clacking on the marble tile as she rushed to take the cart.

"What manners?" Miriam heard Rose mumble. She had not known the sisters to have ill feelings toward anyone, but obviously, they were not particularly fond of Bitsy.

The ballroom was arranged to accommodate a large buffet table covered with a pale pink tablecloth, stacked porcelain plates, and index cards indicating where each course should be placed. Louise was directing the staff where to set the flower arrangements when Miriam, Bitsy, and the Websters entered the room. Her look was one of abject shock.

Bitsy locked her arm through Miriam's and waved at Louise, who turned around and walked quickly toward the kitchen.

"I'll be right back for your cart," Miriam said as she started to follow Louise.

"I'm happy to push it myself," Bitsy said.

Miriam stopped and shook her head. "I'm not sure that's a good idea," she said. "It might be best to keep your distance for a bit."

"What did she tell you?" Bitsy said, pushing her cart to stand beside Miriam. She fumbled for how to reply when Iris appeared at her side.

"Bitsy, my dear, please do come and tell us all about your vacation," she said, taking Bitsy's arm. "We'd love to know how much Nantucket has changed since, of course, we sold the summer house there." As Bitsy began prattling on, Iris looked at Miriam and gave her a wink. Miriam couldn't help but smile at Iris's protective intervention.

"Hi there," Miriam said to Louise as she pushed her cart into the kitchen and unloaded two of the four casseroles onto the prep table. "I need to get the other cart with Jasper's tortes—be right back." Louise just nodded, drumming her fingers on the cutting board. When Miriam returned with the second cart, Louise folded her arms.

"What's the matter?" Miriam asked, placing Jasper's dishes with the others while trying to analyze Louise's scowl.

"I don't know what you're up to, Miriam, but I thought we were friends," Louise said sharply. She leaned over to pull the foil from one of the dishes and wrinkled her nose. "What's that?" she asked, pointing at the first shepherd's pie.

"Um, it's shepherd's pie?" Miriam said, inwardly recoiling at Louise's tone.

"I meant, on the top," Louise said, covering her mouth as if horrified.

"Oh, it's Parmesan mixed with butter and breadcrumbs,"

Miriam said anxiously. "Gives it a real nice texture."

"That's not how Mama's help made it, Miriam. How very disappointing—I can't believe you doctored tradition."

Miriam's shoulders slumped as she tried to think of an appropriate response. "I told you I added cheese to the potatoes, Louise," she said.

"Well, I don't suppose I remembered that," Louise said. "Much like you don't seem to remember my advising you to keep your distance from Bitsy." Hands on her slender hips, she stared at Miriam as if daring her to argue.

"With all due respect, Louise, I am a grown woman. I would like to be treated as such," Miriam said, putting a casserole in a silver chaffing dish for the staff to set on the buffet table.

"I'm only looking out for your best interests, Miriam. Someone must," Louise said, lowering her voice as Matty and Janet entered the kitchen with their dishes. Louise signaled for a server to take the first casserole to the ballroom, then stepped further back into the kitchen, motioning Miriam to join her.

"Louise, I really should put the casseroles in the oven to keep warm," Miriam said, walking to the industrial-sized appliance and adjusting the temperature settings. Louise came to her side, holding one of the dishes a foot in front of her, almost distastefully. Miriam wanted to believe Louise was trying to keep from dripping anything on her red linen dress. She took the dish from Louise and put it in the oven as Louise leaned in to speak into Miriam's ear.

"I'm beginning to wonder if I can trust you," Louise said, her tone laced with menace.

"Louise, please. We're not in high school, okay? Why can't we all just get along?"

"Because that's not how it works!" Louise said. "Pick your side very, very carefully."

"How would I know? The alliances seem to change with

the weather," Miriam said. "I don't want to make any enemies here." She watched Louise cringe as Bitsy flounced into the kitchen.

"Miriam, you're going to sit at my table, aren't you?" she said, looking directly into Louise's eyes.

"I believe she had planned to sit with me, seeing as we're co-chairing the cookbook together, isn't that right, Miriam?" Louise said. Miriam closed the oven door loudly.

"Actually, I promised the Websters I'd keep them company," Miriam said with a firm smile. "They've so looked forward to this luncheon. Now, please excuse me." She heard Bitsy clickety-clacking behind her in sandals better suited for a nightclub than a ladies' luncheon.

"Don't let her boss you around," Bitsy said, tossing back her hair. "You know how she can be."

"I do know she's my friend, Bitsy," Miriam said, checking to see that the dishes were placed appropriately on the buffet.

"Are you sure about that?" Bitsy said, her head tilted and eyebrows raised. "Because I, for one, wouldn't be too confident."

With that, Bitsy sashayed to her table and immediately began chattering with her Fulton Academy friends. Miriam joined the Websters at the table they had claimed for themselves, nearest the buffet, though she really just wanted to go home.

"Are you all right, dear?" Iris said, reaching over and patting Miriam's hand.

"Just when I think I'm finally fitting in here, seems someone always finds a way to throw me for a loop," she said, hanging her head.

"To whom are you referring?" Rose asked before taking a drink of iced tea.

"Louise. Well, Louise and Bitsy," she corrected herself.

"For whatever juvenile reason, you're the newest play toy

they're fighting over. It's all about control and having the upper hand—has been since Bitsy first moved here and became popular. Steer clear of their petty little feud, to the degree you can," Iris said. "Otherwise, you may find yourself picking up the pieces."

Miriam nodded, considering her grandmother's words. She could not know it at the time, but Iris had just spoken prophecy.

34

All things considered, the remainder of Louise's summer was uneventful, even when Emma returned from camp. Emma and Debbie had managed to patch up their friendship, though Louise hoped her daughter had learned a thing or two about whom to trust. For Louise, close friendships were dangerous if one wanted to maintain one's privacy. The only reasons Louise had maintained a relationship with Bitsy were history and convenience, though their dynamic had changed—as had so much else—since Miriam's arrival in Stuarts Landing. She felt as if Miriam had cast some sort of invisible spell, but for the life of her, she didn't understand what it was.

Since the parade, Louise hadn't seen much of Miriam, who was apparently spending most of her spare time with the Websters. At least that's what she heard from a few auxiliary members who seemed to believe the sisters had all but adopted Miriam. To Louise, it was nothing short of odd, but then, so were the Websters, though they were also quite lovable. Since the luncheon, Miriam had been the subject of auxiliary interest largely due to her shepherd's pie, which, even Louise had to admit, was better than her mother's original recipe. She had heard more than one woman exclaim, "Is there anything Miriam can't do?" *Perhaps I should have tried my hand at the domestic arts instead of paying others to do so,* she mused. She was reflecting on her life when her husband interrupted her thoughts.

"Good morning," Clifton said, joining Louise in the solarium with a cup of coffee. "It's Friday, so that must mean you'll be working on the church bulletin today?"

"No, I decided to relieve myself of my responsibilities there," Louise said, stretching her arms casually. "Really, one person can do the job, and besides, I need to put all my focus into the auxiliary. Officer elections are next Wednesday, and I'm going for president."

"You'll be wonderful, as always. I've never known you not to get what you wanted," Clifton said, "one way or another."

Louise put down her cup. "That didn't sound like a compliment."

"Don't be silly, Lu. Of course it was. When you set your sights on something, you're not to be deterred. Look at us, for example," he said, chuckling.

"If I recall, you were the one pursuing me," Louise said, her shoulders relaxing.

"Revisionist history?" he said, grinning as he unfolded the newspaper.

Louise heard the telephone ringing and stood up. "I imagine that's someone from the auxiliary," she said, heading toward the study. She stopped when Pearl opened the French doors.

"Excuse me, Mr. Caldwell, you have a phone call," she said, her hands folded in front of her starched apron. "It's Iris Webster. Are you available?"

Clifton put down the newspaper and rose from his rattan chair. "Yes, of course. I always have time for the Websters," he said, smiling at Louise.

She watched him move quickly into the study and close the door. Awash with curiosity, Louise contemplated eavesdropping, then thought better of it. *Whatever it is, I'm sure he'll tell me,* she thought. She picked up the newspaper and perused the society section as Pearl wordlessly refilled her coffee.

"Thank you, Pearl," she said, turning the page to see a full-sized ad for Butler Automotive, featuring Bitsy in a bathing suit, all but sprawled across the 1980 Buick Electra Riviera. "Unbelievable." She held up the page for Pearl to see. "Has she no shame?"

Pearl merely clicked her tongue. Louise knew Pearl would never say anything negative about her daughter's employer, though she could read Pearl's opinion in that one brief sound.

"Well, at least Bobby didn't have to pay for a model," Louise said.

"Oh, I'm sure he's paying somethin'," Pearl said with a wicked grin. Louise snickered at her quick wit.

Clifton returned to the solarium, carrying his satchel and his suit jacket. "Off I go," he said, leaning down to kiss Louise on the cheek.

"What was that all about?" Louise asked, giving Clifton her most bewitching look.

"Iris asked me to come to their home to discuss a legal matter," he said. "From there, I'll head to the office. What about you?"

"I was thinking of doing a little shopping," Louise said. "What legal matter? Is everything okay?"

"You know I can't discuss my clients' business, Lu," he said, rubbing her shoulder.

"I understand. Attorney-client privilege, blah blah blah. How very noble of you."

"Well, it's kind of the law, sweetheart. You wouldn't want me disbarred now, would you?"

"What? And lose my standard of living? Never!" she said, feigning horror.

Laughing, Clifton headed toward the foyer. "I'll see you this evening," he called over his shoulder. "Dinner at the club?"

"Of course," she said happily, realizing she now had reason to buy a new outfit. *Maybe four.*

***

She was sitting in the great room sipping her "special lemonade" when Clifton came home from work. He set down his satchel as she stood to greet him with a kiss. "Wow! I guess you weren't kidding when you said you were going shopping. You really do look gorgeous in red," he said, taking in her new silk blouse. Pearl entered the room with his glass of Scotch balanced on a sterling silver tray. "Thank you," he said, sitting down before turning his attention back to Louise. "So, you enjoyed your day?"

As she watched him unfold the evening paper and prop it open in his lap, she felt a familiar agitation rumbling inside. As usual, he was being polite, feigning interest in her day. In that moment, though, she realized he needed her to have nothing of any significance to discuss because his focus was on a world very much larger than her own.

"Very much so, though Emma was upset I didn't invite her along," she said, rolling her eyes in an attempt to be light-hearted. "She's always mad about something these days."

"Why didn't you?" Clifton asked, loosening his tie. "She's been away for six weeks, and she starts school in, what, two? Before we know it, our little girl will be off to college, Lu."

"I know, dear, but I just wanted some time to myself. She can be so petulant that it just spoils everything. Besides, I *did* buy her a new dress," she said.

"Did she like it?" Clifton said, bringing the crystal glass to his lips.

"What do you think?"

"You have exquisite taste. Of course she liked it," he said with a smile.

"Nope. She said it's too matronly. I'll have to take it back."

"Then take her along, and let her pick something out," Clifton said in his "case closed" voice. "Problem solved."

"I'll consider it," Louise said, smoothing her skirt. "How was everything at the Websters?" She took a drink to keep from probing further.

"They were as delightful as ever," Clifton said. "Jasper prepared us lunch–Mediterranean, which I've not had before–and it was delicious. We should ask Pearl if she knows any similar recipes."

"Is everything okay with them?" she said. "And did you see Miriam there?"

"Oh, yes, right as rain. They just have a few documents they asked me to prepare," he said, popping a handful of peanuts into his mouth. "As for Miriam, no, she wasn't there."

"Hmm. Are the Websters doing anything with historic preservation?" Louise said, raising her eyebrows.

"Lu, I don't know how many times I have to tell you. I can't discuss my clients' business," he said, finishing his cocktail. "I'm going to change clothes before we head to the club. I assume Emma is joining us?"

"Not tonight. I believe Pearl said she was having a sleepover with a friend," Louise said.

"Debbie?" he said from the doorway.

"I don't exactly know. I'll ask Pearl." She watched him shaking his head and murmuring something as he passed through the foyer to the staircase. *How dare he judge me,* Louise thought, stroking her pearls. *He has absolutely no idea how difficult motherhood can be.*

After finishing her drink, Louise had planned to brush her teeth and refresh her lipstick, but she couldn't ignore the siren song of Clifton's satchel sitting beside his chair. Straining her neck to locate Pearl, she saw her watering the plants in the solarium, obviously preoccupied. Taking a deep breath, she sat down to open the Italian leather satchel she had given him when he passed the Virginia bar exam. After taking a quick look over her shoulder, she removed a legal pad with the words "Webster Estate Revisions" scribbled across the top, followed by several notes, which seemed to be written in code. *How very Clifton,* she thought. She continued scanning the page for clues when she saw the letters "ML" with two arrows underlined toward the bottom.

Hearing Clifton's footsteps on the landing upstairs, she quickly returned the legal pad to the satchel and snapped it shut. Her blood turned cold at the realization Miriam Llewelyn must be exerting some kind of undue influence over the dowagers. *Not if I have anything to do with it. I've known them my entire life. I won't let them be played by anyone, but especially not by HER. I guess trying to mentor Miriam was a waste of my time. You can't teach integrity.*

"Are you ready?" Clifton said, adjusting the pocket square in his sport coat. She took his hand and smiled, her eyes flashing like warning lights at a railroad crossing.

"Oh, I'm *so* ready," she said. He gave her a curious look, but she ignored it. Her attention was on One Webster Way.

35

Miriam had just finished dressing and was clipping on the earrings she bought on sale when she heard someone knocking. She opened the front door to see Iris standing there holding a colorfully wrapped box. She smiled as she invited Iris inside. "Please excuse the mess," she said as she moved her magazines from the couch.

"It looks perfectly spotless to me," Iris said, chuckling as she took a seat. "I hope I'm not interrupting you. I'll only stay for a few minutes." She gazed lovingly at Miriam.

"Would you like a cup of coffee?" Miriam asked. "Or some tea?"

"I would give my right arm for a Tab," she said, lowering her voice. "Rose won't let me have it. She says sodas will give us all cancer. As if!"

"Unfortunately, I only have diet cola," Miriam said.

"I'll take it!" Iris said eagerly.

Miriam went to the kitchen and returned with a bottle of soda for Iris and another cup of coffee for herself. "Would you like a glass? I should have poured it in a glass," Miriam said, turning back toward the kitchen.

"Sit down, my dear girl," Iris said. "This isn't the first time I've drunk from a bottle, though I do need your help opening it," she said. Miriam twisted off the cap and handed Iris the drink.

"Are your hands shaking?" Iris asked, furrowing her brow and setting her soda on the coffee table.

"Oh, probably," Miriam said. "I must admit, I'm a little nervous about the auxiliary meeting today." She caught herself wringing her hands, so she unclasped them and began fiddling with one of the tassels on the throw pillow between them.

Iris reached over and took her hand. "You have nothing to worry about," she said, giving Miriam a meaningful look. "Things always seem to work out as they were meant to, dear. Just hold your head high, no matter what happens."

Miriam gave Iris a wan smile. "I kept telling Bitsy I don't want to be president. It's not right. I haven't paid my dues. I mean, I paid my financial dues... you know what I mean. But she wouldn't listen. Honestly, I think she's planning to nominate me as a way of sticking it to Louise. It just isn't right," she said, repeating herself.

Iris stared at her intently. "Well, of course that's why she's doing it, no doubt about it. But I, for one, believe you absolutely have earned the honor," Iris said. "Look at what you did to save the fashion show. Look at how hard you've been working on the cookbook, not to mention the lovely luncheon you helped orchestrate. By the way, Jasper is almost finished transcribing the recipes. Have I already told you that?"

She had, but Miriam wasn't going to say so. "That's great news, indeed," she said, taking a sip of coffee. "And thank you for your encouragement, Iris. I wish I had your confidence."

Iris handed her the present she had kept at her side. "Perhaps this will help," she said, putting the box in Miriam's lap.

Miriam's eyes welled with tears as she looked at the perfect wrapping. "It's almost too pretty to open," she said softly. "Really, you shouldn't have."

"Go on, dear," Iris said, fluttering her right hand. "I'm not getting any younger!"

Miriam carefully slid her finger along one of the seams, then removed the glittery wrap to find an ornately carved box.

"It's beautiful," she said, turning it around to view it from all angles.

"Yes, well, I got that in Bali quite some time ago," Iris said, her silver bangles jangling as she smoothed back her cropped hair. "But the real gift is inside." She clasped her hands together in anticipation.

Miriam slowly opened the box to find a velvet envelope secured with what looked like a piece of ivory tucked into a delicate satin loop. Inside was the triple strand of pearls Iris had worn on their picnic. Miriam's eyes widened with surprise as tears dripped down her cheeks.

"I've never had anything so beautiful," Miriam whispered, staring at the necklace. Iris handed her a lace-trimmed handkerchief. "I don't know what to say." She dried her eyes while looking at Iris.

"Just say you like them. Would you like me to fasten the clasp for you?" she said, reaching for the pearls.

"Oh, yes, please," Miriam said, turning away from Iris, who was cupping the necklace in her hands. Miriam lifted the hair off her neck.

"I'm imbuing these pearls with Webster mojo, so you'll have a constant reminder of the strength coursing through your veins. My father gave me this necklace for my sixteenth birthday," she said, draping the pearls around Miriam's neck. "They would have been your mother's and then eventually, they would have become yours." Miriam turned around. "They look perfect! Now, would you like to ride with us to the meeting?"

"Thank you so much, Iris, but I have a few errands to run afterwards," Miriam said, gently running her fingertips over the necklace. "I will meet you there, though. And thank you so much for this gift. I will treasure it forever."

"As I hope will you, dear," Iris said, rising from the couch. "See you soon!" She gave Miriam a reassuring hug.

"Go get 'em," she whispered in Miriam's ear.

***

As if she were a jaguar stalking its prey, Bitsy pounced on Miriam the moment she entered the Chamber of Commerce's lobby. "Are you ready?" she said. "I'm just so excited! Nice outfit," she said, assessing Miriam's canary-yellow dress and white wedge sandals. "But we need to get you a pedicure," she said, briefly grimacing. "Those pearls, though, absolute perfection. It's amazing how real costume jewelry looks these days, don't you think?"

Miriam smiled graciously while inwardly cringing at Bitsy's crass remark. "That's nice of you, Bitsy," she said, adjusting the shoulder strap of her purse. "I really want you to think about what you're doing, though. I'm honored you want to nominate me for president, I really am, but you must know there will be consequences, right?"

"I'm only doing what I think best for the auxiliary," Bitsy said, smiling innocently. "Would you like to walk with me?" She nodded amicably at each woman entering the lobby and proceeding toward the meeting hall.

"Actually, I need to powder my nose," Miriam said. "I'll join you in a few minutes."

"I'll save you a seat!"

Miriam had just dried her hands when Louise entered the ladies' room, giving Miriam a surprised look.

"Hi there!" Miriam said, tossing the towel into the wastebasket. Already a tangle of nerves because of what would soon transpire, being in close proximity to Louise made her wish she could run for the hills.

"Hello," Louise said, looking in the gilded mirror as she applied a fresh coat of red lipstick, then returning the tube to her purse. Her eyes zeroed in on Miriam's pearls and

immediately darkened.

"Where did those come from?" she said, glaring at Miriam.

Putting her hand protectively over the necklace, Miriam said without thinking, "They were a gift. From Iris." Immediately she regretted her words and felt her stomach convulse.

"Why on earth would Iris give you something so precious, Miriam? Are you sure you didn't steal them?" Louise said, putting her hands on her hips.

Miriam gasped. "How dare you say such a thing!"

"You've played us all, haven't you? And here, I thought I could help make something of you. But now I see what you're up to, Miriam Llewelyn. And I'm not going to stand for it. Not for a minute," Louise said, stabbing Miriam's chest with her index finger. Miriam reflexively stepped backwards.

"Honestly, I have no idea what you mean, Louise," she said, folding her arms across her chest. *Where was this hostility coming from?*

"I didn't think anything of it when the Websters offered to rent you the servants' quarters," Louise said.

"Their guesthouse."

"Whatever. I just assumed it was the Websters being the Websters. Kindhearted, if not a bit naïve," Louise said. "But now that you've cozied up to them, one might surmise you're no better than the gold diggers they fended off over the years. It's disgusting, quite frankly, and you won't get away with it. Not if I can help it." Her face was now nearly as red as her lips.

"I'm not going to dignify your absurd accusations with a response," Miriam said, turning to exit the ladies' room when Louise grabbed her shoulder.

"Let me put it differently," Louise said, narrowing her eyes as Miriam pivoted to face her. "You've been here, what, six months? I've known the sisters my entire life. I'll be damned if I let anyone take advantage of them!"

Miriam had never heard Louise use profanity, which could

only suggest Louise was deadly serious.

"Louise," Miriam said as gently as she could, "I have become very good friends with the Websters, and I can assure you, I would never do anything to harm them. They've become like family to me," she added, touching her new pearls. "I care deeply about them."

"I don't believe it for a moment. But know this: I'm watching you," she said, brushing past Miriam to open the door.

"You know what, Louise? Just please... mind your own business and stay out of mine," Miriam said forcefully as she followed Louise into the lobby.

She wheeled around and glared at Miriam. "Do you know who you're talking to? Trust me, you don't want me as your enemy," she said, then stomped down the hall as the Websters entered the lobby.

"Well, someone seems to have her panties in a twist," Rose said, giving Miriam a kiss on the cheek. "What was that all about?"

Miriam shook her head. "Just Louise trying to put me in my place," she said, adjusting her headband. "It's nothing. Nothing I can't handle, anyway."

"That's our girl," Iris said, smiling proudly. "Shall we?" She entwined her arm through Miriam's, and the three proceeded toward the meeting.

Miriam wanted to sit with the sisters, but considering Louise's outburst, she decided it was best to join Bitsy, who had saved her a seat. The room became quiet as Kay took the podium, gaveling the meeting to order.

"Ladies, as you know, today's agenda has one item and one item only," she said solemnly. "We're here to elect our new auxiliary officers, who will assume their positions in September. Before I open the floor to nominations, I want to express my profound appreciation to each and every one of you for having elected me your president this time last year."

She placed her hand over her heart and smiled beatifically. "I count it as my life's greatest achievement. Other than my children, that is." Laughter filled the room as Kay chuckled with self-deprecation.

"Now, let's hear a brief word from our president emerita, Iris Webster!" Kay said, clapping her hands as the other women joined her. Miriam watched Iris move gracefully to the podium, her silk tunic and palazzo pants floating behind her in a psychedelic cloud.

"Wherever does she shop?" Bitsy whispered in Miriam's ear.

"Be nice," Miriam whispered back, patting Bitsy's bony knee.

"Good afternoon, my fellow auxiliarists," Iris said, splaying her hands on each side of the podium. "My sister and I have had the privilege of being a part of this most sacred organization for more than fifty years, and I was given the honor of serving as president for numerous terms, so I believe I have earned the right to speak candidly." She paused to look around the room as several women shifted in their seats.

"Many seek positions of power for all the wrong reasons. Today, we're here to elect those women who are willing to put in the hard work and who are committed to service above their personal egos or agendas." She looked directly at Miriam and smiled.

"So, as you make your nominations and subsequently cast your votes, I urge you to prioritize those women you would happily work alongside as they lead the auxiliary into another year of opportunity. Together, we will continue serving our wonderful community. Thank you," she said, bowing her head slightly as the room filled with applause.

Kay returned to the podium. "Well said, Miss Webster." She gave Iris an approving nod. "Now, let us begin with the office of president. I will take nominations from the floor."

Immediately, Bitsy's hand shot up as Miriam's stomach did a somersault. "Mrs. Butler?" Kay said.

Bitsy stood and turned around, waving to the women as if she had just been crowned Miss America. "Ladies, it is my distinct pleasure to nominate my dear friend, a seamstress extraordinaire, and the creator of that delicious shepherd's pie, Miriam Llewelyn, to be our next president! Miriam, won't you stand?" Bitsy said, taking Miriam's arm. Miriam stood and gave the ladies a shy smile, trying to ignore a few murmurs in the crowd.

"Wonderful. Thank you, Bitsy. Do I hear a second?" Kay said, her eyes scouring the room.

Rose stood up. "I second the nomination," she called out, grinning at Miriam.

"Thank you, Miss Webster. Are there any other nominations for president?"

The room remained quiet as the members craned their heads to see if anyone else's hand was raised. "Yes, Mrs. Caldwell?" Kay said as Louise rose from her chair.

Louise lifted her chin and smiled. "I would like to nominate myself for the office of president," she said. "I do believe I've proven my commitment to this organization, which I would be very honored to lead." She looked over at Miriam and gave her a triumphant smile.

"Do I hear a second?" Kay looked around the room nervously as the women remained still. Bitsy raised her hand.

"Mrs. Butler?"

Bitsy stood up. "Point of order, Madame President. Are self-nominations allowed?" she said, looking directly at Louise, whose face had become flushed.

"Thank you for your question. Yes, the bylaws so allow it," Kay said. Bitsy returned to her seat. "Again, do I hear a second in favor of nominating Louise for president?"

Despite Louise's unfounded accusations earlier, Miriam

could not allow her to be publicly humiliated. She raised her hand.

"Mrs. Llewelyn?" Kay called in a surprised voice.

Miriam stood. "I'd like to second the nomination of Louise Caldwell for president," she said as the room was overtaken with whispers.

"While it is highly unusual for a nominee to second the nomination of an opponent, I'll allow it. Thank you, Mrs. Llewelyn. Are there any other nominations, ladies?" She scanned the room once more. "Hearing none, let it be recorded that Miriam Llewelyn and Louise Caldwell are your nominees for president."

Louise looked over at Miriam and gave her a tepid smile. Miriam returned her message with a demure nod.

"What was that?" Bitsy whispered, digging her fingernails into Miriam's thigh. Ignoring Bitsy's question, Miriam covered Bitsy's hand with her own, giving it a gentle pat.

Once nominations had been made for vice president, treasurer, and secretary, Kay instructed the women to use the index card and pen under their respective chairs to indicate their selections for each office. "Please fold your card in half and pass them to your left. I'll collect the cards and tally them while we adjourn for fifteen minutes."

She stepped away from the podium and picked up a large wicker basket, then walked to the end of each aisle to gather their cards. The women rose and shuffled toward the refreshments at the back of the cavernous room.

Miriam saw Louise approaching her, so she turned and walked purposefully to join the Websters, who were stacking a pile of cookies onto their plates.

"While unexpected, that was very kind of you, dear," Iris said, proffering her plate to Miriam, who selected a piece of shortbread.

"I felt so embarrassed for her," Miriam said quietly. "Just

standing there, all alone, she looked vulnerable. I've never seen her like that." She shoved the entire wafer into her mouth.

"We reap what we sow, dear," Rose said, biting into a chocolate chip cookie, then putting it back on the dish. "I'm afraid we've been spoiled by Jasper's cooking. That cookie is as dry as a bone!" She took an unladylike swig of her tea.

"Good afternoon, ladies!" Louise said, joining their circle and smiling as she kissed each sister's cheek. She deigned to acknowledge Miriam with a curt nod. "I understand you all had a lovely visit with Clifton last week. He positively raved about Jasper's cooking, as well as the lemonade."

"We always enjoy seeing Clifton. He's full of so many stories," Iris said. "And such the perfect gentleman. You're a very fortunate woman, indeed. As for the lemonade, Miriam gave us the recipe. It belonged to her mother, isn't that right, dear?"

Miriam merely nodded, feeling taken off guard by Louise's insertion into their conversation.

"I do hope you were able to get everything sorted," Louise said, placing her hand on Iris's arm. Miriam watched her carefully because it seemed Louise was prying into the Websters' private affairs. She looked at Iris, who was closely examining her oatmeal cookie.

"Are those raisins or chocolate chips, dear?" she said, showing it to Miriam.

"They look like raisins," Miriam said.

Iris put the cookie back on the plate just as Kay called the meeting back to order. "Saved by the gavel," she whispered to Miriam as they returned to their chairs. "Good luck."

All eyes were focused expectantly on Kay as she stood at the podium holding a single piece of paper. Bitsy reached over and grabbed Miriam's hand, squeezing it hard. "I'm so excited!" she said under her breath.

"Ladies, thank you for taking your selections for our auxiliary officers seriously. After tallying the votes, I'm very

pleased to announce we have our clear winners, all of whom led by generous margins. When I call your name, please stand and remain standing until I'm finished, then I'll adjourn the meeting and join the officers-elect in the parlor for pictures." She paused to take a sip of lemonade as the women whispered in anticipation.

"Please excuse me," Kay said, dabbing her mouth with a cocktail napkin. "All right, we'll begin with auxiliary secretary. Congratulations, Bitsy Butler!" she announced, clapping politely from the podium. Bitsy jumped to her feet and blew kisses to the women around the room.

"Next, chosen by our members for treasurer-elect is Gigi Reese! Congratulations!" Miriam looked over her shoulder to see Gigi standing proudly toward the back and giving Kay a mock salute.

"Moving to vice president elect, please help me congratulate Matty Walker." She continued clapping as the petite woman stood and gave a slight bow.

"Didn't she make the crab Jell-O thing for the luncheon?" Bitsy leaned down to whisper to Miriam, her curls whipping Miriam's face.

"Yes, it was crab terrine," Miriam said quietly, rubbing her assaulted right eye.

"And finally, I'm proud to announce that with a significant majority of the votes, Miriam Llewelyn has been chosen as president-elect. Congratulations!" she said as Miriam stood shakily. Bitsy wrapped her arms around Miriam and gave her a tight hug as Miriam watched Louise stand and quietly exit the room.

"Officers elect, I will see you in the parlor! Ladies, I will see the rest of you in two weeks. This meeting is adjourned," she said, striking the podium with the gavel.

"Oh boy," Miriam said to Bitsy as they rose from their chairs. "Louise just stormed out of the room. Someone's not happy."

"Well, that's fine because this someone doesn't care!" she said, taking Miriam's hand before flipping her hair over her shoulder. "Madame President-Elect, may I escort you to our photo shoot?" Miriam looked across the room at Iris and Rose, who each gave her their thumbs-up. She waved, then turned to follow Bitsy into the adjoining room, wondering what punishment awaited her in the days and months to come. She put her hand on Iris's pearls and remembered her grandmother's words. *Webster mojo, how I'm going to need you. Please don't let me down!*

36

Though Louise had been overlooked by the auxiliary to serve as its next president, she remained committed to her work with the historical society and the restoration of the old sawmill. With the cookbook sales well underway and Emma immersed in her junior year at the academy, Louise found herself with more free time than usual, which she decided to devote to researching the mill, its origins, and its ultimate demise.

On a crisp fall morning, after drinking a cup of coffee on the veranda with her dogs, Louise dressed in a pair of khakis, a white cotton blouse, a baby blue cashmere cardigan, and her penny loafers, then borrowed a legal pad from Clifton's study to embark upon her fact-finding mission.

Thinking it best to visit the sawmill first, she drove to the outermost part of town, navigating the winding roads until she came upon the property. She parked her Cadillac as closely as possible, then walked around the periphery of what was left of the building. Sadly, there wasn't much beyond its rustic brick slab, three charred walls, and part of the paddle wheel. The mill's remains lay in heaps that appeared to have been left untouched once the blaze was extinguished, some fifty-plus years earlier. Louise didn't know much about the mill since it burned down long before she was born, but she had grown up hearing various rumors about the arsonist having fled town before he could be convicted. People also said the mill was haunted, though Louise didn't put much stock in such ideas. For her, its preservation was essential since it was one of the first buildings in Stuarts Landing. With nothing more to see, Louise returned to her car and headed for the library, where she hoped to find more information.

While she was not an avid reader, Louise loved the old library, which had been built in 1912 with grant money from the Carnegie Foundation. With its neoclassical architecture, including the requisite marble columns, the library was a study in tradition and permanence and, for Louise, an aesthetic delight. After parking, she entered the exquisite building, frozen in time but for the new releases displayed near the checkout area.

"Good morning," she said to the young woman staffing the front desk. "My name is Louise Caldwell. I'm here to do some research, and I'm hoping you can help me."

"Nice to meet you. My name is Laura, and I'm the research librarian. What are you looking for today?"

"I'm a volunteer with the historical society, and I'm interested in learning all I can about the old sawmill," Louise said, taking her legal pad and pen from her tote bag. "I'm not really sure where to begin."

Laura walked out from behind her desk. "Let's start with the index card cabinet," she said. "Please, follow me." Louise walked with her to the back of the library and watched as Laura opened the drawer labeled "Sm-St." A moment later, she pulled out a card. "Ah ha. This should help. It's *The Early History of Stuarts Landing*, and it was written by, let's see, Mr. Thurston Webster," she said. Louise smiled at the mention of his surname—she had no doubt that was the Webster sisters' father. "Looks like it's in the reference section. Do you know where that is?"

"Yes, I do, thank you," Louise said, making a quick note on her legal pad.

"Once you peruse the book, let me know if there are any key dates I might use to search our archived

newspapers, okay?"

"I will. Thank you," Louise said, eager to begin her research.

"I'll be at my desk should you need me. Good luck."

Once in the reference aisle, Louise traced her fingers over every spine until she found the object of her search. Taking the small book from the shelf, she took it to a table to begin reading. First, she explored the index to find anything under "Winston" and was gratified to see her family mentioned several times, including photos of their estate and stories about her grandfather's law practice—the first in Stuarts Landing—as well as her grandmother's founding of the Stuarts Landing Women's Auxiliary. But it reminded her of her lost election, which she did not want to think about, so she quickly flipped the pages to find any mention of the old sawmill in the index, of which there were only three. Skimming each section, she learned the mill had caught fire in October of 1927 and was deemed the result of arson. She hastily took notes, then stopped abruptly as she read who owned the mill.

"How did I not know that?" she asked herself aloud. Grabbing her purse, she hurried to Laura. "Could you pull any *Weekly Gazettes* you have from October of 1927, please? I've set up camp at the table over there." She pointed to the center of the library.

"Sure. Give me a few minutes," Laura said. Louise returned to her spot to continue perusing the history book. She lingered over the photo of her family home, remembering fondly the holidays she celebrated with her grandparents there as a child. Her eyes scanned each page of the slender manuscript until another photo caught her attention. Obviously taken at the annual fall festival, the picture captured a large group of young people enjoying a hayride. She recognized Iris immediately but had no idea about the man sitting beside her, though he somehow seemed familiar. The caption read, "Photo courtesy of the Stuarts Landing Rotary Club." *Hardly helpful,*

Louise thought, shaking her head.

Laura appeared with four folded newspapers and a pair of white gloves. "Please put these on before you handle the pages."

"Thank you. By the way, I'd like to check out this book, please."

"I'm sorry, reference books cannot be removed from the library, Mrs. Caldwell."

"May I buy it then?" Louise said, reaching for her purse.

"Again, my apologies, but all reference materials remain the property of the library," Laura said. "Though if there are pages you would like photocopied, I would be happy to do so. It costs five cents per page."

"Yes, would you please copy this page?" Louise said, showing her the hayride picture. "I'm sure I have a nickel in my purse."

"Would you like to sort through the newspapers first to see if there's anything else you'd like copied?" Laura said.

"Yes. Good idea," Louise said. Laura returned to her station while Louise read two different articles about the fire, then all but jumped when she saw her grandfather's name listed as the attorney for the sawmill's owners. Further down, she saw the reporter had contacted him, but all her grandfather offered was "no comment." She knew from her husband that when someone refused press inquiries, it usually meant there was more to be uncovered. And she knew the only people who might have any answers. After gathering her notebook, the newspapers, the reference book, and her purse, she made a beeline to Laura's desk.

"Could you please copy this photo and these two articles?" she said, removing the white gloves. "Do you by chance have a payphone? I need to make a quick call."

"We don't, but you're welcome to use the one here," Laura said, putting the rotary phone on the counter. "I'll be right

back," she said, walking to the copy machine.

Louise consulted the small address book in her bag, then dialed the number and waited anxiously. When Rose answered, she said breathlessly, "Hi there, it's Louise Caldwell. I'm calling to see if I may drop by in a little while."

"What an interesting surprise," Rose said. "You are more than welcome. We shall see you shortly. Bye, now." She disconnected the line.

Once she paid for the photocopies, Louise scurried to her car and headed north to Webster House.

***

As Louise pulled into the Websters' circular drive, she couldn't help glancing toward the servants' quarters–as she would always know them–to see if Miriam's car was there. Fortunately, it was not, which Louise hoped would mean she would have the sisters all to herself. Jasper greeted her at the door with a slight bow, then motioned her to follow him into the parlor, where Iris and Rose were waiting. "Good afternoon," she said, greeting each of them with a kiss on the cheek before taking a seat on couch.

"Hello, dear," Rose said. "Would you like something to drink? Perhaps, some ginger lemonade?"

Remembering the recipe came from Miriam's mother, she shook her head. "No, thank you. Water would be just fine, please," she said, opening her tote bag and removing the papers.

"To what do we owe the pleasure?" Rose asked, stroking the head of the enormous black cat lying on her lap.

"Well, I wanted to talk to you about the historical society's efforts to restore the old sawmill and perhaps get it listed on the National Register of Historic Places," Louise began. Jasper set her water on the coffee table. "Thank you," she said as he wafted from the room.

"Go on," Rose said. Louise noticed Iris was uncharacteristically reticent. Louise wondered if she was unwell but knew better than to ask.

"We've been able to raise quite a bit of money already, as I believe you know," Louise said.

"Yes, we have donated several times," Iris said. Their Siamese cat was rubbing up against her knee. "Isn't that right, Diva?" She reached down to give the feline a scratch.

"Duly noted and very appreciated. I know Clifton had spoken to you recently about drawing up some documents, and at the risk of being impertinent, I was hoping that may have included making the society one of your beneficiaries."

The sisters looked at each other, clearly telegraphing a message Louise could not interpret.

"For goodness' sakes! Your grandmother must be rolling in her grave, Louise," Iris said. "Weren't you taught, by someone, that it's vulgar to discuss money in this manner? Shame on you!" Reacting to her tone, the cat skittered out of the parlor and up the stairs to the next floor.

"Iris, dear, don't let yourself get worked up," Rose said.

"I just thought, without an heir, you would want your estate to make an impact in perpetuity. And the historical society, well, you know the good work we do."

"We've already recorded our final wishes," Rose said, smiling at her sister. "We're quite pleased with our allocations."

"I'm so glad, though I don't want to even imagine Stuarts Landing without you both," Louise said, attempting to recover the conversation.

"This discussion is so dreadfully morbid," Iris said, rising from her chair. "Please excuse me, but I think I may go lie down."

"Please, can you give me a few more minutes? I have some questions," Louise said. Iris sat back down and folded her arms

but fixed Louise with an uncomfortable stare.

"Let me just say one more thing about your estate, if I may." Louise proceeded cautiously. "I really don't want to see you taken advantage of, either one of you. I've known you forever, and you've always been generous. But people aren't always what they seem. You can be too trusting."

"Are you referring to anyone specifically?" Iris said, raising one eyebrow and licking her lips.

"Well, I didn't want to say anything, but Miriam told me you gave her the pearls she was wearing on the day of the election. We don't really know that much about her background, but it worried me to think..."

"That's enough!" Iris slapped her hand on the side of her armchair.

Startled, Louise said, "All right," and nervously opened her folder. "I went to the library earlier to research the mill. Honestly, I was surprised by what I found. I had no idea your family owned it."

"That was a long time ago," Rose said, glancing at her sister. "After the fire, our father decided to deed the property to Stuarts Landing. We have nothing to do with the fact the township has chosen to let it sit in disrepair."

"I found the book your father wrote about our local history," Louise said. "It was quite remarkable, really, to see the only world I've ever known captured in black and white."

"I don't remember that, dear. What year was it written?" Rose said.

Louise looked at her notes. "It appears to have been published in 1928," she said.

"No wonder. Iris and I were abroad. Do you remember him mentioning it?" she said to her sister.

"I do not," Iris said. "But then, I wasn't here for a few years," she added. "When we returned from Europe, I immediately enrolled at Bryn Mawr. As you must know all too well,

Louise, young people are never as interested in their parents as their parents might wish them to be."

"You make a good point," she said, chuckling. "I read in one of these two newspaper articles that a mill worker was accused of starting the fire, but he fled town before he could be convicted. Did your father know him?" Louise said, then she noticed Iris purse her lips and close her eyes.

"Oh, I suppose it's possible, though Daddy had a foreman overseeing the operations," Rose said.

"What really surprised me the most, though, was seeing my grandfather's name mentioned in conjunction with the incident," Louise said as Iris walked to the mantel and hit the Tibetan gong. Jasper appeared almost instantaneously.

"I'd like a gin and tonic, please," she said. "Would anyone else like something?"

"I'll take one too," Rose said. "Louise?"

"No, thank you," she said, taking a drink of water. Jasper bowed and left the room.

"So, from what I can gather, my grandfather served as your family's attorney—is that correct?" Louise said.

Iris looked at Rose with an anxious expression. "Like I said, we didn't pay much attention to our parents' affairs," Iris said, turning her eyes to Louise. "I suppose it's a reasonable idea since your grandfather had the only law practice in town. Why are you so interested? I don't really see it as any of your business."

"Well, I thought I knew all there was to know about Stuarts Landing, but now, it feels like the town has secrets of its own."

"Doesn't everyone?" Iris said before taking a sip of her cocktail. "Thank you, Jasper."

Louise took the photocopy of the hayride picture from her folder. "It was nice to see this picture of you, Iris," she said, handing the paper to Rose, whose eyebrows shot skyward.

"You were so very beautiful, and the boy you're sitting next to... I didn't recognize him, of course, but there's something so familiar about him." She watched Rose hand the photocopy to Iris, who glanced at it, then put it face down in her lap.

"Did you know him?" Louise said, leaning forward.

"Only briefly," Iris replied, her voice slightly breaking.

"Was he special to you?"

"There are certain things best left in the past, Louise," Rose said as her sister's lower lip begin to tremble.

"But that's the point of the historical society," Louise said, bringing the conversation full circle. "To keep the past alive for future generations!"

"Without wishing to sound rude, my personal life is really none of your business," Iris said. "I would thank you to leave this subject alone."

"Surely you understand," Rose said. "I'm well aware there are aspects of your own life you wouldn't want examined."

Working to keep her facial expression neutral, Louise returned the papers to her tote bag. "You're welcome to keep the photocopy, Iris," she said, rising from the couch.

"Thank you."

"And I appreciate your making time for me," Louise added as she began walking to the French doors.

"Shall I see you out?" Rose said from the couch.

"I know my way," she said. "If you think of anything more, would you let me know?"

Iris was staring at the picture as Louise opened the doors.

"If we remember something that would be helpful, we'll be in touch," Rose said. "Have a lovely afternoon, and please do give our regards to your husband."

Jasper held the front door open for Louise, who strode toward the car, her mind vibrating with the notion the sisters were hiding something. She suspected it was related to the fire, but she couldn't make a logical connection.

At least not until she determined how her grandfather was involved. *All it would take is a look through his old files,* Louise thought as she drove down the tree-lined path toward the main thoroughfare. And she knew just where they were.

248

37

Serving as the auxiliary president proved to be more time-consuming than Miriam had expected, yet she was enjoying the opportunity to introduce some fresh ideas, one of which was revising the organization's membership criteria. In her second official officer meeting as president, she proposed her idea.

"Why should a member's nomination be required for new candidates?" she said to her other officers. "I know Stuarts Landing is a relatively small town, but we can't presume to know everyone. I'm sure there are women who could add a lot of value to the auxiliary. Wouldn't you agree?"

Though Bitsy felt strongly about keeping the auxiliary "exclusive," Matty and Gigi agreed membership should be open to anyone, though they proposed raising the annual dues "just to weed out certain elements." It was a compromise Miriam could accept. So, when the topic came up for the membership vote, she was pleased to see the proposal pass, if only by a slim margin.

Louise was a vocal opponent, but that was to be expected. As Miriam had come to learn, all too painfully, anything threatening Louise's views of how things should be done—"because they've always been done this way"—would be subject to her intervention. The change in bylaws was no exception. Truly, Miriam had never met anyone so averse to change, but Louise would continue being Louise. *Life goes on,* Miriam told herself, *despite Louise's attempts to question my very existence.*

Miriam took her auxiliary position seriously, yet not so much as to leave her job at The Pig. Roy had graciously allowed her to reduce her hours, so she worked on Mondays, Tuesdays, and Fridays, leaving her time for auxiliary business and visits with the Webster sisters. One October morning, she began feeling queasy after breakfast, but she would never leave Roy short-staffed, so she took a hefty swig of Pepto-Bismol before donning her uniform and heading for work.

"You don't look so good," Gloria said as Miriam clocked in. She had been promoted to assistant manager, meaning she had greater authority over Miriam and the other clerks, but was every bit as friendly as she had been on Miriam's first day. She walked up to Miriam and put her hand on Miriam's forehead. "You feel kinda clammy," she said.

"Honestly, I am a bit nauseous," Miriam said, tying her apron. "Probably something I ate. I'll be okay."

She walked from the employee lounge to her register and began counting the money before logging the total in Roy's notebook, all the while trying to ignore her roiling stomach. While she normally loved the bakery smells permeating the air, they seemed almost putrid that morning. She closed her register and quickly returned to the lounge, hoping to find a can of ginger ale or 7UP in the vending machine.

"We're out of sodas?" she said to Gloria, her voice dripping with desperation.

"They change out the machines on Fridays," Gloria said. "Besides, that's no good for an upset stomach. I know what you need—I'll be right back."

Two minutes later, Gloria returned to the lounge and gave Miriam a can of peaches.

"What's this?" Miriam asked, slightly gagging at the thought of chewing something.

Gloria opened the kitchenette drawer and pulled out a bottle opener, then used it to puncture the can. "Drink the syrup," she said. "I promise, it works every time."

Miriam brought the can to her lips and, holding her nose, took three big swallows of the nectar as Gloria giggled. "I used to do that too," Gloria said. "Better?"

Miriam went to the sink to moisten a paper towel, which she draped on the back of her neck. "I think so," she said shakily. "Okay, back to the register." She had taken only three steps before she felt her insides begin convulsing, so she speed-walked to the trash can in the nick of time. Gloria held back Miriam's hair while she violently emptied her stomach until she was panting with relief.

"No idea where that came from," Miriam said, using the towel to wipe her mouth. She stood up and rubbed her temples. "Wow."

Gloria put her arm around Miriam's waist and guided her to the table. "Why don't you sit down for a minute, catch your breath," she said. "Do you think you could keep down some saltines?" Miriam shook her head, putting her head in her hands.

"I feel so strange," she said. "I never get sick like that! My mama used to say I had an iron gut, but, thinking more about it, it couldn't be something I ate since I only had toast for breakfast."

After taking a quick glance at the clock, Gloria took the seat across from Miriam. "May I ask you a personal question?" she said.

"Of course," Miriam said, raising her head to look at her coworker.

"How old are you?"

"I'll be thirty-four in a few months," Miriam said. "January twenty-fourth, to be exact. Why?"

"Is it possible you might be pregnant?"

Miriam could feel herself begin to blush. "There's no way," she said softly. "We tried for years, but it never happened."

"I'm so sorry, Miriam," Gloria said, reaching out her hand to take Miriam's. "I know I sound nosy, but did a doctor tell you it was an impossibility?"

Miriam shook her head. "Quite some time ago, after we had tried unsuccessfully for a few years. I just assumed it was God's will, so we made peace with it."

"I read a story in *People* magazine about a couple who couldn't have children, but they really wanted to adopt. No sooner had they brought home their baby than she found herself pregnant. With twins!" Gloria said. "It could happen, Miriam! Are you, by chance, late this month?"

Miriam gave Gloria a bittersweet smile. "My cycle has always been unpredictable, so I don't put much stock in that, though I am a few weeks overdue. It's not even worth thinking about, though. We've come to accept it's just not in the cards for us."

"Well, not to be bossy—though I am sorta, you know, your boss," Gloria began as Miriam started chuckling. "But you need to take a pregnancy test. We have them in our pharmacy. Want me to pull one for you?"

Miriam knew Gloria was trying to be helpful, yet she didn't want to indulge in the slightest thought she might be expecting. Instinctively, she put her hand over her abdomen, closing her eyes to concentrate on slowing her breath. Moments later, she opened them to find an EPT box sitting on the table in front of her. Gloria remained standing and had her hands on her hips.

"Well, I took your silence as a 'yes.' You want to do it now?" Gloria said, her eyes shining with excitement.

Miriam quickly read the back of the box. "It says I need to take the test first thing in the morning. Great... now I get to obsess over this for the next twenty-one hours. Anyway, it's show time," Miriam said, rising from her chair. "And thank you, really, for your concern."

Miriam elected not to eat lunch since the sight of all the food she rang up during her shift had only made her feel worse. After clocking out, she took her tote and walked to her car, which smelled of the leftover French fries she had bought the day before. She opened her car door and tried to throw up, but her stomach had nothing to offer. The minute she got home, she changed into a nightgown to lie down, overwhelmed by fatigue, yet her imagination would not allow her to rest. Saying a short prayer, she pulled the pregnancy test from her bag, tucked it under her pillow, and soon, she fell into a deep sleep.

When George came through the door two hours later, Miriam was curled up in a quilt on their bed, crying. He sat down beside her and began rubbing her back.

"Sweetheart? What's wrong? Did something bad happen at work?" he said, his voice thick with worry.

Miriam rolled onto her back, then sat up against the pillows.

"Work was fine," she said, rubbing her swollen eyes. "Though I did get sick. I thought it was a stomach bug or maybe something I ate..."

"Whatever it is, I don't seem to have it," George said.

"No, I don't expect you would," Miriam said, her mouth slowly turning upward with a smile. She reached under her pillow for the test, which she cupped in her hands and offered to her husband.

George's eyes squinted with confusion as he looked at the box with wonder.

"Is this what I think it is?" he stammered.

Miriam nodded excitedly, her eyes erupting with more tears. "I wouldn't have even considered I might be pregnant because, after so long, why get our hopes up? But Gloria—I've told you about her—she suggested I take the test. Unfortunately, we have to wait until first thing in the morning though," she said.

George pulled her into a tight embrace, kissing her cheeks, her lips, and her neck before lowering his head to kiss her stomach. "Hello in there, little Llewelyn," he whispered as his tears cascaded down his nose. He wiped his eyes and turned his face toward the ceiling. "Lord, if it's your will, please let this be true."

Seeing her husband so ebullient felt bittersweet. She worried about getting their hopes up, yet this was the closest she felt they had ever come to realizing their greatest wish.

"You'd be the best father ever," Miriam said, hugging herself with anticipation.

"And you'd be the best mother ever," he said. "We should celebrate! Would you like to go to dinner?" Miriam quickly shook her head. "Oops, I wasn't thinking. But when you start getting cravings, I'm here to oblige!"

"If, remember it's still if."

"Of course, if," George said, but he couldn't seem to wipe the smile off his face.

After eating a light supper of chicken soup and crackers, they spent the next few hours playing gin rummy before it was time for bed.

"I'm not sure I can sleep, George," Miriam whispered, coiling herself around her husband's back.

"Close your eyes and imagine rearranging The Pig," George offered.

"That just feels stressful, honey," she said with a giggle, then closed her eyes. "Good night, love." Taking his suggestion, she envisioned the condiments aisle. *Why are seasonings and spices with baking items instead of there?* Her brain began reorganizing the store until she was fast asleep.

When the clock radio began buzzing, Miriam woke with a start. She rolled over, but George's side of the bed was empty. Grabbing her bathrobe from the chair by her nightstand, she

quickly wrapped herself up before putting the pregnancy test in her pocket.

"George?" she called.

"Out here," he hollered. She peeked her head from the bedroom to see him sitting in one of the rockers on the front porch, coffee cup in hand. She went to join him.

"You okay?" she asked, massaging the back of his neck.

"I'm not sure. I was watching the sun rise, thinking how this morning could be the beginning of a whole new chapter for us, Mim. And then I got mad at myself," he said.

"Why?" She moved in front of him and knelt down so she could see his eyes, bleary from little sleep.

"Because I never, ever want you to think my life is less than complete with you. It's not. If you're not pregnant, we'll both be disappointed, and I just need to say that if we're sad, it's not because we're not perfectly fine with the way things are."

Miriam caressed his cheek with the back of her hand. "I feel the same, honey. We are already blessed, in so many ways. I just want you to be happy."

George looked into her eyes and smiled. "I already am. Now go do whatever it is you need to do. I'll be waiting!"

She stood and walked briskly to the bathroom, clutching the EPT box in her left hand, then sat down on the commode and followed the instructions.

Five minutes later, she emerged from the bathroom, poured a cup of coffee, and returned to the porch. George looked at her expectantly, then leapt from the rocking chair when she handed him the test.

"Two pink lines? Does that mean..."

"It *does*!" Miriam shrieked. "It's nothing short of a miracle, George! Oh my heavens... we're having a baby!"

George threw his arms around her and lifted her off her feet before letting out a whoop.

"I never thought this day would happen," she said softly, taking a step back, then rubbing her stomach.

"We have to tell the sisters," George said. "They will be over the moon!"

Miriam took a deep breath. "I thought about that, but don't you think we should wait until I get through my first trimester? Just in case, you know..." she said while trying to mentally cast away any doubts about the viability of her pregnancy.

"They're family, Mim," he said. "And they're right here, which assures me you'll have someone to help if you need anything."

"All right," she said, her smile radiating all the love she felt for her husband and, now, their child. "We can tell the sisters at dinner this Friday. But we're only telling *them*, and I suppose I should tell my boss. Everyone else can find out after I reach that first milestone."

"Deal," George said, playfully extending his hand. Miriam took it and brought it to her lips.

"I adore you, my sweet husband. How very blessed we are," she said. "Now let's get some breakfast before you have to go to work!"

38

The Webster sisters had rarely been ill, which they attributed to a combination of good genes and what they fondly called "the Jasper lifestyle." Lately, though, Rose had noticed her ankles swelling for no reason, and she was frequently light-headed when she stood, all of which she had shared with Iris. Chalking it up to old age, Rose managed the symptoms without comment or complaint, even as Iris continually pestered her to see their doctor.

Because it was Wednesday, the sisters were in their respective bedrooms, dressing for the bi-weekly auxiliary meeting, when Iris heard a loud thud. Dropping her hairbrush, she flew into Rose's room to find her on the floor, unconscious. She knelt and tried to nudge Rose awake before yelling for Jasper, who quickly appeared in the doorway. In one fluid motion, he scooped her up in his arms and placed her gently on her bed. Placing two fingers on her carotid artery, he gave Iris a reassuring smile. Moments later, Rose's eyelids began fluttering, and slowly, she opened her eyes.

"Oh, thank God," Iris said, embracing her sister. "What happened?"

Rose opened her mouth to speak, but her words were jumbled.

"Take it easy," Iris urged, putting her hand on Rose's chest. "Jasper, would you please bring her something to drink?" He bowed, then quickly went downstairs, returning with a glass of orange juice and a straw. After they propped Rose up with pillows, Iris held the glass so Rose could take a sip, but the juice just dribbled down her chin. It appeared one side of her mouth had forgotten how to work. Iris looked at Jasper frantically. "Please sit with her while I call the doctor," she said. "I'll be right back."

She hurried downstairs to their study and flipped open her address book to find Dr. Hawkins's personal number. He was the only doctor in town who still made house calls—at least for the Websters. Iris frantically explained what had happened, and he said he was on the way. She contemplated calling Miriam but thought better of it as she knew Miriam was probably getting ready for the meeting. *No need to upset her unnecessarily,* Iris rationalized. *I'm sure Rose is just fine,* she thought, heading back upstairs.

"Dr. Hawkins should be here in about ten minutes," Iris said. Rose closed her eyes and nodded. "Was she able to drink any juice?" Jasper shook his head. Iris sat down on the bed and curled up next to her sister. "You're going to be okay." She stroked Rose's hair while trying to keep from crying. Jasper quietly left the room, leaving the sisters in unusual silence.

"You know, Mama would tell you to quit being so dramatic," Iris said with a half-hearted laugh. Rose gave her a crooked smile. "What was it women used to get—the vapors?" She sat up and reached for the blanket at the foot of the bed, then covered Rose, who had closed her eyes. "Rose, can you try to keep your eyes open?" As tears began running down Rose's ashen cheeks, she extended her left hand to squeeze Iris's wrist. Rose was never one to cry, which frightened Iris even more. "Are you in pain?" Rose's grip tightened in response. "Just focus on your breathing, dear, just like Jasper taught us." Iris didn't know what else to do.

She put her head on Rose's shoulder, praying silently her sister had simply fainted, yet she feared it was something more serious. "Please, Lord, have mercy," she whispered, then

sat up when she heard the doorbell. Moments later, Dr. Hawkins entered the room, followed by Jasper.

"Thank you for getting here so quickly," Iris said, standing so the doctor could examine Rose.

"I would say it's my pleasure, but that doesn't feel right," Dr. Hawkins said. He pulled the stethoscope from his bag and looped it around his neck, then sat down next to Rose. "Hi there." Rose's eyes fluttered open. "I'm just going to take a quick listen," he said, placing the chest piece over Rose's heart. When Iris saw him slightly frown, she began wringing her hands. He put his fingers on Rose's neck while looking at his watch.

A minute later, he took Rose's left hand. "Miss Webster, if you can understand what I'm saying, please give me a squeeze. Good," he said, looking briefly at Iris, who remained frozen in place. "Can you tell me your name?"

Rose blinked her eyes. "Rzz," she slurred. "Zors." She began to cry once again.

"That's okay," Dr. Hawkins said, patting her arm. "I need to do a few neurological tests. Can you lift your left arm? Great. How about your left leg? Wonderful. Now, let's try the right arm." Iris was horrified to see Rose unable to comply. "Let's try your right leg." Again, no response. "I'll be back in a moment," he said to Rose, then motioned Iris to follow him into the hallway.

"We need to get her to the hospital," he told Iris. "It would appear she's had a stroke, and from the sound of her erratic heartbeat, I believe she may be in atrial fibrillation."

"What's that?" Iris stammered.

"It means the upper chambers of her heart are beating extremely fast and irregularly," he said. "I also noticed the swelling in her ankles, which we call 'edema.' It may be an indication her heart is having trouble pumping blood."

"That sounds serious," Iris said, hoping he would disagree.

"It is, Miss Webster. We need to admit her to see if we can get her heartbeat under control and to run a few more tests."

"Should I have Jasper drive us?" Iris asked.

"We need an ambulance, I'm afraid. Please call 911 and tell them we have a cardiac event and that I'm here with your sister. I will monitor her until they get here, then I'll meet you at the hospital."

"Doctor, is she going to be okay?" She was anxiously wringing her hands.

"I'm afraid it's too early to tell," he said. "But we'll do everything we can."

***

Twenty minutes later, Iris watched silently as a nurse removed Rose's clothing and slipped a hospital gown over her head, leaving it open in front. She then placed a network of electrodes on her chest and neck and connected the wires to a machine, which began beeping wildly. Rose's eyes flashed like a spooked horse, and she tried unsuccessfully to sit up. Dr. Hawkins entered the room and instructed the nurse to begin an IV drip.

"We have to lower her heart rate," he said to Iris, who had begun pacing the tiny room. She winced as the nurse stuck a needle in her sister's arm, taping down the IV port.

"We'll start with saline," he instructed the nurse, "then follow it with an anticoagulant." The nurse had turned to leave the room when an alarm blared.

"Nurse, grab the defibrillator!" he yelled as Iris stared at the monitor. "She's in cardiac arrest!" The nurse rushed the machine to Rose's bedside. He applied the paddles to Rose's chest to shock her heart back into rhythm. After three attempts, he handed the paddles back to the nurse.

"Okay," he said, looking at the monitor. "That did the

trick, though I think we should administer a beta blocker just to be safe."

Iris pulled a chair next to Rose and sat down, her hands trembling, then began stroking her sister's hair. "What now?" she asked the doctor.

"We have to wait and see. If we can't keep her stabilized over the next few days, we may have to consider surgery to check for blockages. And I wouldn't rule out a pacemaker," he said.

"She's never had surgery," Iris murmured. "Are you sure she's strong enough?"

"As I said, we need to give it a few days. At minimum, she's going to need a great deal of physical rehabilitation due to the damage to her right side."

"Will she... will she be able to walk again?" Iris asked.

Dr. Hawkins's eyes radiated kindness as he shook his head. "I would doubt it. But miracles do happen," he said. "We'll pray for that while continuing to do all we can. Is there anyone you would like me to call?"

Once again, Iris thought about Miriam, who would be midway through the auxiliary meeting. "Not at this time," she said, wishing Miriam was at her side. She didn't know how to do this alone, but for now, she would have to stay calm for her sister.

"What can I do for you?" he said softly.

"Give me better news," she said, staring at Rose.

"Trust me, I would if I could."

Rose had fallen asleep, so Iris closed her eyes, remembering the unconditional support Rose had given her as Iris dealt with her pregnancy, the loss of Rusty, and giving her daughter up for adoption.

"We'll get through this," she said to her sister. "One way or another."

39

The day after Louise had gone to the library, then was all but shunned by the Webster sisters when she was only trying to protect them, Louise decided she would continue her research—this time, in her attic. She told Pearl as much while finishing her grapefruit and coffee. Clifton had already left, taking Emma to school before driving to his Richmond office, so she had the house to herself.

"Anything I can help you with, missus?" Pearl asked, clearing away Louise's dishes.

"We don't, by chance, have any gardening gloves? I don't know how dirty it might be up there."

"None I know of, but don't you still have them red leather gloves your mama got in Italy?"

"Right, of course," Louise said, getting up from the table. She went upstairs to her closet and removed the gloves from their original box. Slipping them on, she headed to the end of the hallway, opened the door to the attic, and walked up another flight of stairs. Turning on the light, she looked around at the boxes lining the walls, quilts folded in stacks, a rocking horse her father had bought from FAO Schwarz when Louise was a toddler, her English riding saddle and crop, and myriad other pieces of memorabilia spanning three generations. The attic was a veritable Winston Museum, and while she wanted to breathe in the nostalgia, she was on a mission.

Taking a closer look at the boxes, she zeroed in on three leather cases—the kind attorneys used to transport their files

to court. She spread a quilt on the wooden floor, then put each case on top of it before sitting down to begin reading. Opening the first case, she thumbed through the files, most of which pertained to land sales and business contracts unrelated to the Websters. She unlatched the second case and reviewed its contents—more court filings and pieces of correspondence but nothing of personal interest. With only one case remaining, Louise wondered if her instincts were misguided... perhaps this was nothing more than an exercise in futility? She removed the files from the case and stacked them on the quilt, then examined each label before finding one marked "Thurston Webster."

Her heart began racing as she flipped through each document, many of which concerned the sales of the Websters' various tobacco farms. Then she found a letter dated November 1, 1927, from Thurston Webster to Louise's grandfather.

"It is with a profound sense of urgency that I ask you to handle our most delicate situation, the same we discussed by phone and about which I care not to elaborate in writing for the sake of propriety. I have enclosed a check, made payable to your firm, which I ask that you deposit. From there, please write a check from the firm's account for the same amount to Russell Benson, the former employee at my now destroyed mill, and draw up an affidavit he must sign as a condition of receiving the five hundred dollars, saying he agrees to leave Stuarts Landing immediately and permanently and have no further contact with my younger daughter. Beyond his inappropriate relationship with her, I am willing to say publicly I have every reason to believe he was the culprit behind the fire that destroyed my property, and he needs to be advised he will be so implicated should he choose not to comply with my generous offer. My wife and I are in agreement that this is the best course of action for all so affected. With my sincere appreciation, Thurston Webster."

Louise reread the letter before reviewing the next document in the file, which was the affidavit signed by Russell Benson attached to the canceled check. She thought back to the hayride picture she had shown the Websters and remembered Iris's immediate reaction. *Was the man in the photo Russell Benson?* she wondered, scratching her head. *And had her grandfather been complicit in blackmailing a possibly innocent man?* She wondered why the article she read claimed the arsonist left town before he could be convicted. Then she remembered a conversation with Miriam about Miriam's grandfather several months earlier at the club, and the puzzle pieces began to look useful.

The next morning, Louise dressed in a blood-red gabardine dress and a pair of alligator pumps, planning to arrive at the auxiliary early so she could catch Miriam before the meeting began. At half past eleven, she was waiting in the chamber's lobby when she saw Miriam enter.

"Miriam, do you have a few minutes?" Louise called sweetly. Miriam glanced at her watch, then walked over to where Louise was sitting.

"Of course," Miriam said, taking a seat next to her. "How have you been?"

"Just dandy," Louise said, crossing her legs. "Emma's embroiled in her extracurricular activities, and of course, with my limited responsibilities at the auxiliary, I've had time to devote to other interests. More specifically, the restoration of the old sawmill." She saw the blood drain from Miriam's face and instantly knew her suspicions were on point.

"And how is that going?" Miriam said while taking a package of saltines from her purse.

"Upset stomach?" Louise said, watching Miriam pop a cracker in her mouth.

"Something like that," Miriam said as she chewed.

"I'm sorry to hear it. Too much shepherd's pie?"

"Louise, I don't really have time for your games. Not today," Miriam said, beginning to stand.

"Oh, this isn't a game. I think you'll want to hear what I have to say. I have reason to believe your connection to the Websters is a bit more scandalous than one would have expected," she said. "Who would have thought Iris capable of such a thing?" She shook her head slowly. "No wonder she never married. Ruined, I suppose."

Miriam sat up straighter and glared at Louise. "I do believe I have asked you before to stay out of my business," she said. "Honestly, I have no idea what you're up to, but it must stop. Now. I've done nothing to deserve your harassment."

Louise smiled broadly. "And that, dear Miriam, is where you are dead wrong. I believe you should resign your presidency immediately–an office you never deserved, to be honest. I'm sure you wouldn't want people to know your grandfather, a common mill worker, got a young Iris Webster pregnant and had to leave town in disgrace. What would people say?" Louise said, leaning forward to rest her chin in her hands.

"I truly don't care what you do or say to me," Miriam said, glowering at Louise. "But please leave the Websters alone. They've been nothing but kind, and there's absolutely no reason to drag their name through the mud."

Louise uncrossed her legs, stood up, then looked down at Miriam, who had begun to perspire. "You've just confirmed my suspicions," she said with a satisfied grin. "Consider my offer or let the fireworks begin. See you inside."

Louise turned on her heel and headed for the meeting hall, thinking Miriam would cave to Louise's not-so-veiled threat. She looked over her shoulder to see Miriam nonchalantly eating her crackers, seemingly undisturbed by their conversation as she flipped through her auxiliary notebook. Louise clenched her fists and considered her next move.

After presiding over the auxiliary meeting, which ran longer than usual, Miriam stopped by Butler Automotive to surprise her husband with lunch. Fortunately, the service department was having a slow day, so she and George could enjoy a leisurely meal at the picnic table outside.

"How was the meeting?" George said, unwrapping his cheeseburger and taking a bite.

"Bitsy thinks we should establish a junior auxiliary for high-school girls. She believes it will help improve their chances of getting into better sororities in college, and of course, she wants to be in charge," she said, opening a sleeve of saltines.

"I guess we all have our priorities," George said, chuckling.

"Really, it's not a terrible idea. Bitsy has a real knack for marketing. Oh, you won't believe this," Miriam began, opening her container of tomato soup. "Louise ambushed me before the meeting. She found out about my grandfather and Iris, as if it was any of her business, and I so much as told her that. She's like a dog with a bone, George, and for the life of me, I don't understand why she wants to make trouble. But she threatened to expose Iris—and me, by association—if I don't resign the presidency. Can you believe it?"

"She's still sore about losing the election, honey. Do you really think she'd be foolish enough to risk her friendship with the sisters, not to mention her husband's legal practice, by doing that?"

"Hard to tell with her. I know she wields a lot of influence here—I knew that from the moment I met her. But I never thought she could be so vindictive or stoop to such a level as blackmail and, honestly, what did I do to deserve this? I can't help where I came from. It's as if I did something to her, of all things. I probably need to talk to Rose and Iris, get their take on how to handle this," she said, dipping a cracker into her soup. "Boy, this smells good." She brought the cup to her lips. "I need to check on them after I get home and maybe take a nap. They weren't at the meeting."

"Is that unusual?" George said through a mouthful of onion rings.

"In my experience, yes," Miriam said. "Hopefully, they just forgot, though that's not likely either."

"I wouldn't worry too much, honey. At their age, they've earned the right to do whatever they want, whenever they want," George said, grinning. "Aren't you excited about telling them our news?!"

"You have no idea. I hope I can hold out until dinner on Friday!"

"If you want to tell them today, I completely understand," he said, reaching over to wipe a drop of soup from her blouse.

"I'd rather you be there, but we'll see how it goes," she said. After finishing their lunches, Miriam gave him a quick hug, then drove home sleepily, ready for an afternoon nap.

By the time she reached their house, a gentle rain had begun to fall. Perfect, Miriam thought happily as she changed into a T-shirt and a pair of George's sweatpants. She curled up on the couch with her quilt and the *Ladies' Home Journal*, but she fell into a deep slumber before getting through the first article. She awoke to the sound of someone rapping loudly on the door. Looking at her watch, she was shocked to see she had been asleep for nearly two hours. Stretching, she stood and opened the door to find Jasper on her porch.

"Please, do come in," Miriam said, unlatching the screen door. He solemnly shook his head. Miriam furrowed her brow. "What's wrong?" Her stomach began to churn.

"Come with me," Jasper said quietly, much to Miriam's surprise. She had never heard him utter a single word, which was a shame as he had the most mellifluous voice.

"Come with you where?" Miriam said as her legs began to tremble.

"Come with me. Now, please," he said, folding his hands together as if in prayer.

"Let me put on some shoes and grab my purse. And a sweater," she said before hastily retreating into the living room. A minute later, she was ready to go. She followed him to the Lincoln, electing to sit in the passenger seat beside him. Before pulling out of the drive, he reached into the glove box to retrieve an amethyst the size of a pebble, which he placed in her hand before pantomiming his instruction to hold it over her heart.

"Where are we going?" she said as he drove past the Websters' mansion, then headed away from the property. His eyes remained focused on the road, so Miriam asked if she could turn on the radio—anything to distract her from the panic rapidly consuming her. He nodded, so she found a classical music station playing a series of piano concertos. As they passed the Chamber of Commerce—located in the center of town—she tried to figure out where he was taking her and, more importantly, why. A few minutes later, he turned right, and as they approached St. David's Hospital, her heart lurched to her throat.

"Oh no," she said, her eyes widening in fear. She looked anxiously at Jasper, who brought his fist back to his heart. He parked in one of the spaces dedicated to the emergency room, then opened his umbrella and walked to her side to help her from the sedan. They walked briskly through the

sliding doors, and she was immediately assaulted by the sounds and smells of tragedy unique to hospital settings... a setting she remembered all too well. Still clutching the crystal, Miriam followed him to a room just outside of the nurses' station, silently praying for God to give her strength. When he opened the door, Miriam gasped at the scene before her. Rose was propped up in bed, greenish gray and expressionless, and connected to several machines and IV drips. Miriam felt as if she was replaying the scene with her grandfather, just a year ago. *I can't do this again.* Iris was seated next to Rose, holding her sister's hand. When Iris looked up to see Miriam, she stood and smiled.

"Thank God you're here," she said, exhaling, then reached out to give Miriam a hug. It may have been her imagination, but Miriam thought Iris seemed shorter and frailer than the last time they saw each other. "And thank you, Jasper."

Miriam moved to the side of the bed and leaned down to kiss Rose on the cheek, who blinked her eyes rapidly in response. "What happened?" she said, taking Rose's hand.

"I thought she just fainted," Iris said. "We were getting ready for the meeting, and I heard a loud thud, then I found her on the floor. Dr. Hawkins came quickly and said we needed an ambulance. It seems she had a stroke." She ran her bony hand through her short silver hair.

"Dear Lord," Miriam said as her eyes filled with tears. She looked at the monitors, though she had no idea what the numbers meant, even after all the time she spent in the hospital with her grandfather.

"Is there anything I can get for you?" she asked Iris. "Have you eaten today?"

Iris shook her head. "I'm not hungry," she mumbled, staring at her sister. "She can't speak, Miriam, and she's lost the ability to move her right extremities. I don't know what I'll do without her endless nattering." She dabbed her teary eyes with her sleeve. "It's true what they say, you know. The things that annoy you most about someone are the very things you miss most when they're gone."

Miriam walked to Iris's chair and knelt to look her in the eye. "She's not gone, Iris," she said softly. "You can't give up hope." She looked over at Jasper, who was standing by the door, his head lowered in what Miriam imagined was prayer. Distractedly, Iris patted Miriam's shoulder.

"Tell me something positive," Iris said as Jasper moved a chair beside her, silently inviting Miriam to take a seat. "How was the meeting today?"

Miriam considered telling her about Louise, then realized it would only serve to further upset her already distressed grandmother. "Same as always," she said, slipping the amethyst into her pocket. "You didn't miss much. This isn't the way I had planned to tell you, but I do have some news." She took Iris's hand and smiled shyly.

"Let me guess. George got promoted again?" Miriam shook her head. "No, let me try again. You got promoted?"

"In a manner of speaking. You are going to be a great-grandmother!" she said. Jasper lifted his hands toward the ceiling as Iris stared at Miriam, fresh tears welling in her eyes.

"It's a miracle!" she said, reaching for Rose's hand. "Did you hear that, sister? This means you are going to be a great-great-auntie! Oh, Miriam, we couldn't have asked for a greater blessing. I'm so happy for you and George. Tell me, when are you due?"

Miriam beamed at her grandmother, whose coloring looked slightly improved. "I haven't seen a doctor yet, but by my calculations, sometime next June," she said softly.

"That gives us plenty of time to prepare," Iris said, turning her attention back to Rose, who had begun to cry. "Isn't this exciting, sister?" Rose weakly held up her left thumb, then closed her eyes. Iris wiped the tears from her sister's cheeks.

"Are you hoping for a boy or a girl?" Iris said.

"I haven't given it any thought. Really, it doesn't matter to us as long as the baby is healthy."

"We have Jasper to help with that, right?" Iris said. Jasper clasped his hands together and bowed.

Miriam was about to tell Iris her plans for a baby quilt when the monitors started flashing wildly, setting off an alarm. "What's happening?" Miriam shouted as a nurse rushed into the room. Iris sat frozen as the nurse yelled for a doctor.

"Code blue! Code blue!" the nurse hollered before two white coats rushed in.

"Please, give us room," she ordered Miriam and Iris, who quickly rose from their chairs. They stared at Rose, whose face had gone slack.

"Paddles!" the first doctor ordered as the nurse rolled the defibrillator to the side of Rose's bed. Iris grasped Miriam's arm in a death grip. The doctor placed the paddles on Rose's chest. "One, two, three... clear!" he said, watching the cardiac monitor. Rose's heart did not respond. He reapplied the paddles and tried again as they watched the flat line buzzing across the screen. A second doctor took the paddles and ordered the nurse to increase the voltage.

"One, two, three... clear!" he repeated, then slowly shook his head before looking at his watch. "Time of death, four twenty-seven." Taking off his glasses, he looked at Iris, who had slumped to her knees, then at Miriam, who had begun sobbing into her hands. "I'm so very sorry. May your memories give you peace. Would you like me to call for the chaplain?"

Iris shook her head, then stood up and shuffled unsteadily to Rose's side. "It wasn't supposed to be like this," she whispered, leaning down to kiss Rose's cheek. "You promised me, Rose, you'd never leave me. Remember? Back in Kentucky, at the convent, you swore I'd never be alone. What am I going to do without you?" She sobbed, laying her head on Rose's lap while holding her hand.

Miriam began rubbing Iris's back. "She was a great lady, in every possible way," she said softly. "The world won't be the same without her. But, Iris, you have us. Forever." She reflexively covered her abdomen with her free hand.

Iris's shoulders continued shaking as she cried, holding on to her sister as if willing her back to life. "Would you like a moment alone with her?" Miriam said, blowing her nose. Iris silently shook her head. She looked across the room at Jasper, who was using his scarf to dry his tears. Quietly, he bowed, then left the room.

"Goodbye, my brilliant, beautiful sister," Iris said, her voice breaking. "You always were my strength, whether you knew it or not. We will be together someday. May you bask in God's eternal love until I get there."

Slowly, Iris stood up as Miriam came to her side. Iris threw her arms around Miriam and burrowed her face in Miriam's hair.

"We'll get through this," Miriam whispered, looking over Iris's shoulder at her great aunt. "Thank you, Aunt Rose, for the precious gift of your love and acceptance."

She slowly pulled away from Iris's embrace then put her hand on Rose's leg. "Goodbye," she murmured, wiping another tear from her cheek. "For now."

Miriam wasn't sure how to help Iris, but she silently vowed to do everything she could to fill the void left by Rose's passing. Taking Iris's hand, she carefully led her from the room to join Jasper in the hallway. Together, they left the hospital and remained silent over the course of the drive back to Webster House.

"Miriam?" Iris said, removing her sunglasses as Jasper pulled onto their drive. "Would you stay with me tonight? And George, of course." She gave Miriam an imploring look.

"We would do anything for you," Miriam said.

"You can count on it."

"I am," Iris said softly. "You are all I have left."

Pearl was making blueberry pancakes for Emma and Clifton when Louise entered the breakfast room. "Sit up straight," she said to her daughter, tugging on Emma's ponytail as she walked past her chair.

"Good morning to you too," Emma snarled, glaring at her mother.

"I can see someone woke up on the wrong side of the bed," Louise said, sitting down and putting her napkin in her lap. "Clif, how did you sleep?"

"Wonderfully well. Nothing like a good thunderstorm for a peaceful night's rest. Thanks, Pearl," he said as Pearl set down his plate before serving Emma. "What's on your agenda for the day?"

Despite her repeated requests that he not feed her precious German shepherds table scraps, he gave each of them an entire piece of bacon. She elected to let this transgression pass for the moment. Instead, Louise scooped a piece of grapefruit into her mouth, then winced. "Pearl, honey, would you bring me some Sweet'N Low? This grapefruit is terribly tart." She put down her spoon. "To answer your question, I don't have anything planned, surprisingly. I may see about getting a facial, then possibly go shopping. Can you believe Christmas is just over two months away?"

"Have you ever thought about getting a job?" Emma said, drenching her pancakes with syrup.

"Why on earth would I do that?" Louise said, raising her eyebrows.

"Well, you have a degree in English," Emma said. "I'm sure you could be a teacher or something."

"Again, what would be the point?" Louise looked at her husband, who was absorbed in the sports page.

"To be useful, maybe?" Emma said, giving her mother a snide look.

"Your mother is very useful, Em," Clifton said over the newspaper. "She's done more for this community than almost anyone else I know." He smiled at Louise, folded the newspaper, and scooted away from the table.

"Pearl, these pancakes were incredible, but I can't eat another bite," he said, bringing his half-empty plate to the counter. "I'll see you girls tomorrow. I'm in court all day and again in the morning, so I'm going to stay in Richmond tonight." He rose from his chair, then kissed Emma on the top of her head and Louise on her cheek. *He's been spending more and more nights in Richmond,* Louise thought idly, then tried to banish the suspicions from her mind.

After hearing Clifton close the front door, Louise studied her daughter's sullen expression. "Really, Emma, I'm getting tired of your poor attitude," she said, eating another bite of grapefruit. "Believe it or not, I'm not your enemy."

"You could have fooled me," Emma muttered, stabbing at her pancakes.

"Please hurry up and finish your breakfast. You don't want to be late for school," Louise said as she finished her coffee, then jumped when the phone rang in the kitchen. "Who in the world?" She looked at her watch; it was only seven thirty. She heard Pearl speaking softly but couldn't make out what she was saying. A few minutes later, Pearl came to the table with a distressed look on her face.

"What's the matter?" Louise said, placing her napkin

on the table.

"My friend Tonya works at the hospital," she said. "That was her just now. Seems Miss Rose Webster passed yesterday." She began chewing her bottom lip as Louise gasped.

"No!" Emma yelled, screeching her chair backwards. Louise stood abruptly as her daughter began to cry; she knew Emma had become attached to the older sister after she had spent the afternoon with the Websters. On more than one occasion, she had heard Emma on the phone with them, nattering on about her music and sometimes, God forbid, even playing her guitar for them. But Louise had bigger concerns at the moment.

"What happened?!" Louise said as adrenalin began coursing through her system.

"Alls I know is she came to the emergency room, and a few hours later, she was gone," Pearl said. "I'm so sorry, Miz Louise. I know you cared for her. Miss Emma, you okay?"

Emma had put her head in her hands, her shoulders trembling as she cried. Pearl walked to her side and placed her hand on Emma's arm. "You gotta believe she's in a much better place, darlin'," she said.

"She was the only one who ever showed interest in my music," Emma wailed. "I kept meaning to take my guitar over and play for them, like they suggested, and I just... I just, I never did because I thought you'd tell me I couldn't. I thought I would do it over the holidays and now..." Her voice gave way to her sobs.

"Emma, I know you're upset, but first, please don't make this about me, and second, I really need you to get ready for school," Louise said, fighting back her own emotions.

"I'm staying home," Emma mumbled.

"Is that really a good idea? You have cheerleading practice this afternoon," Louise said impatiently.

"Are you joking, Mom? I didn't know Rose or Iris that long, but unlike you," she yelled, pointing her finger at Louise,

"they got me, you know? Rose, she listened to me. She asked me how I felt about things. What I thought. What I wanted. Through our conversations, I swear they got to know me better than you ever will! Don't you ever consider my feelings?!" Emma yelled shrilly. Louise gave Pearl an anxious look, confused by what to do. Pearl closed her eyes and nodded while staying at Emma's side.

"Fine. Stay at home," Louise said. "But I need to change clothes. I'm going to pay Iris a visit."

"I may be out of line, but don't you think you should give Miss Iris some time?" Pearl said.

Momentarily perturbed by Pearl's unsolicited suggestion, Louise turned and walked out of the room. She thought she heard Emma say, "What about me?" but she knew Pearl would take care of her.

An hour later, Louise pulled onto the Websters' tree-lined drive, narrowly avoiding a gaggle of geese pecking at the gravel. She parked under the porte cochère, then knocked on the side door that led directly into the solarium. Smoothing the front of her black silk dress, she waited for someone to answer. A moment later, she stepped back as Miriam—dressed in a fuzzy pink bathrobe—answered the door.

"Hello, Louise. I wish you had called first, but this isn't a good time for a visit," Miriam said.

As if she owns the place. "What are you doing here?" Louise asked, scowling as she removed her black kidskin gloves. "And why are you wearing your robe?"

"I don't owe you an explanation, Louise," Miriam said, placing her hands on her broad hips. Louise stepped forward, brushing past Miriam to barge into the house.

"Where is she?" she said, spinning around to glare at Miriam. "We got a call this morning, about Rose. I'm here to pay Iris my respects."

"I'm happy to convey the message, but you really should

come back another time," Miriam said while still holding the door open.

"I don't have to listen to you," Louise said, then walked through the solarium with Miriam fast on her heels.

"If you're going to be this way, fine," Miriam said. "She's in the parlor with Jasper."

Louise strode down the hall to the French doors leading to the parlor, Miriam right behind her. When she entered the room, she saw Iris and Jasper sitting with their eyes closed in the lotus position atop two Turkish poufs. "Iris!" Louise said, rushing to her side. Her eyes fluttered open, and her expression morphed from relaxation to annoyance.

"I told her it wasn't a good time for a visit," Miriam said, "but she wouldn't listen."

Louise clenched her fists tightly, digging her nails into her palms. "I came as soon as I heard the tragic news," she said, sitting down in the armchair closest to Iris. "I'm so terribly sorry for your loss, Iris. We all loved Rose." She wondered why Iris was staring at her so coldly.

"Thank you, Louise," Iris said flatly. "It was a great shock to all of us." Jasper rose from his position and poured Iris a glass of tea without offering one to Louise.

"I'm here to help with anything you need," Louise said.

"That's very nice of you, but I have Miriam," Iris said, looking at Miriam with a kind smile.

"You're making a mistake if you believe you can trust her. All she cares about is your money. I won't stand by and let her take advantage of you!" she said. "Especially now."

Iris unfolded herself, stood up, and walked gingerly to join Miriam on the couch. She gazed at Louise, her tired eyes now gleaming like stainless steel. "I don't believe your grandmother—nor your mother, for that matter—would be terribly pleased with your behavior, especially toward Miriam. It's beneath you, Louise," she said. "And if you're not careful, your

bitterness will age you faster than the sun."

Louise tilted her head, reflecting on Iris's disparaging comment. "I have to wonder what my grandmother thought of your behavior, Iris. Did she know about your dalliance with Russell Benson?" She watched Iris closely for a reaction and was surprised to see Iris roar with laughter. *Has she gone quite mad?* Louise wondered as her eyes widened.

"Dear Louise, you must think yourself so clever. While it should surprise me that you've gone digging around in my personal life, it doesn't, sadly. You've always wanted to have the upper hand over everyone, which may indeed be why you failed in your bid for auxiliary president. And as for your grandmother, I have plenty of stories I could share, but my sense of decorum prevents me from sinking to such shallow depths," Iris said.

Louise began ripping at one of her cuticles. "I think you've misread me, Iris. I've only tried to uphold Grandmother Nora's standards and traditions since, clearly, my mother did not choose to," she said, lifting her chin. "Propriety was very important to Grandmother, as it is to me."

Iris set down her glass, then peered at Louise as though she was a strange specimen under a microscope. "What you seem to be missing is some semblance of empathy, Louise. I encourage you to reflect upon that, dear," she said. "I would have thought if you had learned nothing else from Rose, it would have been such."

Louise recoiled at the obvious insult, then her emotions became unleashed. "Was it before or after your father asked my grandfather to blackmail Russell Benson to leave town that you learned about humility?" Louise said, leaning forward to stare Iris directly in the eye.

Iris shook her head slowly, licking her lips. "Of all the days to have this conversation, the first day after losing my sister and best friend is definitely not the one. If you'll excuse me, I have a funeral to plan," she said, looking at Miriam, "with my granddaughter, here."

"Your granddaughter? But how? What?"

"I'm not inclined to go into any details. Besides, I imagine you'll make them up anyway," Iris said with a smile.

Louise's head was spinning. "The child you gave up? Did Russell Benson somehow...? But then..." She couldn't process all of it, but she pulled herself together for the important part. "Well, aren't you concerned about what people will say?" she said, looking from Iris to Miriam for signs of discomfort.

Iris's face broke into a radiant smile. "Truly, I couldn't give less of a damn what anyone here says about me. It doesn't concern me in the least. But what does concern me is Miriam, and one day she will be an exceptionally wealthy woman." Lifting her chin, she gave Louise a triumphant look.

As Louise tried to figure out her next move, Iris stood up. "Jasper, please show Mrs. Caldwell to the door. Thank you for stopping by, but next time, call first."

Louise looked at Miriam, who remained on the couch. "I had no idea," Louise said, attempting to restore some connection. Miriam gave her a wry smile but said nothing.

"Again, I'm sorry for your loss. Both of you, I suppose," she said, then followed Jasper to the solarium.

Before opening the door, Jasper looked at Louise with an expression she did not recognize. "'Ambition is like love, impatient both of delays and rivals,'" he said in a low, soft voice, then bowed. She got in her car as he stood in the doorway, his black caftan blowing softly in the breeze. As she made her way down the long drive, she shuddered as she realized he had peered directly into her psyche.

Iris could not have anticipated how many people would crowd into St. Edward's for her sister's funeral, but every pew was full when Miriam and George escorted her to their dedicated seats. Sitting to the side of the pulpit, Jasper played his sitar softly as people murmured amongst themselves, awaiting the service. Iris thought herself emotionally prepared, but the finality of Rose's passing had not registered until she saw Rose's mahogany casket, beautifully draped with a blanket she had woven just months before her stroke. Its vibrant colors—turquoise, tangerine, crimson, sapphire, and violet—were unabashedly alive amidst the sea of black engulfing the chapel, *much like Rose herself*, Iris thought, smiling. And the flowers... what a wonderful job Miriam had done of choosing the bold and bright arrangements instead of the ubiquitous wreaths of white funeral lilies.

She reached for Miriam's hand as the priest walked to the pulpit, then invited the guests to stand as he read the Liturgy of the Word. After everyone was seated and the choir had sung "Lord of All Hopefulness," the priest invited Iris to eulogize her sister. Taking a deep breath, Iris squeezed Miriam's hand, then slowly ascended the steps, wishing she had written something formal. She gazed at the more affluent members of the Stuarts Landing community who had amassed for the service, wondering if they were there more out of curiosity than celebration of her sister's life. Then her eyes wandered to Jasper, seated next to Miriam in the front row. He put one hand on his heart, holding the other aloft as if blessing her, and smiled. She nodded, adjusted the microphone to accommodate her small stature, momentarily closed her eyes, then began to speak.

"Good afternoon and thank you for joining me in a celebration of Rose Webster's life. One cannot adequately prepare for the loss of a loved one, so I must ask forgiveness if my words are disjointed. My sister was my best friend from the time I was born. With her at my side, I knew I would never have to walk this life alone. Rose found beauty everywhere she looked, taking time to see what others could not. She cultivated people as if they were tender seedlings, always urging them to grow to their fullest height. She was my greatest protector and my fiercest advocate, and while she could have had so much more—namely, a family of her own—she dedicated her life to helping me weather and recover from my own personal storm."

Iris paused to press her handkerchief to her mouth as a tempest of emotions threatened to engulf her whole. She took another deep breath, gathered her composure, and grasped the sides of the pulpit.

"I know many of you thought us eccentric, Rose and me. But that's what made our lives so delightful, really. As a very young woman, I had become a shadow of myself, but it was Rose who taught me what others think of us is never as important as what we think of ourselves. Neither of us wanted to exist in a gilded cage. No. She taught me that life should be gulped, not sipped, and so we did. Traveling, continually learning new things, embracing experiences we were fortunate to have—could we have done all that had we been constrained by public opinion? Maybe, maybe not," she said, her eyes focused on Miriam.

"I had always hoped I would be the one to pass first, since I couldn't imagine my life without Rose. But Fate has a mind of

her own. While I wish Rose had had more time to get to know her great-niece, my granddaughter, she was as overjoyed as I to see a tragic story find a happy ending."

She paused to allow her words to resonate as the congregation began whispering amongst themselves. She rested her eyes on her remaining family and smiled.

"I'm at an age where gossip no longer concerns me, as if it ever really did. People tend to worry about their image, yet we're all human beings, after all, fragile and flawed, no matter our circumstances." She spotted Louise and stared at her as she continued.

"There was a time when loving the wrong person was unforgivable, yet the heart wants what it wants. My love resulted in a baby I could not keep, and during that agonizing point in my life, it was Rose who kept me steady. Without her love and support, I do believe my spirit would have died. She kept me alive. And I credit her for inviting Miriam Llewelyn and her husband to live on our property. Had she not done so, we never would have learned Miriam was my granddaughter," she said, pausing as people audibly gasped.

"If you wish to honor Rose's life, I only ask that you look deeper into yourselves and into others, giving grace instead of judgment, kindness instead of cattiness, and peace instead of posturing. Finally, each and every one of us has the ability to commit our talents, gifts, and blessings toward the betterment of our community. We can all be forces of positive change, even if others may resist. Like a pebble tossed into a pond, our actions can create a positive ripple effect that continues to grow. We only have to be pure of heart."

Taking a pause, she looked at Miriam and placed her right hand to her chest, then smiled and nodded. "Rose," she said, walking to the casket and lightly touching the blanket, "you were a gift to this world and to me, and you will never be forgotten."

As Iris descended the steps, the choir began to sing "Ode to Joy." Miriam and George rose to embrace her as she wiped her eyes, looking out over the crowd, who seemed to be radiating expressions of admiration. All but Louise, who was whispering in Clifton's ear as Emma sobbed, seemingly ignored. Iris sat down and bowed her head, saying a silent prayer asking the Lord's forgiveness before thanking Him for the blessing of family.

"That was beautiful," Miriam said softly, handing Iris a hard caramel. Iris smiled as she popped the candy into her mouth–Rose's favorite.

"As are you," Iris said softly. "I guess the cat's out of the bag now, huh?"

"I could not be prouder," Miriam said, putting her hand on her abdomen.

Once the priest had given the benediction, Iris proceeded solemnly with Miriam, George, and Jasper behind the pall-bearers, walking the casket to the hearse waiting outside.

"With every end comes a new beginning," Iris said as Jasper held open the limousine door. "Let this be ours."

With the tap of her gavel, Miriam called the auxiliary meeting to order. Two weeks had passed since Rose's funeral, and to the best of her knowledge, any gossip about Iris and their relationship had abated. And while she had felt awkward joining Iris for the reading of Rose's will, she was stunned to learn the exorbitant value of her estate, bequeathed mostly to Iris but with generous six-figure sums earmarked for Jasper and Miriam. Never had she enjoyed the sense of social and financial security that wealth provides, but she now understood why the Websters were unconcerned about how they were viewed. The newfound confidence felt liberating, and Miriam intended to make the most of it.

After giving her report on the status of the cookbook sales—which had already well-exceeded their goal, thanks to her carefully negotiated points of sale at the country club and The Pig—Miriam exercised her personal privilege as president to introduce an item not included in the meeting agenda.

"Ladies, I know we are all still grieving the loss of Rose Webster. Her contributions to the auxiliary for nearly fifty years are too numerous to list, but she left an indelible mark on this organization," she said, choking back tears. "For this reason, I would like to introduce a motion to rename the auxiliary meeting hall and ballroom to become the 'Rose Webster Center.' I will now open the floor to discussion."

She had not mentioned her idea to Iris in advance. Though she was not in attendance, Miriam hoped her fellow members would consider what such a dedication would mean to Iris and, by association, to Miriam. True to character, Bitsy was the first to raise her hand.

"I think that's a marvelous idea, Miriam, and such a lovely tribute. Might I ask if we could take the opportunity, should we vote in favor of your motion, to redecorate both areas? They look pretty dated, and I have a fabulous interior designer who would jump at the chance," she said. "Wouldn't that be fun?"

Miriam tapped her pencil on the podium as she considered Bitsy's suggestion. "While I agree the facilities could use a facelift, I'm not sure we have the funds at this time."

"Well, what if we reallocated the money we raised from the fashion show and the cookbook sales?" Bitsy said. With recent events, Miriam had all but forgotten about that project, and with the mill's indirect connection to Iris, her feelings were mixed.

"I don't think that would work since we already promised the funds to the historical society, but we can keep thinking," Miriam said. "Are there any other comments?"

She smiled patiently as Louise rose from her chair. "I understand what you're trying to accomplish, Miriam, I really do," Louise said as she stood rigidly. "And while I believe it to be a thoughtful gesture, I strongly object. You, and many others in this room, may not be aware, but it was my grandmother, Nora Fulton Winston, who had the idea to start this auxiliary some sixty-seven years ago. Well, along with Delilah Webster, I should say. But if anyone's name deserves to be on plaques on our doors, it should rightfully be Nora's. I'm sure you all would agree." She looked around the room for nods of agreement, but the women remained unusually quiet and still.

Bitsy raised her hand once again. "Mrs. Butler?" Miriam said, giving Bitsy the floor.

"With all due respect, Louise, what year did your grandmother die?" she said sweetly.

"I don't see what that has to do with anything," Louise said, "but if you must know, it was in 1962."

Bitsy's face broke into a smile. "And what year was the auxiliary founded? Around 1913?" Louise nodded.

"So, if my math is right, she served the auxiliary for forty-nine years?" Bitsy asked.

"Well, she took inactive status a few years before that, due to her illness," Louise said.

"That would mean she was active for about forty-seven years," Bitsy said. "Fewer than Rose's fifty years, right?"

"What's your point, Bitsy?" Louise said.

"I just think if we're going to be fair, we should name our facilities after our longest-tenured member. That's all," she said, sitting back down.

"Well, I disagree," Louise said.

"Of course you do," Bitsy fired back as other members began tittering.

Miriam rapped the gavel on the podium. "Ladies, let's return to order. Does anyone else have any comments to share?"

Louise raised her hand, then stood. "I propose we amend your motion to call for a vote about the general concept of naming our facilities after someone. If the membership agrees this is important, we then can submit nominations for whom they should be named," she said.

While she knew Louise was being deliberately difficult, she also could understand the logic of her proposal. More importantly, Miriam was committed to keeping this discussion from becoming personal, as everything else had been with Louise lately.

"I agree, Mrs. Caldwell, so let the record show I am amending my motion to call for a general vote about dedicating our meeting hall and ballroom to a longstanding member of this auxiliary. Do I have a second?"

Gigi raised her hand. "I second the motion."

"Thank you. All in favor of the motion, please raise your hand," Miriam said, then quickly counted the hands. "All against?" Clearly, the majority agreed with the idea.

"The motion passes," Miriam said. "Beyond Rose Webster and Nora Winston, are there any other names to be nominated?" she said. She took a sip of V8 juice–her first real craving–as she waited for anyone to raise their hand. "Hearing no other nominations, I will now call for a vote as to whom you all wish to memorialize on the doors to our facilities. All in favor of Mrs. Winston, please raise your hand."

Predictably, Louise's hand shot up first, followed by four others. She looked around the room, glaring at the women who were not in agreement, then folded her arms petulantly.

"All in favor of Miss Rose Webster?" Thirty hands shot into the air.

"By majority vote, the facilities will be renamed to honor Miss Rose Webster," she said, incapable of suppressing her enthusiasm. She fully expected Louise to storm out of the meeting hall, yet Louise remained in her place, though visibly upset.

After completing the requisite committee reports, Miriam adjourned the meeting, eager to dig into the lunchtime spread waiting on the banquet table. Unfortunately, Louise accosted her as she was making her way to the sandwiches. "I know you think you're something special now that you've come into some money, but don't believe for a minute you suddenly have status," Louise said. "You'll always be the Miriam who worked as a cashier at The Pig." She cast a judgmental look at Miriam's homemade outfit.

"I still work there," Miriam said. "There's no shame in making an honest living. But there is shame in putting other people down. Your bitterness is beyond my understanding, but I can only pray you find your way before you alienate

everyone in Stuarts Landing."

Louise squinted her eyes and cocked her head. "So, now you think you're the arbiter of other people's behavior because you've inherited some money? Bless your heart, Miriam. You have so much to learn. Sadly, you won't get that from me," she said.

"I don't expect to, Louise. But this is now twice in one conversation that you've mentioned my money," Miriam said. "I'm not sure how you know, but that doesn't matter. I've never been driven by a desire for wealth. From what I can see, it doesn't guarantee happiness."

"You've never cared because you've never had any," Louise said.

"That's true, but I've been rich in so many other ways," Miriam said, smiling. "Now if you will excuse me, I would like to get a bite to eat."

She had made it to the sandwich tray when Bitsy came to her side. "Ding dong, the witch is dead. I shouldn't say it because I'm really trying to be a different person than who I am around Louise, but I'm glad someone has finally managed to put her in her place. She's gone unchecked far too long around here." She let out an audible sigh. "That was brilliant, Miriam."

While she had intuited for some time that Bitsy held conflicting feelings for Louise, it saddened her to think Louise's failures gave Bitsy pleasure. She supposed their relationship was so steeped in history it was all but impossible for an outsider to understand.

Interrupting Miriam's thoughts, Bitsy changed the subject. "Now, when are you going to talk to Bobby about a new car?"

No longer surprised by Bitsy's brashness, she merely chuckled. "We'll have to see," she said. "Thank you, by the way, for standing up for Rose. I'm sure she's smiling, and

I know Iris will be thrilled."

"It was my pleasure," Bitsy said. "Louise is running out of Winston cards to play, it would seem. My hope for her, as it's been for years, is that she finds a way to lose the shackles of perceived expectation—how she believes things should be—and just, I don't know, figures out who she really is. I'm not sure she knows. Now, when are we going to lunch? I already have some thoughts about a dedication ceremony. After we redecorate," she added with a wink.

44

Having been born and raised in Stuarts Landing, Louise never experienced being an outsider, not even as a freshman at the University of Virginia. Her family names–both Fulton and Winston–represented a dual birthright that ensured smooth entrance and easy acceptance everywhere she went, at least in that part of the state. She had won every election she entered, present circumstance excepted, graduated at the top of her high school class, served as the president of her sorority, and nabbed one of the most eligible fraternity boys on campus as her own. Being in the lead was as natural to Louise as breathing, and she never imagined her perpetually rising star could someday descend. Out of nowhere, Miriam Llewelyn came to town, and in a nanosecond, Louise began to lose her social luster, like the ring of gold on a vintage porcelain plate. With Miriam came a shift in auxiliary dynamics such that Louise no longer felt she belonged. An outsider in the very world she had depended on to keep from descending into the same lonely spiral as her mother had. She didn't yet understand how it had happened, and she had no idea what she could do to resolve it.

Wearing her varsity cheerleader sweater over a faded sorority T-shirt and sweatpants, she was sitting at the dining room table with a martini, poring over her scrapbooks, when she heard Clifton and Emma come through the front door. Wordlessly, Emma sprinted upstairs to her bedroom while Clifton joined Louise at the table.

"Feeling nostalgic?" he said, loosening his tie. "You must have been rifling through the attic." Louise stiffened at the last comment, feeling guilty she had not shared her findings about Iris from her previous trip to their third floor. With Iris's revelation at Rose's funeral, Louise saw no further need to discuss it.

"I suppose I am, in a way," she said, sipping her drink as Pearl placed Clifton's Scotch on the table. "I just don't understand why things must keep changing. I mean, that's part of the reason I insisted we stay here instead of moving into Richmond proper. But Stuarts Landing just isn't the same," she said, rubbing her chin.

"We're about to head into a new decade, Lu. Things are changing all over the world," he said. "I don't think progress is necessarily a bad thing, you know? If we led our lives exactly the same way, year after year, don't you think we'd be bored once we reach our golden years?" He chuckled as Louise considered his question, then shook her head.

"I like things just the way they were, so no, I don't think I'd be bored at all," she said.

"What's really bothering you?" he asked, reaching for her hand, which she placed in her lap instead.

"Not what. Who. Miriam Llewelyn," she said.

"Are you still upset about the election? That was more than three months ago, Lu. There's always next year."

"Yes, I'm still upset and rightfully so. Today, she introduced the idea of naming the meeting room and ballroom after Rose. I objected, then presented my case for Grandmother Nora's name to grace our doors instead. I explained she was the founder and therefore deserved it. Then Ditsy Bitsy, that turncoat, dared to challenge me. Can you believe it? She said Rose had served the auxiliary longer and poof!" She slapped her palm on the table. "Most everyone voted for Rose."

"I can see why that would tick you off," Clifton said. "But

maybe consider that, other than you and the Websters, no one in the auxiliary really knew your grandmother, yet they all knew Rose."

Louise traced her finger over a photo taken of her and her mother in Paris a few years before she became ill. As Louise examined her mother's expression, she could see through more experienced eyes what she had not recognized at the time–a profound sadness even in one of the world's most enchanting cities. Louise wondered if, given recent events, she mirrored that same look. Thinking about what her mother's disregard for social expectations had done to her family, she felt a niggling thought beginning to claw inside her brain, explaining why Miriam had so triggered her visceral disdain toward the too-earnest newcomer. As quickly as the thought came to mind, she mentally brushed it aside.

"I'm thinking about resigning from the auxiliary," she said as Clifton's eyes widened in surprise. "I don't think there's anything left for me there, not now. Miriam has everyone wound around her chubby little finger, and she and I are definitely oil and water. I don't think I can work with her."

Clifton took a slow sip of his Scotch, then sat back and folded his hands behind his head. His expression changed to the attorney-about-to-give-advice look, one which usually meant she would not like what he had to say.

"I suppose that would be the easy way, but is it the right way, Lu? You've worked too long and too hard to just throw in the towel. Besides, Iris would be terribly disappointed," he said.

"I'm not so sure about that. Seems I'm on her bad side too," Louise said.

"I can't imagine Iris being upset with you for anything. She's known you since you were a baby."

"Well, that was before I cautioned them both about Miriam, saying she was only after their money, and then I reiterated that the day after Rose passed, when I paid Iris a visit," she said.

Clifton ran his hand through his hair as his face flushed. Through darkened eyes, he glared at her. "Please tell me you're not serious, Louise," he said, his voice nearly shaking with rage. "They are my oldest and most important clients!"

"I was trying to protect them, Clifton! We didn't know who Miriam was or what intentions she may have had. The Websters have always been like family to me," she said.

"Interestingly, they *are* family to Miriam. Honestly, if you had a concern, you really should have spoken to me about it first. I could have handled the conversation much more delicately than it sounds like you did," he said, raising his voice.

"You wouldn't have taken me seriously."

"I have wanted to say this for quite some time, Louise, and I don't mean to make you feel worse than you already do, but hear me. I believe it would be in your best interests... hell, the family's best interests, if you would pay more attention to our daughter than who's doing what with whom!" he yelled. "Whether you realize it or not, your actions reflect upon all of us. I haven't worried up until now that you don't comprehend this fact. Earlier, you were lamenting about why things need to change, but the truth is, Louise, you need to change before you lose everything." Abruptly, he stood up from his chair. "Please, do nothing further to damage your reputation or mine, as that would come at a profound cost."

"You wouldn't understand," Louise said, putting her head in her hands as he left the dining room. After indulging her self-pity for a few more minutes, she closed the scrapbooks and moved into the solarium with her martini. Staring out the windows at the rose garden, she contemplated her options for some form of redemption.

After changing clothes, Clifton came back downstairs and appeared more relaxed as he rejoined Louise. He had just

opened the latest issue of the *Virginia Bar Journal* when Louise cleared her throat. "I have an idea," she said, "but it will require a bit of an investment."

Clifton closed the magazine and looked at her coolly. "I can only imagine."

"You know how much my work at the historical society means to me, and I've done quite a bit of research on the old sawmill," she said. "We raised a decent amount of money with the fashion show and the cookbook to begin renovation, but a great deal more is needed before the township will likely get started. I was thinking we could pull money from the Winston Trust—say, a quarter of a million dollars—and give it to the township as an earmarked donation specifically for the project. What do you think?"

After taking a sip of Scotch, Clifton studied Louise, who was leaning forward with anticipation. "I'm afraid that's not possible," he said.

"Why not? I know the approximate value of the trust, and as its trustee, you can make it happen, Clif. Won't you even consider it?"

"It's not that. Stuarts Landing no longer holds the deed to the property," he said.

"Then who does?"

"When I met with the Webster sisters to revise their wills and the terms of their trust, Rose asked that I also draw up an offer to purchase the mill back from the township. The township accepted the offer, and shortly before Rose died, she specified in her Memorandum to Executor what should be done with the property upon her death," he said. Louise pulled her knees to her chest, hugging them as she tried to process what he was telling her.

"Okay, I'll bite," she said.

"Rose asked that the property be given to Miriam and George," he said.

"What?! Why would Rose do that?! And what are they even going to do with it? The Llewelyns don't have the money for renovations!"

"Well, Iris does," Clifton said. "I've probably said more than I should, but I wanted to save you from the embarrassment of finding out from someone else. If the historical society wishes to maintain their interest in the mill, then they and you will have to work directly with Miriam."

Louise called for Pearl to bring her another martini, then lay her head back on the chaise.

"We wanted the mill to be restored, then opened as a museum," she said. "Knowing what I found out, there's no way Miriam would allow it."

Clifton looked at her with a bewildered expression. "I'm not sure I want to know," he said.

"I found a letter in my grandfather's files in the attic from Theodore Webster, directing my grandfather to pay Russell Benson to leave town or else be accused of setting the mill on fire. He knew Russell and Iris had had premarital relations, and as we now know, she gave the baby up for adoption. If the mill was renovated, I imagine it would be a daily reminder to Iris of that dreadful part of her life. I don't think Miriam would do it," Louise said, realizing that, once again, her plans would be foiled by Miriam Llewelyn.

"Please tell me you didn't share this information with anyone," Clifton said in a deadly serious tone. Louise began twisting her wedding ring. "Louise?"

"Well, I did, actually," she said. "I told Iris and Miriam."

"Good Lord, Louise. Have you lost your mind?!"

"I simply thought they should know," she said, shrugging her shoulders. "And apparently, they did, so it wasn't a surprise." *Surely, he understands my motives were (mostly) for the good.*

"I don't believe you," Clifton said. "I think you dug around to find whatever dirt you could to get the better of Miriam,

whom you've now decided is your rival. What you don't seem to realize is how heartless this must have seemed to women who've only ever been kind to you. Miriam included, from what I can tell."

"I found mention of my grandfather's name in a newspaper story connecting him to the Websters, so I was curious. That's why I looked through his files."

"Again, I don't believe your grandfather was the subject of your interest. Your jealousy and, quite frankly, your unending need to be idolized will be your undoing, Louise, if it hasn't been already," he said, rising from the couch and moving toward the door.

"Where are you going?" Louise asked as her pulse quickened.

"I have to be in court early, so I'm going to spend the night in the Richmond apartment. Mostly, I need some space to think, Louise. I've put up with your political gamesmanship for a long time without saying anything. But this time, you've made it a point to deliberately hurt people. You've gone too far," he said before storming from the room.

A few minutes later, she heard the front door slam. Emma stomped into the solarium and glared at her mother. "What have you done now? I saw Daddy carrying an overnight bag. Again."

"It's none of your concern. Go get ready for dinner, please," she said, taking a healthy sip of her drink.

"I wish you could see yourself the way others do," Emma said. "I promise, you wouldn't like it."

"Back at you, kiddo," Louise retorted as Emma stomped out of the solarium.

Pearl approached Louise cautiously. "Ma'am, what you doin' ain't right. I've known you a long, long time and ain't never seen you so angry all the time," she said, her voice low with concern.

Louise studied her housekeeper's face while taking another drink of her martini. "When I want your advice, I'll ask for it, Pearl. In the meantime, please leave me to myself."

"Seems everyone else has," Pearl said softly before leaving the room, Louise's dogs closely on her heels.

Yet another betrayal, Louise thought as she listened to their nails clickety-clack on the marble tile in the kitchen. Her eyes brimmed with tears as she replayed the last hour in her mind, analyzing the words that could not be unsaid. Before she could stop herself, she hurled the Baccarat martini glass against the wall, shattering it into dangerously sharp pieces all over the beautiful Aubusson rug.

45

While Miriam had not realized she had been figuratively holding her breath over the course of her pregnancy, it was only because she had been overwhelmed with activity. At Iris's urging, she and George moved into Webster House, taking the previously unoccupied east wing of the home, which included its own living room should they desire more privacy. Miriam had invited Bitsy to orchestrate the auxiliary dedication ceremony honoring Rose, and her efforts were spectacular–Iris could not have been happier, even though she shed a few tears. The cookbook sales concluded with record profits, and the holiday season was an exhausting flurry of parties, none better than the small family celebration at Webster House. By the time Iris and Jasper sent out invitations for the Baby Llewelyn Shower, Miriam felt she could relax–at least until she went into labor.

She and George wanted to be surprised by their baby's gender, so they decided upon an oceanic theme for the nursery, appropriate for a boy or a girl. Iris opted to follow suit with her plans for the shower, so she instructed her caterer to create a cake resembling a sandcastle complete with fondant shells and starfish. She also ordered a wide assortment of hors d'oeuvres, including shrimp kabobs, crab cakes, mini lobster rolls, and tuna melt hand pies in puff pastry, all of which were arranged–along with several cold salads–on the dining table Iris had festively covered with beach towels.

Jasper had placed the crystal punchbowl full of Hawaiian Blue Punch on the buffet, which Iris decorated with armies of paper umbrellas. Shortly before their guests were due to arrive, Iris called Miriam and George into the solarium.

Dressed in a silk aqua caftan, five strands of pooka shells in varying lengths, and a pair of white leather sneakers upon which she had painted schools of tropical fish, Iris appeared every bit the picture of celebration.

"There you are!" she said as Miriam and George entered the room. Miriam was amused that George had dressed as a cruise captain but was delighted to see him so excited about the party. She tried not to feel like a big Beluga in her own seafoam dress, but she didn't let her self-consciousness spoil her mood.

"The house looks magical, Iris," Miriam said as George helped her onto the rattan settee, then sat next to her with his hand on her ripe belly. "And that cake—I've never seen anything so detailed!"

"Thank you, my dear. I only wish Rose could see it, but I know she'll be with us in spirit," Iris said. "I'm sure you will receive a bounty of lovely gifts today, yet selfishly, I wanted to give you the first. Jasper?" Her eyes twinkling with anticipation. A moment later, he came into the solarium carrying a large present wrapped in iridescent paper, at once gold, then shifting to various shades of blue and green. He propped it against the side of the settee, then bowed. As he began moving toward the door, Iris asked him to sit down.

"You're every bit a part of this family," Iris said, "and this is a special moment." He floated to the papasan chair next to Iris's and took a seat.

"It is my desire that my great-grandchild be sur-rounded not just by love but by beauty, which I believe is so important as the world becomes uglier. I hope my gift brings a lifetime of peace to the angel growing inside you.

Please, go ahead and open it!"

Miriam had not expected another gift from Iris, who had paid to install a saltwater fish tank in the nursery, already full of beautiful creatures mesmerizing to watch. George put the gift between them, holding it as Miriam carefully removed the wrapping. She blinked back tears as she gazed at the painting before her, a peaceful seascape resplendent in hues of lilac, gold, blue, and pale pink. Then she noticed the signature.

"Oh, my goodness!" she exclaimed, looking at Iris with an awed expression. "Are you kidding?" George wrapped his arm around her shoulders as she began to weep.

"When I saw it come up for auction, I simply had to acquire it for the baby," she said, clapping her hands gleefully. "Do you like it?"

"Are you actually asking me if I like an original Monet?" Miriam said, giggling as the tears dripped on her dress. "I'm blown away, quite honestly! Thank you, thank you! I'd leap up to hug you, but I'm afraid I'm not that flexible."

"Then I'll come to you," Iris said, rising from her chair and walking to Miriam before leaning down to embrace her. "There's nothing I wouldn't do for you both or this sweet baby." She placed her hand protectively on Miriam's stomach. Miriam stared at the painting, imagining what stories their child would see in it over the years.

"Jasper, George and I have been talking, and we'd like to ask you a serious question," Miriam said after carefully sliding the painting to George to prop against the settee. "You have been as much of a blessing to us as Iris and, of course, Rose. I know the breathing exercises you've taught me will come in handy during labor and well throughout my parenting journey." She caressed her abdomen. "And the meals you have prepared to keep me and the baby healthy, there are no words. Even George has commented how good he feels—his boss had warned him about sympathy weight gain, but he hasn't added an ounce." She laughed.

"Bobby was sure I'd be up by about twenty pounds." George chuckled. "He said he put on fifteen when Bitsy was pregnant with Debbie. Thank you, Jasper."

Jasper put his palms together and bowed in his seat.

"We want you to be a part of our child's life, which is why we're asking if you would agree to be Baby Llewelyn's godfather," Miriam said, clasping her hands together and grinning.

Iris reached over and took Jasper's hand, beaming. "This is exactly what I had hoped you would wish," she said to Miriam and George. "Though it may require he give up his vow of silence." Jasper's face broke into a smile.

"I speak when it is necessary," he said softly. "In this moment, it is necessary for me to humbly accept your most sacred invitation."

"Thank you," Miriam and George said in unison, then they all turned as they heard the door chimes.

"It's party time!" Iris said, rising with Jasper. George helped Miriam to her feet, then carefully picked up the painting to take to the nursery.

***

Miriam tried to mingle with her guests, but her lower back was aching, and her feet were painfully swollen, so she took her post in one of the armchairs in the parlor. George dutifully brought her a plate of hors d'oeuvres and a crystal tumbler full of water, then sat down to join her while Iris chatted with various auxiliary members.

"I cannot get over our good fortune, honey," she said. "Our family, this new little life inside of me, the love that surrounds us. And I was so surprised that Gloria and Roy even showed up! I didn't know if they'd attend since I had to quit my job at The Pig." She took a bite of the crab cake.

"My word, this is delicious!" She fed George the other half.

"Everyone adores you, Mim, but no one more than I," he said, kissing her shoulder.

"Did you see that Emma came? That was a shocker," she said, shaking her head. "It looks like she even brought a gift. Honestly, I don't know if she did it to defy her mother or if she just wanted an excuse to get out of the house, but it's lovely to see her."

"Did Iris invite Louise?" George said.

"She wasn't going to, but I asked that she do it as a favor to me. You know I don't hold grudges, but I suppose Louise does. Anyway, this is a wonderful party."

Their conversation was interrupted by Bitsy, who sat down on the red chaise with a glass of rum punch. "What a fabulous shower," she said, crossing her legs. "I'm so glad Louise isn't here to ruin it. Tell me, have you all considered names?"

Miriam looked at George and smiled. "We have, but of course we won't know for sure until the baby arrives," she said.

"Are you going natural? Please tell me 'No' because I assure you, it's brutal," Bitsy said. "When I was in labor with Deb..."

"I am so looking forward to sharing birth stories after our baby is born," Miriam said. "But for now, I'm already scared out of my mind. I'd love to hear all about your experience in a few months. We can compare notes." She bit into her lobster roll, then closed her eyes and said, "Mmmmm."

"How foolish of me," Bitsy said, recrossing her legs. "But all I can say is, you see how Debbie turned out. You'll be fine!"

Iris entered the parlor and walked to the mantel to gently tap the Tibetan gong, then took her seat across from Miriam and George. The catering company had arranged skirted chairs around the spacious room, more than enough to accommodate the thirty-plus people who had accepted the invitation. Jasper guided their guests from the dining room into the parlor, then stood by the credenza laden with gifts.

"Thank you all for coming today," Iris said as she stood. "If anyone had told me a year ago how drastically my life would change, I would have thought they had one hookah puff too many." The room erupted in laughter. "To have found my granddaughter and her husband, and to now be awaiting the arrival of my great-grandchild, well, it's an embarrassment of riches. Miriam," she said as her eyes became misty, "you have made my life and our entire community better in so many ways. I love you with all my heart. Now, let's open some presents!"

Over the next hour, Jasper handed Miriam and George each a gift, which they opened with delight and took time to enjoy. Precious little onesies, a veritable aquarium of plush fish and dolphins, luxurious blankets, a Tiffany piggy bank and silver spoon, an ocean-themed mobile, and so much more. Finally, only one gift remained, which Jasper handed Miriam, then placed his hand on his heart.

"This is from you?" Miriam asked. He smiled and bowed.

Miriam opened the carved wooden box to find inside an elaborate garland of flags, though she did not understand their significance. She looked at Iris. "Those are Tibetan prayer flags. They are used to promote peace, compassion, strength, and wisdom. Jasper, I can't think of a more perfect way to welcome a new life into this world," Iris said, beaming.

"Thank you, Jasper. You all have been so generous," Miriam said to their guests, taking George's hand. "We are humbled and so very grateful. I know we're where we are supposed to be—Stuarts Landing feels like family, thanks to all of you." She dabbed her eyes with her napkin. "Is everyone this emotional when they're pregnant?"

A chorus of women shouted, "Yes!" Miriam smiled, looking at Iris and wondering how she had felt, but she would wait to inquire.

As if reading Miriam's mind, Iris stood up. "I do believe our mother-to-be needs to rest," she said. "Thank you all for coming and being part of our joyous celebration." The guests rose from their chairs, lining up to give Miriam and George their best wishes. Miriam noticed Emma standing alone in the back of the room, holding a tote bag as she watched the guests slowly depart. Once everyone had left, she approached Miriam awkwardly.

"Well, hello there!" Miriam said, giving Emma a bright smile. "I do believe you're getting more beautiful by the day!"

Emma reached into the bag to remove a small package, which she then handed to Miriam. "I'm so sorry for how my mother has been acting," Emma said quietly. "If it makes you feel any better, it really doesn't have anything to do with you. I think she's just jealous."

"How is she doing?" Miriam asked, holding the package in her lap. "I haven't seen her in ages."

"She says she's just taking a break from the world, but honestly, I think she's becoming a recluse. All she does is watch television and drink her 'special lemonade,'" Emma said, making air quotes.

"I'm truly sorry to hear that. Are you getting by okay?"

"It's fine," Emma said, shrugging. "I'll be heading off to college in a little over a year, then I won't have to deal with her."

Miriam hated hearing Emma so indifferent to her mother and silently prayed her own child would never feel the same.

"Enough about her. Please, open it!" Emma said, now practically bouncing with enthusiasm. Miriam unwrapped the tissue paper to find a turquoise wool throw.

"It's exquisite," Miriam said, "and so soft! I love it, sweetie!"

Emma beamed with pride. "I knitted it myself," she said. "Pearl taught me!"

"Well, you are obviously a quick study, Emma. It will be perfect in the nursery," she said, handing the blanket to George so he could feel it for himself.

Iris approached Emma and gave her a hug. "Thank you, precious girl," she said, kissing the top of Emma's head.

"Emma, if you ever want to talk, you know where to find me," Miriam said. "You're always welcome here."

"Amen! Now, we need to get Miriam to lie down. Please give my best to your mother," Iris said as she walked Emma toward the French doors.

After hearing Jasper close the front door, Miriam let out a sigh. "What a celebration, Iris!" she said, working her way to a standing position. "I know I shouldn't, but I think I'm going to head back for another piece of cake. I need strength to get started on my thank-you notes!"

As they were walking toward the dining room, Miriam felt a slight cramp in her abdomen, and before she knew it, she had expelled water all over the hardwood floor. Panicking, she grabbed George's arm before apologizing to Iris for the mess.

"Dear girl, I believe it's show time," Iris said. "Jasper? Please pull the Lincoln around!"

"You're coming with me, aren't you?" Miriam whispered as she felt her contractions beginning.

"I wouldn't miss it for the world."

46

Iris sat in the walnut rocking chair, looking down at the exquisite bundle asleep in her arms, and thought–not for the first time recently–how miraculous life could be for those paying attention. With her ethereal skin, Cupid's bow mouth, strawberry blond hair, and bluish-green eyes, her great-grand-daughter looked like the perfect amalgamation of Miriam, George, and Rusty Benson. As Iris rocked gently, stroking the baby's head, she began wondering how her life would have been different had she run away with her one true love, married, and raised her daughter with him.

Miriam walked groggily into the nursery and sat down on the ivory loveseat, rubbing the sleep from her eyes. "How's little Poppy?" she asked, stifling a yawn.

"She's just as perfect as ever," Iris purred. "She hasn't cried once! Having her here filled an emptiness I didn't even know I had, not really, anyway. I only wish Rose could have lived to meet her. We must be sure to tell stories about her when the baby gets a little older."

Miriam looked at Iris thoughtfully. "I will have to rely on you for that," she said softly. "I didn't get to know her as well as I had hoped, but I can attest to her adventurous spirit and her compassionate heart. Both of which I hope Poppy inherited."

"She already has a twinkle in her eyes, just like my sister. You can be sure she'll be a little firecracker!" Iris said as the baby began to stir. Miriam stood to take Poppy from Iris, then rocked her back and forth in her arms.

"It's only been three weeks, dear, but I can already say you're a wonderful mama," Iris said. "Just as I'm sure your mother, Althea, was as well."

Miriam returned to the couch, cradling Poppy in her arms. "Mama was a sweetheart, though she battled through her bouts of melancholy–depression, as we call it now. She never talked about it, but I know Granddaddy worried about her," she said.

"Did she know Rusty was her real father?" Iris said.

"I don't think so. But she adored him. He took good care of us once Daddy left and, really, even before that. I haven't known how to talk to you about this, Iris, because I haven't wanted to bring up painful memories, you know?"

"That's very kind of you, dear, but the pain truly vanished the moment we realized who you were. You can ask me any-thing you wish," Iris said. "I have no secrets left to hide."

Miriam took a deep breath. "Did you want to keep my mother?"

Iris took off one of her silver hoops and began massag-ing her ear lobe. "Very much," she murmured. "But it was in early 1928, and things were so very different back then. What I had done was scandalous, at least in my parents' eyes, and I couldn't bring shame to the family name. I did what I was told to do–and it's funny because my mother kept trying to convince me, once I gave up your mother and earned my col-lege degree, that I would still be a 'catch,' as we used to say. That is, if nobody knew about my being damaged... another of our antiquated euphemisms. After Rusty, I couldn't imagine ever loving another man nor giving birth to another child. I thought it would be a betrayal of sorts, so I resigned myself to being a spinster."

"Do you regret it?"

"Sometimes. When I watch you and George together, I

wonder what would have happened if I had fought harder to be with Rusty. George is so much like him. Quiet, kind, gentle. But it's no use entertaining regrets, honey. We do the best we can to make the most of our lives. Looking at you now, holding my exquisite great-granddaughter, I know everything worked out as it was meant to," she said.

"Do you wish you had gone back and tracked him down?" Miriam said softly.

"Part of me does, but what would have been the point? As I told you before, Mother would never approve of my continuing any sort of relationship with him. Nor would my father, honestly, though he was fairly progressive for the time. I try not to think of what further lengths they would have gone to separate us. I had to let him go," she said as her chin quivered. "But I'm glad you were blessed to have him in your life."

Poppy began to cry, so Miriam stood and began pacing the nursery, patting the baby's back.

"Did you get to name my mother?"

"The only two things I could give her were the dogwood brooch from Rusty and, yes, her Christian name. Althea was my grandmother and one of the strongest women I've ever known," Iris said. "I wanted that innocent baby to be a survivor, so I named her after Grandma. It sounds like she lived up to it."

Miriam smiled. "As well as she could," she said.

"Now, I'd like to talk about you," Iris said, getting up from the rocker. "What are your dreams for the rest of your life?"

"That's a heavy question!" Miriam said, continuing to pace. "First and foremost, I want this little one to grow up healthy and happy. And I'd like to continue serving Stuarts Landing through the auxiliary, though I must admit, it sometimes feels like what we do is frivolous."

Iris chuckled at Miriam's candor. "The auxiliary serves a purpose, though it's often more for the members than it is for

the community," she said. "Women's organizations became a thing around the turn of the century, decades before we gained the right to vote. They afforded women the opportunity to make a difference, to work for a greater good even as we were politically mute. But I agree, given my long affiliation with the auxiliary, that it became more social in nature. Perhaps you could explore more meaningful ways for the auxiliary to improve Stuarts Landing."

"I'll think about it," Miriam said, sitting back down on the loveseat.

"What else?"

"When George and I owned the hardware stores, I loved every minute of it. Well, until we took our eyes off the business when Granddaddy became ill. I liked making important decisions and getting to know our employees. I liked our store being a place people frequented, not just because of what we sold but because of the culture we created. Sometimes, folks just stopped by to chat and didn't buy a thing. It never bothered me because I figured they were lonely," she said.

"If you were to have a business now, what do you think it would be? You could be a fashion designer, you know... I'll never forget your outfits in the fashion show," Iris said, putting her earring back on.

"Oh, my sewing will be devoted to little Poppy here," Miriam said, hugging her baby. "But I actually think it would be fun to have a restaurant, you know? A place that serves nostalgic comfort food using old recipes that have been forgotten by our fast-food world. Not too fancy... just comfortable. A place where people want to come for good meals and camaraderie."

"One of the things I loved most about Europe was how complete strangers shared tables," Iris said, reminiscing. "Rose and I met some of the most fascinating people that way. It's a lovely idea that would be a nice addition to Stuarts Landing."

"Just a pipe dream," Miriam said as Poppy sucked on her pinkie.

"It doesn't have to be. You were at the reading of Rose's will. She bequeathed you the old sawmill," she said, her eyes sparkling. "It sits on the riverfront. Can't you just see it? It would make a beautiful restaurant. What do you think?"

Miriam tilted her head, staring at the Monet as her mental wheels began to spin.

"It would take a small fortune to renovate the mill," Miriam said. "And wouldn't that bring back uncomfortable memories for you?"

Iris laughed. "Rusty only worked there," she said. "We never, you know, *there*."

Miriam giggled, then felt herself blushing. "I don't need to know," she said, holding up her hand. "But something I've wanted to ask for a long time is why they were so quick to blame him for the fire? I never told you that the first person I met here, the manager over at the Cardinal Inn, even hinted that Granddaddy's name was still considered 'mud' around here and that I best keep it to myself."

Iris shifted in her seat, trying to answer a question she had never allowed herself to explore. Not for the first time, she wished Rose were still there to help sort her thoughts. She closed her eyes, trying to steel herself from the painful memory.

"I guess the most direct answer I can offer is that it was expedient and convenient. Why bother trying to investigate what really happened when getting Rusty out of town served my parents' purpose?" Iris rubbed her eyes, trying to erase the mental image of her mother's enraged expression when she—with Rose at her side—reluctantly confessed her condition. Even after all these years, her blood still chilled when she remembered her mother's words: "For what he has taken from you, we shall take from him three-fold."

Lost as she was in her thoughts, Iris jumped when she heard Miriam's voice. "Was the fire before or after they found out about..."

Iris inhaled sharply before answering. "It was the next day," she murmured. "And two days hence, he was gone."

"You never got to say 'goodbye'?" Miriam said, stroking the top of Poppy's silken head.

"I did not. I was expected to go to the convent, as my mother instructed, then never speak of it again. So I didn't. But I never stopped thinking about what might have been, foolhardy though that was. At least I still have a bit of Rusty in you and sweet Poppy here. That's more than I could have wished for," she said, settling her eyes on her great-granddaughter and smiling wistfully. "Let's go back to discussing your ideas for a restaurant... I'd rather talk about memories in the making, wouldn't you?"

"I would, but I'm still troubled by who committed the crime my granddaddy was falsely accused of," Miriam said. "It's just so wrong!" She began chewing her bottom lip as a lone tear snaked down her cheek.

"All I can say is that the world is full of people who will happily get paid to do the evil bidding of others. And since the 'others,' in this case, are long since deceased, there's no reason to exhume the past. The sawmill, though, once stood for the beautiful simplicity that was life here, regardless of what happened. *That*, my dear, is why it's worthy of salvation. And I used that word quite deliberately," Iris said, leaning forward and clasping her hands together. "So?"

Miriam shifted Poppy to a different position in her arms before responding. "It's a big idea, and maybe even a silly one, to think I could launch a restaurant here. Besides, Louise was so focused on turning it into a museum. I don't need to further invite her wrath."

Iris rubbed her chin, remembering Louise as a young woman who could have, should have been broken by her mother's untimely death. That she had managed to exhibit such resilience, well, Iris would always acknowledge Louise's strength because she had seen it within herself. "Louise has her own demons, sweetheart, and one day, she may actually face them. But while I'm not particularly concerned with Louise Caldwell, given her most inappropriate behavior toward you—and us, to be frank—why couldn't you do both? Decorate the restaurant with old pictures of Stuarts Landing and its early residents. It could be a living museum with wonderful food!" Iris said, growing more excited by the idea.

"I could never afford the renovations, Iris. And I've never run a restaurant. Plus, I have Poppy to consider. She's my top priority," Miriam said, stroking her daughter's back.

"Well, I can afford it," Iris said. "You and George have run a business before, and Jasper once owned a tofu bar in Sedona. Among the lot of us, we could do it. Shall we hire a contractor and see what it would take?"

Miriam closed her eyes, and at first, Iris thought she had fallen asleep. But then, she could see her granddaughter's mental wheels turning, so she stayed silent despite having a great deal more to say about Louise. *That can wait for another day,* she thought. She slowly rose and began walking toward the door when she heard Miriam's voice.

"Okay. Let's do it!"

Iris pumped her fist as Poppy spit up on Miriam's shoulder.

"Is this a sign?" Miriam asked, laughing as she reached for a hand towel on the changing table.

"I view it as an exclamation point from the great beyond," Iris said, her eyes moistening. "Rose always did know how to get people's attention."

During her senior year at the Fulton Academy, Emma spent more time away than at home. Louise wanted to believe her daughter had grown sentimental in preparation to attend the University of Virginia and was taking every opportunity to make new memories with her friends. In her more self-aware moments, Louise knew Emma just wanted to avoid her. Had Clifton not been so eager to buy her a car—a brand-new Buick coupe from Butler Automotive—Emma would have been more tethered to home and family. Louise clenched her teeth every time she considered how her own husband had been complicit in Emma's estrangement.

After graduating near the top of her class, Emma spent most of the summer with Debbie and the Butlers, taking weekend trips to their home in Virginia Beach, enjoying lavish pool parties, and going on shopping excursions to build her college wardrobe. While Louise welcomed the peace and quiet afforded by Emma's absences, she felt silently judged by both Clifton and Pearl for her unwillingness to connect with her daughter before she left home. When such thoughts emerged, Louise had taken to numbing them with vodka, a bottle of which she kept beneath her bathroom sink.

A few days before Emma was scheduled to move into her dormitory room at the university, Louise was roughly awakened by Clifton sitting down heavily on their bed. Sleepily, she looked at the clock and saw it was already ten in the morning. She had not remembered going to bed the night before,

and from the acrid taste in her mouth, she obviously had not brushed her teeth.

"Louise, we need to talk. Now," Clifton said gruffly as he stood.

"Why aren't you at work?" Louise asked, trying to focus her bleary eyes on her obviously angry husband.

"Because I'm taking Emma to lunch at the club," he said, "so she knows at least one of her parents will be sad to see her leave. I'd ask you to join, but I want Emma to enjoy herself, and that wouldn't be possible with you drinking your meal."

Louise sat up and tried to cross her legs primly, pulling her nightgown over her knees. "Don't be absurd, Clifton. It's not like you don't have a cocktail at lunch," she said defensively.

Clifton walked into their bathroom, returning a moment later with her half-empty bottle of Smirnoff and slamming it on her nightstand. He folded his arms and stared at her with contempt.

"Why are you snooping around in my cabinet?" Louise shouted.

"I was looking for mouthwash," he said. "I certainly didn't expect to find this, though I know from Pearl that you've been enjoying your 'special lemonade' earlier and earlier each day. I don't say this lightly, Louise, but something must change before it's too late."

Louise got out of bed and brushed past Clifton on the way to the bathroom. Closing the door, she sat at her makeup table and stared at her face, which looked puffy and pale. "You need a facial," she said to her reflection. "And maybe a massage."

***

For Emma's last dinner before leaving for Charlottesville the following morning, Pearl had spent the entire day in the kitchen whipping up Emma's favorites. As she placed the platters of barbecued pulled pork, potatoes au gratin, green beans almondine, buttermilk biscuits, and blackberry cobbler on the table, Clifton eyed Louise, who was finishing her second glass of pinot noir. Seemingly oblivious to any tension in the dining room, Emma eagerly loaded her plate as Louise reached for the wine bottle.

"Louise," Clifton said sternly, "I think that's enough."

Emma looked up from her plate as Louise defiantly refilled her glass. "Mom, c'mon. It's my last night here for a while. Can't you enjoy it without getting wasted?"

Clifton gave Louise a supercilious look but did not rise to her defense.

"How dare you disrespect me! Did it ever occur to you that I'm struggling with the thought of you moving away?" Louise slurred. "You're my world, Em. You have to know that!" She began to cry.

Emma shoved a forkful of potatoes into her mouth, glaring at Louise as she chewed methodically, like a heifer working its cud.

"Everything I've done has been to give you a leg up," Louise said, taking a gulp of wine and spilling an errant drop on her cotton house dress. She no longer spent time worrying about what she was wearing since she so rarely left home.

"Keep telling yourself that, Mother. Because from my vantage point, you've only cared about your social status, which, as I'm sure you've noticed, has taken quite the hit," Emma said.

Louise recoiled as if punched in the solar plexus. "Take that back!" she yelled. "You have no idea what you're talking about!"

Clifton held up his hand. "Louise, that's quite enough."

"Who came to your defense when you made that ridiculous attempt to boycott cotillion, hmm?" Louise inquired.

"Um, the same person who missed every single football

game this year, the last time I'll ever be a cheerleader? The same person who failed to help serve at our seniors' breakfast? The same person who asked me if I was a lesbian because I don't have a boyfriend? Shall I continue?" Emma raged, her face growing red.

"You did what?" Clifton said, glowering at Louise.

"It was a fair question. I wanted to be sure she felt supported if that was, indeed, the case. Fortunately, it's not," she said, giggling.

"Go on and laugh," Emma said, her eyes ablaze with fury. "I'm not going to miss this. Not one fucking bit!" She plunged her spoon directly into the pan of cobbler and brought it directly to her mouth.

"Manners, please," Louise snapped, spooning a few green beans onto her plate, then picking one up with her fingers and sucking on it. "Delicious! You won't get meals like this at school, that's for sure."

"I wouldn't have gotten meals like this at home if it weren't for Pearl," Emma retorted.

"Then consider my work here done," Louise said, pushing back her chair and clumsily standing. Grabbing her glass of wine, she called for Pearl.

"Pearl, honey, I think I'll take a tray in my room," she said, weaving her way over to Emma and placing a firm hand on her shoulder. "One day, you're going to miss me," she mumbled, then she ruffled Emma's hair, getting her diamond ring caught in one of Emma's locks.

"Ouch! You're hurting me!" Emma exclaimed, reaching back to grab Louise's wrist. With a yank, Louise extricated her hand along with several strands of Emma's hair.

"I'll see you in the morning," Louise said, leaning down to kiss Emma's cheek and missing as Emma pulled away. "Nighty night!" She wiggled her fingers as she stumbled out of the dining room.

When she awoke the next morning, Clifton's side of the bed was empty and undisturbed. Apparently, he had slept elsewhere. Unsteadily, Louise got up and put on her satin robe before brushing her teeth and hair, then going downstairs. She followed the sound of voices to the solarium and found Emma sitting with Clifton, a Tiffany box in her lap.

"Daddy, I don't know how to thank you," she said, touching the diamond studs in her earlobes.

"You are more precious to me than all the diamonds in the world," Clifton said softly. "When you wear them, please remember how very much I love you." Emma threw her arms around his neck, then looked up as Louise approached them.

"What a beautiful surprise," Louise said, raising her eyebrows at Clifton, who quickly averted her gaze. "They suit you well."

After carefully putting the robin's egg-blue box and white satin ribbon back into the Tiffany bag, Emma stood. "I still need to tell Pearl goodbye," she said, sauntering past Louise with Clifton in tow. Louise followed them to the kitchen, where Pearl was putting several plastic containers full of cookies into a tote bag.

"Don't need you starvin'," Pearl said as Emma hugged her from behind. "I done heard 'bout them sorority girls goin' all stick-figure skinny. You's perfect, so be sure to eat!"

"I don't know what I'd have done without you, Pearl," Emma said as her eyes became misty. "You helped keep me sane." She shot a look at Louise.

"I love you like my own," Pearl said, turning around and enveloping Emma in a tight embrace. "I promised I wasn't gonna cry, but jeez oh Pete, I's gonna miss my girl." She stepped back and wiped her eyes with her apron.

"I love you too, Pearl. And just in case you were wondering, you can send me care packages any time you like," Emma said, grinning. "Daddy, will you walk me to my car?"

Louise stood motionless as Clifton took Emma's hand. "Emma? Don't you want to say goodbye?"

Emma strode toward Louise and patted her shoulder. "I already have," she whispered, then turned on her heel to walk with Clifton to the front door. "See ya!" she called over her shoulder.

Louise looked imploringly at Pearl, hoping for some word of advice. Pearl pursed her lips, then, shaking her head, began silently wiping down the counter. Louise poured a cup of coffee and went out onto the veranda, watching Clifton and Emma make their tearful goodbyes. A few minutes later, he joined her and sat silently as they watched Emma drive away.

"Louise," Clifton said, "you will, of course, keep this house, since it's been in your family for generations, but I've had enough. I can't live like this anymore. You have more than you could ever possibly need in the Winston Trust, which I'm happy to continue managing, or you can find someone else to do it. But I'm finished. I want a divorce."

Louise dropped the porcelain cup onto the tile, shattering it to pieces.

"You can't be serious!" she shrieked, looking at him with desperation. "I've just had a rough patch. I can make this work!"

Clifton shook his head sadly. "I can't. Not anymore." With that, he went into the house and slammed the door. She hurried after him and watched as he removed an already packed bag from the hall closet. Before she could stop him, he stormed from the house. Standing in the front doorway, she solemnly watched as his Mercedes sped down their driveway and on to a future without her. In the space of thirty minutes, her family had completely abandoned her.

Miriam had just put Poppy down for her mid-morning nap when she heard the telephone ringing in their bedroom. When they first moved into Webster House, Iris had insisted upon giving them a dedicated line in their wing, which proved highly convenient given the volume of auxiliary-related calls Miriam received each day. No longer president, though still an active member, she spent significantly less time fielding calls. Answering the phone on the fourth ring, she heard Bitsy breathlessly ask if she could stop by in a few hours.

"Why don't you just join us for lunch? Jasper and I made gazpacho, and I believe he's working on some crab cakes now," Miriam said as her mouth began salivating.

"I don't think I've ever had gazpacho," Bitsy said. "Is it fattening?"

"Anything but," Miriam said. "It's basically chilled vegetable soup, and I promise, you'll love it. See you around twelve thirty?"

"I can't wait!" Bitsy said. "See you then."

After hanging up, Miriam trotted downstairs to find Iris in the solarium, working on a new painting. "Did Poppy put up a fuss about her nap?" Iris asked.

"Not in the least, thankfully! Bitsy just called, and I hope you don't mind, but I invited her to lunch with us today," Miriam said. "I'm sure we'll have plenty."

Iris put down her paintbrush and smiled. "Sweetheart, I've told you before. This is your home. If you want to invite

people over, you're more than welcome to do so! You don't need my permission unless, you know, you're planning some kind of Dionysian love-in. That might require some different elements," she said, slapping her knee as she laughed.

"Good grief, Iris. You're too much!" Miriam said, rolling her eyes.

"So I've been told, dear. I wear it as a badge of honor!" She chuckled, returning to her watercolor. "I'm making this for Poppy," she said.

The painting was only partially finished, but Miriam was mesmerized by the brilliantly colored ballet of seahorses Iris was creating. "Poppy's going to love that, Iris!" Miriam said. "I'll tell Jasper we're having a guest for lunch. Shall we eat in the gazebo?"

"Perfect idea," Iris said. "Poppy always enjoys playing outside!"

Two hours later, Jasper led Bitsy into the parlor. Wearing a patchwork dress and a pair of wedge sandals, Miriam thought Bitsy looked as though she had just stepped off the cover of *Vogue*. "Bitsy! I've missed you this summer!" Miriam said, rushing to give her a hug. "And that outfit. It's so chic."

Bitsy smiled as Iris approached with her arms outstretched. "Hello there," Iris said, kissing Bitsy on the cheek. "I take it you've had a lovely summer? Your tan is positively radiant! Let's sit down, shall we? I think Jasper is putting the finishing touches on lunch."

Iris took her favorite peacock chair while Bitsy and Miriam sat on the divan. "I think we're missing someone," Bitsy said, looking around the room with a smile. "With Debbie off to college, I need a baby fix."

"She'll be awake any minute," Miriam said, looking at the Cartier watch that had once belonged to her great-aunt.

"I didn't mean to ignore your question, Iris. Yes, we took advantage of every second we had with Debbie, spending quite a bit of time at our beach house," she said. "With the new general manager Bobby hired for the dealership, his schedule has become so much more flexible. Though I really wish he would find a hobby instead of following me around like a puppy."

Iris removed her glasses and gave Bitsy a sly grin. "It's smart to keep a handsome husband in your sights," she said, wagging her index finger.

"I'm not worried," Bitsy said. "We were made for each other. I have so much more to tell, but I really must see the baby!"

"She's fifteen months old already." Miriam chuckled as she rose from the couch.

"I know, but they will always be our babies, even when they're grown," Bitsy said wistfully.

"Let's move to the gazebo, Bitsy, and Miriam can bring Poppy outside to join us, though I warn you, she's quite the talker," Iris said, getting up from her chair.

After changing Poppy's diaper and dressing her in a romper she designed, Miriam carried her squirming daughter down the stairs. "Me walk! Me walk!" Poppy insisted, tugging Miriam's sleeve.

"No, my sweet angel. I've already told you that you're not quite ready for the stairs," Miriam said. When they reached the solarium, Miriam put Poppy down, and the minute she saw Jasper outside in the gazebo, she began running for the door.

"'Sper! 'Sper! 'Sper!" she yelled, flying outside as Miriam tried to catch her. By the time she reached the gazebo, Poppy had attached herself to Jasper's leg as he tried to pour everyone a glass of Sauvignon Blanc, peering shyly at Bitsy.

"She is just precious!" Bitsy said. "And that curly red hair! She's going to be quite a beauty."

"Well, we're actually more focused on her being kind and clever," Iris said, taking a drink of wine. "But beauty certainly

never hurts, as you well know."

After prying Poppy away from Jasper, Miriam put her in the highchair next to Iris, who handed Poppy a banana slice from the fruit salad. "It's the only fruit she likes at the moment," Iris said.

Jasper ladled their gazpacho from an Italian ceramic tureen into matching bowls, then placed a small plate of crab cakes with jalapeño tartar sauce in front of everyone except Poppy, who was banging her little fists on the highchair. "She wants her macaroni and cheese," Miriam said to Bitsy as she put the bowl in front of her toddler.

"I don't blame her," Bitsy said, dipping her spoon into the soup bowl and tasting the gazpacho. "Good gosh, I think I've died and gone to heaven!" She pretended to swoon. "This may be my new favorite food!"

Iris took a bite of her crab cake and nodded. "Oh, yes, Jasper, adding the jalapeños to the sauce gives it just the right amount of heat!" she said, dabbing the sides of her mouth.

As Miriam tried to enjoy her lunch while keeping an eye on Poppy, Bitsy leaned forward, her eyes sparkling. "Ladies, I've been made aware of a most tragic piece of news," she said, grinning.

"Dare I say that your message and your countenance are not aligned?" Iris said as she offered Poppy another slice of banana.

"Why does this sound like you're about to dish up some dirt?" Miriam asked, giving Bitsy a concerned look. She had told Bitsy before that she found gossip to be destructive since Miriam herself had been fodder for the rumor mill from the moment she arrived in Stuarts Landing. *Apparently, Bitsy had forgotten that conversation,* Miriam mused as she cut into her crab cake.

"I prefer to call it 'information sharing,'" Bitsy said. "I got a call this morning from Debbie..."

"How's she liking the university?" Iris interrupted. "I thoroughly enjoyed my time in college. It's where I really started to find myself, as people say nowadays."

"You know Debbie. She's all about her social life, and it seems to be thriving there, especially now that she's in a sorority," she said, brushing her hair off her shoulders. "But she called about Emma."

Miriam sat up straighter as her maternal instincts sounded an alarm. "Oh no, is she okay?" she asked, wiping Poppy's messy cheeks. Poppy gave her a toothy grin before upending the bowl on her tray. "I guess little Poppy's had enough!" Miriam offered her another banana, which Poppy decided to try putting in her nose. "Sweetheart, not in the nose. In the mouth." Poppy giggled. "Silly girl!" Miriam said, tickling her under her chin. "I'm sorry. Back to Emma. What's going on?"

Bitsy leaned back in her chair. "As Debbie explained to me, Louise and Clifton paid Emma an unexpected visit yesterday. They took Emma to lunch, and over dessert, they told her they were getting... are you ready? They are getting divorced!" Bitsy said.

Miriam looked at Iris, who merely shook her head, then turned back to Bitsy. "Holy cow—that's terrible!"

"I could have predicted it," Iris said under her breath.

"How so?" Bitsy said, finishing the last of her gazpacho.

"Over the course of my rather long life, I've learned that people who are so tightly wound they can't cede control or adapt to change are harboring deep insecurities," Iris said, dabbing her lips with her napkin. "And those insecurities must find an outlet—usually, an unhealthy one. I have watched Louise venture down a dangerous path, starting – quite sadly– when Miriam brought new life to the tiresome auxiliary. I believe it was the beginning of her unraveling."

Miriam brought her hand to her mouth. "Are you saying this is my fault?" she said, her eyes widening with anguish.

"Of course it's not your fault, dear," Iris said, taking off one of her silver bangles and handing it to Poppy, who immediately put it in her mouth. "Louise has spent her life trying to compensate for her mother's deficiencies, at least as perceived by Louise's Grandmother Nora. She's led a relatively shallow life, prioritizing her social stature over everything else. When you live for what other people think, you're not really living. And honestly, I think it was best for the auxiliary she didn't become president, but for her, that was a public humiliation she didn't know how to get past. A shame, really."

Miriam considered Iris's explanation, feeling marginally assured she was not the villain in Louise's story. She looked at Bitsy, who was idly chewing a piece of crab cake.

"So, how did Emma take it?" she said.

Bitsy folded her napkin and placed it on the table. "That's the best part of the story, really," she said, crossing her legs suggestively as Jasper removed her dishes. "Apparently, Emma told Louise she was glad they were getting a divorce and that she never wanted to see or speak to Louise ever again! I would stroke out if Debbie ever said that to me."

"A rather poor choice of words," Iris said, clearing her throat.

"Oh, right. I'm sorry! But can you imagine? I knew Emma and Louise had their problems, I guess. I just had no idea how deep those problems were," Bitsy said.

"Further to what I was saying," Iris said, taking another sip of wine.

"Emma told Debbie that Louise was getting drunk all the time. Even during the day," Bitsy said. "No wonder we haven't seen her around."

Miriam took the tray off the highchair and scooped Poppy into her arms, hugging her protectively as she looked at Bitsy. "Do you think we should pay her a visit? Let her know we're here for her?" she said, bouncing Poppy in her lap.

"I wish I could be a better person, Miriam, I really do. But given how Louise has treated us, I think it's up to *her* to make amends," Bitsy said. "If she wants our help, she needs to ask for it."

"And she won't," Iris said. "Her pride is her Achilles' heel."

"But shouldn't we try?" Miriam said.

Bitsy smoothed her dress over her knees, seeming suddenly self-conscious. "I've known Louise for more than twenty years," Bitsy said. "You're only asking for a fight if you try helping her. She'll rip out your throat as soon as look at you. Best to leave it alone."

Once the women finished their crème brûlée, Bitsy thanked them for lunch and departed, leaving a trail of sadness in her wake. "Louise will get through this," Iris said, finishing her wine. "But you can't do it for her, nor would she want you to. Besides... we have a building to renovate and a business to birth!"

Miriam wished she shared Iris's pragmatism, but something told her things would only worsen for Louise.

After returning from her trip to Charlottesville with Clifton to inform Emma about their divorce, Louise spent the next two weeks in bed, despite Pearl's gentle attempts to coax her outside or, at least, to the kitchen. She recently had taken up smoking, which, in addition to her increased vodka intake, served only to fuel her self-loathing, yet her bad habits gave her something to anticipate—the next drink, the next cigarette—throughout her dreadfully lonely days. Every time she replayed Emma's hateful words in her mind, not to mention her conversation with Clifton on the way home, she inwardly cringed and then cried.

"I'm glad Daddy's divorcing you!" Emma had shouted, oblivious to what the other restaurant patrons may have thought. "All you've ever cared about is yourself, *Mother*. I hate what you did to this family, but now, you're as free as a bird. I will never see you or speak to you again. And that's a promise!" She stood from the table, then Clifton rose from his chair and walked Emma to her car. Louise watched as they hugged for what seemed like five minutes before Clifton came back inside, motioning to Louise that it was time to leave. During the ninety-minute drive back to Stuarts Landing, she tried to make conversation with her soon-to-be ex.

"How do you feel?"

"I feel just fine," he said, keeping his eyes on the road.

"I can't believe she said those things," Louise said, examining her ringless left hand.

"She'll be staying with me in Richmond on her college breaks," Clifton said. "I've already bought a house. And I will be sending the movers to your house to clear out my closets and my office. Just so you know. It will probably be next week."

"We could try counseling," Louise said.

"I'm afraid it's too late for us, but I would encourage you to explore that. You need to do something to pull yourself together."

When he pulled into her driveway, she looked at his clenched jaw and furrowed brow and felt her heart breaking all over again. "I'm so sorry, Clif. For everything."

He turned to her slowly, his eyes telegraphing unadulterated pain. "I fell in love the moment I met you, Louise, and from that moment on, I would have done just about anything for you," he said. "So many times, I've tried to determine what, if anything, I did to get us to this point, and truthfully, I always come up empty. It didn't have to be this way if you had turned to me instead of the bottle." He paused to clear his throat; Louise wondered if he, too, felt remorseful before he interrupted her thoughts. "But the way you've treated people, including our daughter and me, is beyond the pale. I do hope, for *your* best interests, that you can pull yourself from the abyss into which you've fallen."

Louise turned in her seat to stare at his profile and watch him grind his teeth as she tried to recall how he may have contributed to their demise. Truthfully, life had been a blur the last year or so, but she also knew he had begun distancing himself long before this conversation. That he had not thought enough of their marriage to let her know how he was feeling in the moment felt like an insult; that she was blindsided felt like an injury. *Or was I not paying attention?* She rejected the thought as soon as it arrived.

"It must be nice to feel so superior," Louise said, unfastening her seat belt and opening the passenger's door.

"Good luck decorating your new house. I'm sure your secretary will be more than happy to help. You can lie to yourself all you want, but I know the real reason you want a divorce. Don't think I didn't notice all the nights you stayed in Richmond." She slammed the car door, then watched as he drove away slowly, realizing it was likely the last time he'd ever be there.

And in the ensuing two weeks, nothing she could think of would undo that. Staring out the solarium window, Louise thought about her life and realized nothing mattered to her anymore. Even her beloved dogs, who had taken to shadowing Pearl instead of adhering to Louise's side. Louise assumed they had joined the ranks of all who had abandoned her.

"Mizzus, I brought you some homemade chicken soup and a grilled cheese," Pearl said, placing the tray on what had been Clifton's side of the bed. She moved to the windows and began opening the curtains. "It's time to stop your wallowin'. C'mon now."

Louise took one look at her lunch and immediately felt nauseated. "Not hungry," she mumbled, pulling the sheet over her head.

"When's the last time you done take a bath?" Pearl asked, emptying Louise's overflowing ashtray into the wastebasket. Louise ignored her. "You think you's the only person in the world ever hit bottom?" Pearl said, sitting down on the bed. "Well, you ain't. But the way you're going, I'm afraid you may reach the point of no return." Finding Louise's hand under the covers, Pearl took it into her own. "Dear Heavenly Father, I come to you prayerfully and ask you to show Miz Louise here a way out of her darkness. May you shine your most abundant light on her spirit..."

"Just stop it, Pearl," Louise said, yanking her hand from Pearl's grasp. "I think God has more important things to worry about than my disastrous life. I'm fine, though I wouldn't mind

some of your lemonade."

Pearl stood up from the bed, put her hands on her hips, and pursed her lips. "I don't make that no more," she said.

Louise looked at her angrily. "You will do as I ask," she said, untangling her legs from the sheet and trying to stand. Her body gave way to gravity, and she dropped to the floor, then began laughing as she examined her abraded knee.

"I looked the other way longer than I oughta have. Shoulda said something sooner, but I thought you'd pull yourself together. I'm gonna say, though, you ain't goin' the way of your mama. Not on my watch!"

"You don't wear one," Louise said, rocking herself as she giggled.

"You're losing your ever-lovin' mind," Pearl said, marching into the bathroom. Louise heard water begin filling the bathtub. Pearl returned to Louise's bedroom and reached down to pull Louise from the carpet. "I swear to God Almighty, I will drag your bony butt into the bath, and don't think I'm joking," Pearl said. Louise faltered as Pearl led her toward the tub. "Easy there, Mizzus." She tightened her grip on Louise's arm.

Louise looked at her expansive bathroom, now devoid of any of Clifton's toiletries, and exhaled dramatically as Pearl helped remove the nightgown she had worn for five days straight. As Pearl helped Louise into the tub, her face contorted with concern.

"Mizzus, what's that?" she said, pointing to a rash on Louise's breast as she sank into the water.

Louise looked down at her chest and shrugged. "I don't know," she said. "The mark of the beast?" She laughed much too loudly.

"Now I know you've done gone crazy," Pearl said. "And it ain't funny. I'm calling the doctor. We need to get you examined."

Louise submerged her entire body underwater, drowning out the sound of Pearl's incessant harping. Holding her breath, she thought of her teenage competitions with Bitsy to see who could stay under the longest. When she came up for air, Pearl had vanished. After washing her hair and body with a bar of hand soap, Louise awkwardly climbed from the bath, wrapped her body in a towel that still smelled like Clifton, and retreated to the chaise in her cavernous closet. After taking a swig of vodka from a bottle she had hidden in one of her shoe boxes, she cocked her head and gazed at all the clothes memorializing a life now long gone. As she was taking another pull from the bottle, Pearl reappeared.

"We're gonna get you dressed," she said. "Either you tell me what you want to wear, or I'll pick something, but we're goin' to the doctor. Now."

"Nope," Louise said, wrapping her towel more tightly around her gaunt frame. Pearl leaned down, peering into Louise's eyes.

"You've done run everyone out of your life," Pearl said. "From where I sit, I'm all you got left. I was gonna retire, and I can afford to, believe you me. I've been saving, but I know you need me, even though you'd never actually admit it. Now get your butt up and get dressed. We're leaving in ten minutes. Else, well, you're on your own." With that, she turned and stomped out of the closet.

Ten minutes later, Louise joined Pearl downstairs. Dressed in fraying sweatpants, a cotton oxford, and a pair of flip-flops, Louise knew she looked unkempt, yet she didn't care. Pearl raised her eyebrows but wordlessly took Louise's arm and guided her outside to her Cadillac. "You okay me driving?" she asked. Louise shrugged as she got into the backseat.

"I s'pose that's a yes. I ain't never driven such a fine car," Pearl said, easing the sedan down the driveway. Louise leaned back against the headrest and closed her eyes.

Fifteen minutes later, Pearl pulled into the parking lot of Louise's doctor's office. Louise awoke with a start, then began trembling. "I changed my mind," she said, folding her arms in front of her chest.

"Yeah, well I haven't. If you can't see me trying to help you, well, Lord forgive me, but I give up," Pearl said, glowering at Louise in the rearview mirror.

"Fine!" Louise said, opening the passenger door. "But I'm only doing this for you."

Pearl remained at Louise's side as Dr. Grinstead examined her breast, then inquired about when she first noticed the discoloration and how she had been feeling.

"I didn't really notice it," Louise said, pulling the medical gown closed. "Pearl here did."

"I don't want to alarm you, but we really need to do a mammogram," Dr. Grinstead said, taking off her glasses. "I'm not liking what I'm seeing."

"It's probably just a bruise," Louise said, looking at Pearl, whose face had frozen.

"Have you fallen recently?" the doctor asked.

"Probably," Louise said, snickering. The doctor looked at Pearl, who shook her head.

"All right. I'm sending you to the diagnostic center next door," she said, making a note in Louise's file, then pressing a button on the wall to summon a nurse. "Emily," she said when the nurse entered the room, "please call Mizel and tell them I have a patient who needs to be screened immediately. Diagnostic mammogram."

Emily left the room swiftly as Louise looked over to Pearl, then at the doctor.

"What's happening?" she asked as her hands began shaking.

"We'll know in a little while," Dr. Grinstead said gently. "Go ahead and get dressed. I don't know if you've had a

mammogram, but they can be a tad uncomfortable." She rose from her stool and patted Louise's bruised knee. "I'll be in touch." As the doctor left the examination room, Louise's eyes met Pearl's.

"Have faith," Pearl said. "You's okay."

After Pearl left the room, Louise began dressing, choosing to avoid the mirror.

***

The mammogram was more painful than Dr. Grinstead had explained, but Louise dutifully complied with the technician, wincing as her breasts were flattened like hamburger patties while trying to hold her breath.

"Please wait in the lobby until the radiologist has a chance to evaluate your screening," the technician said after escorting Louise back to the dressing room. Though raised in the church, Louise knew her faith had lapsed. Changing back into her street clothes, Louise touched her breast and said a brief prayer for hope. She didn't have faith her prayer would be heard.

Pearl was sitting in the lobby, reading the latest issue of *Redbook* as Louise took a seat next to her. "I'm liking the looks of this corn chowder recipe," Pearl said, giving Louise a sideways glance. "Might be just what you need to put on some weight." She gave Louise a kind smile.

Louise stared straight ahead at the framed inspirational posters on the wall, then looked at her watch. "I hate corn," she said mindlessly as she fidgeted in the stiff chair.

"Well, I can puree it, and you'll never know," Pearl said, flipping the pages of the magazine. "You good?"

Louise adjusted her bra strap. "Right as rain," she said, then instantly thought of Clifton.

Fifteen minutes later, the technician walked into the

waiting area. "Mrs. Caldwell? The radiologist would like to have a word," she said. "Please follow me."

Pearl reached for Louise's hand, but Louise swatted her away.

"I'm coming with you," Pearl said, pulling herself up from the chair. "Here we go."

The women proceeded to the radiologist's office at the back of the clinic. After taking their seats, the radiologist appeared holding Louise's scans.

"There's no easy way to say this," he said, looking over his glasses. "You have a significant mass in your left breast that looks to me like cancer. I'll call Dr. Grinstead, but your next step—urgently, I might add—is to see an oncologist. I'm so sorry, Mrs. Caldwell."

"Call me Louise," she said, gripping the sides of her chair. "Is it bad?" Her body began shaking.

"You need to see an oncologist," he said, rising from his chair. "I'm sorry."

Silently, Louise and Pearl left the clinic. As Pearl was driving them back to Winston House, Louise looked out the window, taking in the town she had known since birth. Once Pearl pulled into their driveway, Louise rolled down the window to breathe in the crisp fall air.

"Pearl, you deserve to retire and enjoy your life," Louise said. "I'm letting you go." She opened the passenger door. "I think it's best. For both of us." After closing the door, she strode to the front door.

"You're gonna need help," Pearl called out, wiping her eyes.

"I'd rather just handle it myself," Louise hollered back. "Go home and enjoy your family. While you still can. And please—I don't want anyone else to know."

She slowly unlocked the front door, dropped her bag on the table in the foyer, and went to the bar to make herself a

drink while she contemplated her options. She wanted to call Clifton, yet she knew he would think it was a ploy to lure him back, and she knew Bitsy would not respond. Sitting in the great room, she lit a cigarette and faced the bitter truth. Other than her two beloved dogs, looking up at her with confused expressions, she was completely alone for the first time in her life. And she was terrified.

50

Miriam lifted Poppy from her car seat in the Lincoln while Jasper unfolded her stroller, then helped get the toddler strapped in and situated. "This September sun is unforgiving!" Iris said, opening her umbrella and putting on her sunglasses. "Miriam, did you bring Poppy's sunbonnet?"

"Got it right here," she said, patting her tote bag. She removed the pink hat and attempted to secure it on Poppy's head, but the child was having none of it.

"No! Don't want it!" she said, shaking her head angrily.

"Poppy," Iris said, bending down to look her precious great-granddaughter in the eyes. "See? Ri-Ri wears a hat too!" Iris pointed to her own hand-painted visor. "You can be like me!" Poppy stopped resisting, smiling at Iris as Miriam tied the bonnet under her chin. "Let's go check out the progress!" Iris said.

Though Miriam wished George could have joined them, he was busier than ever at Butler Automotive, having been promoted to general manager at the dealership's second location. From what she could see, she knew George would be as pleased as she was with what the contractors had already accomplished. They walked over the repaired bridge, passing the waterwheel to reach the main door into the mill, which now had a fortified foundation and a newly constructed wooden exterior designed to mirror the original structure. Inside, they found a full crew laying hardwood planks on the floor.

"It's really taking shape," Miriam said, pushing Poppy's stroller toward the added space that would become the kitchen. Iris followed along, taking in the windows that had been installed so guests could enjoy a view of the river.

"Do you think we should add a deck? For outdoor seating?" Iris said, seeming to marvel at the natural beauty surrounding them.

"I love that idea," Miriam said, imagining a crowd of happy customers dining *al fresco*. "Just like inside, I want community seating." She envisioned people making new friends as they enjoyed all her menu would have to offer.

Iris opened a box of animal crackers for Poppy, giving her two at a time, as had become their routine. "Tanks you, Ri-Ri! Look, Piggy!" she said, holding the cracker up before stuffing it into her mouth.

"That's right! You're so clever, Poppy," Iris said, smiling.

"Good afternoon, Mrs. Llewelyn, Miss Webster," Jack said as he approached them, adjusting his ballcap. "Whaddya think?"

"I think we couldn't have found a better contractor," Miriam said, extending her hand. "Have you found any issues we should be aware of?"

"Nothing terribly concerning. Once we rebuilt the foundation, which was no small doing, things have gone pretty smoothly. Our biggest challenge was getting the building plumbed for the kitchen and restrooms. Folks that worked here, before the fire, must have used an outhouse, though I can't find any evidence of it," he said. "Likely got lost in the blaze."

"I notice you added a new feature," Iris said, pointing to the stone fireplace with its exquisitely carved mantel. "Given the mill's history, are we sure it's safe?"

Jack put his hand to his heart. "I give my word, it's as sound as it could be. I hired the best masons I could find from

Richmond. No need to worry," he said. "I also went ahead and checked with the township regarding maximum capacity. I was told you'll be able to accommodate about a hundred people inside."

"We're thinking about adding a deck outside," Iris said. "Is that possible?"

"Absolutely! If we build it along the western wall, folks will get a nice view of the river and the sunset. Brilliant idea! That should give you seating for at least another thirty people or so," Jack said.

Miriam felt her stomach turn a somersault as the reality of their endeavor—just a daydream years before—was taking shape before her eyes.

"I need an animal cracker," she said, holding out her hand. Laughing, Iris gave her the whole box as Poppy protested loudly.

"Mine!" she shouted. Miriam gave her a gentle look. "Pwease?"

"We'll share, Poppy," Miriam said, laughing while handing her daughter another two cookies.

"Do you have any other questions?" Jack said, looking over his shoulder as the flooring crew moved closer to where they were standing.

"I guess the million-dollar question is, when do you think we'll be finished?" Miriam said.

Jack took off his cap and scratched his head. "It's September now." He looked up at the ceiling. "By my calculations, we should have all the renovation work completed by November, including the deck. From there, we'll need to move on to interior design. Have you thought about a firm you'd like to use?"

Miriam turned to Iris and Jasper, grinning. "You're looking at it!" she said. Jack raised his eyebrows.

"Oh, we have ideas," Iris said. "Believe you me!"

"Well, depending on how quickly you decide what you'd

like so we can get everything ordered and arranged, I think you could be ready to open as early as February. Let me know your ideas as soon as you can."

Iris clapped her hands excitedly, her bangles jangling in harmony. "Miriam, imagine–a grand opening on Valentine's Day! Wouldn't that be divine?"

Miriam put her hand to her throat. "I'm not sure I'm ready," she whispered.

Jasper walked to Miriam's side, putting his hand lightly between her shoulder blades. "Breathe," he murmured.

"Well, if you have no other questions, I need to get back to work. Let me know when you're ready to discuss your designs. Have a nice afternoon," Jack said before returning to the space designated for the kitchen.

Thirty minutes later, Iris and Miriam were sitting on the veranda at home, enjoying their iced tea while watching Jasper push Poppy on the swing he had made. "I can't believe this is really happening," Miriam said.

"Rose would be so proud of you, Miriam." Iris lifted her glass in a toast. "She knew you would do something wonderful with the property, and here we are, on the downhill slide to the opening!"

Miriam opened the leather journal Iris had given her, then took a pen from the pocket of her overalls. "I think we need to start brainstorming," she said, "but first, I want to ask your permission for something."

Iris looked at Miriam with a curious expression. "I can't imagine denying you anything," she said as she adjusted her glasses. "Shoot!"

"While it probably makes more sense, from a historical perspective anyway, to call the tavern The Old Sawmill, I think I have a better idea," Miriam said, bouncing her knee. "Would you mind if we named it 'Rose's'?"

Iris's mouth widened in a dazzling smile. "I could not possibly think of anything more apropos," she said, holding her hand in the air to give Miriam a high five.

"I'd like to hang some of her woven pieces throughout the interior, along with your watercolors, if you'd allow it," Miriam said as Iris nodded enthusiastically.

"Yes, wonderful! And you know her favorite color..."

"Absolutely. The walls must be turquoise," Miriam said, making notes. "And the front door—it has to be fire-engine red!"

"Would you like a few paintings from our collection to incorporate into the design?" Iris asked. "I'm not parting with the Picasso, but we have a few Dalis that could work."

Miriam scratched her cheek. "I think that might be too much," she said, chewing her lip. "What if we allowed local artists to display their works for sale?"

"Now you're talking," Iris said, sipping her tea. "That would definitely bring a greater sense of community to the place, and it would be great PR. Let's talk about the bar area... I think that's where we should display photos from Stuarts Landing's early days, if the historical society will allow us to make copies."

Miriam nodded, frantically scribbling in her journal. "I like that, but I'd like them to be consistently framed—maybe gilded? Too formal?"

Iris shook her head. "I think they should look rustic, honestly. I'd go with dark wood to match the paneling we'll have in the bar. And I'd love to see some potted palms, just to add some feng shui to the design."

"Fung what?" Miriam said with a chuckle.

"Oh, leave that to Jasper," Iris said with a smile. "Now, let's talk menu. What are you thinking?

Miriam closed her journal and tried to envision her future guests and what they might be eating. "I want the food to be comforting and savory, nothing too trendy... though we

can introduce new items depending on seasonal produce." She closed her eyes as she imagined various dishes.

"There were so many wonderful recipes from the auxiliary cookbook," Iris said, rubbing her temples. "Perhaps they'll provide some inspiration. But you must serve your mama's ginger lemonade."

"Well, that's one menu item," Miriam said, tapping her pen on the journal. "May I add Jasper's crab cakes and hummus? Oh, and his French beef stew?"

"I can't imagine he would mind. This is a good start, dear."

"I'd love to include the shepherd's pie I made for the auxiliary luncheon, remember? But the original recipe belonged to Louise's mother, so that doesn't really feel right. I doctored it back then… if I changed it up a bit more, do you think I should put it on the menu?"

Iris's attention turned to Poppy, giggling on the swing, and she smiled.

"Look at that child," Iris said. "Not a care in the world, happy as a little lark. It's funny. I felt that way when I was very young, and now, in my older years, I feel that way again. If I could figure out how to bottle it, well, wouldn't that be something? About the shepherd's pie… it does fit with the vibe you want to create. But if you add it, I think you need to credit the inspiration–Louise's mother–and that might set her off. It's hard to know since she seems to have disappeared." She seemed lost in thought for a moment. "I know! Make it completely yours. Start from scratch and reimagine it. The name is common enough, and people will likely order it based on the idea of comfort food. Then when they taste what you've created, they'll come back for more!" She began massaging her temples once again.

"You're right! I can start with some tender beef chunks and maybe try a bit of cream in the gravy. What vegetables should we use? Something tasty but different. I'm sure Jasper can help me come up with something."

"Of course he can. He's got some great ideas."

"Now, potatoes will need to go on the top, but what if we tried a sweet potato mash or maybe purple potatoes..." She stopped when she saw Iris grimacing. Miriam leaned closer, worried something was wrong. "Are you okay?"

"Oh, just getting a migraine, I think. I'll be fine," Iris said, closing her eyes.

"Okay. Let me run inside and grab you a hat." After choosing a bright pink hat from her grandmother's coat closet, Miriam heard Jasper yelling her name. Frantically, she ran through the solarium, her heart pounding as she imagined Poppy somehow injured. She threw open the door and found Jasper on the ground next to Iris, his expression contorted in anguish. She rushed to their side as Poppy began to wail, hiding behind Jasper.

"What happened?" Miriam said, looking at Iris lying lifeless on the tile. Jasper looked at her, clearly in despair.

"She fell from her chair," he said softly, cradling Iris's bloody head in his arms. Miriam picked up Poppy to comfort her, though her eyes never left Iris. "It happened too fast," he murmured.

"I'm calling an ambulance!" Miriam said, turning back toward the solarium.

"It's too late. She's no longer with us," Jasper said before reciting a Tibetan prayer.

Shocked and heartbroken, Miriam sat down next to Iris, holding Poppy tightly in her lap, and began to sob. Poppy looked up at Miriam and patted her cheek. "Don't cry, Mommy. Don't cry." Miriam buried her face in her daughter's curls, unable to speak.

She felt a hand on her back. "Go inside. I will call the funeral home," Jasper said, wiping the tears from his eyes.

Miriam stood up with Poppy, walking shakily into the house and wondering how she could possibly go on without her beloved grandmother's guidance.

Though profoundly hungover, Louise dragged herself from bed in time to dress, eat a strawberry Pop-Tart, and drink a cup of black coffee before calling a taxi. Despite her protests, Pearl frequently phoned to inquire how Louise was feeling and ask what she could do to help—each time, Louise tried to assure her she was managing just fine. The last thing she wanted was to be pitied by anyone, especially her former housekeeper, whom she knew would have gladly driven her to her first chemo appointment had Louise asked. *I managed to recover from the lumpectomy by myself. I got through ten months of radiation by myself. I can get through this.* With her divorce now behind her and Emma still estranged, Louise knew she only had herself to rely upon, even as the concept was a foreign one.

"Where to, ma'am?" the driver asked, looking at her in the rearview mirror as Louise slid into the back seat. He was an older gentleman who spoke with a thick Jamaican patois. Louise met his eyes in the mirror—gentle and kind, as if he held in his heart all the secrets of life. Louise leaned forward to ensure he could hear her.

"We're going to Richmond," she said. "The address is 915 Broad Street."

He nodded as he pulled the cab away from her home. "Are we going to a business or a residence?"

Louise folded her hands in her lap. "It's a business," she said. "A clinic, actually."

"My name is Sam," he said, giving her a kind smile.

"I'm Louise. Do you mind if I smoke?" she said, rolling down the window. "I'm a bit anxious."

Once again, their eyes met in the mirror. "I'll allow it, though you know it's bad for your health," he said, his smile fading as he gave her a concerned look.

Though her hands were trembling, Louise managed to light her cigarette, leaning her head back against the seat as she took a long drag. "Might be too late for that," she said, looking out the window while contemplating her mortality. Though she had not attended the funeral service, she had been deeply saddened to hear of Iris's death just one month earlier. She regretted that their last interactions had been contaminated by Miriam's presence, as if Louise's family's history with the Websters was without value. Now, as an heiress happily married and with a daughter, Miriam seemed to be living the life Louise once enjoyed. *Had she never come to Stuarts Landing,* Louise thought bitterly, *I wouldn't be all alone.*

A few minutes later, Sam broke the silence. "Would you like to talk about it?" he said, easing the cab onto the highway.

"Not really, but what the hell," Louise said, tossing her cigarette butt out the window before rolling it up. "Today is my first chemotherapy session." She realized it was the first time she had uttered the dreadful word aloud.

"Whoo boy," Sam said, letting out a heavy sigh. "That must feel quite frightening. My wife, she had the cancer. We found that ganja made it easier for her to endure her treatments."

Louise gave him a quizzical look. "Ganja?" she said, lighting another cigarette.

"Oh, that's what we call it at home," he said with a chuckle. "Marijuana or weed, as you would say here."

Louise immediately thought of the dope-addled teenagers passing joints behind the gym when she attended Fulton Academy. "That's not really my scene," she said, bringing her hand to her neck and shaking her head.

"You may feel differently," he said in a knowing voice. "It helps with the nausea. I'm curious, if I may ask, why you called a cab instead of having a loved one accompany you?"

She took a pull from her cigarette, looking out the window at the curtain of Virginia pines flanking the highway. "The only person I could have called is my former housekeeper," she said, "and I don't want to burden her in her retirement."

He gave her a sad look. "No other family? Friends?"

Louise shook her head. "Not anymore," she said. "My friends abandoned me years ago, as did my husband and daughter. Honestly, I don't understand why, but here I am."

Sam nodded thoughtfully as his eyes once again met hers in the mirror. "We have two sayings in Jamaica you may wish to consider. The first is 'Good frien' betta dan pocket money.' It means true friends are more important than any material item you can ever possess," he said, his eyes fixed steadily on the road. "The second is one I've relied on several times, and believe me, 'tis true. 'Ole fiyah tick easy fe ketch.' It is easier to rekindle a relationship than begin another with someone new."

Louise pulled a shawl from her bag and draped it around her shoulders. "What became of your wife?" she said.

"Abigay? Oh, she went into a brief remission, but the demon cancer returned with a vengeance," he said. "She died very peacefully, surrounded by family as the sun set over the Caribbean. It was beautiful."

Louise closed her eyes, trying to steady her breathing.

"She was happy, my girl," Sam said. "Up to the very end. She always say she led a life of no regret, just joy in every day, no matter the circumstance."

Wringing her hands, Louise contemplated his words. She could not imagine life being so simple. They rode in silence for the next thirty minutes as she tried to predict how her

first session would go.

"Here we are," Sam said, pulling up to the clinic's entrance. "Miss Louise, would you like me to stay with you?"

Louise looked at him in the rearview mirror, and her eyes began to well with tears. How could a perfect stranger treat her with such kindness? Oddly, it was harder to accept than the abandonment of her family and friends.

"Sam, that is very nice of you," she said, reaching into her wallet and handing him a one-hundred-dollar bill. "But I'll be okay."

"This is too much," he said. "The fare was only thirty-five dollars."

"It's just the right amount," she said, opening the passenger door. "Thank you for talking to me. I had forgotten what it was like." She gathered her purse and tote bag.

He handed her a card with his name and phone number. "I would be happy to pick you up, Miss Louise. Just call me when you're ready," he said.

Louise nodded noncommittally. "I appreciate that," she said, putting it in her bag.

"Just remember. There is always something to be grateful for, no matter what your imagination tells you," he said as she stepped from the car. "I will pray for you."

Louise walked slowly into the clinic, turning around to give him one last wave, but he had already driven away.

"My name is Louise Caldwell," she told the nurse at the front desk as her legs began to shake. "I'm here for my, um, appointment." She tried to swallow the lump in her throat.

"Right this way," the nurse said, guiding Louise into a brightly lit room full of women in leather recliners, their bodies attached to IV drips. Louise couldn't help noticing how many of them were wearing head scarves. She averted her eyes as the nurse settled her into her chair. "Please roll up your sleeve," she directed before inserting the needle into Louise's arm and securing the line with medical tape.

"How are you doing?" the nurse asked as the poison began flooding Louise's bloodstream.

Louise tried to remember Sam's words, but she was too frightened for philosophical quotations to make any difference. "I'm just ready to get this over with," she said, putting on her sunglasses and closing her eyes. In that moment, she didn't know if she was referring to the treatment session or her life.

52

After giving herself a few weeks to process Iris's passing, Miriam threw herself back into the tavern, as that was the only thing—other than her daughter—that helped assuage her gut-wrenching grief. While Iris had conveyed in her estate wishes that she did not want any kind of service after she died, Miriam had hosted a small celebration of life at Webster House. Louise declined to attend, but Clifton was there, along with Emma, the Butlers, and a few elderly members of the auxiliary. Miriam had displayed many of Iris's framed watercolor paintings on the dining room table, explaining they would be installed in her tavern, which seemed to have inspired Bitsy's eager request to help with the final details.

"Just tell me what I can do, and I'm there," she had said.

"Be careful what you ask for," Miriam responded at the time. Three weeks later, they were in Bitsy's car, heading to Richmond to troll various antique stores in search of furniture.

"I want the tavern to feel as eclectic as Rose and Iris always were," Miriam said. "I think that will make the tavern more inviting, don't you?"

Bitsy swore at the driver tailgating her before responding. "I think we should at least try to keep the woods all the same, you know? Like, let's commit to walnut tables or oak. Definitely not pine—too soft," she said, changing lanes. "Are you going to want to refinish them or leave them as we find them?"

"I suppose it depends," Miriam said. "To be honest, I hadn't built that into the timeline," she added. "What do you think?"

Bitsy swerved to avoid running over a garbage bag in the road. "I think I need a drink after this drive! I'm sure your budget will accommodate any work the furniture may need, but give me a pair of good rubber gloves, and I can strip with the best of them!" Bitsy said with a giggle, nudging Miriam with her elbow.

"I can only imagine," Miriam said, laughing. "And I'd rather not!"

"So, for the soft opening, I was thinking we could make it an auxiliary event?" Bitsy asked, looking at Miriam for agreement. Now that Bitsy had become president, Miriam knew she was exploring opportunities to make the auxiliary more involved in supporting Stuarts Landing businesses. Her idea of offering members discounts at Butler Automotive had paid dividends to the dealership. *Truly, she has a keen mind for marketing,* Miriam thought.

"I love that idea," Miriam said as Bitsy pulled into the parking lot of the first of five antique stores on their list. "We could do a fixed menu, maybe amp the price just a tad and donate the profits to a local charity?"

"Yes, yes, and yes!" Bitsy said, honking her horn for emphasis. "Okay, let's get to shopping!"

The first store offered little in the way of furniture that would work, though Miriam did find several sets of vintage china in varying patterns that coordinated with the color scheme she and Iris had envisioned. At their second stop, they purchased several tables in various shapes—arranging for white-glove delivery to the tavern—as well as an assortment of milk glass vases and a wire bird cage (because it was cute). By the time they had paid out at the fifth store, they had purchased more than enough tables to fill the tavern's interior.

"Now I really need a drink," Bitsy said, loading a pile of wicker baskets into the trunk of her car.

"We don't have any chairs," Miriam said as Bitsy pulled out of the parking lot. "And I'm not sure what to do with seating on the deck."

"I think you have time for that," Bitsy said. "It's still pretty chilly in February, so I don't think people will want to sit outside, at least for a few months. As for chairs, that may be the one area where we have some consistency. If the walls are going to be turquoise, what would you think about some lovely red leather club chairs?"

Miriam closed her eyes and tried to imagine how it would all come together. "I like it," she said. "But I have no idea where to begin."

"My decorator can get it taken care of," Bitsy said. "One less thing for you to worry about."

"Go for it," Miriam said as Bitsy pulled in front of the Jefferson Hotel.

"They have the very best drinks here," she said as the valet attendant opened her front door. She unfurled herself dramatically as he all but salivated looking at her long legs.

"You really are something," Miriam said, laughing, as they walked to the bar.

After they had ordered their drinks—a screwdriver for Bitsy and a glass of Prosecco for Miriam—they looked at each other and smiled.

"You know, you were the first person to make me feel welcome when I moved here," Miriam said. "So much has happened since we came to Stuarts Landing, it's hard to wrap my head around it."

Bitsy looked at her with a tender expression. "I can't imagine what it was like to be a newcomer here as an adult. It was hard enough as a teenager to find traction. I will always credit Louise for taking me under her wing, though it came at a high price," she said, shaking her head sadly. "As long as I followed her lead, everything was just peachy keen. If I dared to, in her mind, steal her spotlight, well, all bets were off."

Miriam thanked the waiter for her Prosecco, then raised her glass to clink Bitsy's. "I'm glad you never allowed her to kill your spirit," she said. "Gosh knows, she certainly tried to take me out a few times. I wonder how she's doing though, with the divorce and all."

Bitsy took a sip of her drink. "Well actually, it seems she may have lost her mind. Jackie told me Louise dismissed Pearl after all these years. So, I guess she's just rattling around in that huge house by herself," Bitsy said. "And I never knew her to have any real hobbies outside of her volunteer work. How long has it been since she's been to an auxiliary meeting?"

"I couldn't tell you. Same with church. It's like she's vanished."

"Are you going to invite her to the grand opening?" Bitsy said.

"I'm still thinking about it. Maybe it would do her some good to feel included, get out of the house?"

"Or she could make a scene," Bitsy said, raising her eyebrows. "You just never know with her."

"Isn't that the truth. Bits? I hope you'll take this right, but I wanted to tell you how much I've seen you change recently," Miriam said with a smile.

"Really? How so?" Bitsy leaned forward and rested her elbows on the table, clasping her hands together.

"When I first met you, I wasn't sure if you were, how shall I say, friend or foe. Watching you and Louise, well, at times I felt like I was a pawn for both of you, you know?"

Bitsy grinned. "You just said quite a mouthful. I don't think either of us was conscious of it at the time, but you kind of drew everyone out of their comfort zones around here."

"I certainly didn't mean to," Miriam said, furrowing

her brow.

"Oh, in a good way," Bitsy said, reaching over to pat Miriam's hand. "You are so guileless, so sincere, so genuinely kind... you kind of became my role model, even though I didn't always show it. Old habits die hard, as they say, but I did want to change, and I think you're right. I have. Thanks to you."

"Thank you, Bits. That means a great deal to me, as does your friendship. Now, let's get back to work!"

***

One month later, Miriam met Bitsy at the mill so they could oversee the installation of the furniture Miriam had purchased, including the red leather chairs Bitsy had ordered from a custom furniture maker in North Carolina. Miriam had already hung Iris's paintings, as well as the photos she had duplicated from the historical society. From there, it was a matter of fine-tuning the décor and, more importantly, finalizing her menu, hiring staff, and getting ready for the soft and grand openings.

"It's really taken shape," Bitsy said, plunking down into one of the club chairs. "You must be so pleased!"

"You know, it was Iris who asked me about any big dreams I still had. I didn't expect to say, 'Oh, for sure, I want to open a restaurant,' but it felt right from that moment on. I'm just sorry she couldn't see our shared vision—with your amazing help—come to life," Miriam said, gazing at Iris's watercolors.

Bitsy reached into her bag and pulled out a sketchbook. "I hope you don't mind, but I created a design I think would be perfect for your logo," she said, handing it to Miriam. "I think we have plenty of time to have a sign made to sit over the front door."

Miriam opened the sketchbook to see a beautifully rendered peacock wearing red sunglasses, turquoise beads, and a pair of pink ballet shoes. Her eyes welled up with tears as she brought her hand to her mouth.

"You don't like it?" Bitsy said, reaching for the sketchbook. "I have other ideas..."

Miriam wiped her eyes. "It's positively perfect," she said. "The only thing I'd like to add is the tavern's name: Rose & Iris's. Other than that, let's go with it!"

Bitsy raised both arms in the air, letting out a loud whoop.

"You've really missed your calling, Bits," Miriam said, staring at the drawing. "You could make a living doing this!"

Bitsy twirled a strand of her hair before taking another sip of her drink. "I just might," she said.

***

Once the holidays passed, Miriam worked with Bitsy on the logistics of the February seventh trial run, one week before the official grand opening. "We must invite the mayor," Bitsy said, "and the president of the rotary club. Anyone else you can think of?"

"Besides the women in the auxiliary and their husbands? I think we may have our hands full!" Miriam said, dabbing the perspiration from her forehead.

"Okay, most important question: What are you going to wear?" Bitsy said, watching Miriam as she paced around the tavern.

"I haven't given it a thought," she said with a chuckle. "I'll let you advise me on that."

"Red," Bitsy said. "You must wear red!"

"Okay, I'll wear red. What are we missing?" Miriam asked, returning to the table and obsessively checking her list.

"Nothing I can think of. And besides, it's the things that go askew that make for the best stories!"

Miriam grimaced. "Lord, help me!"

When February seventh arrived, Miriam knew she had done all she could to ensure the soft opening would be a success. As she was dressing in a crimson velvet pantsuit, George came into their bedroom, already outfitted in a new tuxedo he had bought for the occasion.

"You look stunning, Mim," he said, kissing her neck. Poppy had followed him and was bouncing with unbridled enthusiasm.

"He got you a present!" she said as he reached into his interior pocket, removing the iconic Tiffany robin's egg-blue box with a white satin ribbon.

Miriam gave George a curious look–he was never one to be spontaneous. "What is this?" she asked as she sat down on their bed. Poppy immediately jumped in her lap, clapping her hands.

"It's a surprise, Mommy!" Poppy said. "And pretty, just like you!"

Miriam opened the box to find an opal ring as fiery as the sun.

"For my forever shining light," George said as Miriam put it on. "I am so incredibly proud of you, not just for the tavern but for the wife, the mother, the woman you are."

Miriam stood and examined her reflection in the mirror. "I feel like a princess," she whispered, turning around and embracing her husband and daughter. "Thank you seems so inadequate." She gave them each a kiss.

"We probably need to go," George said. "Jasper has the Bentley pulled out front."

"One last thing," Miriam said, opening her jewelry box. After pinning her dogwood brooch on her jumpsuit–the one Iris had pinned on baby Althea's blanket–she turned around. "I'm ready!"

Together, the three walked downstairs to meet Jasper at the car. As he opened the door for Miriam, Jasper leaned in and whispered, "They breathe blessings into this night and into your endeavor, both sisters. You are covered by their love. Forever."

53

As she flipped the sign from "Closed" to "Open" on the fire-engine red wooden door, Miriam could not believe her good fortune. Though her tavern, Rose and Iris's, had officially been in business for two weeks now, it seemed like yesterday when she first conjured the idea of turning the abandoned sawmill into a promising business. And because of its history, the mill would always represent a meaningful–if not tragic–part of her history too. Shaking her head to clear the memories, she turned her attention to the kitchen, where the staff chattered while finishing their prep work for the lunch crowd.

Gloria approached her with a yellow legal pad, and Miriam smiled–Gloria had proven to be an excellent manager, which allowed Miriam time to focus on the creative aspects of the business. Miriam knew from her first encounter with Gloria at The Pig that she was more talented than anyone would have assumed given her humble upbringing. Especially in Stuarts Landing.

"It looks like we're going to be two servers short today," Gloria said, tapping the tablet with her pencil. "Do you want to take care of the front or the back of the house?"

She handed Miriam the schedule, pointing to the names of those whose shifts they would have to cover.

"This isn't the first time they've called in at the last minute," Gloria said. "Perhaps we should consider letting them go?"

Miriam looked at her thoughtfully, massaging behind her ear with her index finger. "They're in college, Gloria," Miriam said. "I know they need the money. Could be they've got a big deadline or something. I mean, I wouldn't know since I didn't go to college, but they're good kids."

"That's fine and dandy, but they're not being very reliable," Gloria said, pursing her lips.

"I say we ask them what might be going on in their lives and give them another chance. Besides, it'll be fun to serve our customers!" Miriam said, tightening her apron. "If you don't mind overseeing the kitchen, I'll handle the front."

Gloria noddedm then smiled. "What're you going to do with the tips?" she said.

"What do you think? Pool them for the kitchen staff, of course!"

"Really, Miriam, the world needs more people with a heart as big as yours," Gloria said, turning to head back to the kitchen.

"At least you didn't say 'derriere'!" Miriam hollered. Gloria responded with a snort.

***

By noon, the tavern was full of happy patrons eating and laughing while the fireplaces popped and crackled. Miriam glanced around the room and once again felt humbled that she—with plenty of support—had turned her improbable dream into a living, breathing business. The décor, an eclectic blend of furniture and artwork, supported the inviting ambiance Miriam had desired—a vibe that encouraged people to check their concerns at the door and simply relax with a hot meal, a cold beverage, and lively conversations. A community—that's what Miriam strove to create, and for now, she believed her endeavors to have been successful.

The bell over the front door tinkled, and she turned to see Louise step tentatively into the spacious front room. Miriam nearly dropped the tray of dirty glasses she was carrying back to the kitchen. No one had seen Louise in ages, though plenty of rumors enshrouded her and her disappearance. Miriam trusted Louise would adhere to the sign encouraging patrons to seat themselves and took the tray quickly to the kitchen.

"You okay?" Gloria said while shredding more lettuce for their house salad. "You look like you've seen a ghost!"

Miriam wiped her hands on her apron, then stared down at her school bus-yellow sneakers. "That's not far from the truth," she said. "Guess who just came in?"

"Hmm... let me think. Elvis?" Gloria said, scooping the lettuce into an enormous stainless-steel bowl.

"Good one," Miriam said with a chuckle. "But sadly, no. Louise. Louise Caldwell!"

"She's still around? Hadn't heard her name in a long time," Gloria said, looking up at Miriam. "Didn't her husband dump her?"

Miriam gave a half-hearted shrug. "Seems I heard something, but you know I don't like gossip."

Gloria looked at her thoughtfully. "Weren't you all pretty close at one point?"

Miriam momentarily reflected on her complicated relationship with Louise over the years. "Yes, for a minute, then everything went south."

"Well, you better get out there. We don't like to keep our patrons waiting!"

"Yes, boss," Miriam said, grabbing a single menu from the kiosk before returning to the dining area. Taking a deep breath, she slowly approached Louise's table and couldn't help noticing how frail the woman had become.

"Well, hello, Louise!" Miriam said in her most cheerful voice. "What a lovely surprise!"

Louise furrowed her brow, then scowled at Miriam. "Really? You were the one who invited me to your grand opening," she said. "I, of course, had a prior commitment. I do hope it went well." Her mouth broadened into a feral smile.

"We had a wonderful turnout, thank you. May I bring you something to drink?" she said, handing Louise the menu.

"Why yes, I believe I'll have an extra dry martini," she said. Miriam resisted the urge to check her watch; very few of her lunch patrons asked for alcohol, unless they were tourists.

"Coming right up," Miriam said, turning on her heel to walk to the bar. She heard Louise mumbling to herself and could feel Louise's hawkish eyes boring into her back. When she returned with the icy glass in hand, she noticed Louise's hands shaking as she perused the lunch menu.

"Everything okay, Louise?" she said, placing the drink on the cardboard coaster branded with the Rose and Iris's logo.

Louise picked up her drink with both hands and took three thirsty gulps before putting it down and smiling. "Of course. Why wouldn't it be?"

She's behaving oddly, Miriam thought to herself, *even for Louise*. Miriam couldn't pinpoint what she was feeling, but she knew her instincts were trying to warn her... of something.

"Would you like to hear our lunch specials?"

"Don't you own the place?" Louise said. "Can't you afford help?" She took another hearty swig of her martini, then wiped her mouth with the back of her hand. *Was she already intoxicated?* Never, in all the years she had known Louise, had Miriam witnessed her doing something so profoundly uncouth. Her concerns continued to mount.

"I can come back if you'd like more time," Miriam said, putting her pen behind her ear.

"No, I'd be interested in hearing what you'd recommend," Louise said. Her eyes, shining like quicksilver, were lasered on Miriam's.

"Our quiche is very good—today, it's mushroom and spinach," Miriam said. Louise wrinkled her nose. "We also have a lovely corn beef and cabbage special, which has been very popular." Louise shook her head, and Miriam couldn't help noticing several strands of her blonde hair falling onto the placemat.

"Really, I can come back," Miriam said.

"No!" Louise said, holding up the menu and stabbing it with her index finger. "That. That's what I want," she said, indicating the shepherd's pie. Miriam involuntarily shuddered as she realized why Louise was here.

"Excellent choice," she said. "I'm eager for you to taste it since I reimagined the recipe! It will be out in just a minute."

"I'll take another drink," Louise said. Miriam nodded, went to the bar, retrieved the shaker from the refrigerator, and poured another martini, which she brought nervously to Louise's table. Louise remained silent as she brought the fresh glass to her lips.

Walking purposefully, though shakily, into the kitchen, Miriam placed the order in front of Gloria, then went to the faucet to pour a glass of water. She had just taken a drink when Louise stormed into the kitchen, her fists clenched. "Am I just a big joke to you?!" she said, loud enough that the dining area fell into an immediate hush.

"I'm not sure what you're talking about, Louise." Alarmed, Miriam looked over her shoulder at Gloria, who was standing perfectly still. Louise inched closer, a crazed look in her eyes as she wielded her right index finger like a weapon pointed directly at Miriam's face.

"Why did you have to do it, Miriam? Why did you have to take away everything that was mine?" Louise railed. Miriam took a step backward, unsure what was happening.

"Again, I don't know what you're talking about it!" she said, holding up her hands as if in surrender.

"My life was fine; Stuarts Landing was fine. Then you come along, and in a heartbeat, you took my place. You stole the auxiliary presidency right out from under me, then you took Bitsy, who was *my* best friend. Was that enough? Of course not! You took the Webster sisters, who I've known since I was born, then this!" She swung her arms wildly to indicate the building. "This was my dream, Miriam... my dream to make this a museum! Not some, some watering hole with second-rate food," she said, panting. For a moment, Miriam worried the hysterical woman would faint, she looked so unsteady.

"Louise," she said, taking a step closer to the woman, who was hugging herself tightly. "It was never my intention to take anything from you. I just wanted to be happy, that's all, but never at your expense. You must believe me."

"Are you?"

"Am I what?"

"Happy?!" Louise spat. Miriam watched Gloria slip quietly from the kitchen to reach the telephone stationed in the bar. Gloria raised her eyebrows, but Miriam shook her head, mouthing, "It's okay." She returned her attention to the shrunken woman standing before her.

"I am happy," Miriam said softly. "But not at seeing you so distraught. Is this about the shepherd's pie? It's a completely different version, but I can take it off the menu if you wish."

Louise began to laugh. "That's what you think I care about? What a riot, Miriam. No, I'm distraught, to use your word, because you got away with it, unchecked."

Now, Miriam was even more confused. *How much has Louise had to drink already?*

"You've lost me, Louise," Miriam said, shaking her head.

"Oh, I lost you some time ago. Right about the time you became an heiress," she said, sounding downright serpentine as she drew out the last syllable.

"That's not what I meant. I don't understand what you're

trying to tell me," Miriam said, dabbing her forehead with the handkerchief she kept tucked in her apron.

"You broke all the rules here, and yet you still came out on top," Louise sputtered as she began to cry. "You didn't care about anything I tried to teach you, and I guess it didn't matter after all. But why… why couldn't that've been my mother's story too? It didn't work when she bucked the system. So, why couldn't she just conform? Would that have been so bad? Why did they have to send her away?" She dropped her head and covered her eyes with trembling hands as her shoulders convulsed.

Miriam's heart jumped to her throat as she watched Louise silently implode.

"Why don't you come with me," Miriam said gently, reaching to take Louise by the elbow. Before she could react, Louise swung her handbag at Miriam, hitting her squarely in the jaw. She recoiled, rubbing the side of her face as Louise lunged toward her, swinging her bag and knocking a full tray of dirty glasses off the kitchen counter. A large shard rebounded from the tile floor and sliced the top of Miriam's ankle as she cried out in pain.

"*Stop!*" Gloria said as she raced into the kitchen, grabbing Louise in a bear hug as the woman tried to fight back.

"Let go of me!" Louise said, struggling to escape Gloria's arms.

Miriam had never witnessed anything like the scene unfolding, and she hoped she never would again. She remembered something her granddaddy had told her so many long years ago. "The one thing everyone has in common is longing. What separates us is what we long for," he had said. And in that moment, Miriam suddenly understood Louise. What she didn't understand was how to help her. So she did the only thing that came to mind and called Pearl to come and get Louise. Ten minutes later, she watched Pearl help

Louise get into the old pickup truck.

"Whew," Gloria said. "What was that all about?"

"It's a really long story," Miriam said. "And I'm still trying to make sense of it all."

54

Miriam knew Louise's life had taken a series of unfortunate turns in the last year or two, but her erratic behavior at the tavern was beyond anything Miriam could have anticipated. Once the shock of Louise's outburst had dissipated, Miriam couldn't help feeling sorry for her. After calling George at the dealership to tell him about the episode, his first question was whether Miriam had been hurt.

"Not terribly, though she did hit me in the head with her purse and I have a pretty nasty cut on my ankle," Miriam said, rubbing her temple. "Emotionally, though, yeah—she basically accused me of ruining her life. And then she told me I had gotten away with breaking the rules here while still, how did she put it? While still coming out on top. Then, she just broke down, George. I watched as she just fell apart, like a brick wall crumbling, crying for her mother. And all I could think was that I had no idea she was so fragile and that my very being caused her to shatter. I had wanted us to be friends, but I guess she could never see me that way. She compared me to her mother, who refused to conform and, from what I understood, that led to her death. She still isn't over it."

"That's too bad about her mom, but you are who you are. And you have plenty of people who love and cherish you, Mim," George said. "I wouldn't worry about Louise."

Miriam replayed in her mind the scene of Louise sinking to the floor of the tavern's kitchen, contrasting it to when she first met Louise, once regal, even patrician in her appearance and behavior. The unhinged and unkempt woman who stormed into her tavern was exactly the type of person Louise would have publicly shunned.

"I feel I owe it to her to help, somehow."

"And this is why people look up to you," George said. "Most people would want their pound of flesh."

"You know I don't derive pleasure from another's tribulations, sweetheart. It's bad for the soul."

"You've been hanging out with Jasper too much!" George said, chuckling. "I'll see you tonight. I'm assuming you'll have Gloria close up?"

She looked over at Gloria, who was putting together the waitstaff schedule for the following week, and smiled. "Yes, she'll handle the closing. We'll have a nice family dinner at home. All right, gotta run. I love you," she said before hanging up the phone.

***

They had just finished eating when the doorbell rang. Poppy jumped out of her chair to run full tilt to the door with Jasper hurriedly following behind. Miriam gave George a concerned look.

"You're not expecting anyone, are you?" she said, folding her napkin and placing it beside her plate.

"I was going to ask you the same thing," he said.

A moment later, Jasper ushered Pearl into the dining room, holding Poppy's hand.

"Pearl, please come in! Have you eaten?" Miriam said, standing to give Pearl a hug.

"Aw, thank you, Miz Llewelyn, but I'm good. I need to talk to you, and I'm sorry for not callin' first," she added, shuffling nervously side to side.

"Poppy, honey, stay here with Daddy and Jasper while I go

talk to Miss Pearl, okay?" Miriam said, kissing the top of her daughter's head. Poppy nodded happily, snatching another piece of bread from the table.

Miriam led Pearl to the parlor and closed the door.

"I never been here before," Pearl said, looking around the eclectic room in wonder. "Is that..." she said, pointing at the centerpiece of the parlor, her mouth agape.

"Oh, yes, it's a Picasso," Miriam said. "It belonged to the sisters. They actually met him!" she added, smiling at the memory of that conversation.

"Well, I'll be," Pearl said, staring at the painting with awe. "I learned about him at one of them artist talks at the museum in Richmond. Can't say I understand his work, but it sure is somethin'."

"They did love their art," Miriam said, motioning to the couch. "Let's sit down, Pearl. Are you all right? Is Jackie okay?" She took a seat, inviting Pearl to sit down next to her.

"Oh, she fine, that one. Never gives me a worry, never has. She doing real well at the beauty shop, all while still working a day a week for Miz Butler," Pearl said, smoothing the front of her modest dress. Miriam had never seen her in street clothes and realized that, in her simple outfit, she looked younger than she had in the uniform she wore while working for Louise.

"How have you been?" Miriam said, trying to help Pearl feel comfortable as she was clearly distressed about some-thing. "Enjoying retirement? Bitsy told me you were no longer working for Louise."

"It's been nice. I got more time to work at the church, which I enjoy. Started a little shop, Water From the Rock, for women needin' nice clothes to find work but who ain't got money. We take donated clothes, repair and clean 'em if need be, then give the women vouchers they can use to get what they need for free," she said proudly.

"You're doing the Lord's work, Pearl," Miriam said, patting

Pearl's hand. "Let me know how I can help."

"Oh, you bet I will. But that ain't why I'm here, Miz Llewelyn."

"Please, call me Miriam. No need to be formal," Miriam said with a smile.

"Um, okay, Miriam," Pearl said. "I'm real glad you called me to come help with Miz Louise, but the way she was shocked me to my shoes."

Miriam shifted on the couch, unsure where the conversation was heading. "Yes, Louise seems to be struggling, though I hadn't seen her in ages until today," Miriam said. "Probably not since before Emma left for college. What's that, like, two years?"

"Sound 'bout right."

"I don't know how much she told you about what happened today," Miriam said.

"She done say nothin'."

"Well, she came to the tavern and made some accusations," Miriam said carefully, as she knew Pearl's allegiance would always be to Louise. "Then she seemed to have some kind of breakdown, and she walloped me with her purse before swinging again and sending a tray of bar glasses flying. My manager, Gloria, wanted to call the police, but I thought it better to call you."

Pearl began rubbing her eyes. "Oh, dear Lord. She done lost it, Miriam," Pearl said, looking at her sadly. "She done made me promise I wouldn't tell no one, but she sick."

Miriam leaned forward. "Is it serious?"

Pearl nodded. "She got the cancer," she said softly. "And she don't want my help."

"Is anyone there for her?" Miriam said, rubbing her eyes.

"Not that I can see. She a proud woman, that Miz Louise. You know."

"We need to go see her. Now," Miriam said, standing up

quickly. "I'll put together some leftovers from tonight, if you give me a few minutes."

"Ah, now, I don't think she would want that," Pearl said, shaking her head. "She gonna think I done violate her privacy."

"Well, it's a good thing you don't work for her then," Miriam said, walking to the French doors. "I'll be right back."

After explaining the situation to George and Jasper, Jasper helped her assemble a container with lasagna, salad, and French bread to take with her.

"Are you sure about this?" George said. "Especially after today?"

Miriam looked into his eyes. "I couldn't live with myself if I didn't try to help her," she said, putting her head on his shoulder. "I don't know how long I'll be. I love you."

"Mim? Be careful," George said.

She picked up the food and headed toward the parlor. "Ready? Let's go out front. Jasper's pulling my car around," Miriam said as Pearl stood.

"I ain't got a good feeling 'bout this," Pearl said, following Miriam to the front door.

"We'll be fine," Miriam said, walking down the steps toward the Lincoln. Pearl got into her truck, and together, they convoyed to Louise's house.

When they arrived, the house was dark, though Miriam could see the yard needed tending. Her fingers twitched at the thought of getting in there to weed and prune, but she followed Pearl to the front door instead. Pearl pressed the doorbell, then looked anxiously at Miriam. The only sound they heard was the two German shepherds barking frantically from the foyer. They waited for a few minutes before Pearl pressed the bell again.

"You don't have a key?" Miriam whispered.

"I do, but that don't feel right," Pearl whispered in response.

"Let's walk around back, see if her car is there." They hurried to the porte-cochère and found the Cadillac in its spot.

"Does the key work on this side door?" Miriam said. "It goes into the solarium, right?"

Pearl opened her pocketbook and took out her keys, fumbling to find the right one. Quietly, she unlocked the door, and together, they tiptoed inside, closing the door softly behind them.

Miriam could not believe her eyes. The solarium was littered with pizza boxes and empty liquor bottles, paper napkins strewn about the floor, piles of dog excrement soiling Louise's prized Persian rug. She raised her eyebrows at Pearl. They moved into the kitchen, turning on the light so Miriam could put the food on the counter. The sink was full of dirty dishes, and the floor was splattered with grease and other stains Miriam could not identify.

"Where is she?" Miriam whispered as she walked toward the great room. It was empty.

"Most likely in her bedroom, if I had to guess," Pearl said. "Follow me."

Together, they ascended the stairs and walked down the long hall to Louise's room. When they opened the door, they saw Louise sitting in bed gazing out the window, a vodka bottle in hand, her nightgown covered in vomit.

"Oh, Miz Louise!" Pearl said, rushing to her bed. Louise gave her a hazy look, then turned her head and squinted at Miriam.

"Louise? It's me, Miriam," she said, approaching her. The bedroom was littered with dirty clothes, and to Miriam, it smelled like death.

"Why are you here?" Louise slurred, trying to get out of bed. "Wasn't today enough for you?"

Miriam went to the bathroom and noticed a battalion of pill bottles lined up on Louise's vanity. She quickly grabbed a washcloth, ran it under the faucet, and brought it back to

Pearl, who was trying to remove Louise's nightgown.

"Leave me alone!" Louise said, twisting as Pearl tried to settle her. She was behaving like an animal ensnared in a net. Miriam helped get Louise changed, then watched as Pearl cleaned her face.

"Pearl told me," Miriam said, sitting down on the bed.

"Dammit, Pearl!" Louise yelled, then began coughing violently. "I didn't want anyone to know!" She reached for the bottle of vodka and brought it to her mouth as a trickle of blood began running from her nose.

"That's it, Louise. You can hate me all you want, but we're getting you to the hospital," Miriam said, taking charge.

"Over my dead body," Louise said.

"You may be dead sooner than later if we don't get you looked at," Miriam said.

"Like anyone would give a damn," she said, wiping the blood from her nose.

"I would," Miriam said. "Now, we're going to help you downstairs, and I'll drive us to the hospital." She put her arm around Louise's skeletal waist.

"I don't want to die," Louise mumbled, "but I'm not sure what I'm living for anymore." She stumbled as they tried to help her down the hall.

"Then, we'll figure that out. Together," Miriam said. "If I've learned nothing else, it's never too late to make a different life for yourself."

Louise awoke to find herself in a hospital bed, plugged into several monitors while liquids flowed into her bloodstream through two separate IVs. Her head was pounding, her mouth felt chalky, and she was perspiring profusely. She had no memory of what brought her there nor how she arrived. She closed her eyes, only to be jolted by a wave of nausea so severe she grabbed the blue, kidney-shaped emesis basin from the side table and held it under her mouth. Though her stomach convulsed, all she could do was heave up bitter-tasting bile. She was panting from exertion when the doctor entered her room, followed by Pearl and... Miriam?

"Good morning, Mrs. Caldwell. I'm Dr. Morris, and I'm the attending physician on duty. I'm glad to see you awake," he said, looking at the monitors. "You were in pretty bad shape when your friends brought you in last night. In addition to an extremely high blood alcohol level, your liver enzymes are dangerously elevated, and you are dehydrated to boot. We're giving you electrolytes to settle your system down and glucose to manage your hypoglycemic shock. How are you feeling?"

Louise tried to sit up but felt too weak. She stared at the ceiling instead. "Like I've been hit by a train. Twice," she said, wiping her mouth with the back of her hand.

"I understand you're being treated for cancer," Dr. Morris said. "Did your oncologist not explain to you that alcohol consumption is strongly discouraged during chemotherapy? Or advise you about the importance of maintaining good

nutrition to give your body strength?"

Louise looked over at Pearl and Miriam, then turned her attention back to the doctor. "Of course he did," she said, running her hand through her dirty hair, only to see several clumps fall to the sheet. "I don't need to be scolded. I'm not a child." Her hands began to tremble.

"I'm going to ask you a question, and I need you to answer honestly," he said, "as your health absolutely depends on it. How much do you drink each day?"

Louise's eyes welled with tears as her entire body shook. She felt she was being tormented from the inside out, as if every cell was warring against her, hungry for her demise. *What the hell, Louise! What do you have to lose? Tell the truth!*

"I drink vodka, mostly," she said, her eyes finding Pearl, who was studying her with maternal warmth. *How did I take her for granted?* Louise chided herself, awash once again with sadness at what had become of her life. "Sometimes Scotch or wine but mostly vodka." Pearl nodded encouragingly. Miriam remained quiet but was looking at her with an expression of kindness Louise knew she did not deserve.

"How much do you drink?" Dr. Morris repeated, his tone deadly serious.

"I go through about a fifth of vodka every two days or so," Louise said. "And I usually have a few glasses of wine with dinner." She folded her arms over her chest.

"Thank you. We're going to have to keep you here for a few days as you go through detoxification," he said. "Cancer and chemo are hard enough on your system. Alcohol consumption only exacerbates your disease state. And while the detox process puts your body through the wringer, it's necessary for the chemo to do its job. Any questions?"

Louise looked at him angrily. "You can't keep me here against my will," she said, her voice rising with agitation.

"True enough. But I can also say your prognosis—if you

continue down the path you've been on—is not good. Not good at all," he said, making a note on her chart.

Miriam stepped forward. "Louise, I really think you need to do as Dr. Morris says."

"I'm sure you're relishing every moment of this," Louise said, closing her eyes.

"In a manner of speaking, yes, Louise, I am," Miriam said, holding her head higher.

Louise's eyes flew open. "As I expected," she snarled. "'How the mighty have fallen!' Isn't that what you're thinking? Isn't that what everyone's been thinking?"

"I relish the opportunity to *help you*, Louise. To help you find your way back to health and to life. That's what I relish and hope for," Miriam said.

Pearl nodded enthusiastically. "Exactly what she say, Miz Louise. We all want to see you strong cuz we care 'bout you. How you not know that?"

Louise started crying, which turned into sobbing, as the doctor left the room. Miriam cautiously sat on the side of Louise's bed; Pearl stood behind her.

"I've lost everything," Louise said through her tears. "My family, my friends, my reputation, my health, my sense of who I am. I've got nothing left." She blew her nose indelicately.

"How about hope? Have you lost that?" Miriam said, putting her hand on Louise's bony thigh.

"Yes," Louise whispered, covering her eyes with her hands.

"What happened to your faith? Your imagination? Your take-no-prisoners attitude?" Miriam said. "I know who you are, even if you can't see it right now."

"I don't like who I am," Louise mumbled, then began chewing on her thumbnail. "Haven't for a very long time."

"Then learn to be someone you like," Pearl said. "You is a sweet child of God. Quit acting the fool!"

Louise closed her eyes, then drifted off into a deep sleep.

When she awoke, Miriam was sitting in a chair by her side, her fingers furiously knitting what appeared to be a cap.

"Where's Pearl?" Louise asked as her voice cracked. She reached for a cup of water, but her hand was shaking too much for her to bring it to her mouth.

"Let me," Miriam said, taking the water and helping Louise drink a few sips. "There. Good. Pearl went home to take a nap. She said she'd be back later. Oh, and she has your dogs at her house. For now."

"That's good. What time is it?" Louise said, squinting to see the clock.

"It's a little after two in the afternoon," Miriam said, looking at her watch.

"How long have you been here?"

"Since we brought you in last night, around eight," Miriam said.

"You've been here for eighteen hours? Why on earth would you do that? Don't you have a family and a business to tend to?"

"My business and my family are just fine. You needed me more. You're just too stubborn to realize it," she said with a chuckle. "I expect the next few days are going to be pretty rough, but you don't have to go it alone. I promise."

Miriam reached out for Louise's hand and squeezed it. The warmth of her touch almost frightened Louise, and she initially pulled away. But when Miriam didn't flinch, she relaxed ever so slightly. "I have so much I want to say, but my mind is all cluttered."

"There's plenty of time for that," Miriam said with a smile. "Mama used to always tell me the rearview mirror is smaller than the windshield, because what's in front of us is more important than what's behind us. Words to live by, don't you think?"

Louise closed her eyes and smiled, placing her hand over her breast. "Yes," she whispered. "Yes, I do."

376

56

Miriam visited Louise each of the nine days she spent in the hospital, wincing at times as she watched Louise navigate the ugly throes of detox. Sometimes angry, often irritable or weepy, and usually shaking uncontrollably, Louise seemed a shrunken version of herself, yet Miriam was pleased to see her fighting through her misery. On some occasions, they sat quietly, watching afternoon television (which they both agreed was mindless). Louise had lost considerably more hair, so Miriam always brought her knitting needles and yarn, whipping up as many cute hats as her fingers would allow so Louise would have plenty of options.

Two days before she was to be discharged, Miriam and Pearl visited together, having planned to bring Louise lunch from the tavern. Miriam opted against the shepherd's pie and instead packed a picnic basket with spinach and mushroom quiche, tomato parmesan soup, mini baguettes, and chocolate mousse, all of which she served as Louise eyed the food hungrily.

"It looks like your appetite has finally returned!" Miriam said as Louise dug into the quiche.

"Oh, Miriam, this is to die for!" Louise said after swallowing. She brought the container of soup to her mouth and took a big sip. Miriam smiled, noticing Louise's hands had stopped shaking.

"Eat up now, Miz Louise," Pearl said, nodding as Louise took a baguette and slathered it with butter.

"Is this from Rose & Iris's?" Louise asked as crumbs dropped on her chest. Grinning, she brushed them onto the floor.

"Yes," Miriam said. "That's a new soup recipe I'm trying out. Thought you'd be my official taster!"

"Absolutely, positively put this on the menu," Louise said, dipping her baguette into the cup. "Divine."

"I'd like to talk with you about something," Miriam said, sitting down in the chair next to the bed. Pearl pulled another chair beside hers and sat down, folding her hands in her lap. "You've still got a ways to go with your treatment, so I'd like you to come stay with us."

Louise furrowed her brow and put down her fork. "Don't you trust me to be alone? Honestly, after what I've been through, the mere thought of alcohol makes me sick," she said.

"It ain't that, Miz Louise," Pearl said, leaning forward. "We trust you just fine. We just think you'd get better faster if you ain't all by yourself."

"Then why don't you come back to work?" Louise said.

Pearl shifted in her seat. "That's mighty nice of you, Miz Louise, but I'm too old. And if you fall, I'm afraid I ain't strong enough to pick you up. But I'll come visit you at Miriam's," she said, giving Miriam a wink.

"You're always welcome," Miriam said. "Louise, I promise if you think this lunch is good, you'll swoon when you taste Jasper's cooking... you'd never know you're eating health food. After Rose died, he helped Iris keep her strength—the tai chi and breathing exercises he teaches did wonders for her, for all of us, really."

Louise stuffed another piece of baguette into her mouth and looked out the window. Miriam turned to Pearl, who merely shrugged. Finally, Louise turned her attention back to them as she plunged her spoon into the chocolate mousse.

"I don't want to be a burden," she said, bringing the spoon

to her mouth. "Oh, God, this is sin! Can I have this every day?" Her face mirrored that of a child eating ice cream for the first time.

"Well, this is kind of a special treat," Miriam said. "The doctor told me you need to watch how much sugar you consume."

"Yeah, yeah, cancer loves sugar," Louise said, defiantly shoveling another large spoonful into her mouth while smiling impishly. "I'll only stay until I get my strength back and not one minute longer."

Miriam smiled broadly. "That's wonderful! Poppy will definitely keep you amused," she said, clapping her hands. "But I'd like you to promise you'll stay until your chemo is over and we know you're cancer-free." She looked to Pearl for agreement.

"That's right," Pearl said. "Then you can get on with being you."

"Oh, I have no plans for that," Louise said, giving Miriam a meaningful look. "I plan to get on with finding who I was meant to be all along."

"Hallelujah!" Pearl said, holding her hands to her chest and closing her eyes. "All praise to you, sweet baby Jesus!"

"Damn right," Louise said with a chuckle.

"Now, Miz Louise, it ain't right you be cussin' right after we done thanked our good Lord," Pearl pretended to tease. Louise stuck out her tongue, then all three broke out into laughter. To Miriam, it was the sound of friendship.

***

After thoroughly cleaning Louise's house, Pearl packed two suitcases worth of clothes, shoes, and accessories she thought appropriate for Louise's convalescence then took them to Miriam's. "Do you think she'll have trouble with the stairs?"

Miriam said as they arranged Louise's clothes in the closet.

"I can't say for sure, but I know they got her doing some exercises in the hospital. Knowing Miz Louise, she'll be fine," Pearl said, hanging Louise's silk robe on a hook in the bathroom. "You made the room look real nice. Them plants is a nice touch."

Miriam smiled. "That was Jasper's idea. He says plants help clean the air. Isn't that something?"

Pearl nodded. "God know what he's doin'. And, Miriam, I just have to say, anyone ever ask me for an example of livin' in Christ, it'd be you. Most people woulda turned a blind eye to Miz Louise, especially if she done them like she done you. You about the kindest woman I've ever known."

Miriam smiled. "Let he without sin…"

"Cast the first stone," Pearl added.

Two hours later, Jasper drove Miriam to the hospital to pick up Louise, who was waiting eagerly in a wheelchair—attended by a nurse—under the awning of the circular drive. Her cheeks pink from the chilly weather and bundled in one of the caps and a blanket Miriam had knitted, she looked healthier than Miriam would have anticipated.

"Hiya!" Miriam said, leaning down to give Louise a hug. "Ready for your next adventure?"

"I was born ready!" Louise said, taking a deep breath of the crisp air. After thanking the nurse, Miriam wheeled Louise to the Lincoln.

"Hi there, Jasper!" she said happily as he helped her into the car. He nodded and bowed, opening the other passenger door for Miriam, who climbed in next to Louise.

"Poppy is positively giddy to meet you," Miriam said, turning to look at Louise. "And you'll never have to wonder what she's thinking, that's for sure."

"She sounds like my Emma," Louise said, pulling her wool cap a little lower on her forehead.

"Have you called to let her know what's going on?"

"Heavens no. We haven't talked in about two years. Besides, she's long since written me off. I don't blame her, not really," she said, nervously bunching the blanket in her lap.

"Why would you say that? You're her mother. That's a bond that can't ever be broken."

"You know, being confined to a hospital bed for nine days gave me plenty of time to think and reflect, Miriam. And that wasn't necessarily a good thing... that's the whole reason I took up drinking in the first place," Louise said, looking at Miriam. "She and Clifton were right. My priorities were in the wrong place. All I cared about was my image, being in charge, being admired—envied, even—by everyone else. The last thing I wanted to be was like my mother, who let the social pressure of this town drive her to a nervous breakdown. I thought I was doing right by my Grandmother Nora, who I didn't even like. Can you imagine? I didn't realize how much I was neglecting what mattered most."

Miriam took Louise's hand. "Remember what I said in the hospital? It's never too late to change."

Jasper spoke up unexpectedly. "'Tis true. According to Buddha, 'Every morning we are born again. What we do today is what matters most.'"

Louise seemed as surprised as Miriam that Jasper had spoken. "He does that sometimes," Miriam said. "But he only says what's necessary."

"Essentialism," Jasper said, smiling at them in the rear-view mirror.

"Then I think it's essential, before we get much farther, for me to apologize to you, Miriam," Louise said as she wiped an errant tear from her cheek. "How I treated you was despicable. At first, I judged you for being so different than anyone I'd ever met. Then, I resented you for being so authentic, for not seeming to care what people thought of you... just like my mother, who willed herself to die in the mental institution when I was thirteen. And then, I became jealous of you—everyone warmed up to you, while turning from me. When I found out your connection to Iris, I got even more jealous. If I could turn back the clock, I would have tried to be more like you instead of being so desperate to hold on to my ways." She paused, coughing into her tissue. "All I can say is I'm sorry, and I ask your forgiveness."

Miriam had remembered once discussing Louise's mother and her unfortunate death, which Louise had attributed to cancer at the time. Hearing it was a form of suicide, well, no wonder Louise was so fragile yet worked so hard to disguise it. She hurt for Louise, knowing how deeply the death of her own mother had nearly felled her but for her granddaddy's steady presence. It did not seem Louise had any such anchor at a time she needed one most, which made Miriam feel even more protective of her.

"Of course I forgive you," Miriam said, leaning over to give Louise an awkward hug. "But you also need to forgive yourself, honey. That's the only way you will find true peace."

"Namaste," Jasper said as he turned onto One Webster Way.

"Translation?" Louise asked, smiling.

"The Divine in me honors the Divine in you," Miriam and Jasper said in chorus.

As Jasper pulled into the circular driveway, the door flew open, and Poppy dashed down the steps, followed by Pearl and George, who held a bouquet of flowers. Jasper helped Louise from the car as Miriam swept Poppy into her arms. George handed the flowers to Louise, who gave him a friendly hug before her eyes met Pearl's. "Thank you," Louise said to the woman who had been a constant in her life since she was thirteen. "Thank you for not giving up on me."

"I'm never one to give up on no one," Pearl said, smiling.

"Least of all you."

"Welcome home!" Poppy shouted, wriggling in Miriam's arms. She put her daughter down, and Poppy immediately ran to Louise's side. "Be my new friend?"

Louise's eyes filled with tears. "Would you like to call me Aunt Louise?" she said, looking hopefully at Miriam, who clasped her hands together and nodded.

"Can I call you Aunt LuLu?" Poppy said, her eyes sparkling.

"I think that's a brilliant idea," Louise said, cupping her hand under Poppy's chin. "A new name for a new life."

Poppy took Louise's hand as they all ascended the stairs into the house. Miriam noticed Louise walking a bit taller and with more confidence than she had seen in a long time. She smiled, tipping her head to the sky and mouthing a silent "Thank you" to Iris and Rose as her family became one person larger.

EPILOGUE

Miriam and Louise did one last walk through Webster House, adjusting a few of the illuminated garlands hanging over each doorway and inspecting the festive spread on the buffet in the dining hall while awaiting their guests' arrivals. Miriam raised her glass of sparkling cider in a toast.

"What a journey this has been," Miriam said, her emotions feeling as effervescent as the beverage she had just poured. "Here's to you, Louise. You fought, and you won! See ya, cancer. We won't miss you!"

Louise looked into Miriam's eyes as they clinked glasses. "I couldn't have done it without you," she said, embracing Miriam in a warm hug. "The grace you've shown me is more than I could have expected and was clearly more than I deserved."

"We've already talked about this, LuLu," she said, adjusting the elf hat she had sewn the night before. "It's called 'friendship,' plain and simple. Now, please, put yours on," she said, pulling a matching hat from her apron pocket. Louise grimaced.

"My hair is just now starting to look decent!" she said. Miriam handed it to her anyway. Grumbling, she put it on as Poppy came racing into the dining room.

"When's everyone getting here?" she asked, holding her basket of candy canes. Miriam had asked her to help Jasper greet everyone at the door. "I'm in my party dress and everything!" she said, twirling around like a ballerina.

"There's my little princess," George called as he entered the room. Giggling, Poppy ran to show him her new red patent leather shoes. "You are a vision, my little princess," he said, swooping her into his arms.

Jasper wafted through each room, lighting the cinnamon-scented candles. He, too, had been enveloped by the spirit, sporting a forest-green caftan over a pair of red parachute pants. "Don't you look charming!" Louise said as he stoked the fire in the solarium. True to character, he put his hands together and bowed.

"You're welcome," Louise said, grinning.

As George put the cassettes of Christmas music into the tape deck and adjusted the volume, the doorbell rang, signaling the arrival of their first guest.

"Let's go!" Poppy grabbed Jasper's hand and tugged him to the door. With a look from Miriam, she added, "Pwease."

"She's becoming more like Rose every day," Miriam said to Louise as they moved to the parlor. "So bossy!"

"And yet so precious," Louise said softly, her expression suddenly changing. Miriam imagined Louise was thinking about Emma.

"Well, hello, Pearl!" Miriam said as Pearl handed her a wrapped loaf. "You weren't supposed to bring anything!"

"It's my 'nana bread," Pearl said, beaming happily. "Merry Christmas! Miz Louise, I got one for you, too, out in the car."

"You better eat yours fast, Miriam," Louise said, eyeing the loaf greedily. "I don't know her secret recipe, but it's downright decadent!"

"No one'd believe me if I told 'em," Pearl said.

The bell rang once again, followed by Poppy leading Roy and Gloria into the parlor. "Roy! I'm so glad you're here!" Miriam embraced him warmly, then turned to see Pearl noticing him with apparent interest. Putting her hand over her mouth to keep from chuckling, Miriam took Roy by the arm.

"Roy, do you know Miss Pearl Washington?"

"Very pleased to meet such a lovely woman," Roy said. "How haven't I met you before?" Miriam gracefully moved away to let them get acquainted, hoping the first of the schemes she had planned for the day would turn out for the best.

"You're looking quite fetching," Miriam said to Gloria, who was sipping her mulled wine.

"Dang, this is good," Gloria said. "We may have to put this on the menu! At least until February or so. Oh, and thank you, Miriam," she added with a mock curtsy.

"I don't think I've seen you in a dress! It suits you perfectly," Miriam said, noticing how well the wool knit accentuated Gloria's voluptuous figure.

"Is that one of your creations?" Gloria asked, looking at Miriam's emerald velvet evening suit.

"It is, actually," Miriam said, putting her hand on the dogwood brooch fastened to her lapel. "And this, this was Iris's."

Gloria leaned in to look at the enameled piece, then pulled Miriam into a hug. "I wish I had known her better, but based on what you've told me, she was one courageous woman. I see where you get it."

As Jasper ushered the Butlers into the parlor, Miriam noticed Jasper noticing Gloria, now twirling her braids. *Holiday magic is definitely in the air,* she thought to herself.

While George and Bobby huddled in the corner, likely discussing either sports or cars, Miriam greeted Bitsy with a kiss on the cheek. "Where's Debbie?" she said, looking around the room.

"Oh, she found Poppy lickety-split! She's in love with that child, you know," she said, taking the glass of Prosecco Jasper offered her.

"Goodness, Poppy probably has her locked in her bedroom playing dolls," Miriam said. "She loves her babies, as she

calls them!"

"And Debbie is probably in hog heaven," Bitsy said, turning as Louise came into the parlor.

"I was off powdering my nose," Louise said, giving Bitsy a hug. "Bits, loving your outfit!"

Dressed in a gold crushed velvet pantsuit, Bitsy looked like champagne personified. "Why, thank you, Louise." She looked over at Pearl and Roy. "Get a load of that! I see a love connection," she whispered conspiratorially as Louise softly giggled, taking a sip of her sparkling cider.

A few minutes later, Jasper softly tapped the Tibetan gong, indicating it was time for the guests to move to the dining hall for dinner. While she had considered placing name cards, Miriam decided to let their guests sit where they wished. After going upstairs to wrangle the girls away from their dolls, Miriam took her seat at the head of the table across from George on the opposite side. Pearl and Roy continued chatting as they sat down, while Bitsy and Louise flanked Miriam. Debbie sat with Poppy, and Gloria joined George and Bobby, still probably talking sports. Jasper looked at Miriam as if waiting for her cue to begin serving, but she subtly shook her head.

Standing, she gently tapped her wine glass with her spoon. The room fell to a hush. "When I think of Christmas, I think of family, and for a while, it was just me and George. Well, after Granddaddy died, anyway," she said, smiling at her husband. "And while we were blessed to have each other, we are even more blessed now. We are *all* family, you know." She paused to dab her eyes. "We've been through the ups, the downs, and the sideways, sometimes together, sometimes not, but today and forever forward—hopefully—we will always have each other. I'd like to raise a toast to all of us for the bonds we have created with one another. Cheers!"

After everyone clinked glasses and took sips of their

drinks, Miriam removed an envelope from her pocket. "Rose and Iris were the most extraordinary women I've ever known, and to have had them in my life–if only briefly–well, it was an education in how to truly live each day to its fullest. They also believed, as I do, that there are more important things than money. They valued experiences and adventures, and that got me to thinking. How can we open the doorway to experiences and adventures for young girls who come from limited means? It's really Pearl who started me thinking about this."

"Like me?" Poppy yelled, holding up her hand as the room erupted in laughter. Debbie reached over and tickled her, reducing Poppy to a velvety bundle of giggles.

"As I was saying," Miriam said, pretending to ignore her bewitching child, "it occurred to me we have an opportunity, right here in Stuarts Landing, to help our young girls thrive. That's why I am asking Louise to serve as the president and managing director of a new foundation, the name to be determined." Louise brought her hands to her mouth. "It should be complimentary to what Pearl already has going with Water From the Rock." Pearl smiled and nodded.

"Louise, this check should be enough to get us started," Miriam said, handing her the envelope. "Will you accept my offer?" Louise opened the envelope and gasped. Everyone clapped as the two women embraced.

"Speech! Speech! Speech!" The guests began chanting. Poppy banged her fork on the table, laughing.

"I honestly don't know what to say," Louise said as her voice wavered. "While I spent a good share of my adult life volunteering, I don't know as I ever felt an emotional connection with the actual work I was doing. This, though, this idea of yours, Miriam, is so very like you... generous, kind, and desperately needed here. I would be honored to head this foundation, with some help." She looked at Bitsy, whose face

was aglow. Bitsy nodded and clapped as the women sat down. "Pearl, can you teach me how to relate to these young girls? I'm not sure I know where to start."

"Of course, Miz Caldwell."

"I think it better be simply Louise from now on."

"All right. Then, of course, Louise." Pearl nodded, beaming from ear to ear.

"You're something else," Louise said to Miriam as Jasper began serving their first course.

"I believe in you," Miriam said. "Pretty simple."

"And you know I want to help," Bitsy said, taking a sip of Prosecco. "Whatever you need me to do. Except lick envelopes. Those days are over."

Everyone had begun eating their lobster bisque when the doorbell rang. Louise looked at Miriam, who put down her spoon. "Excuse me," she said softly, rising from her chair to leave the dining room—but not before leaning down and giving George a kiss on the top of his head.

Miriam walked purposefully to the foyer to greet their late arrival. "I didn't know if you'd make it," she said. "But I am just so incredibly happy to see you. Are you ready?" Miriam asked as Jasper took her coat. She nodded nervously. Miriam took her clammy hand and led her to join the other guests.

"Merry Christmas!" Miriam announced as she escorted Emma into the dining room. In the few years since Miriam had seen her, she had blossomed into a stunning woman who walked with confidence and purpose. Louise dropped her soup spoon on the floor as she struggled to get out of her chair.

"Oh my heavens! Emma!" she said, flying toward her daughter and wrapping her in her arms. As the tears streamed down both their faces, they remained locked in an embrace for several minutes, rocking back and forth as everyone in the room wiped away their tears.

"I missed you, Mom," Emma said softly, pulling away and

looking into Louise's eyes. "You should have told me, you know, about everything." She took her mother's hand.

"Everything happens as it should," Louise said, kissing her daughter's forehead. "And what a coincidence? There's an empty chair right beside me." She looked at Miriam with a smile. "Once again, Miriam works her magic."

Emma sat down next to her mother as Jasper served her a bowl of lobster bisque. "Oh, I didn't do it alone," Miriam said, looking down the table at Pearl. "I had a little help."

"Always loved both of you, and it ain't never gonna change," Pearl said, saluting Louise and Emma with her French bread before turning her attention back to Roy.

Louise took a deep breath and exhaled slowly. "What could possibly make this day any better?"

Miriam cleared her throat, then smiled. "I'm so glad you asked, LuLu. After dinner, we have a special treat in store. Emma, would you like to tell everyone?"

Miriam smiled at Louise's daughter, so mature, so beautiful, with her entire life of adventures ahead of her, then looked at little Poppy, who was busy shredding a dinner roll. She said a silent prayer, asking for time to slow down, if only for a moment.

Emma winked at Miriam. "Mom, remember how I always wanted to have an all-girl band?"

Louise blinked quickly, then shook her head. "I don't know as I knew that, sweetheart. I'm so sorry."

"Well, I started one with two of my sorority sisters. We've played in a few little dives in Charlottesville, and we've developed a decent following. Tonight, we're going to play for all of you! When they get here, that is."

Louise enveloped Emma in a hug. "I'm so unbelievably proud of you, my beautiful girl. I always was, really. I just never told you, and for that, I can't tell you how sorry I am, but I promise to do better. So, what is the name of your band?"

Miriam looked at Emma, and they both began to giggle uncontrollably. "Are you going to tell her, or should I?" Miriam said.

"Go ahead," Emma said. "Brace yourself, Mom."

With every eye focused on Miriam, she held up her glass and said, "Tonight, our featured entertainment will be The Auxiliary."

Louise threw her head back and laughed until tears rolled down her face. "I'm afraid to ask. What kind of music do you play?"

At her question, Miriam and Bitsy grinned and raised their eyebrows in unison, cocking their heads while waiting for Emma's response. Emma merely smirked.

"Well?" Louise said, dabbing her eyes with her napkin.

"We play the blues, Mom," she said, playfully punching Louise's arm. "The blues!"

"That seems strangely fitting, doesn't it, Miriam?" Louise said.

"In so many ways!" Miriam said. "And Emma, Gloria and I will need to talk with you about booking the band for some upcoming... what do you call them? 'Gigs'?"

Emma lifted her glass in affirmation. "We're down!"

"Here's the thing," Miriam said. "Despite what's happened in the past, we have so much to look forward to, together."

As her guests raised their glasses and said, "Amen," Miriam's heart nearly exploded with gratitude. *Thank you, Granddaddy, for sending us here. I questioned your motives for quite a while, but now I see the life you always wanted for me. It's more beautiful than I could have imagined, and I have you and Iris to thank for that. I hope you have united once again and that Rose is keeping you both out of trouble.*

THE END

ACKNOWLEDGMENTS

My desire to become a novelist began while I was an English major at The University of Texas at Austin. After my first creative writing class with Peter LaSalle, the author-in-residence, I was fortunate to be selected for a one-on-one honors tutorial with him the following semester. That opportunity instilled in me a deep love for storytelling, and at the age of twenty, I began writing my first novel. Oh, what a mess it was... so, I put it away only to begin some four other uninspired novels over the ensuing decades. In hindsight, I should have heeded Peter's advice to me at the end of our time together: "Whatever you do, don't pursue a career through which you'll be writing every day, as it will kill your desire to see your name on the spine of a book." Did I listen? Nope... I spent the next thirty-six years working in marketing communications during which, yes, I wrote constantly. But always for someone else's benefit (though the paychecks were nice).

Fast forward several decades and an early retirement and here I am, a debut novelist doing what I've always dreamed of: writing my stories while helping other authors hone their craft. And I've learned that despite my earlier misconceptions, writing and publishing a book truly is a team sport, and I have many people to thank for helping me reach this point.

First, my patient and supportive husband, Noble Groves, who happily listened as I read each chapter aloud, helped me brainstorm as needed, and kept the meals coming when I was too preoccupied to cook... words cannot adequately convey my appreciation (and to think I'm a writer). Gabrielle Cottraux, my wonderfully brilliant grown daughter, also provided much needed encouragement and love as

I navigated my way through numerous edits, revisions, and momentary crises of faith. Yes, I raised her well!

I was fortunate to have two accomplished editors help me whip my manuscript into shape: Mary Ellen Bramwell and Megan Turner. At times, I know I balked at your suggestions, but you helped me see the proverbial light. This book is better because of you.

My beta readers have been invaluable not only in helping me see areas where the book could be strengthened, but also for giving me confidence to keep pushing forward. To fellow authors Lee Orlich Bertram, Del Blackwater, and KJ Fieler, along with my dear friends Marianne Bosshart, Anne-Marie D'Alia, Jon Julnes, and Debbie Schall: thank you for believing in me and in this story and giving so freely of your praise.

Finally, I am grateful to my team at Atmosphere Press. Your professionalism, support, and enthusiasm for this book made working with you a genuine delight.

BOOK GROUP DISCUSSION GUIDE

- Do you think this story is more about triumphing over one's detractors or choosing not to give them any relevance?

- This book explores generationally held beliefs, specifically Miriam's and Louise's. Which, if either, of their value systems resonated with you? And if yours have changed, what precipitated that change?

- Did you relate to Louise, either as yourself or as someone you know? If so, explain.

- Is Bitsy a sympathetic character and if so, why?

- How did you feel about Clifton leaving Louise?

- Have you ever been estranged from one or more of your children, as Louise was from Emma? What happened?

- If you were either Rose or Iris, what if any decisions would you have made differently?

- What keeps Pearl so devoted to Louise, even as she's no longer in Louise's employ?

- In some small way, would you consider this a feminist book?

- Is there a specific quote or passage in the book that spoke to you? What about it stood out, and why do you feel it resonated with you?

- Do you have a favorite quote or scene from the book? Why does this stand out to you?

- Which character would you most like to meet and why?

- If you were making a movie of the book, who would you cast?

- If you could ask the author one question, what would it be?

- What do you think happens to the characters after the story ends?

ABOUT THE AUTHOR

As the daughter of an Air Force officer and a federal attorney, Suzanne Groves grew up relying upon her imagination, creativity, and innate curiosity to weather several early-life relocations and family challenges. An avid reader from a young age, Suzanne went on to earn her BA in English from The University of Texas at Austin and, twenty-six years later, an MA in History from The University of Texas at Arlington. She parlayed her English degree into a successful marketing communications career, during which she received numerous national and international awards for creative excellence. In 2020, she was named a "Top Woman in Communications" by Ragan Communications/PR Daily in the inaugural year of the national award.

The author of two nonfiction books, Suzanne now writes women's fiction and facilitates two critique groups for other authors finetuning their manuscripts. When she's not writing or editing, you can find Suzanne continuing her twenty-seven-year journey of genealogical research, experimenting with new recipes, traveling with her husband, keeping up with her perpetually shedding German shepherd (and cat), and engaging in literary shenanigans with her fellow authors.

You can contact her through her website:
https://www.suzannegroves.com